May It Please Your Lordship

Toby Potts

Monday Books

A CIP catalogue record for this title is available
from the British Library

ISBN: 978-1-906308-56-8

Typeset by Andrew Searle
Printed and bound by CPI Group (UK) Ltd,
Croydon CR0 4YY

www.mondaybooks.com
http://mondaybooks.wordpress.com/
info@mondaybooks.com
www.tobypotts.com

ABOUT THE AUTHOR

Toby Potts is the *nom de plume* of David Osborne, barrister, author, public performer, and public speaker. Some years ago, he hit the headlines nationwide and made legal history when he delivered his final speech to the jury entirely in verse. For this *tour de force* he was dubbed 'The Barrister Bard' by the popular press. He followed this with the publication of a short humorous book on advocacy entitled *No Holds Barred*, written under the pseudonym of Ivor Bigg-Wigg QC. He has appeared on radio and television as a legal commentator, and has written a number of articles for the national and regional press as well as various journals.

In the recent past, David has also written and presented legal revues (to full houses). He is regularly in demand as a Public and After Dinner Speaker, and has written a short book entitled The Art of Public Speaking. He is married with four children and lives in Somerset.

This is a fictional work. The characters portrayed are either the product of the author's imagination or they are used entirely fictitiously. Any resemblance to persons living or dead is entirely coincidental – apart from Hugh Grant and Prince Harry, who appear as themselves but in a wholly fictional capacity.

To Sally

CONTENTS

Chapter One

COMETH THE HOUR, COMETH THE MAN

'I DO HEREBY call you to the Bar and do publish you utter barrister.'

The Master Treasurer of the Honourable Society of Gray's Inn took my outstretched hand, shook it limply, and turned to the next student.

Poor old buffer, not long for this world, I thought, as I made my way back to my seat, hot and uncomfortable in white tie and tails, and looking for all the world like a tailor's dummy.

In spite of the heat and discomfort, I was barely able to contain my excitement. In those few short words, I had been transformed from chrysalis to butterfly.

A question fluttered briefly through my mind – cabbage white, or red admiral?

But I dismissed it. I had no doubts. The legal profession, one of the oldest and most revered in the civilised world, was about to be shaken to its very foundations. How I envied those whose good fortune it would be to instruct me in their cause, to fight the good fight and emerge triumphant or, *tant pis*, to be comforted in the knowledge that their life savings had been well spent.

Only dimly aware of the ritual unfolding around me, my thoughts wandered back to that fateful day when I had taken my first hesitant steps on the path towards a career at the Bar.

I was in the lower sixth at school when old 'Tripod' Biddle, the Head of Physics who also doubled as the Careers Master, had organised a Careers Day in the Great Hall. Various stalls were set out to promote suitable careers for the sons of gentlefolk, and we washed around aimlessly in the best traditions of gormless adolescents without a single creative thought between us.

It must have been a depressing sight for all those old boys who had taken the time and trouble to sell their wares in return for drinks and lunch with the Headmaster and Governors.

I was about to resign myself to an agreeable life of debauchery when Tripod bounded over and took me gently by the arm.

'Hello, Potts,' he said. 'Seen anything you fancy?'

'Frankly, sir, not a lot.'

'Then take my advice. If you can't find a proper job, how about the law? According to Jean Giraudoux, there is no better way of exercising the imagination than the study of law. No poet ever interpreted nature as freely as a lawyer interprets the truth.'

He chuckled, and bounded off in search of another lost soul.

During the holidays, I mentioned my nascent interest to my father.

'Splendid idea, my boy,' he said, with an indulgent beam. 'A good solicitor is the pillar of his community, and highly respected.'

'Well... actually, I was thinking of becoming a barrister.'

'Good God,' he spluttered, the beam disappearing in an instant. 'Whatever for? They're pompous idiots in fancy dress, who talk the hind leg off a donkey and charge the earth for saying bugger all. What you need is a *proper* job.'

And that was his last word on the subject.

My father was an accountant, and rather good at it. He was senior partner in a long established City firm. Solid without being showy, it had probably been around in Scrooge's time. Now in his mid-fifties, I imagined him as an older version of the man he had been in his mid-twenties – kind, measured in thought and speech, and also solid without being showy. He had joined the firm as a trainee, and, man and boy, had worked his way slowly and methodically to the top.

My mother, in contrast, had always been something of an orchid in a nettle bed, a delicate flower to be nurtured and cosseted. She had met my father in their late teens, and courted for years as they weighed up the options; two years after the nuptials, and carefully planned like a good balance sheet, I came along. My mother was an avid collector of Toby jugs, which she dotted around the house on every available surface, so it was no surprise that I was named after her abiding passion. I was her only child – a difficult birth put paid to a repeat performance – but my father seemed content with his lot, and, as he was fond of reminding me, one child is so much more affordable.

Over the weeks and months following the Careers Day, I found my mind returning time and again to a mental picture of myself in a fetching horsehair wig, hands grasping the lapels of my barrister's gown for dramatic effect as I made some important speech or other to a rapt jury. It was a picture I found increasingly compelling; in fact, despite my father's strictures, my determination to qualify as a barrister surprised even me.

There are four Inns of Court dating back to the dawn of time – Lincoln's Inn, Inner Temple, Middle Temple and Gray's Inn, all nestling within hailing distance of the Royal Courts of Justice, and occupying a large slice of prime London real estate. Within their hallowed cloisters were ancient libraries, chapels, barristers' chambers, and huge dining halls festooned with the coats of arms of the Great and the Good. As I discovered, all aspiring barristers had to join one of the Inns of Court before they could be called to the Bar. I can't think why, but for me at least, Gray's was *primus inter pares*, and the most prestigious of the four.

As I was soon to discover, membership of an Inn entailed various bits and pieces of arcane ritual, one of which was that of dining in Hall. Before being called to the Bar, I had to dine formally a dozen times as a student member during my three years at University. I threw myself enthusiastically into this custom. I will never forget my first dinner. I had arrived early to soak up the atmosphere, and, as I walked into South Square, I stood for a few moments gazing up in wonder at the Georgian façades, behind which I pictured learned counsel poring over grave and weighty opinions as they prepared for their next High Court appearance. This was the stuff of which dreams were made, and I was soon to be a part of it.

As the Hall doors were open, I made my way inside and was intercepted by the Under Butler who, judging from the expression on his face, took me for a tourist.

'May I help you, sir?'

'I'm here to dine,' I replied, feeling rather grand.

'Not without a gown, sir.' His manner was dismissive.

Following his directions, I made my way to the cloakroom, grabbed the first gown that came to hand and returned, chastened but unbowed, to join the queue that had formed in my absence. As I waited, the Head Butler, resplendent in a purple frockcoat trimmed with gold braid and important enough to be addressed in Capital Letters, caught my eye and walked smartly over.

'Kindly follow me, sir,' he said, plucking me from relative obscurity as he began to escort me to the top table. Flattered as I was by his attentions, I had a mounting sense of foreboding as all eyes followed my progress the length of the Hall, or so it seemed to me.

'May I enquire when you were called, sir?' he asked as we reached the top table. I felt the blood rushing to my cheeks.

'I think there's been some mistake,' I stammered foolishly, 'I'm a student member.'

'A *student* member?' he repeated, doing a passable impression of Lady Bracknell. 'Then pray tell me why you are wearing a barrister's gown?'

I was escorted back the length of Hall like some common criminal, hoping the ground would open and swallow me up. The cloakroom attendant, too little too late, helped me select an inferior student's gown, and I was eventually seated on the bottom table near the door where the Head Butler could keep an eye on me. I had already been branded a troublemaker, but there was worse to come.

I had barely recovered my composure when three loud bangs of the gavel brought us all to our feet. A pair of ancient doors swung open behind the top table, and a parade of octogenarians filed slowly into Hall.

'Who are they?' I whispered in a spirit of enquiry.

'Benchers,' replied the know-all to my right. 'Retired judges and barristers who've long since passed their sell-by-date and who sit around all day drinking port and waiting to die.'

After grace – in Latin, *nimirum* – everybody sat back down again and the meal was served. As ill luck would have it, I found myself seated as head of my Mess. Each Mess consisted of four students, and in front of me was placed a sheet of paper. On this I was required to list the names of the other three students who formed my Mess, as well as the names of the four students above me forming the Upper Mess, and the names of the four students below me who formed the Lower Mess. At an appropriate moment, somewhere between the brown Windsor soup and the lamb cutlet, I had to ask permission of the Head of the Upper Mess to toast their Mess, each and every one by name, but not before each and every one had toasted each and everyone else in my Mess, and then repeat the performance with the Lower Mess. The Upper and Lower Messes would then toast each other and then my Mess in return. In this way, we all drank a lot of wine and ate precious little of the rapidly congealing cutlet.

After dinner, there was to be a debate in Hall and, once the octogenarians had tottered out to their decanters of port, I sat back exhausted to await the evening's entertainment. The President of the Debating Society introduced the speakers and then turned to the motion.

'The motion for tonight's debate,' he announced over the hubbub of conversation, 'is that this House deplores sexual discrimination at the Bar, and I now call upon Clarissa McCarthy to speak in favour of the motion.'

A big girl with pursed lips and hair in a tight bun rose heavily to her feet.

'Gerr 'em off!' bellowed some lout at the back, to roars of approval from his male companions.

'Male chauvinist pigs!' McCarthy bellowed back. 'And you know the one thing pigs are good for? Woffal!'

There were roars of approval from the females present, and as insults were traded across the floor the debate rapidly degenerated into farce. So much for the cut and thrust of rapier-like wit. I stuck it out to the bitter end and then, just before ten, the Under Butler mercifully brought the evening to an end by turning off the lights. It was a memorable introduction to the arcane ceremony of dining in Hall.

The gavel shook me out of my reverie as we rose noisily to our feet.

'Members of Hall,' intoned the Master Treasurer, 'the toast is Domus.'

This was the first of many toasts at many dinners that had us up and down like a pair of tart's knickers. We toasted each other, Gray's Inn and Good Queen Bess, got drunk on port, sang songs and did various silly things as we rang down the curtain on our student years.

Chapter Two

THE SEARCH FOR PUPILLAGE

AFTER AN AGREEABLY long summer vacation – too long, by several weeks, for my father's liking – I began the search for pupillage.

In common with all aspiring barristers, I had to undertake this glorified, year-long apprenticeship under the eye, watchful or otherwise, of a practising pupil master, whom I would follow round like a faithful lapdog. He, in turn, would show me the ropes and smooth my passage to fame and fortune. I had no right of audience – to speak in court – for the first six months, so this was a time of eating idle bread, much to my father's displeasure. But, in my second six months, I could stand on my feet as a real grown up barrister, or so I hoped, and if all went well, a tenancy – a permanent seat in Chambers – beckoned, and with it the big time.

As I boasted no legal background or connections, I had to start from scratch.

Gray's Inn, forward thinking as ever, had appointed a Master of Students, whose task it was to place newly-qualified members with suitable pupil masters. The Bencher who had drawn the short straw had had a distinguished career at the Chancery Bar, poring over the complexities of corporate insolvency, intellectual property and Trusts, and was now seeing out his twilight years on the High Court Bench, so he was right at the cutting edge of youth culture.

I made an appointment to see him.

'And have you chosen your field of specialisation?' he asked with no visible sign of enthusiasm, as he peered through his half-moon spectacles at my application form.

'Yes, Master, I'd like to specialise in crime.'

'Good God,' he said, recoiling as though at the sight of something unpleasant. 'Whatever for?'

'I rather fancy the cut and thrust of advocacy,' I replied brightly. 'Defending the innocent, the down-trodden, the oppressed, holding high the sword of...'

'Yes, yes, quite so,' he interrupted, rather testily, 'although, in my experience, they're all as guilty as sin. I'll do what I can, but frankly I don't know any criminal barristers, so let patience be your watchword. They also serve who only stand and, er, wait. If it was good enough for Milton, it's good enough for you.'

Not an auspicious start.

My name was duly entered on the Register; after what seemed like an eternity, I received a letter inviting me to meet one Ronald Berger in his Chambers in the Temple, promptly at nine in the forenoon, with a view to a possible pupillage.

I arrived with ten minutes to spare, found Hare Court after a number of false starts, and marched purposefully up the stairs to the clerks' room.

Hare Court, unlike many parts of the Temple, had been spared the worst excesses of the Blitz and remained as a lasting testament to late Georgian/early Victorian architecture. Stone floors and stairs, off-white tiles and cast iron balustrades were as they had been when Hare Court opened for business all those years ago. It all looked and smelled like a converted public lavatory.

There were three clerks serving the best interests of twenty barristers, seated in a cold and cheerless room at desks which mirrored their seniority and importance. After establishing my credentials, I wedged himself between two antediluvian filing cabinets to await my prospective pupil master's pleasure.

At a quarter past nine, the senior clerk interrupted his call to his bookmaker and glanced towards me. 'Mr Berger will see you now,' he sniffed. 'Jason will show you to his room.'

Jason was a 16-year-old youth with tea-stained hands who had his foot on the first rung of the ladder, and whilst waiting for the call to come on up he had to content himself with the role of Chambers gopher. Every chambers had one: they were like mascots, though some were luckier than others. I followed him along a gloomy corridor to a back room, which Berger shared with two others.

Seated behind a tiny desk was a grey-haired man of advancing years and diminutive stature with pink, well-scrubbed features and a large pair of gold-rimmed spectacles. Judging from the substantial deposits, dandruff was a major problem, but one which, with commendable fortitude, he had chosen to ignore. He was dressed in pinstripe trousers, worn permanently at half-mast, a black waistcoat and jacket, and cut a somewhat Dickensian figure, with overtones of Uriah Heap.

I had to admit that my first impressions of Berger and his Chambers fell far short of what I'd imagined, and the pervading air of seediness was a serious depressant. But then, as this was the first criminal barrister I'd ever met, perhaps they were all like that?

'Thank you, Jason,' said Berger in a high-pitched voice, as the youth retired. 'You must be Potts.' Sharp as a sausage. 'And you're looking for a pupillage in crime?'

My first inclination was to deny any such ambition and return, cap-in-hand, to the Master of Students for an in-depth reappraisal, but that would have been defeatist, and pupil masters, good, bad or indifferent, were hard to come by.

'Yes, indeed,' I replied, with as much enthusiasm as I could muster in the circumstances.

'Good, good,' he nodded, clasping his small, chubby hands over his ample stomach. 'If you'd like to start on Monday, phone the clerks and they'll tell you where to find me.' He stood up and consulted his watch, rather like the White Rabbit in Alice in Wonderland. 'Now I must be on my way or I'll be late for court.' And so saying, he gathered his wits and papers, not necessarily in that order, and scurried off.

The interview was over; in those few short minutes, I had wed myself to a complete stranger for the next six months.

In reflective mood, I made my way slowly up Chancery Lane to Ede & Ravenscroft, Robemakers to the profession since 1683. Like a Matador donning his Suit of Lights, I was transformed from head to toe by an unctuous assistant smelling strongly of mothballs.

The list of apparel, like the bill, was enormous. Two pairs of pinstriped trousers, two black jackets with matching waistcoats, six white collarless shirts, six white starched day collars, six white, starched wing-collars for court, six white pairs of bands to wear around my neck when appearing in court, two sets of collar studs, one barrister's gown and, finally, one snowy white wig with personalised box which had to be specially ordered and would take at least three weeks to arrive.

ONE LAST STOP before returning home to prepare my father for the shock of paying for all of this was Butterworth's Law Bookshop in Bell Yard, where I purchased the latest edition of *Archbold*, the criminal practitioner's bible and an indispensable tool for the successful advocate. Booted, kitted and spurred, I was ready to do battle.

Unfortunately, I was at home when the bills hit the door mat, and my father hit the roof.

'Good God, Toby!' he spluttered, doing the mental arithmetic as a man of numbers does. 'This is more than I earned in the whole of my first year as an accountant!'

'Well, that was a long time ago, father,' I replied lamely. 'And besides, as a barrister, I must look the part.' He looked thoroughly unconvinced, not to say fuming, so I added hastily, 'I'll pay you back, of course, once I'm established. Perhaps you can look on it as an investment in my future.'

'Future what, is more to the point!' he said. 'If only you'd taken my advice and become a solicitor. Look at this!' He stabbed his finger at the bill from Ede & Ravenscroft. 'Five hundred pounds for a wig, and a further three hundred pounds for a box to keep it in! Why on earth do you need a wig box? To stop it escaping I suppose!'

'Well...'

'And one hundred and seventy-five pounds for a gown! So by my calculations' – he was seldom wrong in these matters – 'your fancy dress is costing me nearly a thousand pounds, and all for the privilege of talking the hind leg off a donkey. And that's assuming,' he added, witheringly, 'you get the chance!'

'It'll all come right, I assure you, so...'

'And from what you tell me, for the first six months, you won't earn a penny! It beggars belief!'

Mercifully, my mother came to my rescue, as mothers are wont.

'Don't be so mean, George,' she said. 'Toby has to look the part, and I'm sure he'll look an absolute poppet in his wig and gown.' She smiled encouragingly. 'I can't wait to see you in action. We'll both be so proud!'

'Don't hold your breath, dear,' said my father, though he was a beaten man. 'You'll have to wait a good six months, if not longer, and, who knows, by that time poppet here may want a whole new outfit!'

As somebody said, and it wasn't my father, you can't put a price on success.

Chapter Three

AT THE BAILEY

THAT FRIDAY EVENING, as instructed, I phoned Berger's Chambers.

'Mr Berger will be at the Bailey on Monday,' garbled the senior clerk, in between mouthfuls of tea and ginger nut crunchies. 'So if you care to meet him in Chambers at nine o'clock sharp, he'll walk down with you.'

I put down the phone with a frisson of excitement as I contemplated my first day in pupillage – and at the Bailey, no less. I had obviously underestimated my learned pupil master.

Berger of the Bailey! What a thrill!

According to my frequently boring lectures on the history of the English legal system, the Bailey – or, more precisely, the Old Bailey – was the highest criminal court in the land, and had been since 1673. It was where murderers, rapists, and other felons were prosecuted, convicted and then taken to a place of execution to be hanged by the neck until dead, and may God have mercy on their souls. Man, woman and child, guilty and innocent alike, were charged, condemned and dispatched to their Maker by Judges who had only a passing acquaintance with the law, and who went about the more pleasurable business of eating and drinking and fornicating without a moment's reflection on the plight of those less fortunate than themselves.

Juries fared no better. They were threatened, cajoled and suborned into returning guilty verdicts regardless of the evidence, and those who had the temerity to kick against the prick were kept without food, drink, heat, or other creature comfort, until they saw the error of their ways.

I was as nervous as a kitten all weekend, and greatly relieved when the momentous day dawned. I was awake to greet it, which was just as well as it took me the best part of an hour to strap myself into the starched white collar, which was as stiff as a board and totally unyielding. I reflected that a dry run might have been a good idea, as the collar and I fought each other, neither willing to yield. But if I were to become a successful barrister I had to meet adversity head on. No good falling at the first hurdle. *Vires in adversum,* and all that.

Once locked into place, it felt like a medieval tourniquet. To make matters worse, I found it nigh on impossible to turn my head independently of my body, attracting a number of very strange looks and a helping hand across the road from an elderly lady as I made my way to the Underground. Hot and bothered, I alighted at the Temple and hurried along to Hare Court.

Berger was there to greet me, and, after the briefest of exchanges, we set off down Fleet Street to walk the short distance to the Bailey.

The security was impressive, if somewhat heavy-handed. After all, I was a fully-qualified barrister, but that cut no ice at all as I was searched and patted down before being allowed inside the main building. From there we made our way to the fourth floor, and the relative sanctuary of the robing room, the inner sanctum reserved exclusively for barristers, and away from the prying eyes of solicitors, clients and witnesses, where they could put on their formal robes undisturbed whilst chewing the fat, discussing the merits or otherwise of their cases, and studying the runners in the 3.30 at Kempton Park.

This was the moment I had been dreading all morning. I had to release myself from my starched white day collar and replace it with an equally starched wing collar and bands. To avoid attracting attention to myself, I moved around the room as though deep in thought.

My very smart Gray's Inn tie was the first obstacle. In my efforts to remove it from the vice-like grip of the collar, it became firmly knotted around my neck and the loop was not quite wide enough to lift it over my head, as I discovered when I attempted the manoeuvre. It looked to the innocent bystander – a rare commodity at the Bailey – as if I'd decided to end it all.

Next came the problem of trying to separate the collar from its restraining stud. The two were locked together in mortal combat, and it took all of my strength to prise them apart. My composure was slipping by the minute, but fortunately Berger had shuffled off to the lavatory and was not witness to his pupil's discomfort. At last, with numb and aching fingers, the offending restraint was torn from my neck and I collapsed, exhausted, into a chair.

The reverse performance with the wing collar had barely begun when Berger, refreshed and ready for the day's drama to unfold, poked his head round the corner. 'I'll go ahead,' he whined, in that high-pitched voice of his. 'We have a clear start in Court One, and I want to check if all our witnesses are here.' I nodded with difficulty, speech being all-but out of the question. 'And don't be late.'

Easier said than done, I thought, as I returned to the uneven struggle.

'Having trouble?' I turned to see a tall, distinguished man with a friendly face smiling indulgently in my direction.

'I'm afraid so,' I gasped, swallowing hard. 'I can't seem to get the hang of this collar.'

'Let me help,' said my saviour, and, with years of practice, he soon had me battened down and laced up. 'You must be a pupil,' he continued, standing back to admire his handiwork.

'First day,' I confessed.

'Never mind,' he replied. 'It can only get worse. Who's your pupil master?'

'Ronald Berger.'

He chuckled. 'Known affectionately in the profession as "Ham" Berger,' he said, 'but don't tell him I said so. He's not renowned for his sense of humour.' He glanced up at the clock. 'You'd better get going, it's nearly half past ten. Good luck.' And with that, he swept majestically out of the robing room.

Donning my snowy white wig and black, well-pressed gown, I made my way purposefully, and with as much expedition as the dignity of my profession would allow, to the ground floor and thence, after helpful directions from a passing usher, to Court One. Opening the door as quietly as possible, I tiptoed in and glanced around for Ham. He was nowhere to be seen. To my left were rows of seats dotted with a few members of the public; to my right were more seats, fortuitously unoccupied. As I was beginning to feel conspicuous, they seemed as good a place as any to sit and observe the trial process.

BARELY HAD I SAT down when Ham burst into court with his gown billowing behind him and clutching his brief, ready to do battle. Before I could catch his eye, a loud bang of the gavel announced the arrival of the judge.

'All rise,' intoned the judge's clerk, as the judge emerged from behind the impressive solid oak throne to take his seat in the place of judgment. As I was later to discover, this was the Honourable Mr Justice Boniface, known as 'Sourpuss', and one of Her Majesty's High Court Judges. He wore a robe of scarlet red, fetchingly trimmed with ermine, and clutching a pair of white gloves. A small wig perched precariously on his bald pate, and nearly slipped off as he bowed to the court. Pink, fleshy and bejowled features glared out at the assembled multitude, only breaking into a fleeting and wintry smile as he acknowledged defence counsel.

The court clerk rose, as did the Defendant, a dignified fellow with thinning, grey hair.

'Are you Adrian Donald Fortescue Browne?' asked the clerk, in a loud and sententious voice.

'I am,' came the reply.

Startled, I looked harder at him. *Could* it be? It *was*! I tried not to stare. The man in the dock, this Fortescue Browne chap, was the former Director of Public Prosecutions, and the object of intense press and media speculation. Not a bad start to my career – albeit if I were merely to be an interested observer in the unfolding drama.

Calm and composed, he stared straight ahead as the gentlemen of the Press began scribbling feverishly. This was very exciting indeed.

'Sit down.' Mr Justice Boniface glowered at Ham. 'Is this to be a trial, Mr...' He glanced down at the slip of paper containing the names of counsel, 'Berger?'

'It is indeed, my lord,' replied Ham, confidently.

'So be it,' said Sourpuss, with no discernible enthusiasm. 'Then summon the jury panel.'

It took a good ten minutes for the jury panel to assemble in court, brought as they were from the catacombs of the building usually reserved for filing cabinets, refuse disposal and miscellaneous. As they stood, blinking in the cold light of the court, and totally disorientated, Mr Justice Boniface glared over at me, and then back at Berger.

'Mr Berger.' The Judge was plainly not amused. 'There is a young man fully robed sitting in the well of the court.' He nodded towards me. 'Have I missed something, and if so, what part is he to play in these proceedings?'

Ham leapt to his feet, shot a glance over to me, coloured visibly, and started to jerk his head uncontrollably in my direction. Defence Counsel rose slowly to his feet, bowed, and turned towards me.

To my amazement and relief, it was the same tall, distinguished and friendly face from the robing room. He leant down towards me and whispered, 'Don't worry, old chap, but you're sitting in the jury box. Why don't you go and sit behind Berger?'

This was the worst day of my life – or so I thought, naïvely, at the time. I clambered out of the jury box, all eyes upon me, and made my way down to Counsel's benches. Ham, for his part, was apologising profusely, which, in the circumstances, was the least he could do.

'Mr Potts is my pupil, my lord,' he whined, 'and this is his first day in court. He is obviously unfamiliar with our ways.'

'A self-evident observation, Mr Berger,' snapped his lordship, 'and precisely why pupils have pupil masters – to show them the ropes.'

The unspoken criticism of Ham was lost of no-one. He looked uncomfortable, and glowered at me.

'Now shall we get on?'

'Quite so, my lord,' Berger stammered, shuffling through his papers. 'The Defendant stands charged with the grave offence of persistently importuning in a public place for immoral purposes, and on arraignment, pleaded not guilty.'

"The gravity of the offence is for me to decide, Mr Berger, not you or the jury as well you know. But now that you mention it, I have in all my years on the Bench tried many grave offences, and have handed down some *very* severe sentences.' Ham smiled weakly. 'However, I can state without fear of contradiction that I have never been called upon to try a case as grave as this. So I ask, in a spirit of enquiry, why me, and why is this case here?'

Was it my imagination, or had the judge taken against Ham Berger?

'My lord,' said Berger, at his most unctuous, 'as your lordship will recall, the murder trial listed before your lordship this morning has been vacated to enable the defence to instruct their own forensic expert, so by hap' chance this trial was allocated to your lordship at very short notice. The case is here because, as your lordship may know, this offence was committed within the bailiwick of the Bailey, which is the only court having jurisdiction to try it.'

'Very droll, I'm sure.' There was the faintest of smiles playing around the judge's mouth.

'I'm sorry, my lord?'

'Within the bailiwick of the Bailey, very droll, Mr Berger.'

Berger stood open-mouthed, the fleeting moment of his own unintended wit going right over his head.

'Never mind, never mind,' said his lordship, with some irritation. He sat back and closed his eyes. 'Get on with it.'

The jury duly empanelled, Ham rose to his feet to open the case for the prosecution.

'Mem' jury,' he began, 'I appear on behalf of the prosecution in this case, and my learned friend Sir Archibald Scott-Malden QC appears for the Defendant.'

I drew in my breath sharply. My saviour, and the distinguished man with the friendly face, was none other than the former Attorney-General who, after the last General Election, had stood down to return to private practice. This was history in the making, and I was there to witness it. Whatever else, Berger was hopelessly outgunned. A distinguished Defendant, an even more distinguished defence counsel, and a hostile judge. An irresistible combination.

Good luck, Ham, I muttered to myself, *you're going to need it.*

'At approximately nineteen thirty six hours...'

His lordship threw down his pen and pushed back in his chair. 'What is this gibberish, Mr Berger?' he snapped irritably. 'Nineteen thirty six hours? The purpose of an opening address by prosecution counsel is to illuminate, not obfuscate. The jury and I are totally bemused, and, I dare say, so is your neglected pupil.'

'My lord.' Ham was going down for the second time, and he was still a long way from the shore. With grim determination, he plunged on. 'At approximately seven thirty six in the evening, the defendant was seen in a notorious red light district of London, driving his motor car slowly along the street. You will hear evidence that he stopped and was approached by a lady of easy virtue.'

'A *lady of easy virtue,* Mr Berger?' snapped Sourpuss, barely disguising his impatience. 'What on earth does that mean? Do you mean a prostitute?'

'Er... yes, my lord, I suppose I do, but...'

'Then say so. This is not some eighteenth century soap opera dreamt up by Dame Barbara Cartland over a box of soft-centred chocolates. We are in the twentieth century, for goodness sake, and we are all familiar with prostitutes, are we not, members of the jury?'

I wasn't quite sure if that was what Sourpuss meant to say, but it produced a few titters.

'Very well, my lord.' Berger returned to the jury. 'As I was saying, mem' jury, the Defendant was approached by a... prostitute, there was a brief conversation, and the defendant drove on. The Crown say that he was importuning for an immoral purpose.'

I noticed that Ham had now broken into a gallop. In fact, he was babbling like a baboon, such was his anxiety to conclude his opening speech without further interruption.

'At approximately nineteen....I mean seven forty four, he stopped for a second time, was again approached, and before he could agree terms he was arrested. With your lordship's leave,' he panted, triumphantly, 'I will call my first witness. Miss Dolores Del Fabro.'

There was an audible stir of anticipation in the court as Dolores entered, drenched from head to toe in a strongly-scented, not to say overpowering, perfume. My eyes began to water with the sheer intoxication of it as she swayed seductively past me on her way to the witness box. Dolores, otherwise known as Sharon Turner, was a dyed-bright redhead on the wrong side of 40, plump, with a painted face worthy of Toulouse-Lautrec. Mutton dressed as lamb, I thought uncharitably, as she minced her way to the witness box in a provocative polka dot minidress which was only just decent by anybody's standards. His lordship's eyes lit up, and his welcoming smile had an almost lascivious edge to it. He was beginning to enjoy himself, and it showed.

Dolores took the oath in a quiet, demure voice, gave the judge an engaging smile, and then sat down.

'Please state your name and address,' said Ham, totally unmoved by this vision of loveliness.

'Dolores del Fabro,' she said, before adding 'Miss', for good measure. 'Of 24 Eaton Square, London. Do you want my phone number as well?' She giggled, displaying a row of pearly white teeth.

'I think not,' replied Ham, colouring visibly.

'Eaton Square?' asked the judge. Dolores nodded. 'What a coincidence,' he continued, smiling warmly. 'We're near neighbours.'

'I thought your lordship looked familiar.'

There was an audible chuckle from the public gallery as the judge cleared his throat and regained his composure. 'You were saying, Mr Berger?'

'Madam,' he began, putting both feet right in it. Even I could see that one coming.

Dolores immediately burst into tears. '*Madam?*' she exploded through hysterical sobs. 'Who do you think you are, calling me Madam? I didn't come here to be insulted by an ignorant little moron like you!'

His lordship rushed to her side – metaphorically-speaking, of course. 'Please calm yourself, Miss del Fabro, no slight on your character was intended, I am sure. The ignorant little moron is prosecution counsel who is duty-bound to ask you questions, and we must all bear with him – for the time being, at least.'

The judge stared icily at Berger. 'Shall we try again, Mr Berger, and this time with a little sensitivity?'

'As your lordship pleases,' Ham whined, and turned back to Dolores. 'Were you in Argyle Square on the night of the eleventh of November?'

'No, my lord,' said Sir Archibald, rising from his seat. 'That, as my learned friend should know, is a leading question, and is not permitted under the rules of evidence.'

Young and inexperienced as I was, I knew that leading questions, which suggested the answer, or which contained information Counsel wished to have confirmed, were strictly 'verboten'.

His lordship nodded. 'Quite right, Sir Archibald. Mr Berger, it is a basic rule – a very basic rule – of evidence that you cannot lead your own witness. Even your pupil knows that.' I winced. 'Rephrase your question.'

'I apologise, my lord.' Back to Dolores. 'Where were you on the night of the eleventh of November last?'

'That's nearly a year ago, how can I possibly remember? I'm a very busy girl.'

'Busy at what?' snapped Berger, beginning to lose his composure.

'That's none of your business,' Dolores snapped back.

'Yes it is.'

'No it isn't.'

'Really, Mr Berger,' interrupted the judge as Sir Archibald was on the way up again, 'this is getting us nowhere. I suggest you try another approach.'

Ham smiled thinly. 'Very well, my lord.' Taking a deep breath, he plunged on. 'Do you know the defendant?' he asked, pointing to the dock.

This time Sir Archibald was up like a jackrabbit. 'Again, my lord, and with respect to my learned friend, identity is in issue, and there has been no formal identification in this case.'

'Is that right, Mr Berger?' His lordship was not amused.

'Well... er.' Ham was going down for the third time, 'Sir Adrian Browne is a well-known public figure, arrested in Argyle Square whilst persistently importuning for sexual favours...'

'Yes, yes, that, as you explained in your opening address, is your case.' Sourpuss was losing patience. 'The question, however, for the jury, is can you *prove* it on admissible evidence? The jury are not remotely interested in what you *say*, it doesn't amount to a row of beans.'

There was a long pause, the silence broken only by the ticking of the court clock, as Berger took stock of his hopeless situation. 'But, but…' he whined.

'*But, but* will not do, Mr Berger. Have you any admissible evidence connecting the Defendant with Miss del Fabro, and, more to the point, any evidence that Miss del Fabro was even there on the night in question?'

Going down he might be, but Ham could picture his prosecution practice sinking without trace, and taking him down with it. He was not going to do so without a fight. There was now an irritable note to his whine. 'My lord, had Miss del Fabro come up to proof, and given evidence consistent with her witness statement, the question of identity would not have arisen. She is obviously a recalcitrant witness, and I apply to treat her as hostile.'

According to my law lectures, still fresh in the memory, a hostile witness is one who is deliberately distorting the evidence, and who refuses to tell the truth. If Ham's application was successful, he could cross examine Dolores and put her witness statement to her. I was also taught that a hostile witness was next to useless as a witness of truth, wholly discredited and unlikely to be believed by the jury. It was a high-risk strategy.

Sourpuss's eyebrows had shot up like fireworks. 'Do you agree, Sir Archibald?' he asked.

'No, my lord, I do not,' came the reply as Sir Archibald rose from his seat. 'My learned friend has not even begun to lay the foundations for such an application. A forgetful witness is not, and can never be, a hostile witness under any circumstances.'

'Sir Archibald is quite right, Mr Berger,' said Sourpuss, 'and I rule against you. So where does that leave you?'

One last headlong rush into the Valley of Death. 'I have another prostitute to call…'

Dolores was about to explode, but Sourpuss waved her down. 'Mr Berger, this is intolerable. You have not proved that Miss del Fabro is a prostitute, so even if your next witness surmounts that particular hurdle, do you have any admissible evidence of a formal identification? I thought not,' he continued, before Ham could reply. 'And besides, where is your evidence that the defendant was persistently importuning for immoral purposes? "Persistently", in my vocabulary at least, suggests more than once. Am I right, Sir Archibald?'

Sir Archibald rose with all the dignity that his high office and professional esteem could muster. 'Your lordship is, as ever, a Solomon come to judgment,' he purred. Game, set and match.

Sourpuss turned to the now totally bemused jury. 'There you have it, members of the jury. On the admissible evidence called before you, the Crown haven't even begun to establish a case for this defendant to answer, and I direct you to return a verdict of not guilty. The defendant may leave the dock without a stain on his character. I shall rise.'

I accompanied Ham back to the robing room for the briefest of post mortems. I had to hand it to him, he had a skin like a rhinoceros, and seemed completely unfazed by the mauling he'd just received. 'Well,' he whined, 'now you've seen the cut and thrust of advocacy at its highest level, has it whetted your appetite for a life of crime?'

Frankly, I couldn't think of anything to say in reply.

'I'm going back to Chambers,' he continued. 'I've brought my own sandwiches' – no expense spared – 'so I'll see you later.' And, with that, he was gone.

I WATCHED HIM go. I would have liked to discuss the case, and perhaps learn something from what had gone wrong, but I judged that now was not the time. Instead, after performing the dance of the starched collars in reverse, I made my way up to the Bar Mess, the dining room set aside for barristers. Over by the window sat Sir Archibald with assorted acolytes, deep in animated conversation. Seeing no familiar faces, I selected the *plat du jour* and sponge pudding with custard, and sat down on my own, trying not to draw attention to myself. I had just finished when, to my trepidation, I saw Sir Archibald making his way over. I immediately stood up.

'Please sit down, young man. Do you mind if I join you?'

'I.. I.. I…'

'I didn't quite catch your name when we met earlier,' he said, sitting down opposite.

'Potts, sir, Toby Potts.'

'Please, Toby, call me Archie,' he said, smiling kindly. 'And where is your pupil master?'

'Gone back to Chambers to eat his sandwiches,' I blurted out, immediately feeling disloyal.

'Ah, that's Berger for you, not one for socialising. Still, it takes all sorts. So, what did you make of this morning's high drama?'

'I was rather confused, to be honest,' I said. 'I don't pretend to understand all the rules of evidence, but the case seemed to fall apart with the first witness. The prosecution made certain assumptions about her evidence that they were clearly unable to prove.'

Sir Archibald chuckled. 'A very perspicacious observation.'

'I mean, I hadn't read the papers or discussed the case with Berger before going into court,' Sir Archibald raised his eyebrows, 'but it seemed an open and shut case.'

'On the face of the papers, you are right. We all know Miss del Fabro earns her living staring up at the ceiling, but knowing it and proving it are not always one and the same thing. My advice to you, Toby, starting out on what I hope will be an illustrious career at the Bar, is that you can never over-prepare. Never assume that some fact or other will prove itself, always be *ready* to prove it, just in case your star witness loses the plot.'

'So should Sir Adrian have been acquitted?'

'Under our system of justice, yes. The prosecution must prove the guilt of the accused to a very high standard, and even if the guilty are acquitted from time to time, you don't throw the baby out with the bathwater. Our system may not be perfect, but it's the best we've got. God help us if our lords and masters get their way, and abolish trial by jury. Although it worked for the defendant today, can you imagine anything worse than being tried by Sourpuss on his own?' I smiled deferentially. 'And as for Sir Adrian, whatever else, he behaved foolishly, his career is in ruins, and he'll never rise to high office again. That is his punishment, so justice of sorts has been done.'

Sir Archibald paused. 'So, your first day with Ronald Berger? Can't say I know him well, an honest journeyman rather than a shooting star. To quote Robert Louis Stevenson, "Here stands one who meant well, tried a little and failed much: that should be his epitaph." Should make it to the Circuit Bench in a few years' time.'

'Really?' The surprise in my voice didn't go unnoticed.

'Being a good or able advocate is no longer an essential prerequisite to judicial advancement, and more's the pity. If you keep your nose clean, don't upset anybody on the way up, and toe the party line, you've got as good a chance as the next man. Not so long ago it was different. Judges were appointed on ability, and usually after a distinguished career at the Bar. They had a feel for it, and the Bench was the richer for it. Sourpuss is a case in point. He can be intimidating, but despite his gruff manner he's a good judge, and, above all, he's fair. Nowadays, all sorts of nonentities are getting appointed.' I laughed, and wished I hadn't. 'They get their idiot guides printed for them by the Lord Chancellor's department, together with their specimen directions, and even their hours of sitting. You can't get a feel for the case if you don't observe human nature. It's not what a witness *says*, it's the *way* he says it, the body language, that can make the difference between truth and lies, conviction or acquittal.'

I sat transfixed as Sir Archibald glanced down at his watch. Should I ask him for his autograph, or perhaps a photo opportunity for posterity? What a story to tell my friends and parents – 'This one is of me and my good chum Archie... you know Archie? The former Attorney-General?' If only...

He stood up to go. 'It's been a pleasure chatting to you, Toby, but I've detained you long enough. Let me leave you with one final piece of advice – never settle for second best. Why be ordinary if you have it in you to be extraordinary. Good luck!' And with that he was gone.

Chapter Four

MY FIRST OUTING

HORSEFERRY ROAD MAGISTRATES' Court. Within chiming distance of Big Ben, and a stone's throw from Smith Square and Lord North Street in the heart of Westminster Village, where the real business of government is done behind closed doors and heavily draped curtains.

But I had other things on my mind as I travelled to court, clutching my first ever brief. I had duly completed my first six months' pupillage with Berger. They had not been a conspicuous success, even by Berger's modest standards, and they had seemed to drag on forever. Sadly for me, Berger's big day out at the Bailey was the high point in an otherwise undistinguished and mundane practice, fed as it was on an unremitting diet of low-grade crime, always prosecuting, always whining, winning some and losing some, keeping his nose clean and waiting for the call to come on up onto the Circuit Bench. An ideal candidate, if Sir Archibald were to be believed.

I couldn't move fast enough to wave Berger goodbye, and with luck on my side, I found a second pupillage in Brick Court, another converted Victorian lavatory. My new pupil master, Nick Ridley, was cut from a different cloth altogether, - he was dynamic, upwardly mobile, with a good solid practice in serious crime, and tipped, by many, for elevation before long to the ranks of Queen's Counsel. Becoming a QC – or 'taking Silk' as it was called after the silken gowns worn by the chosen – was the passport to the senior ranks of the profession, achieved by a labyrinthine process of recommendations, nods and winks, and bestowed on those able junior barristers who had slaved away with distinction at the sharp end for at least ten years.

After a week or three of getting to know each other and bonding, I found myself passing the clerks' room one evening, just before close of play, when the senior clerk called me in.

'I'd like you to help me out, sir,' he said.

I didn't know what to expect, and I was rooted to the spot. For the senior clerk to address me at all was privilege indeed.

'Chambers solicitor can't make it to court tomorrow, so I've agreed to cover it. It's plea before venue at Horseferry Road Magistrates Court, client charged with making off without payment. Straightforward case, you'll be on your own, but I'm sure you can handle it. Here's the brief. Meet the client at court.' And so saying, in that seminal moment when the Heavens conjoin, the brief was ceremonially handed over to me, in much the same way, I imagine, as Jehovah handed down the Ten Commandments to Moses. All that was missing was the burning bush and the deep and manly voice of Charlton Heston.

My hands trembled as I took possession of the backsheet, fondly enclosing two pages of instructions, and lovingly tied together with pink ribbon. I smiled weakly, and, like a dog with a favourite bone, scurried off to worry over it and digest the Sisyphean task ahead. I could picture it already. The short and pithy statement on the steps of the court to the waiting press, announcing to the world that my client was innocent of the heinous charge levelled against him, that justice would prevail, and he would leave court with his head held high and singing my praises. What a glorious start to a glorious career!

That night, as I burned the midnight oil, I studied the brief, reading and rereading my instructions, which were commendable for their brevity, if nothing else. They described how the defendant, one Anthony Hercules Smith, had disgorged himself from a taxi owing ten pounds and sixty pence on the meter and had, to put it crudely, legged it, followed in hot pursuit by the irate driver. Rounding the corner in full flight, the hapless Smith had barrelled straight into PC Plod. After a moment to take stock of the situation, Plod had nicked, cuffed, and spanked the defendant in short order, dumping him unceremoniously into the back of a passing police van, and thence into custody. In the fullness of time, Smith had been charged with making off without payment, and bailed to appear at Horseferry Road Magistrates' Court to await the full majesty of the law. My cue to enter stage right.

Incessantly picking up the brief and putting it back down, almost reverentially, I thumbed through *Archbold* and made detailed notes about plea before venue, something to do with the Defendant's right to elect trial by jury if, of course, the offence was 'triable either way'. What did that mean? Why couldn't the editors of *Archbold* write in plain English?

After a lengthy trawl, I found what I was looking for, and read to my horror that on conviction (an unlikely event with my firm hand on the tiller, but one that had to be countenanced in case of an incompetent tribunal or a perverse jury), a person (presumably my client) shall be liable, for an offence under section 1 or section 2 of this Act, (what's this got to do with anything?) to imprisonment for up to five years (What?!) and for an offence under section 3 of this Act, to imprisonment for up to two years (that's better, but not much).

I read on, more in hope than expectation of enlightenment, to discover that this section (whatever) is printed as amended by the Magistrates Court Act section 154(1) and Schedule 7 paragraph 170. For section 32 of the Act, see *ante* § 1 - 30. Finally, to add to my misery, I discovered that section 5(3) was repealed by the Extradition Act section 37(1) and Schedule 2. Section 5(4) included offences under the Act (which Act?) in the schedule to the Visiting Forces Act 1952, which defines for England and Wales 'offence against property' for purposes of exclusion in certain cases of the jurisdiction of the United Kingdom courts.

I should have followed my father, and become an accountant.

I was seized with a rising sense of panic. My instructions told me nothing about Smith's status in this our sceptred isle. Smith was a common enough English name, but not conclusive. Perhaps Smith was an alias. After all, what right-minded Anglo-Saxon parents name their son Hercules? Was my Smith an illegal alien? That might explain his sudden dash for freedom. If so, was he liable to extradition? Was he part of the visiting forces, and if so, what visiting forces, and where was he visiting from? Did the court have jurisdiction, and was legging it without paying the fare an 'offence against property'? At first blush, I thought not, but remembering Sir Archibald's words of wisdom about being prepared for every eventuality, I plunged back into *Archbold*, and, in the Table of Statutes, wedged between Visiting Forces (British Commonwealth) Act, and the Wages Act, were at least a dozen further references to the Visiting Forces Act 1952.

It was past two in the morning when I finally got to bed. I slept fitfully, waking each hour on the hour, and forcing myself back to sleep. By six I abandoned the uneven struggle and prepared myself for my date with destiny.

AS IT WAS the Magistrates' Court, I was not required to robe, so I dressed in my suit, white shirt with double cuffs and a sober, quasi-regimental tie. Kicking around my small apartment off Earls Court Road, I forced down a bowl of cereal, and then, fortified for the task ahead, gathered up the brief, counsel's notebook, and my copy of *Archbold*, and, bracing myself, took one last look in the mirror:

> *I see you stand like greyhounds in the slips,*
> *Straining upon the start. The game's afoot,*
> *Follow your spirit; and upon this charge*
> *Cry 'God help me! England and St George!'*

As ill-luck would have it, a points failure down the line had me sitting, powerless and frustrated, for a good fifteen minutes before arriving at Westminster Underground Station. My carefully laid plans had been shot to pieces. It was now twenty to ten, and, with the court sitting promptly at ten, there was no time to lose. The illegal alien would be pacing the court precincts, glancing anxiously at his watch, waiting for his Armageddon, and with no sign of his saviour. I walked as fast as I could, almost trotting but not quite, conscious as I was of the dignity of my profession, and determined to arrive with my *gravitas* intact. A damp shirt and beads of perspiration starting out from my forehead was hardly the image I was hoping to cultivate, and not good for client confidence.

I was only dimly aware of the roar of traffic past the Mother of Parliaments where, one day, in the not-too distant future, I might be appearing in the highest court in the land, a pleasure in store for their lordships as I charmed them with my brilliant and incisive advocacy. All that and more as I turned into Horseferry Road and up the steps to the court. Ten minutes to spare.

I emerged into the waiting area and found a bun fight at the OK Corral in full swing. It seemed as if all the flotsam and jetsam of humanity were washing aimlessly around the assembly area, with screaming kids running amok, disinterested mothers staring vacantly into the middle distance, and defendants, friends, relatives and solicitors all milling about. It was like a Hogarth cartoon. Matronly ladies from the Women's Royal Volunteer Service were manning large trolleys, from which they dispensed refreshments to all comers, innocent and guilty alike, they cared not. It was gumboot territory only, as the recipients of this largesse waded in and out, relieving the ever-increasing tension of not knowing whether their loved ones would be coming home with them.

I glanced anxiously around. How was I to identify Mr Smith from all these likely candidates? After a moment's reflection, I thought it best to find the court and work my way back. This was easier said than done. All four courts were sitting that day, and a list of defendants of biblical proportions was posted on a board between Courts Two and Three. The scrum around the board made easy access impossible as I peered over countless shoulders, hoping to catch a glimpse of my client's name. No sooner had I managed to jostle my way to the front, when the court tannoy crackled into life: *'The case of Smith will now be heard in Court One.'*

A combination of blind panic and rising nausea gripped me, my mouth went dry, and for a moment, I felt I might lose my composure

– such as it was. Taking a deep breath, I hurried to Court One, almost stumbling through the double doors and into court.

Seated on the dais at the far end in an imposing chair embossed with the royal coat of arms was the Chief Magistrate of England and Wales, otherwise known in these circles as God, who, from his countenance, was in no mood to brook any nonsense. In his late fifties, he cut an imposing figure, his pallid complexion, thinning hair and aquiline nose on which were perched half-moon spectacles gave him the look of a bird of prey as he glowered at the file of papers handed up to him by the court clerk. His bristling moustache and regimental tie gave him the appearance of a military man, used to doing everything by numbers. In front of him, on the advocates' benches, sat an array of solicitors and acolytes, shuffling papers, conferring with colleagues in hushed whispers and ready to snap to attention when their case was called on. At the back of the court was the dock, encased in bullet-proof glass, with steps leading down to the cells.

As I stood, wondering what to do next, there was a loud clanging of keys, the door at the back of the dock opened, and in walked the defendant flanked by two dock officers. On any view, he was not the sort of man one would wish to meet in a dark alley late at night. His short-sleeved shirt revealed arms the size of hams, both heavily decorated with assorted tattoos proclaiming love and hate in equal measure, with serpents locked in mortal combat around Satan and his hordes from Hell. With no sign of a neck, his shaved head sat brutishly on massive shoulders, gold studs adorned his small, pink ears, and his mouth, snapped permanently open, displayed a set of uneven and discoloured teeth.

I had to do something, anything, to redeem the situation, so I sidled over to the dock, hoping I wouldn't be noticed, and pressed my lips between the cracks in the glass.

'Mr Smith?' I whispered.

'Yer.'

'My name's Toby Potts. I'm Counsel, and I'm here to represent you. Sorry I couldn't speak to you earlier, but leave it to me, and we'll have a chat afterwards. Alright?'

Mr Smith stared blankly back, but I didn't have the time to dawdle. Making my way to the front of the court, I squeezed myself onto the end of the advocates' bench. All the other advocates had to shuffle along as the Chief Magistrate glowered at me and this unforgivable interruption to the smooth running of Her Majesty's business.

The court clerk addressed the defendant. 'You are charged that on divers days between the thirteenth and fifteenth of May you did murder one Jane Margaret Kershaw. You may sit down.'

I was stunned and appalled in equal measure. Not only was my client a fare-dodging illegal alien, he was also a murderer most foul. I was wholly unprepared for this dramatic turn of events, and the thought of flicking through *Archbold* 'on the hoof' whilst at the same time wading so far out of my depth was an unattractive option. There was nothing else for it but to brazen it out and seek the court's indulgence, so I rose to my feet at the same time as the learned prosecutor down the far end of the bench. I was not to be outranked as I waved my colleague back down. The Chief Magistrate stared at both of us, seeing but not believing.

'What on earth is going on,' he snapped, addressing himself to me, 'and who and what are you?'

'I apologise for interrupting my learned friend, sir,' I began with as much composure as I could muster under difficult circumstances, 'I am learned counsel and I appear here today to represent this defendant. This new and very grave charge has taken me and my client totally by surprise. We are here to face a charge of making off without payment, yet without any prior warning or notice, a charge of murder has been added to the indictment which, I would respectfully submit, is a denial of natural justice.' A nice touch, I thought, it always impresses the punters. 'In the circumstances, I have no option but to ask for an adjournment, so that I can see my client in conference and take instructions.'

There followed a crashing silence as the Chief Magistrate contemplated my application. He glanced down at the list of advocates in front of him, and then looked up. 'Mr Throgmorton, do you have anything to add?'

Mr Throgmorton, a local and respected solicitor well known to the court, rose slowly to his feet. 'My learned friend's application takes me by surprise, sir,' he began, obviously bemused. 'I have certainly not instructed him in this case, nor would I contemplate doing so. If my learned friend can be persuaded to withdraw his application, we are ready to proceed without further delay.'

'This is intolerable. You are?' The Chief Magistrate looked hard at me.

'Potts, sir, Toby Potts of counsel.'

'And you believe that you are instructed to represent this defendant, Brian George Smith, on a charge of making off without payment?'

'I... I... I...'

As I flapped helplessly, dawn's early light began to break through the confusion. If only I could rewind the tape and start all over again. I picked up my brief, studied the name on the backsheet, which I knew off by heart anyway, and looked up. 'There may have been some mistake, sir,' I stammered. 'My client's name is Anthony Hercules Smith. It hadn't occurred to me until now, but perhaps there is another Mr Smith appearing at court today.'

'An understandable mistake,' he sighed heavily. 'Mister Clerk?'

The court clerk took out the list of cases for the day, and found that Anthony Hercules Smith, charged with making off without payment, was listed to appear in Court Three.

'Well, there we are, Mr Potts, out of chaos comes forth order. Don't let me detain you any longer.'

'I am so sorry, sir.' I bowed reverentially, and made to leave.

'Blues and Royals?' asked the Chief Magistrate, fingering his regimental tie.

'Er, actually, no, sir. Marks and Spencers.'

The Chief Magistrate threw his head back in disgust as Potts the poseur withdrew. I was about to leave court when the defendant stirred from his seat in the dock. ''ang on a minute,' he grunted. 'Where's me brief off to?'

I quickly made my way to Court Three. Although I didn't know it at the time, as I walked in, walking out past me was Anthony Hercules

Smith who, in spite of assurances given to him by his solicitor the previous day, had appeared, unrepresented and unloved, to face the serious charge of making off without payment. Without my guiding hand, he had pleaded guilty, and had been fined £250 with costs and compensation, and warned as to his future conduct.

I never received another brief from that solicitor, but in the fullness of time, and to my surprise and delight, I was rewarded for my *tour de force* with a brief from Mr Throgmorton. Even the worst day has its compensations.

Chapter Five

PRIDE AND JOY

FORTUNATELY, MY SHAKY start didn't turn out to be career threatening. After a few days in purdah, I was soon back in the saddle and whetting my appetite on several mentions, applications, and even one plea in mitigation. Confidence returned, and I was beginning to feel ready for the big time.

In this positive spirit came the case of the Crown versus John Gray, charged with the criminal damage of two rare Amazonian Blue parrots, which the local press dubbed 'Pollycide'. He was also charged with criminal damage to a stately pleasure dome, now nothing better than matchwood, and using threatening words and behaviour.

I knew – and know – very little about birds.

My Great Aunt Maud once had a canary, very briefly, which she christened Chirpy, because he chirped a lot.

The dear woman was a bit batty, and didn't realise that if you let a bird out of its cage, it is the devil's own job to get it back in again, and the more he flew around the room, in a heightened state of agitation, the looser became his bowels. Great Aunt Maud was very house proud; in fact, living on her own and with little else to do, being proud of her house was a full-time obsession, so Chirpy's bowel problems became a significant issue. Further, Chirpy's habit of emptying the bottom of his cage onto Great Aunt Maud's best Persian rug didn't help.

After mature consideration, she decided Chirpy should do his poos outside in the garden, and that was the last she saw of him. For days after, at all hours of the day and night, and much to the annoyance of her neighbours, Great Aunt Maud would stand outside her garden door, calling Chirpy's name. Great Aunt Maud had a particularly shrill voice. But I was soon to discover that Chirpy and his little peccadilloes were as nought compared to the Amazonian Blue.

A conference had been arranged in Chambers ahead of the hearing, listed before the Justices at Surbiton Magistrates Court.

By convention, conferences were arranged at four thirty in the afternoon, on the assumption that able counsel would be fully occupied in court during the day, and this was the earliest opportunity to see the client. The fact that I had no court commitments that day, indeed no commitments whatsoever, cut no ice with the clerks, but no matter. At least it gave me plenty of time to prepare before the Grays, together with their solicitor's representative, arrived in chambers ready for a full and frank exchange of views.

The brief contained a wealth of information. Besides the statements of complaint, my client and his wife had both made detailed background statements leading up to the incident giving rise to the charges.

In addition, a page helpfully photocopied by my solicitor from the National Geographic told me as much as I needed to know about our feathered friends.

I learned that, in the parrot world, the Amazonian Blue is a wondrous thing indeed. Its gaily-coloured plumage, predominantly blue, hence the name, marks it out for special note. It's also becoming increasingly rare, and so, to combat the dearth of acceptable partners, the male has developed a particularly ear-piercing screech. Not to be outdone, the female returns the male's screech with an equally ear-piercing screech of her own. In this way, contact is established.

The complainants were Paul and Marion Pratt. They were bird fanciers, but not your common-all-garden variety. Digging deep into their savings, they acquired a pair of mating Blues – or that's what they were told by the local pet shop. With healthy chicks selling for up to a thousand pounds a time, they couldn't go wrong, so they thought.

The Pratts did nothing by half measures, and nothing was too good for their newly-acquired money machines. In anticipation of their arrival, the rear garden of Number 26 Acacia Avenue was transformed into a veritable bird paradise, with a stately pleasure dome of epic proportions replacing the purple sprouting broccoli in the former vegetable patch. Fully climate-controlled, the dome was equipped with everything an Amazonian Blue's heart could desire, including 'his' and 'her' perches, walkways, the ubiquitous bell and mirror, foliage to remind them of happier days in the wild, and a well-appointed nesting box with all the creature comforts for the deposit and incubation of the hoped-for eggs.

John and Liz Gray, with an 'A', had bought Number 28 Acacia Avenue some eight years previously, intending it to see out their retirement years. They were not exactly unsociable, but they certainly preferred their own company. They acknowledged the Pratts on the chance encounter, such as the car washing ritual and the stroll to the newsagents on a Sunday morning, but that was about it.

John Gray had risen to the rank of regional sales manager of a well-known double-glazing firm, had lived frugally, invested wisely, and retired relatively comfortably. As a leaving present after all those years in service, John's firm had replaced all the windows at Number 28 with their end-of-line Georgian effect double-glazed, condensation-proof PVC windows, which Liz had decorated with matching net curtains. John had added a conservatory and decking in the rear garden, which, according to the estate agent, caught all available sun; come rain or shine, it was to become their second home. A patio set of all-weather furniture and a gas-fired, top of the range barbeque completed their suburban Shangri-La.

The arrival of Pride and Joy, as the Pratts had christened their Blues, was an eagerly-awaited affair. Once bedded down, out came the digital camera, and a brand new photo album in pristine condition was unwrapped, ready to record all those memorable moments to treasure in the years to come.

One problem not immediately appreciated by the Pratts was that Amazonian Blues are creatures of habit, and habits acquired over centuries of flying free in remote forests die hard. As they and the Grays were to discover in very short order, Amazonian Blues wake up and greet the dawn with a screech that can shatter a glass goblet at fifty paces. In the summer months, dawn usually arrives in Acacia Avenue at between four and four thirty in the morning.

To make matters worse, Amazonian Blues continue to screech all day long, the fact that Pride and Joy were perched right next to each other being of no consequence whatsoever.

Amazingly, the Pratts took all this screeching in their stride – as a sign, perhaps, that their investment was bearing fruit. Not so the Grays. Relations, never warm at the best of times, rapidly became arctic. Words were not immediately exchanged, which simply added to the tension that was finally to explode.

As the summer wore on, other irritants besides the screeching began to rankle. To achieve some semblance of sleep, the Grays had to spend the nights with their end-of-line Georgian effect double-glazed condensation-proof PVC windows hermetically sealed, which simply added to their discomfort. When the wind was in the west, the overpowering smell of bird droppings stung their nostrils as they sat, grim-faced, on their patio, glowering at the laplock fence dividing their two gardens.

Eventually, the Grays mounted a deputation of two and presented themselves at the Pratt's front door. It was not a happy encounter, and whilst there ensued a full and frank exchange of views, including doubts cast upon their respective progenies, nothing was achieved to the satisfaction of the Grays. John concluded the lively exchange by announcing that they hadn't heard the last of this, and Paul telling John to eff off. Not a man to mince his words was our Paul.

Marion, who hadn't had an intelligent conversation with Paul for as long as she could remember, took to chatting to Pride and Joy at every opportunity, and her persistence was soon rewarded. She discovered that Amazonian Blues were excellent mimics, and by constant repetition, one of her strong suits, the three of them were screeching away in no time at all.

The laplock fence, unlike the end-of-line Georgian effect double-glazed condensation-proof PVC windows, provided no effective sound barrier to this constant chattering. It wasn't as if it could be remotely described as interesting or informative. It started predictably, with Marion asking, 'Who's a pretty boy?' and 'Who's a pretty girl?' – directed, it has to be said, in a somewhat random fashion at whichever bird looked remotely interested in this gibberish. No fault of Marion's, as the sexing of Amazonian Blues is notoriously difficult. It progressed down the etymological scale to 'give us a kiss', perhaps invoking distant memories of her courting days with the monosyllabic Paul, and Marion's all-time favourite, 'birdy birdy num-nums'.

Eventually, the Grays could stand it no longer. On that fateful summer's evening, John took matters into his own hands. The pleasure dome was reduced to matchwood, and the parrots dispatched to their Maker.

ONCE AGAIN, AND thanks to *Archbold*, I had researched the law and procedure relating to criminal damage. To my chagrin, I had discovered that, by virtue of section 22 of the Magistrates Court Act and Schedule 2, where the value of property damaged or destroyed fell below the benchmark of £5,000 the offence was summary only – that is, able to be tried in front of magistrates only, and not (as with an 'either way' or 'indictable-only' offence) a Crown Court jury. As the value of the two Pollies and their incredibly naff hut were a derisory £3,000, summary trial was the order of the day.

Never mind, at least I could reassure Mr Gray that, in the event of conviction – and, at first blush, I couldn't spot the defence – the sentence was limited to a maximum of three months' imprisonment, instead of the ten years available to the sentencing judge after trial by jury. However, as I was soon to find out, conviction was the last thing on Mr Gray's mind.

I read on. Property, I discovered, means property of a tangible nature, whether real or personal, including wild creatures which have been tamed or are ordinarily kept in captivity if – but only if – they have been reduced into possession which has not been lost or abandoned.

Whatever did that *mean*?

But wait! I paused in my reading as I spotted a faint glimmer of light at the end of the tunnel. The brace of Pollies were obviously kept in captivity, but not 'ordinarily', and had the Pratts left open the pleasure dome door they would almost certainly have flown the coop. This was interesting and a possible line of defence. As I could hear myself submitting to the court with compelling logic, could anyone prove that they had actually been tamed? True, they could screech complete gibberish – but this was far from conclusive.

Self-induced intoxication was no defence. More's the pity, for the sangria-soaked defendant; he'd have been home and dry if it were. I concluded my researches by reading a convoluted definition of 'lawful excuse', which made no sense whatsoever, hammering on as it did about proprietary rights and interests and consent and reasonableness, so I decided to put it on the back burner and return to it only if absolutely necessary. Wrong decision, as it turned out.

Promptly at four thirty, Mr Gray, accompanied by his wife Liz, was shown into the conference room, together with Debbie, their solicitor's junior clerk, there to take notes and report back. Drawing on my experiences in pupillage, I decided, after the usual pleasantries, to allow Mr Gray to open the proceedings by speaking his mind, so that I could see which way the wind was blowing, before asserting myself and proposing the way forward, firmly but fairly. No point in exciting the punter's expectations if there was nothing to get excited about.

Gray was a stubborn and self-opinionated man whose body language and attitude brooked no contradiction; he was not used to taking 'No' for an answer, a habit born of years of persuading legions of home owners to buy replacement windows they didn't want or need. Liz turned out to be his echo. Everything he said, she echoed, an irritating habit which reminded me of the two dead parrots. By the end of their opening remarks, I was ready to throttle both of them.

Gray was off and running in no time at all, and quickly warmed to his theme. 'We tried reasoning with them, neighbour to neighbour,' he said, 'but they weren't having none of it. It was time for affirmative action.'

'Affirmative action,' nodded his wife.

It sounded like something out of *Star Wars* to me.

'We'd taken to keeping a log, with duplicate copies dated and countersigned by my good lady wife for presentation to the Environmental Health department of the council.'

'Duplicate copies,' she said.

'Eventually, after several phone calls and letters, they send some spotty youth to investigate.'

'That's right, some spotty youth.'

'I mean, what good was that?! He was even younger than you, no offence intended.'

'Even younger.'

'No offence taken,' I lied, through gritted teeth. 'At least I don't have spots. Please continue.'

I hoped he might drop dead like the parrots, but my luck was not in.

'Anyway,' he continued, 'Sod's Law took over. We went into the back garden where, moments before, the fucking parrots had been screeching away, only to be met with a wall of silence. I mean, you could have knocked me down with a feather.'

'Could have knocked him down with a feather.'

I burst out laughing. 'Very witty, Mr Gray.'

Gray didn't see the wit of it at all. 'This is no laughing matter, Mr Potter, I can assure you.'

'I'm sorry, Mr Gray, I interrupted you.'

'Yes. Where was I?'

'I remember this bit,' Liz chimed in excitedly. 'You kept jumping up and down, screaming at the parrots and hurling abuse, but not so much as a squawk. The air turned positively blue,' she added with a giggle.

Amazonian blue, perhaps?

'It's not funny, Liz,' said Gray, with a scowl.

'No dear, it's not funny.'

'Anyway, the spotty youth put us down as troublemakers, the cheeky bugger! But you know what?'

'What?'

'No sooner had he driven off, the fucking parrots started up again. I mean, Sod's Law or what?!'

'Almost spooky,' I said.

Gray nodded vigorously. 'That's what I said to the wife.'

'That's what he said to me.'

This conference was taking on Jarndyce proportions. Enough of the cabbage: time to concentrate on the meat and potatoes.

'So tell me what happened on the day in question, Mr Gray,' I said.

'I'm coming to that,' he snapped back. He paused to compose himself. 'Now where was I?'

'Sod's Law, dear.'

'Yes, that's right. Anyway, the final straw came when Pratt taught the parrots to screech 'Fuck off John' over the garden fence.'

'Are you sure?' I asked. I must confess I was struggling to keep a straight face.

'Of course I'm fucking sure. Clear as a bell. I could hardly believe my ears, and not just once or twice, but all day long. The wife's a refined lady, and not used to hearing that sort of language. It's a fucking outrage!'

'That's right, dear, it's a… it's an outrage.'

'So what did you do?'

'I wrung their fucking necks!' Gray was almost shouting. 'I wrung their necks, that's what I did, and I'd do it again!'

'He'd do it again.'

There was a long pause as I allowed him time to compose himself.

Then I picked up Pratt's witness statement. 'According to his statement, he claims you flattened his laplock fence…'

'That's half mine, so he can go screw himself!'

'Half ours.'

'Well,' I continued, trying to calm Gray down, 'there's no charge of damaging the fence, so we can forget about that. However, he goes on to say you were drunk…'

'I'd had a couple of sangrias, where's the harm in that?'

'Couple of sangrias.'

'…and that he saw you running headlong towards the parrot cage, trampling his prize display of dahlias on the way. Again, no charge,' I added quickly, before Gray had time to reply. 'He then describes how you flung open the door, grabbed hold of Pride, or Joy, and wrung its neck. You've already dealt with that.' I pressed on. 'Seeing what was happening, he leapt from his chair, and hurtled down the garden, only to see you grabbing the other parrot, Joy or Pride, it doesn't matter. He cannoned into you, and the three of you went down in a heap of feathers and droppings as the cage collapsed around your ears. Sad to report, he concludes, that Joy, or Pride, died shortly afterwards of shock.'

'And good riddance to both of them, is what I say. No jury in the land is going to convict me, unless we get twelve bird fanciers.'

'Well,' I interjected hastily, before Liz could repeat anything. 'I'm afraid you can't elect trial by jury. It has to be tried in the Magistrates' Court.'

'Poppycock!' An unfortunate word in the circumstances. 'I know my rights, and it's my inalienable right to be tried by a jury of my peers. It's guaranteed under the Magna Carta!'

'It's his right.'

'The law has moved on since the Magna Carta, Mr Gray,' I said. It was time for me to assert myself. 'I can assure you that in this case there is no right to trial by jury.'

'What do you say, young lady?' Gray snapped at Debbie, who blushed and smiled weakly. Debbie was her firm's equivalent of Jason. She made the tea, answered the phone, took notes in conference, and reported back.

I rode quickly to her rescue. 'There's no need to involve Debbie at this stage, Mr Gray.'

'Why not! I'm paying for legal advice, you're giving me the wrong advice and she's giving me no advice at all. Why buy a dog and bark yourself, that's what I want to know!'

'That's what you want to know, isn't it dear?'

I felt an enormous groundswell of sympathy for the Pratts, but with an agreed fee of £100, already spent, I wasn't about to kiss it goodbye – not yet anyway. I decided to try another tack. 'How are things between you and the Pratts now? I wonder if there's any room for compromise?'

Wrong tack. Gray's face went a brighter shade of puce. 'Compromise!! You must be joking! My only regret is I didn't wring Pratt's scrawny neck along with his fucking parrots!'

'I have every sympathy with your predicament,' I lied, trying to calm the situation, 'but as I see it, you can't enter your neighbour's garden and throttle his parrots without lawful excuse.' As soon as I'd said it, I wished I hadn't.

Gray's dark mood suddenly lifted like the early morning mist as he slammed his fist down on the desk. 'That's it!' he bellowed triumphantly, 'You've got it in one. Why didn't you say so first off? Well done, Mr Potter, we'll go with lawful excuse!'

'That's right, dear, lawful excuse,' Liz chimed in, without the faintest idea what she was talking about.

She was not alone. I stared back, with a rictus grin and a mounting sense of panic. Having left it on the back burner, I couldn't now start flicking through *Archbold* to bone up on 'lawful excuse', with the punter sat opposite and his £100 hanging in the balance. If in doubt, cut and run. 'Well,' I said, with as much authority as I could command, 'we've had a full and frank discussion, and unless you have any more questions…' Dear Lord, please, no more questions! '…I suggest we adjourn, and I'll see you at court.'

Two days later, on a warm afternoon in the leafy suburbs of Surbiton, the warring parties assembled in the foyer of the court, ready to do battle. Debbie was there, keeping her distance, as was Paul Pratt, who turned up wearing an orthopaedic collar and a pained expression. You could cut the atmosphere with a knife.

By now I had boned up on 'lawful excuse', and as I suspected, it didn't apply. I had also considered, and rejected, all other defences, so it fell to me to break the news to Gray.

The client was far from amused. 'You told me I had a defence!' he said, with a glare.

This was going to be difficult. 'Actually, all I said was that "lawful excuse" was *a* defence. I didn't say it was a defence in *your* case.' It sounded lame, and I knew it.

'So what's your advice now?'

There was no alternative. I plunged in. 'I'm afraid you have no defence to killing the parrots, so I must advise you to plead guilty.'

'Over my dead body!' bellowed an outraged Gray.

'That can be arranged!' Paul Pratt bellowed back from across the foyer, and it was only the timely intervention of the court staff that prevented another ugly incident.

Gray's inclination was to fight each and every charge to the last breath in his body, all the way to the House of Lords and beyond if necessary, such was his sense of grievance, but wiser counsel eventually prevailed, and after protracted consultations between me and the prosecutor, he pleaded guilty to Pollycide, and the remaining charges were dropped.

At Gray's insistence, and by way of mitigation, I played the tapes of Pride and Joy in happier times in full 'Fuck off John' mode, but this fell on deaf ears. The injustice of it all!

Gray was fined £500 and ordered to pay £2,000 compensation. He left court muttering darkly about incompetent lawyers, but at least he was comforted in the knowledge that peace and tranquillity would now fall like a warm blanket over Number 28 Acacia Avenue.

Some weeks later, I got a phone call from Debbie, putting me on red alert. She told me that Gray had been in touch, ranting and raving and demanding immediate action. Shortly after he had paid the fine and compensation, he had been out in his garden when he had heard the sound of hammering in the garden at Number 26. Standing on an upturned plant pot and peering over the recently repaired laplock fence, he saw to his horror the odious Pratt putting the finishing touches to a brand new stately pleasure dome which had risen, Phoenix-like, from the ashes of its predecessor – and, to add insult to injury, paid for by him!

Oh dear, oh dear, oh dear! Here we go again!

Chapter Six

AT THE SCRUBS

'Mr GAZZARD WILL SEE you tomorrow at two o'clock sharp,' and so saying, Fred, the senior clerk returned to the business of the day.

For me, it was high noon, or two o'clock to be precise, when I would find out if I were to be offered a tenancy in Brick Court, or cast adrift on a sea of troubles. It was make or break time. A tenancy would secure my future at the Bar for the rest of my professional life, or so I hoped, an invitation to join the club as a fulltime member and to begin the climb, *per ardua ad astra*. The alternative didn't bear thinking about.

I had completed my second six months in pupillage and had done as well as could be expected, or so I believed. Chambers solicitors had, for the most part, spoken well of me, I'd kept my nose clean, my shoes shined and my mind focused on the task in hand.

Fortunately for me, Nick Ridley, my pupil master, supported my application, and had put in a good word with other senior members. I was confident, but not over confident, about my chances, but Nigel Gazzard, the Head of Chambers, had a reputation for being eccentric and unpredictable, and if he didn't like what he saw, there was no chance.

'One thing to bear in mind, Toby,' said Nick when he heard the news. 'Nobody gets into these Chambers unless they can recite by heart the case of Palmer against Camley Borough Council. You may remember it from your lectures on Tort.' I nodded, wishing that I did. 'Bone up on it, and you should be alright.'

Off I went like the wind to the library and found the case, locked into a dusty law report from the early 1960s. Mr Palmer, a grumpy old man in the twilight of his years, was walking down the street in Camley, glaring at one and all as was his wont, when he fell into an open manhole and injured himself. Step forward one Nigel Gazzard, son of Nigel Gazzard, Queen's Counsel, and grandson of Nigel Gazzard, Queen's Counsel, who had founded Brick Court Chambers. Not much originality of thought went into naming the male line in the Gazzard family.

Gazzard's father had made shed-loads of money advising large corporations on how to spend their employees' pension funds and get away with it, was burnt out by 50 and dropped dead three weeks short of his 51st birthday. The present Gazzard was cut from a different mould, but carried an illustrious name, which helped, and over the years had carved out a solid if unspectacular practice in general common law.

Enter the grumpy Mr Palmer, Gazzard's golden ticket, as it turned out, to fame. Acting on counsel's advice, Palmer sued Camley for negligence.

Gazzard lost in the High Court and then the Court of Appeal – their lordships taking the view that if grumpy old men were stupid enough to be wandering down the street not looking where they were going, then they had only themselves to blame. I could see their point, but Gazzard, nothing if not tenacious and stubbornly undeterred, took the case to the House of Lords. Happily for Gazzard, and Mr Palmer, that court was composed entirely of grumpy old men who spent every waking moment glaring at one and all, so they allowed the appeal and awarded modest damages and costs.

Gazzard never looked back. Mind you, he never looked forward, either – though, after innumerable applications to the Lord Chancellor, he was eventually rewarded for his persistence and appointed Queen's Counsel. The shock was almost too much to bear. He went into semi-retirement, became a grumpy old man, and saw out the remainder of his days living comfortably off his father's shed-loads of money, bossing the snot out of his long-suffering wife Mildred and discharging his duties as Head of Chambers when the mood took him.

The next afternoon, promptly at two, I presented myself for his inspection.

'So,' Gazzard began, 'you want to join chambers.'

I nodded enthusiastically. 'One of the best sets in the Temple.'

'*One* of?' he snapped back, glaring at me. 'One of? *The* best set in the Temple, young man.'

'Yes, yes, absolutely.'

There was a long pause. 'I gather from Ridley that you wish to specialise in crime. Humbug! All this nonsense about bamboozling the jury into acquitting the guilty, and what do they do? They go out and do it again!' I'd heard that somewhere before. 'I can't be doing with it!' This was not going at all well, and not what I was expecting. 'A solid common law practitioner is what these chambers need. It did me no harm,' he continued, looking wistfully into the middle distance. Another long pause. 'I suppose you've heard of the case of Palmer against Camley Borough Council?'

Here I was on firm ground, having memorised it down to the last detail only the previous evening. 'Yes indeed,' I began, 'one of the leading cases on public liability negligence…'

I realised my mistake almost before those weasel words were out of my mouth, but Gazzard pounced before I had chance to retract them. '*One* of?' he snapped, again. '*The* leading case, young man!'

'Yes, yes,' I hurried on, 'and a ground-breaking case, if you'll forgive the pun.'

As it turned out, Gazzard would not forgive the pun. In fact, he was not remotely amused, and glared at me in the manner of a particularly fastidious and short-tempered diner studying a foreign body floating in his soup.

'Very well,' he said, at last. 'I shall consult senior members of chambers and let you have my decision in due course.' I got up to go. 'A word of advice, young man.' I turned back. 'Don't try and be clever, it doesn't become you. There's no room in these chambers for clever people.'

I retired to Ridley's room to lick my wounds. The interview had been disastrous, and I knew it. To while away the time, I flicked listlessly through the Chambers Vacancies section in *Counsel Magazine* as my mood of depression deepened. Just as the clock moved towards six and close of play, Ridley walked in, clutching a bottle of champagne and two glasses.

'A toast to the new member of chambers!' he beamed. 'Congratulations!'

I didn't know whether to laugh or cry, so I did both as Ridley slapped me warmly on the back. 'And the icing on the cake,' he continued, 'and awaiting you in the clerks' room, is your first jury trial brief. A fine start to a glorious career, I'm sure of it. Cheers!'

I couldn't stop shaking, so I sat down to compose myself. 'I can't begin to thank you enough, Nick,' I stammered.

'No need, dear boy. Now, when you've finished your champagne, I suggest you collect your brief and we'll have an early supper at my club. Tonight's for celebrating, tomorrow's another day.'

And indeed it was, as I unfolded the brief and peered bleary eyed and hung over at the case of Darren 'Tosser'Willis who, together with Matt 'The Knife' Lucas, Luke 'Puker' May and John 'Jo-Jo' Radcliff, was charged with affray. After a night on the razz, the four amigos were pitch forked out of the Cock and Bull public house into the cold night air, well-lashed and spoiling for a fight. They trod the well-worn path to Dellers Nightclub, the local hotspot for spare totty and lashings of vodka and Red Bull. Tosser had only just finished a six-month ban from the club for previous misunderstandings, so the bouncers were keeping a close eye on him. True to form, as he lolled, semi-comatose, at the bar, somebody jogged his drinking arm, and the rest, as they say, is history. Chairs, glasses, skin and hair flew in all directions as the bouncers ran around like headless chickens, trying to restore what passed for decorum.

They failed miserably, so they called in the cavalry, and the next thing Tosser remembered was the friendly face of the duty solicitor peering at him out of the gloom of a police cell. Not feeling his best, he elected to say nothing when interviewed, an invariable practice cultivated over years in police custody, so he was duly charged and remanded to appear next morning at the local Magistrates' Court. Their Worships took one look at his record, refused him bail, and committed his case for trial to the Crown Court.

There was closed circuit television footage taken of the incident from the club's in-house camera. A tape had been produced, which

I loaded into the chambers video recorder. It was like watching the moon landing, one giant step for mankind, only worse, as silent blurred images flitted across the screen in lapsed time, and as I had no idea what Tosser looked like, it told me nothing. So far, so good. Tosser's defence, courtesy of the duty solicitor who'd drawn the short straw and wished he hadn't, was ambivalent to say the least. He wasn't there, and if he was, he didn't do it.

THE CONFERENCE HAD been arranged that very afternoon, at four thirty sharp, in the depths of Her Majesty's Prison at Wormwood Scrubs. It was my first visit to Wormwood Scrubs – the first of many – and it lived up to its rather depressing name. A Victorian creation on the outer margins of west London, where decent folk feared to tread, it had been built to house four hundred and eighty of the Good Queen's less fortunate subjects but, with the advance of a more civilised society, was now home to over eleven hundred, all crammed together in small, unhygienic cells like a German holiday camp in the Canaries. In spite of later additions and some updating, the prison still retained its original crenulated façade, totally out of keeping with the squalid mass of squirming humanity behind its high walls. A slate grey sky and a biting wind which assailed me as I hurried, coat up around my neck, to the main entrance simply confirmed my first impressions: this was hell on earth, and the sooner I was out of it, the better.

Entry to the Scrubs was a performance in itself, proving – if proof were needed – that getting out was a good deal easier than getting in. I produced my letter of authority at the gate, and, after careful scrutiny, I was escorted across the yard, together with twenty or more of the inmates' nearest and dearest, all clutching their visitors' vouchers, to a sort of holding pen.

My first and lasting memory was the overpowering smell of body odour and strong disinfectant as we all shuffled forward to be searched. When it came to my turn, I was confronted by a female prison officer

– it was the skirt that gave her away – built like a brick barn and sporting an incipient moustache. As she'd clearly had her sense of humour surgically removed on or before taking the job, you stepped across her shadow at your peril. After I had removed every metal object I could think of, I walked through the electronic gate, which of course bleeped. To a groundswell of hostile mutterings behind me, back I went, and everything I had to my name was deposited into a plastic dish and pored over like the droppings of a sacred cow. After what seemed like an eternity, I was given a clean bill of health and moved on to the final hurdle, the conference admissions officer.

'I have a conference booked with Darren Willis,' I said. I was trying to be at my most charming while staying on the right side of obsequious. No point upsetting the natives, although my patience was being tested to its limits. 'I am his counsel.' Might as well pull rank.

'Are you indeed?' The admissions officer, unimpressed, picked up his clipboard and ran his finger down the list. 'Willis, you say?'

'That's right. W-I-L-L-I-S.'

The admissions officer gave me an old-fashioned look, and returned to the clipboard. 'Sorry, but I've no record of a conference booked with W-I-L-L-I-S.'

This was not going well. I was about to protest, when the admissions officer's supernumerary detached the enormous mug of tea from his lips and offered his two bit's worth. ''ang on a minute, George,' spake the Oracle, 'ain't that Bootsy Farmer's collar? Yer know, Tosser?'

George's brow furrowed as the thought processes cranked into gear. Back to the clipboard and the descending finger. Eureka! Got it at last! 'Tosser… why didn't you say so? Room Seventeen. Mr Farmer's with him, 'as been for the last twenty minutes'. George looked up. 'You're late, squire.'

I was about to say something, thought better of it, and hurried down the corridor to Room Seventeen. Ex-Detective Sergeant 'Bootsy' Farmer was a big man with gnarled features and a disposition to match. He'd spent the best years of his life in the Met, kicking several shades of the proverbial out of any villain who had the temerity to stray onto his patch. One kick too many had forced the

Commissioner reluctantly to part with his services, with full pension and benefits naturally, and Bootsy found himself out on the street with nothing to do. Considering his options, Bootsy decided to offer his gamekeeper skills to the poachers, and touted himself around to solicitors as their outdoor clerk. Some, with personal experience of Bootsy from the good old days, found the pill too bitter to swallow, but a doughty band from the twilight zone provided him with enough work and more to top up his pension and keep him ticking over.

It was not particularly onerous work. Bootsy was delegated to sit in on interviews with suspects during unsocial hours at the local police station, to attend conferences with counsel, and to sit in court, taking notes and reporting back. Of course, taking accurate notes had never been his forté; during his time in the Met he had tended to make them up as he went along. But no matter; it was better than nothing, which wasn't saying much.

Bootsy and Tosser were in animated conversation as I walked in, and I had the feeling I was interrupting a private conversation. Both were smoking, Bootsy dragging on a disgusting Panatella that smelled like old socks, and Tosser about to roll his third smoke from his stash of Old Holborn shag. My eyes were watering before I sat down and opened my Counsel's notebook, containing as it did various bullet points, flow charts, and diagrams, all designed to put flesh on Tosser's paper-thin defence.

'Sorry I'm late,' I began, tentatively, 'but the security in here is something to be believed.'

'That's strange,' said Bootsy. 'I didn't have any problems.'

I ignored the slight and pressed on. Directing my remarks to Tosser, I continued. 'My name is Potts, Toby Potts, and I'm counsel instructed to represent you at your forthcoming trial.'

Tosser stared back vacantly. Twenty-eight years old, with more convictions than you could shake a stick at, he was an unedifying spectacle – scrawny, with a sunken, sallow complexion, and a grade two haircut exaggerating his protruding, studded ears.

'Now,' I said, trying to sound positive, 'there are a number of matters we need to discuss if we're to fine tune your defence.'

'Look, Tobe,' Tosser interrupted, the note of familiarity jarring with a sense of my own self-importance, 'me and Mr Farmer 'ere 'ave been 'aving a little chat, d'yer know what I mean?'

I didn't.

'Now, me and Mr Farmer go back a long way, d'yer know what I mean, 'e first felt me collar when I was no more than seventeen.' Bootsy nodded fondly. ''e was an 'ard bastard, d'yer know what I mean?' Bootsy stopped nodding fondly, and blew a cloud of noxious smoke over the cheeky little sod, but Tosser was on a roll and nothing was going to stop him now. 'An 'ard bastard, but a fair one, and when Mr Farmer tells me to cop a plea, then I cop a plea, simple as that. D'yer know what I mean?'

There followed an awkward silence as I absorbed the enormity of Tosser's peroration. What should I do?

The silence was broken by Bootsy, who leaned forward and, placing his massive forearms on the table, stared intently at me. 'The way we see it, Mr Potts,' he said, warming to his theme, 'is that Tosser doesn't have a prayer, not even with you representing him.'

A nice touch, wholly lacking in sincerity.

'So if Tosser cops a plea, with credit and time spent on remand, he'll do twelve months tops and be out before he knows it. After all,' he continued, waxing lyrical, 'as Churchill once said, you can fool some of the people all of the time, but you can't fool all of the people all of the time. D'yer know what I mean?'

'Actually, it was Abraham Lincoln, not Churchill,' I said, in what, as it turned out, was my only significant contribution to the conference.

'Yeah, yeah, whatever, you're the scholar, Mr Potts' – a backhanded compliment if ever there was one – 'I could see that the moment I clapped eyes on you, but Tosser and me, we're streetwise, ain't we Tosser? And there are times when that counts for everything.'

And that was it. I thought about asserting my authority as learned counsel, but as I had none there seemed little point. And besides, with the oxygen supply dipping dangerously low, and a rising tide of nausea welling up from the pit of my stomach, I couldn't get out fast enough.

After a clammy handshake, Tosser sloped off to his cell and Bootsy gave me a friendly slap on the back. 'See you at court, then, Mr Potts.'

Over my dead body, I thought, smiling weakly. Bootsy accepted the offer of an enormous mug of hot sweet tea with the admissions officers, leaving me to make my own way out. As fast as I could, I went back through security and eventually, gasping for breath, out into what passed for fresh air. I took one last, lingering look at the Scrubs, shuddered, counted my blessings, and hurried back to the Temple.

Never mind, I thought, *you win some, you lose some. Was it General Custer who said that?*

Chapter Seven

AT THE ASYLUM

SNARESBROOK CROWN COURT seemed to me like the last outpost of the Empire, and for a while, in those early days of cutting my professional teeth on unpalatable fare, it became my second home. It was buried at the outer margins of civilisation and close to Epping Forest, where more than squirrel nuts had been buried over the centuries. For some, it hadn't been buried deep enough, such was its reputation.

My first outing to Snaresbrook was hardly auspicious, and remained in the memory for all the wrong reasons. The Crown Prosecution Service uses counsel from time to time when it suits their convenience, and when their own team of lawyers are otherwise engaged. And so it was that, one evening, I was summoned into the clerks' room and handed my first prosecution brief.

'Nothing special,' observed the senior clerk, 'but the CPS are short-staffed and I've agreed to help out. Besides,' he added, 'if you pull this one off, there'll be more to come.'

I nodded gratefully, and went off to my room to study the brief. The backsheet looked like a map of Ireland, with Tippex erasing the names of my predecessors in title who had picked up the brief, run with it and then dropped it. No matter, it was mine now, and it promised a chance to prove myself as the Hammer of the Ungodly.

My instructions were light on the facts, directing me as they did to the case summary, and heavy on the law. There were *pro forma* pages about human rights and the advocate's duty to the court, sentencing procedures and, most important of all, the advocate's duty to apply for costs. Finally, in bold type, were strictures against the advocate making any decisions of his own. All decisions had to be referred to the reviewing lawyer, whose telephone number was appended, again in bold type. So much for the independent Bar.

The case summary, commendable for its brevity if nothing else, described the defendant, Wayne Pedder, a serial shoplifter who, on the day in question, helped himself to a DVD player courtesy of his local one-stop shop and made a dash for the exit. Sadly for him, the automatic doors failed to respond to his fleet of foot, and he barrelled straight into them and bounced back into the waiting arms of the pursuing security staff. He was charged with theft and attempted criminal damage to a pair of automatic doors.

Fair enough, I thought, *bang to rights*.

Even the reviewing lawyer seemed to agree, and a guilty plea had been indicated. Every prosecution case has a reviewing lawyer, a senior member of the Service who, together with the investigating officer, is responsible for collating the evidence and advising on further evidence where necessary. He or she also takes into account any admissions made by the accused, and then gives his or her 'learned' opinion on the likely outcome when the case reaches court.

I ARRIVED EARLY, and, after a brisk walk from the station, decided on a stroll around the extensive and well-manicured grounds. The court had been converted from one of those magnificent Victorian monstrosities built to contain the mad, the bad and the abandoned, with an abundance of crenulated walls, and fetching little turrets rising majestically into the perpetual grey sky. It looked like a lunatic asylum, and it certainly fitted the mould. Long, drafty corridors, antiseptic paint everywhere, obviously a job lot, and completely soulless.

Although it was winter, there was a watery sun reflecting off the enormous lake, the squirrels were busy collecting nuts, and a large flock of Canada geese were paddling and hissing along the shore. It was an idyllic scene totally out of keeping with the past and present occupants.

My reverie was rudely interrupted by a loud bellow.

Looking up, I saw a strange figure, dressed in an old knitted cardigan, standing on one of the crenulated parapets of the court. Obviously one of the former inmates. I cupped my hands to my ears.

'Get off the grass!' bellowed the strange figure.

Poor old fool, better humour him. I gave him a cheery wave and strolled towards the main entrance.

Having found the robing room, small and crowded, I was about to be exposed to some old-fashioned sandbagging, although I didn't know it at the time.

'Are you Potts?' I turned round to be confronted by a short, wiry man in his early forties, with greying hair, pursed lips, and an aggressive demeanour. 'I defend Pedder,' he continued before I could answer, 'and I'm led to believe that you prosecute.'

'Yes, that's right.'

'My name's Cantwell.' I nodded. 'Now, the defendant will accept a bind-over if you offer no evidence. Done and dusted, and we can be on our way by eleven. After all, some of us have better things to do than fart around here all day. So what do you say?'

'I'm afraid it's not my decision,' I replied, remembering my instructions. Even if it had been, I wouldn't have accepted a bind-over – effectively, a slap on the wrist with a promise from the defendant to be a good boy in future in return for being allowed to walk away, whistling. 'Anyway, I'd say your man is as guilty as sin.'

Cantwell scoffed, derisively. 'A minor consideration, and one I do not entertain. Nor, for that matter, does my client.'

'What about his previous convictions?' I continued. 'Your client's a prolific offender.'

'And just how do you intend getting that into evidence?' said Cantwell. 'His previous convictions are irrelevant, as well you should know.'

He had a point, and I knew it: there are strict rules forbidding the disclosure to the jury of a defendant's previous convictions, on the basis that you don't give a dog a bad name and hang him

'Anyway,' he said, not waiting for a reply, 'I can see that we're wasting each other's time. We'll let the jury decide where the truth lies.'

And with that, he flounced out of the robing room.

Noël Cantwell, I later discovered, was almost a permanent fixture at Snaresbrook. He lived locally, so it suited him. He had three golden rules – never prosecute, never plead guilty, and never fraternise with the prosecution, who were the enemy, to be tolerated as a necessary evil, but never to be humoured. All of this ensured that he got regular and remunerative work from local defence solicitors, whom he kept on a very tight rein.

As I made my way to Court Thirteen, I contemplated the prospect of my first jury trial with understandable trepidation. I was hardly prepared for the task ahead, through no fault of my own. I thought about the reviewing lawyer's clear belief that there would be a plea of guilty. Some review! Some lawyer! And to cap it all, Cantwell as my opponent, with the bit between his teeth. I'd have to be at my sharpest to win the shining hour. But then, the evidence did seem overwhelming.

With five minutes to go, there was no sign of the CPS law clerk, who was supposed to hold my hand and steer me effortlessly through the stormy waters. As I was contemplating my next move, the usher popped her head around the door. Addressing nobody in particular, and in the manner of a fishwife shouting the odds, she bellowed, 'The case of Pedder will be heard in Court One!'

Bellowing was almost endemic at Snaresbrook Crown Court.

I shuffled into court, with Cantwell barging his way forward and studiously ignoring me, all the time under the watchful gaze of His Honour Judge 'Bonkers' Clarke, the Resident Judge.

Snaresbrook was not exactly the jewel in the Crown Court hierarchy, and finding a resident judge to hold sway and bring much-needed gravitas to the post proved almost a bridge too far. However, more by luck than good judgment, word reached the Mandarins in the Lord Chancellor's department that His Honour Judge Bonkers Clarke, recently separated from his wife following unfounded salacious revelations in the tabloid press, had been advised to look for a change of scene well away from his usual watering hole if he were ever to enjoy his index-linked pension. Such advice from the

Lord Chancellor was not to be lightly discarded, so, after a suitable period in retreat, he was duly installed. The fact that he was known by one and all as Bonkers from his earliest days on the Bench made the appointment almost apocryphal.

> 'The judge, without knowing how or why,
> Made still a blund'ring kind of melody,
> Spurred boldly on, and dashed through thick and thin,
> Through sense and nonsense, never out nor in.
> Free from all meaning, whether good or bad,
> And in one word, heroically mad.'

After ten years at the helm, Bonkers modestly accepted the Honorary Recordership of Epping Forest, bestowed upon him by the grateful burghers. He was nothing if not fully committed to his resident status, throwing himself energetically into every aspect of court life. Arriving each morning at the crack of dawn, and sporting an old knitted cardigan, he was regularly to be seen patrolling the corridors, noting down broken light bulbs and unemptied waste bins, bringing his own brand of order out of chaos. He was accompanied, as always, by Max, his faithful black Labrador, who possessed a wet and inquisitive nose as many a court usher would attest. An irresistible combination.

I was about to take my seat when Bonkers addressed me. 'Now, let me see, Mr... er... Potts,' he began. 'I don't think much of this indictment. How do you justify the count of attempted criminal damage to an automatic door?'

'I agree, your Honour,' smarmed Cantwell, rising from his seat.

'Not yet, Mr Cantwell, you'll have your turn, I'm sure of it. Who was the idiot who drafted that particular count, Mr Potts?'

I turned to the law clerk, Tracey by name, as I was subsequently to discover. She might as well do something. After all, this was supposed to be a team effort. 'Who was the idiot who drafted that particular count?' I whispered. 'Can you help?'

'That'll be our Mr Newman,' she whispered back, and took out a form, ominously headed, 'Advocate's Evaluation'.

So be it, I thought, *if you can't stand and fight, better cut and run.* 'I am instructed that it was our Mr Newman, the reviewing lawyer. If your Honour will rise for five minutes, I can take instructions.' Tracey was not amused, and made a note to that effect on the form – 'found wanting under fire'.

'Bunkum!' scoffed Bonkers. Clearly he was even less amused. 'I shall enter a verdict of not guilty on that count.'

Could he do that? I wondered, plunging into my *Archbold*.

'You can close that book now, Mr Potts. I am the law in this court!' There was no answer to that. Then Bonkers paused, peering intently at me over his spectacles. 'Have we met before?'

I peered back, and a vision of the strange figure on the parapet, bellowing at me as I strolled across the grass outside, loomed large in my mind's eye. 'Er... I don't think so, your Honour. This is my first appearance at Snaresbrook.'

There was a long pause. 'Very well,' he said, at last. 'Let's hope it's a memorable one. Now, Mr Cantwell, what's the defence to the charge of theft? The defendant was caught red-handed.'

Cantwell oiled his way to his feet. 'The defence will be placed fairly and squarely before the jury in the course of the trial...'

'Yes, yes, I have no doubt, but what is it?'

'Your Honour presses me.'

'I do.'

'Very well, the defendant will say that whilst on a legitimate shopping expedition in the One-Stop Shop to buy a DVD player, he was suddenly caught short following a particularly powerful vindaloo curry the night before, and, in his understandable anxiety not to disgrace himself, he made a dash to the nearest evacuation point, forgetting he still had the DVD player under his arm. His progress was thwarted by the malfunctioning automatic doors, with the result that, after the inevitable acquittal of this spurious charge, he has engaged my services to sue the store for negligence and the replacement cost of a pair of soiled trousers. Your Honour will be familiar with the case of Palmer and Camley Borough Council?'

In all his years on the Bench, Bonkers thought he'd heard it all, but this was the best by far; he raised his eyes to the ceiling in total disbelief.

'And what about the confession he made when he was arrested?' Bonkers looked down at the case papers. '"It's a fair cop, guv." What does the defendant say about that?'

Cantwell was equal to the task. 'He didn't say it, your Honour, but, if he did, the word he used was "shop", not "cop".'

'What? He said "It's a fair shop, guv"? Is this what you are telling me?'

Bonkers' eyebrows were now hovering several inches above his head.

'Your Honour has it in one,' smarmed Cantwell, totally unfazed by the absurdity of his instructions. 'But, pausing there, do I detect a certain scepticism about the defence in your Honour's remarks?'

'You do indeed, Mr Cantwell. This is a complete waste of public time and money.'

'Then may I remind your Honour, with the greatest of respect, of course' – Cantwell was now positively dripping – 'that the defendant is entitled to a fair trial in front of a jury of his peers, regardless of the apparent merits or otherwise of the defence...'

'Don't lecture me on the law, Mr Cantwell. I am perfectly well aware of the defendant's rights, and as for merits, as you so delicately put it, there are none. That said,' he continued with a full head of steam, 'I have no intention whatsoever of wasting my time trying this case.' He glanced down at his court list. 'I shall release it back to Court Nine and Mr Recorder Twigg,' and, so saying, he slammed the file shut and threw it at the court clerk. 'Don't let me detain you,' he glowered. 'Call on the next case.'

MR RECORDER TWIGG was in the full blush of youth, barely old enough to shave. With a substantial personal injury practice, he knew nothing whatsoever about the criminal law, and so, in the eyes of the Lord Chancellor, was an ideal candidate to preside over the cut and thrust of life at the coalface. Equipped as he was with a large, red folder fetchingly entitled '*An idiot's guide to the criminal law – Judge's copy*', he was ready for anything.

On any view, my first jury trial was a disappointment. The jury, to a man, looked either catatonic or positively hostile. The evidence went as predicted. After my opening speech, I called the security person as my star witness, who looked for all the world like a character from a Gilbert and Sullivan operetta. His uniform was straight from The Pirates of Penzance, the very model of a modern Major General, with epaulettes and tassels and lanyards and badges fit to burst.

Fortunately for me, Mr Security was a seasoned campaigner. He'd seen it all before, so immediately after the event he'd made a witness statement, which he'd memorised by heart before giving evidence. If it was in the statement, it had happened. If it wasn't, it hadn't, or if it had, he couldn't remember. He was not going to give an inch.

The defendant's evidence, as trailed by Cantwell, was true to form, as he trotted out the Vindaloo Defence. My incisive cross-examination, a model of its kind if I say so myself, was brief and to the point. 'A tissue of lies,' I heard myself suggesting at one point. The defendant disagreed, as they do, and I sat down with a flourish as Twigg scribbled away in his notebook. Never once did he look up, to get a feel for the case or to study human nature in the raw. For him it was nothing more than a forensic exercise, so he kept well out of the evidential arena. It was antiseptic justice with a capital 'A', devoid of all emotion, but, with the help of his Idiot Guide, unobjectionable down to the last comma and full stop.

The jury were out for a full twelve minutes before returning to find the defendant not guilty as charged. Another notch on Cantwell's belt as Tracey scribbled furiously on the 'Advocate's Evaluation' sheet. So much for my prosecution practice as I returned, crestfallen, to the Temple. What had I done wrong?

On the train back, I was joined by an older and wiser colleague who'd seen it all before. 'Don't blame yourself,' he said. 'It's an impossible nut to crack. The CPS have an indifferent bottle of *vin mousseau*, which they keep in their vaults, to be opened when any defendant is convicted of an offence of dishonesty. It isn't going to happen.'

'I don't understand. I mean, the law is the law.'

'Not in Epping Forest, it isn't. At least, not our idea of the law. Think about it. Years ago, we locked them away, for no good reason, simply because they blighted the landscape and bruised the sensibilities of middle class suburbia. Then we let them all out again, and expect them to behave like model citizens. Old habits die hard, so when they're not out thieving and wheeling and dealing and getting nicked, they're sitting on juries. Whatever else, there's honour amongst thieves, so is it any wonder they stick together?'

A sobering thought, but how was I going to sell that to Paul Newman and the senior clerk? Even now, I could picture Tracey putting the final touches to the Advocate's Evaluation form, at best, damned with faint praise.

Oh well, too late for regrets. And, besides, tomorrow's another day.

Chapter Eight

TALLY HO

Mᴦ DISMAL FAILURE to secure a conviction at Snaresbrook left me in *mal odeur* with the CPS. They briefed counsel on results, not good looks or advocacy, and those who fell at the first hurdle were deemed unworthy to wield the trusty sword of justice. To add insult to injury, Paul Newman, the reviewing lawyer, was singularly unimpressed with the Advocate's Evaluation form, duly completed and filed by our Tracey. Words like 'dismissive' and 'discourteous' jumped out from our Tracey's copybook handwriting, always a pleasure to read.

As I waited in the wings for my next call to centre stage, life went on much as before, the world continued turning, and it was business as usual at Brick Court.

But there was trouble brewing out in the Sticks, and it was soon to present me with my greatest challenge.

To my surprise, and trepidation, the brief to represent the Earl of Brockenhurst came into chambers, in my name no less, and marked with a thousand guineas on the brief. A king's ransom! I couldn't believe my eyes. Surely some mistake? I was at a complete loss to know why I'd been chosen, so I phoned the Earl's solicitor, Peter Simkins.

'Ah, yes, Mr Potts, you come highly recommended.'

'I don't understand.'

'Then let me explain. His lordship had a chat about the case with his old friend, Sir Archibald Scott-Malden QC. I believe the two of you are acquainted?'

I didn't know what to say, but immediately stood up. This was not the sort of phone call to be taken sitting down.

'Anyway, Sir Archibald felt unable to take the case personally, due to a conflict of interests. They were at Eton together, don't you know, and have remained firm friends ever since. Added to which,

Sir Archibald has ridden regularly with the Hunt whilst staying as a weekend guest at Sandle Manor.' I was swooning in awe. 'Sir Archibald felt this was a case where we should keep as low a profile as possible. No offence intended, Mr Potts,' he added hastily.

'And none taken, Mr Simkins, I assure you.'

'Splendid, splendid, I knew you'd understand. The Press will have a field day, whatever happens, and if Sir Archibald were there as well…' He paused. 'I'm sure you get the picture.'

'Of course.' I felt a little deflated, but it quickly passed.

'Splendid, splendid. Now, we have a conference booked with you tomorrow morning at eleven thirty in your chambers. His lordship is staying at his London house even as we speak, so it will suit his convenience, and he is greatly looking forward to meeting you. As am I.'

After I had gathered my wits, it was time for some serious research in the Chambers edition of *Who's Who*. The Earl's entry occupied the best part of two pages. Charles Marjoribanks Dalziel Cholmondeley Fitzherbert, twenty-third Earl of Brockenhurst, known affectionately to his small but eclectic circle of friends as 'Buffy', could trace his ancestry back to the Norman Conquest. For services rendered to the usurper King William, his forebears were granted lands in Hampshire which stretched as far as the eye could see and beyond.

Over the centuries, and with judicious unions arranged on the nuptial couch or in the stables, the Brockenhursts added to their lands and possessions in equal measure, and thanks to fee tails and entails, held in trust for successive generations, their power and influence remained undiminished. At the last count, the Brockenhursts were the third greatest landowners in the country, after HM of course, and the Cavendish boy.

Sandle Manor was the family seat, situated in magnificent parkland at the end of a long tree-lined drive. The house itself was mainly Tudor, built at much the same time as the ill-fated Cardinal Wolsey was putting the finishing touches to Hampton Court.

History relates that Good Queen Bess, not this one, that one, spent a night at Sandle Manor during one of her whirlwind tours.

It was the time of papist plots and social unrest, so she was testing the loyalty and hospitality of her courtesans. As the Brockenhursts were one of the premier Catholic families in the country, a visit was inevitable.

Having been shown to her apartments for a wash and brush up before dinner, she observed, in idle chit-chat, how much better the view from her window would be without so many trees.

As soon as she had retired for the night, hundreds of estate workers were dragooned into felling an equal number of mighty oaks. They laboured ceaselessly all night, groping their way from tree to tree, trying to keep the sound of chopping and the crashing of newly-hewn timber down to a dull roar, interspersed with the occasional oath, and by dawn's early light an avenue of sorts had been created for Her Majesty's pleasure.

The Good Queen breakfasted lightly on pheasant, swan, pigeon and quail, washed down with champagne, but she was in poor spirits and a pale shadow of her former, already pale self, having spent a restless night to the accompaniment of chopping, crashing and cursing, which she found most aggravating.

History does not relate what comment, if any, she made about the newly-created avenue, or even if she noticed it, but Sandle Manor was well-stocked with firewood for the next two hundred years. The earl's ancestor kept his head and his estates, and, mercifully for both parties, the Queen never visited again.

On his twenty-second birthday, Charles's father called him into the study and announced he was to marry. A suitable bride had been chosen for him from the society pages of *Country Life*, a handsome filly with good bone structure and impeccable antecedents and, most important of all, not yet broken to the harness. Arabella Fotheringay-Smythe married Charles in a fitting ceremony at St Paul's Cathedral, and, after a honeymoon being eaten alive by the midges on the Fitzherbert estates in Scotland, they settled down to a life of married bliss. Ensuring the blood line of the Fitzherberts began slowly, but once Charles had got the hang of it there was no stopping him, and five children were born of their union.

So much for the life and times of the Brockenhursts.

Now to my instructions, to see what hand fate had dealt me.

To Charles, fox-hunting was a way of life, as it had been for centuries. It was more than just a good day out, it was a pageant to be enjoyed to the full, nobs and peasants alike. Whilst Oscar Wilde may have declaimed it as 'the unspeakable in pursuit of the uneatable', he was a girlie fop with long hair, who had never saddled a horse in his entire life, and who should have stuck to what he did best, which was writing mediocre plays and fooling around with young men half his age.

There had been fox-hunting at Sandle Manor for as long as there'd been foxes, which was as long as there had been Sandle Manor, and before. Charles had become Master of the Sandle Manor Hunt upon the death of his father, and it was one of the finest in the land, patronised by Royalty no less.

But not everybody shared his enthusiasm, least of all Steve Gardner, part-time lecturer at the Southampton Polytechnic-as-was, and full-time hunt saboteur. He saw it as his mission in life to save God's furry little creatures, and nobody was going to get in his way. What was good enough for Walt Disney was good enough for him.

As was customary during the season, the Hunt met on the first Saturday of the month. On this particular Saturday, Steve had decided to make a stand. A small but noisy demonstration was held at one of the main gates, kept back by the local constabulary. Banners were unfurled, horns and whistles blown, together with some good-natured chanting. But with the main house some two miles away up the avenue dedicated to the memory of Good Queen Bess, it had little impact.

In any crowd, there were always the occasional hotheads, determined to cause mischief, and even though the estate was surrounded by high walls, a small band of protestors, led by Steve, managed to clamber over and into the grounds.

Later that afternoon, a formal complaint was lodged at the local police station by Steve. He had been viciously assaulted by his lordship, and he had the marks to show for it. And he had. Two livid red welts across his back bore testimony to his earlier confrontation. When asked what he was doing on private land, he claimed that it was his duty as an animal lover to prevent the commission of a heinous act of barbarity.

The Duty Sergeant's first inclination was to send the odious Gardner packing with a flea in his ear, and he was about to do so when the phone rang. It was a newshound from the local paper, and before sunset it would be all over the national press. Against his better judgment, the Sergeant decided Gardner must have his day, so in the fullness of time his lordship was charged with assault occasioning actual bodily harm, and respectfully requested to appear at Little Hampton Magistrates Court on a day to be appointed, at his lordship's convenience, of course, to answer the charges.

CHAMBERS WAS already abuzz with the news, and, for the first time since I had joined, Fred, the senior clerk was almost deferential. 'All is ready for the conference, Mr Potts,' he said, positively drooling. 'I shall sit in, of course, to take notes and ensure everything goes like clockwork. Chambers' best china is being washed and polished by Paul even as we speak, and fresh coffee and a selection of biscuits will be available. You'll use Mr Gazzard's room, naturally, and Paul will give it a good hoovering and dusting before he goes home tonight, won't you, Paul?' Paul, the chambers gopher, grunted. 'Now, if there's nothing else...'

Just then the phone rang, answered by the first junior clerk. As he listened, the colour drained from his face and he started shaking.

'Who is it, Mike?'

'It's... It's Sir Archibald Scott-Malden, and he wants to speak to Mr Potts.'

There was a deathly hush as the clerks' room absorbed the enormity of that statement. I turned to Fred, who was gaping like a fish out of water.

'Do you mind if I take it in here?' I said.

'Not at all, sir.'

What a signal honour.

I walked over and took the receiver. 'Is that you, Archie?' I couldn't resist it. 'Thank you so much for recommending me to his lordship.' I listened for a minute. 'Yes, of course, I shall pass on your best wishes, and I look forward to thanking you in person when we next meet.'

My star never shone so bright as I replaced the receiver and smiled graciously at one and all. 'Until tomorrow then,' I said, as I swept majestically out of the room. It was a moment to savour.

I had no particular axe to grind in either camp when it came to hunting, shooting and fishing. For my part, I couldn't see the point of big sweaty horses, with big sweaty riders, galloping around the countryside for the sheer hell of it. I was inclined to agree with the poet William Shenstone, who remarked that 'the world may be divided into people that read, people that write, people that think, and fox-hunters'. On reflection, though, I decided that perhaps I should keep that opinion to myself.

I had tried riding, briefly, in my student days, when I was anxious to impress a girlfriend who was devoted to the sport. I bought all the gear, at considerable expense, including riding boots that took me over an hour to remove, and breeches that took an hour to put on, and enrolled at my local riding school.

I was allocated an enormous brown horse called Bertie, which farted a lot, and was as stupid as they come. The nag had the unnerving habit of walking backwards, which was scary, and had no interest whatsoever in my wish to bond. Each ride out consisted of Bertie, with his nose up the lead horse's bottom, and oblivious to my blandishments, going at a snail's pace, until the command from the riding mistress to return to stables. Up went Bertie's ears, and off he went at a full gallop, farting all the way back, with me holding on for dear life. After six lessons, Bertie, the girlfriend and I parted company.

Whatever else, and despite my reservations, I was determined to be supportive, as the twenty-third Earl of Brockenhurst arrived promptly at eleven thirty, decanted onto the steps of Brick Court from a magnificent Rolls-Royce Phantom VI. The car park attendants had been forewarned, so there was a lot of running around and tugging of forelocks as his lordship smiled graciously and was ushered inside by Fred, wearing a frock coat no less. The only thing missing was a trumpet fanfare.

I stood up to greet his lordship, accompanied as he was by Mr Simkins, and the earl's personal secretary, delegated to attend to his lordship's every wish. The Earl cut an impressive figure. Tall, well-built, silver haired, yet fit looking for his 63 years, his tanned complexion suggested many hours in the saddle, or on the moor. He was immaculately dressed in a tweed three-piece suit, and he held himself in the manner of a man who brooked no nonsense.

'So you're the young chap who's going to see off this pack of mongrels baying for my blood?' he said, fixing me with piercing blue eyes. 'Splendid, splendid.' He beamed at Simkins. 'Now, what's our line of attack?'

'I assume your lordship is familiar with the case and the charge you have to answer?' I began, trembling slightly and trying to sound confident.

'Of course.'

For the next half hour, I went through the evidence and the law, with his lordship grunting occasionally, and Fred scribbling furiously. Although I was as nervous as a kitten, I tried to sound confident and composed, and hoped I was succeeding. After a while Paul arrived to lighten the mood, bearing the best chambers' china with the promised coffee and custard creams.

At last, with the conference over, his lordship glanced over at Simkins. 'The court clerk has been in touch, very good of him, wishing to fix a date for my convenience... and yours, of course, Mr Potts,' he added, almost as an after-thought.

Fred immediately interjected. 'Mr Potts will make himself available at your lordship's convenience,' he grovelled. 'I shall see to it personally.'

'That's kind of you, but I know how busy Mr Potts must be, as a successful criminal practitioner.' I smiled winningly at Fred, who averted his gaze. 'Johnson.' The Earl's secretary slid effortlessly to his master's side and produced a large, leather-bound book, embossed with the Brockenhurst Coat of Arms. His lordship flicked through. 'Fortunately we are out of season,' he said. 'However, I have a week's shooting pencilled in at Sandringham after Christmas.' Fred almost fell to his knees. 'Then a couple of weeks off in the Caribbean with the Dollamores.' He looked up. 'My old bones need a spell of winter sunshine to relieve the monotony of this dreadful climate,' he chuckled, as did one and all. 'So I suggest Thursday the seventeenth of February at two in the afternoon. Does that suit?'

I turned to Fred. 'Do you have my diary available, Fred?'

I was loving every minute of my new found fame, and determined to milk it.

'That will be fine, your lordship,' replied Fred, 'and I shall mark it in the diary forthwith.'

'Splendid, splendid, then let battle commence.'

His lordship passed the book back to Johnson and stood up. We all followed suit. 'You'll come on down and stay at the house the night before, Mr Potts. I insist on it.' I wasn't about to refuse. 'We can have another little chat and fine tune our plan of campaign. It'll probably be pretty chaotic, so take us as you find us. Until then.'

As Fred escorted the Earl down the stairs, I felt mixed emotions and a dull, aching feeling in the pit of my stomach. Regardless of the outcome, for the Earl this was, at most, a minor irritant. Life would go on afterwards as it had for centuries. For me, however, with the national media crammed into the courtroom, it was a more serious affair. But the thought of a night at Sandle Manor, where Royalty and the highest born in the land had set foot... strolling along the south terrace, with one of the Earl's lovely daughters on my arm, muttering sweet nothings, and perhaps a lingering kiss beneath a moonlit sky. The fact that it would be darkest February was of no consequence – after all, true love knows no bounds, and, as my mother was fond of saying, time to find a nice girl and settle down.

My reveries were interrupted by Fred's return. He was at his most effusive, literally trembling with excitement. 'What a gentleman, the noble earl, such quality, and what an honour and privilege for you, and chambers as a whole. What a feather in your cap if you pull it off!' He paused, and his expression changed. 'My Gawd, what happens if you don't?'

LITTLE HAMPTON COURT was surprisingly quiet, almost deserted, as I arrived with Mr Simkins at a quarter to two and introduced myself to the usher. The plan, hatched the night before, was for the Earl to arrive after us, promptly at two, to avoid the media scrum.

In truth, the night before had been something of an anti-climax.

The Countess and her children were abroad, skiing, so his lordship and I had dined, informally and alone, in the small green dining room. So much for the budding romance, nipped in the bud. There were roaring fires in the dining room and the drawing room, but the rest of the house was as cold as charity.

With the ordeal of the day ahead uppermost in my mind, and with my host and client at my elbow, this was not the time to overindulge, so I held back on the wine and brandy, and had very little of both. Fortunately, the small sip of brandy that I did allow myself saved me from hypothermia in the night. There was frost actually on the inside of my bedroom windows when I retired, and the bed was no warmer. I was all in favour of crisp white sheets, but this was ridiculous.

At least I was rewarded with a full English breakfast the next morning, and by eleven I had thawed out sufficiently as to take a turn around the house. Two hours later, and with no sign of his lordship, I set off alone for court.

As we stood in the assembly area, waiting for the Earl, I turned to Simkins. 'It's very quiet,' I said, anxiously. 'I wonder if we've got the right day?'

Mr Simkins smiled. '*We* have, *they* haven't. His lordship is very astute, as you will have observed, so we put it about that the hearing had been postponed to another date to put the papparatpack off the scent. It looks as if our little subterfuge has worked a treat.'

Although I tried to hide it, I was disappointed, to say the least. How could I have my hour of fame if there was nobody there to record it for posterity? Still, all was not lost: I spotted the cub reporter from the local paper, ready to report grave and weighty misdemeanours such as speeding through the village, and the growing litter problem outside the Post Office.

Promptly at two, his lordship alighted from Johnson's Fiat Panda – the man really was a master of the art – and strode into court. The case was to be heard by a Lay Bench of Magistrates, consisting of three local worthies, imbued with a smattering of the law, and assisted by a qualified clerk.

The Chairman, ruddy-faced, quite jovial-looking, obviously liked a pint, and, from his appearance, I guessed he was a local Yeoman farmer, and probably onside. To his left, and with a new, light blue perm for the occasion, sat a woman of indeterminate years who looked as if she sucked lemons for a living. A difficult nut to crack. To the Chairman's right sat a youngish, nervous man who fidgeted a lot – possibly a trainee bank manager. I put him down as a floating voter, he could go either way.

After the formalities, the case for the prosecution was opened by one Gordon Bennett of the Crown Prosecution Service. He took himself very seriously indeed. After a short but pithy rehearsal of the facts, with Lemon Face sucking away, he called his star witness.

Steve Gardner had scrubbed up for the occasion. Gone were the greasy hair, jeans, open-toed sandals and T-shirt proclaiming the right to life of all God's creatures. He was wearing a jacket and tie, and the pained expression of a martyr who had suffered much for the cause and was ready to suffer again.

Bennett took him through his evidence, competently delivered, if somewhat emotive. He came up to proof, and there was a case to answer.

Then it was my turn to cross-examine. I rose slowly and placed my notebook onto Gazzard's lectern, which I had 'borrowed' to give myself extra *gravitas*.

'Now, Mr Gardner,' I began, trying to sound wise beyond my years, 'you are a seasoned campaigner against blood sports, are you not?'

'I am,' replied Gardner smugly, directing his answer to the Bench.

'And in furtherance of your campaigns, you attend many Hunts, do you not?'

'Yes I do. Dumb animals have rights as well. Just because somebody thinks he's God Almighty doesn't give him the right to do as he pleases!'

He glared at his lordship.

'Quite so.' I was at my most charming: the velvet glove wrapped around the iron fist. 'And would you describe yourself as a law-abiding citizen?'

Gardner's eyes narrowed, but it was too late for turning back. 'Yes, I would.'

As I mentioned earlier, in relation to the wholly incredible tale of the diarrhoeal Snaresbrook Crown Court shoplifter, barristers are not, generally, allowed to raise a defendant's previous convictions in open court. But there are exceptions to this rule, and one of these is where a defendant claims, untruthfully, to be of good character. Poor old Steve had wandered straight into my rather obvious trap.

'And yet, according to this document' – I held it up, doing a passable impression of Neville Chamberlain returning from Munich – 'you have seven previous convictions recorded against you over the past four years.'

Bennett was up like a jackrabbit. 'Where did you get that document?' he snapped. 'Who gave it to you?'

'Is Mr Bennett suggesting that Mr Gardner's previous convictions should not have been disclosed to the defence?' I said, smugly. 'If so, I know of no authority for that proposition. Justice has to be transparent.'

I smiled at the Bench, and even the Lemon Sucker nodded in agreement.

'Well... well... I... I...'

'Thank you, Mr Bennett.' I turned back to Gardner, who was looking increasingly uncomfortable. 'These convictions show that, in the course of your campaigning against blood sports, you have been found guilty of assaulting a constable, of wilful obstruction, and of using threatening words and behaviour. Is that not right?'

Gardner was on the defensive, and it showed. 'There are times when a law-abiding citizen has to stand up and be counted for what he believes,' he said, defiantly. 'If that's a crime, then I'm guilty and proud of it!'

'So you have no hesitation in breaking the law when it suits you, is that what you're saying?'

He was about to reply, but thought better of it.

'Turning now to the day in question,' I said, 'are you familiar with the law of trespass?' Again no answer. 'Do you accept that when you climbed over his lordship's wall, you were trespassing?'

'Of course, I'm not an idiot.'

'So you say, Mr Gardner.' A nice touch, I thought.

'But there are times when the means justify the end,' he added. 'If you know what I mean.'

'You claim that when you trespassed on Lord Brockenhurst's estate, it was to prevent him and his companions from fox-hunting, is that right?'

'Yes.'

'And it was your intention to disrupt the Hunt, regardless of your right to do so, is that correct?'

'Correct.'

'And when you approached Lord Brockenhurst, it was your intention to drag him from the saddle?'

'No.'

'No?' I paused for dramatic effect. 'Then what were you doing when you say you were struck by Lord Brockenhurst?'

'I was trying to grab his horse's reins to prevent his lordship from riding off, that's all.'

'That's all?' I said, with just the right note of indignation. I had the scent of blood in my nostrils. 'The horse was terrified, and began to rear up. That's right, isn't it?'

'So what? If the cause is right, it's a sacrifice worth making.'

'What? For you, or the horse? You've just told the Bench that dumb animals have rights as well.' Another nice touch. 'And yet, there you are, on your own admission, violating those rights! You can't have it both ways, Mr Gardner.'

'It's all in a good cause,' replied Gardner, feebly.

I pressed my advantage. 'At the time when Lord Brockenhurst struck you across your back with his riding crop, you still had hold of his horse's reins, correct?'

'Maybe, I can't remember.'

Wrong answer.

'And as the Bench will know' – I might as well get them onside – 'the law allows a person to defend his own property, and that's precisely what Lord Brockenhurst was doing when he struck you. That's right, isn't it? No further questions,' I added, before Gardner had the time to reply.

I turned to the Bench as Gardner slunk off to lick his wounds. 'I submit there is no case to answer, sir, and I invite you to dismiss the charge.'

One is never sure, but I felt that I had done enough as I waited nervously for the Bench to return from their deliberations. I exchanged a few pleasantries with Lord Brockenhurst and Mr Simkins, both speaking fulsomely of my forensic skills. His lordship, in particular, seemed relaxed and confident about the outcome.

Happily, his confidence was not misplaced: the Bench returned before long and dismissed the charge, together with one hundred pounds awarded to his lordship, to be paid by the CPS.

It was a great victory, and I felt elated. The cub reporter faithfully recorded the proceedings, and the case was taken up by a select few of the national dailies. Sadly, no mention of me.

His lordship took his leave, Johnson handed over the cheque for services rendered, and I prepared for the long journey home. That was the last I saw of Lord Brockenhurst.

What his lordship and Mr Simkins didn't know was that Sir Archibald had sent me, in confidence, a copy of Gardner's previous convictions, together with a list of questions that might win the day. The Old Boy network was alive and well.

Thank God Almighty for friends in high places, eh? Now, who said that?

Chapter Nine

THE TEMPLE OF GLOOM

BEWARE OF CLERKS who say, 'Just a short application, straight in and out, no problems, and you'll be back in Chambers by eleven.'

This I was to discover to my cost.

I had just celebrated my first six months as a member of Brick Court, and it had gone passably well. There had been highs and lows, as with any barrister feeling his way, but that was to be expected, or so I told myself. I wasn't in the 'fat cat' club, as yet, and my modest earnings seemed to dissipate at an alarming rate. There was value added tax to be paid at the end of each quarter, travel to and from court, chambers rent, clerks' commission and then, of course, the dreaded income tax. It all left me perilously short at the end of each month. Still, I thought, it was only a matter of time.

The euphoria surrounding my day of fame in Little Hampton Magistrates Court, rubbing shoulders with the Great and the Good, was but a distant memory. No invitations were forthcoming to join the Earl and his party at Henley, or Ascot, or the glorious twelfth on the extensive Fitzherbert estates in bonny Scotland, in fact, not even a postcard for old times' sake, so the wedding plans to the fragrant Lady Lucinda, or whoever, had to be put on hold.

In spite of effusive promises after the case, no work, either, from Mr Simkins. All that heady praise about a star in the making and a glittering career were nothing more than puffs of wind. It was a strange old world, and there was nothing stranger than solicitors. One minute they were all over you like a cheap suit; the next minute they were but a distant memory.

I was shaken out of my dark mood by a knock at the door, and before I had time to answer in sloped Paul bearing a brief, which he plonked down unceremoniously on my desk. 'Brief for tomorrow,' he grunted. 'Short application, straight in and out, back in Chambers by eleven.' Before I could reply, he sloped back out again.

The head note on the backsheet was enough to stiffen my sinews, and more, as I read to my horror: 'In the Court of Appeal, Criminal Division.'

This can't be right. Nobody appears in the Court of Appeal Criminal Division, or *any* Division, for that matter, without months of painstaking preparation. After all, for most practitioners, the Court of Appeal was the highest court in the land. Yes, of course, there was the House of Lords, but few indeed, with the obvious exception of Gazzard, sought fit to jolt the old fossils out of their judicial torpor. The Court of Appeal was the business end of the law in action, where the buck stopped, and usually with a full stop.

I read on. The defendant had been charged with murder most foul and had pleaded guilty to manslaughter on the grounds of provocation. The plea had been accepted by the prosecution, no doubt after referring the matter to the reviewing lawyer, and he had been sentenced to seven years' imprisonment.

Many might feel he'd got off fairly lightly at that, all things being equal, but not this defendant – and when I read the facts of the case I was minded to agree with him. On the advice of leading counsel, Queen's Counsel no less, he had sought leave to appeal the sentence. His application had been considered by a single High Court Judge, and refused, so he was exercising his right to renew his application before the full court. Queen's Counsel, having been paid handsomely for his input, had long since moved on to his next forensic triumph, leaving his hapless junior to pick up the pieces.

An addendum psychiatric report had been requested by the defence, but would not be available for at least another four weeks, so I was instructed to apply for the application to be adjourned until such time as the report was available, when the application would be renewed.

Fair enough, I thought, with a feeling of relief. Up on my feet, application to adjourn the application, application granted, sit back down again, and back in chambers by eleven. A doddle, and an appearance at the Court of Appeal on my CV.

IT WAS NO MORE than a stone's throw from the Temple to the Royal Courts as I crossed The Strand, through the neo-gothic portals and into the impressive main hall. I eventually found the robing room, presided over by Whistling Jack, the attendant who spent every day listening to the radio and whistling along with the better-known tunes. He seemed to do nothing else.

I checked the court lists, found my application third on in Court Seven, and went off in search of the cells. A few words of introduction and explanation wouldn't come amiss, especially as legal aid didn't extend to the defendant's solicitor. After what seemed like an eternity, bolts and keys rattled in the original studded door, the hatch window opened and a close relative of the Amazon from Wormwood Scrubs peered out at me. I smiled winningly, the hatch was slammed shut, more rattling, and then the door was opened.

'I'm Counsel representing Mr Smith, listed in Court Seven. Is he here?'

Without saying a word, the Amazon moved slowly and deliberately over to her list, ran her finger down, found the name, and requested me to sign in. Actually, it was more like an order. I wasn't about to argue.

I sat in the small interview room, waiting patiently for the defendant's arrival, and flicking idly through my papers. Suddenly the room darkened as a ghost from the past stood, menacingly, at the doorway. I stared, Brian George Smith stared back, and then, almost simultaneously, the penny dropped.

Smith spoke first, his face creasing into a smile of recognition. 'Gawd 'elp us, as I live and breathe, it's me brief from 'orseferry!' There was a bone-crunching handshake as he clattered into a chair.

'Where've yer bin? Yer pushed off like a rat up a drainpipe! But yer 'ere now, and that's what counts.'

I didn't know what to say, and I didn't want to relive that particular nightmare. It would take too long, and now wasn't the time.

Patiently, I explained what was going to happen, and that trial counsel would be available when the case was listed for the renewed application. Smith was disappointed, but if that's what Mr Potts advised, then it was good enough for him.

I shuffled into court and took my seat just as their lordships entered. I decided to sit in on the first two appeals, to gauge the mood and see which way the wind was blowing. By all accounts, it was blowing from the Arctic.

By convention, there were three appeal judges, with a Lord Justice of Appeal presiding. Today it was Lord Justice 'Prickly' Thorne, who had risen to the High Court on the back of a successful libel practice. He had the added advantage of a large *château* in France, which he made available to friends in high places, including the Lord Chancellor and the Master of the Rolls – not, of course, that this had made any difference to his appointment, no, that was made wholly on merit.

The bookends were Mr Justice Hare, a relative newcomer and keen to impress, and Mr Justice Burke, who was neither.

The first appeal, even though presented eloquently by experienced counsel, was blown out of the water in pretty short order. Their lordships were scathing about the merits of the appeal, and made it plain from the outset. They didn't even consider it necessary to retire after hearing submissions. They simply huddled together for a minute or two, conferring, like the three witches in Macbeth:

> *'When shall we three meet again*
> *In Thunder, lightning or in rain?*
> *When the hurly-burly's done,*
> *When the battle's lost and won,*
> *Fair is foul, and foul is fair;*
> *Hover through the fog and filthy air.'*

Just as the second appeal was being called on, the usher came up to me. 'Their lordships were wondering if you'd received a copy of this,' she whispered, handing me a four-page document. 'It came by fax last night. You may need it.'

I glanced down at the document headed 'Addendum Psychiatric Report'. My mouth went dry, and I broke into a cold sweat. Quickly, I flicked through it. In essence, the psychiatrist had nothing further to add to his first report, prepared for the original sentencing hearing, but – expensive holidays not paying for themselves – had taken four pages to say so.

What to do? I found myself between a very uncomfortable rock and an extremely hard place. Smith, for reasons only he knew best, thought I was the bee's knees, so I couldn't withdraw on that account. The brief contained all the information required to advance the application, including the judge's sentencing remarks, together with the original psychiatric report. The only two variables in the equation were the absence of trial counsel, and my manifest inexperience. I sat, rooted to the spot, as the second appeal went the way of the first, and before I knew it, the clerk was on his feet.

'The application of Brian George Smith.'

Smith was brought into the dock, where he stood for a moment, blinking, as he took in the unfamiliar surroundings. He spotted me, smiled, gave me the 'thumbs up', and sat down.

'Yes, Mr Potts?' Lord Justice Thorne addressed me as I rose to my feet.

'May it please your lordship,' I began, more in hope than expectation, 'I am instructed to apply for an adjournment of the defendant's application to renew his application for leave to appeal against sentence.'

'Why so, Mr Potts?'

'Well, my lord…' There was no point beating about the bush. 'The basis of the application was to await the addendum psychiatric report, so that trial counsel could address you on the merits.'

'And you were not trial counsel, is that it?'

'Quite so, my lord.' A shaft of light at the end of the tunnel, but a fleeting one.

'Have you now received a copy of the addendum report?'

'I have, my lord.'

'And it adds nothing to our store of information, do you agree?'

'Well, no, my lord.' I was down but not out. 'That may be so, but I'm not sure if I can do justice to this application.' Better to be up front, whatever the consequences.

Lord Justice Thorne glanced at the bookends, and then turned back to me. 'You have all the information you require, so the only question remaining is whether you have the confidence of your lay client, the defendant?'

Smith stood up, unprompted. 'Yeah, 'e's me brief, is Mr Potts!'

Lord Justice Thorne smiled. 'Well, there you have it, Mr Potts. Kindly proceed.'

I took a deep breath as he tried to marshal my thoughts. It was seat of the pants time, and I knew it. 'My lord, I apply for leave to appeal against sentence on the ground that it was manifestly excessive.'

So far, so good, but not for Mr Justice Burke. 'How can you say that?' he snapped. 'The sentencing judge applied the guidelines to cases such as this.'

'Well, my lord,' I stammered. 'Guidelines are only guidelines, and they don't always take into account compelling mitigation.'

'And what is your compelling mitigation, Mr Potts?' interjected Lord Justice Thorne.

From his body language, Mr Justice Hare had decided to sit this one out, and was doodling on his notebook, no doubt reminiscing about the glory days when he was earning six times his present salary and not having to listen to some wet behind the ears youth chuntering on about this, that and the other. Mr Justice Burke, however, remained ever vigilant, ready to jump in with some withering remark. It was almost as though he were relishing the prospect.

'My lord,' I began, slowly, 'the defendant pleaded guilty at the first opportunity to the manslaughter of his common-law wife. I submit that the learned judge did not give sufficient weight to the circumstances surrounding the events of that fateful day.'

'The defendant killed his wife, Mr Potts,' snapped Mr Justice Burke. 'That's the reality. How can you say he didn't deserve every day of the sentence passed?'

'If your lordship will allow me.' I wasn't going to be browbeaten. 'Here was a thoroughly decent, hard-working man, the father of three children, who worked every hour God sent him to provide a good life for them all. He was a long-distance lorry driver, taking him away from home for days on end. On that fateful day, he arrived home unexpectedly to find his wife in bed with another man. I doubt, my lord,' I added, addressing Mr Justice Burke directly, 'if any man, let alone the defendant, could not fail to be affected by that sight.'

Burke was about to say something, but a glance from Lord Justice Thorne silenced him. Taking advantage of the moral high ground, I pressed on. 'In a fit of blind fury, he lashed out, struck his wife a blow, sent her reeling, and she banged her head against the wall. As your lordships will have seen from the papers, she died two days later in hospital, never regaining consciousness.'

Their lordships were strangely silent. Was that a good sign or not? 'So,' I continued, 'he has lost everything: the wife he loved and adored, the children he loved and adored, and who are now in care, and his life is in ruins. Nobody regrets more than the defendant what he did that day, no punishment can bring his wife back. But your lordships can ease the pain by tempering justice with mercy. After all, justice without mercy is no justice at all.' I'd heard Nick Ridley use that line before and had squirreled it away for just such a moment. 'Those are my submissions.' I sat down, drained of all emotion.

'Thank you, Mr Potts,' said Lord Justice Thorne, and the three went back into their huddle. After a few minutes of whispered discussion, they stood up. 'We will retire to consider your submissions.'

I SAT AND waited. Had I done enough, or had their lordships merely slipped out for coffee and biscuits? I glanced over at Smith in the dock, and gave him a reassuring smile. It was like one of those hospital dramas: 'Your life in their hands'. Such was the weight of responsibility on my slender and inexperienced shoulders. If only that wretched addendum report hadn't been faxed through, if only trial counsel had made himself available, if only...

There was a loud knock on the door behind the Bench, everybody rose, and their lordships filed back into court. Lord Justice Thorne spoke. 'We have decided to grant the defendant's renewed application for leave to appeal, and will treat this hearing as the full appeal. I shall ask Mr Justice Burke to deliver the judgment of the court.'

My heart sank. It was doomsday, and no going back. 'We have listened carefully to the able submissions made on behalf of the defendant by Mr Potts. He has submitted that the sentence of seven years' imprisonment was manifestly excessive, given all the circumstances of the case, and what Mr Potts has described as compelling mitigation. The sentencing judge had before him the original psychiatric report and, no doubt, the same compelling mitigation submitted to him by eminent Queen's Counsel, appearing for the defendant at the time. Mr Potts did not appear in the court below, so he comes fresh to the task set him in different and difficult circumstances. The sentencing judge applied the guidelines handed down by this court in cases similar to this, and we cannot fault his reasoning or the sentence he passed.'

Oh well, I thought, at least I tried, but I was bitterly disappointed. Smith deserved a kinder fate.

'However, there are cases which, in exceptional circumstances, fall outside the guidelines, and we are persuaded that this is one. We are further persuaded that the sentencing judge did not give sufficient credit for the compelling mitigation placed before us by Mr Potts. A single blow in extreme provocation led to disastrous and tragic consequences, which could not have been contemplated by the defendant when he acted as he did.'

A glimmer of hope against all adversity. I listened, spellbound.

'Therefore, as an act of compassion, tempering justice with mercy,' Mr Justice Burke allowed himself a wintry smile as he looked down at me, 'we shall allow this appeal and reduce the sentence to one of three years' imprisonment.'

I wanted to throw my papers in the air, such was my relief and elation. As the next appeal was called on, I bowed low to their lordships, Lord Justice Thorne gave me an encouraging nod, and after a minute or two to catch my breath outside court, made my way back down to the cells.

Brian George Smith stood for a moment in the doorway, and then walked over and embraced me in a large, sweaty, bear hug. As he held me, he sobbed quietly and uncontrollably on my shoulder. There was no need for words. Then, breaking away, he touched me lightly on the cheek, and was gone. It was all I could do to keep my composure.

Back in chambers, Fred looked up. 'Everything went well, I hope?' he enquired.

'Yes thanks, Fred, very well indeed.'

'Good. Now tomorrow, I've got you down for a custody time limits application for the CPS at Snaresbrook. Doesn't pay much, but we've got to get you back onside. Here's the brief, ten sharp in front of Bonkers.'

I sat staring out of the window in reflective mood. Brian George Smith would be out in less than a year, with time served and good behaviour, to rake over the ashes and get on with what remained of his broken life. As for me, life also moved on, to the next challenge and the next mountain to climb.

And what of the future? To the likes of Mr Justice Hare, as he sat doodling and counting his millions, the Criminal Bar was an irrelevance, and the first repository of the intellectually challenged. He had never met the likes of Brian George Smith, with his big sweaty hands and his tattoos, and had no wish to do so. To him, the Bar was a money machine, and if you couldn't afford him, then you couldn't have him.

But there had to be more to it than that. To me, it was all about real people, with their weaknesses and hardships, their sweat and tattoos, their poverty and sheer hopelessness. Even with the constant struggle over legal aid, inadequate payment, arguing over the pennies, if that was what it was all about, if the next case was just another meal ticket, then it wasn't worth the candle. You might as well give it all up and become a lorry driver.

Now there's a thought!

Brian George Smith made it all seem worthwhile.

I had done something good and noble, and had given hope to a man who had lost it all.

Chapter Ten

GONE TO POT

I HAD NEVER been into drugs, not even at university, where they were supposed to be freely available. Well, to be strictly accurate, I'd been offered a spliff at a party once, but, like all those people in high places who set such a good example for lesser mortals to follow, I hadn't actually inhaled; according to my friends in the know, this defeated the object of the exercise.

In my professional capacity, drink and drugs formed a sizeable part of my practice, from yobs in town centres drinking themselves senseless, assuming they had any sense in the first place, to lowlife on dark street corners offering coke, and brown, and hash, and speed, and E's and anything else that took your fancy. It was very depressing, as it was to the bobbies on the beat who found themselves in the front line, night after night, when they weren't back at the station filling in forms.

My first outing into the twilight zone concerned Dave 'Dogface' Brown, a small time dealer in heroin working his patch in Lambeth. By all accounts he was doing well. He had a nice flat, furnished expensively in a tasteless sort of way, with a top of the range stereo system that would knock your socks off at thirty paces.

Dave liked his gadgets.

With a face like a bloodhound, and instincts to match, he'd always managed to keep one step ahead of the law and the competition. However, nothing lasts for ever, as Dave discovered to his cost. Following an undercover operation, he had been charged with supplying a controlled drug of Class A to another, and possession of a small quantity of cannabis resin, and remanded in custody to stand trial at Southwark Crown Court.

I arrived early at Court, to see him in conference and prepare for trial. Counsel originally instructed was detained elsewhere, as his trial had overrun, so I had inherited the brief the night before. I'd long since reconciled myself to second or third choice in the pecking order, but work was work, and I was beginning to get my fair share of the pickings.

Southwark Crown Court was one of the newer, purpose-built courts, just south of Blackfriars Bridge, wedged between anonymous office blocks, and decked out with chrome and neon and garish carpets. A truly forgettable building, but justice was justice wherever it was administered, and at least there was a decent wine bar just around the corner.

Once robed, I presented myself at reception on the ground floor. Time to touch base with my solicitor's representative.

At my behest, the tannoy crackled into life. *Would the legal representative of David Brown please report to reception.*

To my horror, bearing down on me from the other side of the foyer, loomed the formidable figure of Bootsy Farmer, smiling broadly with his hand extended. 'What a pleasure, Mr Potts. We meet again, and another lost cause if I may say so. Still, as Churchill used to say, we also serve who only strut and fret our hour upon the stage.'

Very droll, I'm sure, I muttered under my breath. Poor Churchill, poor Shakespeare, and, more to the point, poor Dogface at the sight of Bootsy the Bard bearing down on him, ready to give him the full treatment and get him to plead guilty. Worse still, had Bootsy already seen him and carved a deal? The instructions, on this point at least, were clear. Dave didn't plead guilty to anything. For him it was a matter of principle. *Fair enough*, I thought, though I couldn't spot the defence to possession. A lump of cannabis resin found where the sun never shines, wrapped in cling film, didn't just get there on its own. Supplying a Class A drugs was in a different league altogether, attracting a long sentence of imprisonment if convicted, but Dave had a defence, of sorts, and it would be my task to present it.

I was determined to assert myself from the outset and not play second fiddle again. 'Good morning, Mr Farmer,' I said. 'How nice to see you again. Have you seen the defendant yet?'

"Fraid not, Mr Potts. I got here early for that specific purpose, but the prison van was late, and he's only just arrived. Shall we go and pay our respects?'

What a blessed relief.

I walked purposefully ahead towards the Custody Suite as it was called, determined not to be nobbled by Bootsy on the way. Dave was brought into the interview room, and after the usual niceties, the conference began.

'The main evidence against you comes from the two women police officers, PCs Black and White.'

'Yeah. Nice girls, big boobs, been transferred to Islington, last I 'eard. Won't see them again for a while, more's the pity.'

Was it my imagination, or was Dave high on something? He looked remarkably laid back.

'They say you sold them three wraps of heroin?'

'Yeah. You're not telling me nothing I don't already know, dude.'

'I appreciate that,' I continued, 'but as I've stepped in at the last minute, I need to be sure I've covered all the angles, and this is your chance to bring me up to speed.'

'Hey, if it's speed you want, dude, then I'm your man,' replied Dave, chuckling.

This was not a promising start. Dave was a child of the sixties, flower power, Woodstock, make love not war and all that, who used to get stoned on Jefferson Airplane and had never moved on. What he couldn't smoke himself, he sold to others.

THE POLICE OFFICERS, Linda Black and Clare White, had been inseparable, even at school. They played together, pulled together, got drunk together, and had sat together through one of those career mornings in their last year, presented by some poor Plod who'd drawn the short straw and had been delegated to persuade the local kids that it was better to uphold the law than to break it. For the most part, it was stony ground, with lots of snide comments from the back row about 'If pigs could fly, New Scotland Yard would be an airport'. Not original, but hurtful nonetheless. Each year, more in hope than expectation, the Plods of this world went through the motions, smiling through gritted teeth and making a mental note of the troublemakers. Their time would come. It was all part of building rapport with the wider community, before giving the cheeky little buggers the cuffing they richly deserved.

But every now and then, like a beacon in the night, somebody stood up to be counted, and in that memorable year, Linda and Clare took the forms together, enrolled together, trained together and passed out together, before being posted together to Lambeth Police Station, that jewel in the armpit of south London.

Their first two years as fully-fledged police officers were uneventful. They were spat on, had lager poured over them, were assaulted in the street, mainly by drunks and addicts, were sexually harassed and generally abused, in keeping with their new-found status. All part of a day's work, but they persevered, and eventually their perseverance was rewarded.

Chief Inspector Derek 'Hot Hands' Spinks, their Station commander, so-named because no female bottom or bosom was safe from his persistent groping, had risen through the ranks, more by devotion to duty than by conspicuous talent, and had his eye on the main chance and a well-turned ankle. When he wasn't form-filling and sifting through statistics and meeting targets, he was dreaming of becoming Commander Spinks, or even, Commissioner Spinks. Why not? After all, if the present incumbent, a complete plonker, could reach the top of the tree, there was hope for them all. Imagine the honour and the glory – Commissioner Sir Hot Hands Spinks, a trip to the Palace, his photo in all the tabloids spouting garbage about law and order and his vision of making the streets of London safe for decent law-abiding citizens to walk at night, and attending Gala dinners with the frightful Lady Hot Hands in close attendance. Better still, leave her at home, and invite some gorgeous arm candy almost as eye-catching as his array of service medals.

Hot Hands had devised a force initiative, to grab the headlines and thrust himself into the limelight, where he would modestly take all the credit for a job well done. The peddling of drugs was reaching epidemic proportions on his patch, and it was time to act decisively. He summoned Linda and Clare into his office. He motioned them to sit down.

'Now, girls,' he began, momentarily distracted as they both crossed their legs, together. 'Er... you've done very well in your first two years, and reports from the station sergeant are most encouraging.'

'Thank you, sir,' they replied together, giving him a winning smile.

'So I've decided it's time to give you a leg up, so to speak, a chance to show what you're made of and to display your obvious talents.'

Linda and Clare exchanged nervous glances.

'I'm going to recommend you both for some undercover work.'

Linda and Clare exchanged even more nervous glances. Hot Hands, as they both knew, was not averse to a bit of undercover work himself.

'We don't quite understand, sir.' Linda spoke for them both.

'Of course you don't,' he snapped, 'but if you'll stop interrupting, I'll explain.' The momentary scowl quickly gave way to a munificent smile, almost a leer. 'I'm setting up a task force to target drug dealers on my patch. It's becoming a scandal, and I want it stamped out!' He slammed his fist on the desk to underline his determination. 'Now, as you know, as soon as the uniformed branch approaches the dealers they scuttle for cover like rats up a drainpipe, and the few collars we feel aren't worth the candle. I want the big-time dealers caught and put behind bars. We're going to hit 'em' – his voice rose to a crescendo – 'and hit 'em hard!'

As Hot Hands leaned back in his executive, simulated leather, fully-rotating, chair, he could almost taste the press conference on the steps of the town hall, with that dreadful little scrote from the *Lambeth Evening Herald* scribbling something positive for a change. 'And that's where you girls come in.' They sat there, breathless with anticipation. 'I want you to go undercover, find the dealers, and collar the lot of them. Are you up for it?' he asked, rhetorically.

'Yes sir,' replied the girls together, both springing to their feet.

'Good. I knew I could rely on you, and who knows, if you pull it off' – an unfortunate turn of phrase – 'there might be a promotion in it for the two of you. Now report to Sergeant Major, and good luck.'

Len Major was the long-serving and long-suffering station sergeant who, since his promotion several years ago, had resigned himself to what passed for witticisms about his name and rank. But he had broad shoulders and a stoical disposition, and he'd been called worse in his time, so he took it in his stride, as he did most things that happened on his daily tour of duty. Very little ruffled Sergeant Major.

The girls were clearly excited about the challenge that lay ahead as they reported for briefing. 'Right, girls, settle down and listen carefully,' he said. 'This could be a dangerous assignment, so keep your wits about you at all times. You'll be playing the part of slappers, so you'll have to dress appropriately.' Linda and Clare were even more excited. It would be like their last year at school all over again – vertigo-inducing platform shoes, short skirts, and low-cut blouses. 'The lower, the better,' advised Sergeant Major, 'as it distracts the dealers and catches them off-guard. As they say,' he added somewhat crudely, 'if you've got them, flaunt them!' The girls giggled together. Lashings of makeup and cheap perfume would complete the look/smell. If the low-cut blouses didn't overwhelm the dealers, then the cheap perfume should do the trick.

'Last but not least,' said Sergeant Major, reaching under the counter, 'you'll each carry a handbag, but not just any old handbag. These bags are state of the art hi-tech with a concealed mini-recorder and camera.' He paused whilst the girls absorbed the enormity of this statement. 'All your dealings with the low life need to be filmed and recorded, so you've got it on tape. Otherwise, with some poncy, overpaid barrister arguing the toss with the jury, it's your word against theirs, and that may not be enough.' The girls nodded together. 'You simply press this button on the clasp, here, to start recording, and press again to stop. It's as simple as that.'

Famous last words.

The next evening, promptly at six, the girls tottered into the station, looking every inch the part. Dressed like that, they were bound to score, drugs or no drugs. Sergeant Major wiped his brow, took a long drink of cold water, put them through their paces, handed over the handbags containing marked bank notes, and off they went into the gathering gloom.

Wandering up Mare Street in the general direction of Clapham, they spotted a creature from the dark side of the moon selling copies of the *Big Issue*. He was certainly dressed for the part – matted, greasy hair, a three-day stubble, filthy old anorak and faded jeans. If he wasn't on drugs, then he should be. A good place to start. He was accompanied by his ever-faithful hound, the mangy Biggles, specially trained to sniff out Plod, and who growled menacingly as the girls approached.

'Quiet, Biggles,' said Scruff Bag, smiling winningly at the girls as they approached him. 'Can I interest yer in a copy of the *Big Issue*? This week it's all abart police brutality and corruption in 'igh places.'

Cheeky bugger. 'Yeah, OK,' said Linda. Might as well start somewhere.

'You girls looking for business?'

'What sort of business?' asked Clare, not yet into the part.

'Well, sweetheart, looking like that, 'ow many businesses are y'in?' He gave her a nudge and a wink.

'Maybe later, mate,' replied Clare, blushing to her roots, 'but what we need now is a little smack. Can you help?'

''appy to oblige the both of you,' said Scruff Bag, thinking Christmas had come early by several months. 'You drop 'em, and I'll smack 'em. Best offer I've 'ad all day.'

'That's not what she meant,' said Linda, glowering at Clare, as she tried to redeem the situation. 'We're after a score.'

Scruff Bag's yellow eyes narrowed as he looked them up and down, and then glanced around. 'Don't use the stuff meself,' he lied. 'Disgustin' 'abit.' He paused, and, from his expression, was obviously performing mental gymnastics within a very limited repertoire. 'Alright,' he said, at last, with his beady eyes fixed on the girls' ample software. 'But what's in it for me?'

Linda looked at Clare, who nodded. 'Maybe a deal, depends on the quality.'

'Yer on. Follow me.'

Scruff Bag ducked down a side street, all the time looking around him, and led the girls to a seedy block of flats on the Trelawney Estate. He pushed a button on the grimy intercom, and after several minutes, it crackled into life.

'What yer want?' came a disembowelled voice.

'Dave, it's Mick. I've got a couple of slappers want a bit of brown. Are yer dealing?'

'For fuck's sake, Mick, keep yer fuckin' voice down! Why don't yer shout it from the fucking roof tops!'

'Sorry, Dave.'

There was a long pause. 'Can yer vouch for 'em?'

'The real thing, Dave, and play yer cards right, they might give yer a freebie.'

'You can cut that out right now,' said Linda. Freebies were definitely not in the job description.

'Alright, come on up.'

With the lift long since broken, they climbed the stairs to the seventh floor, pausing on each landing for Scruff Bag to catch his breath. As they approached Dave's door, Linda signalled to Clare to press the recording buttons on their handbags. Immediately there was a perceptible whirring noise from the depths within, fortunately masked by Scruff Bag's heavy panting. He rang the bell, which didn't work, so he knocked loudly. Within a few seconds, the door was opened, and there stood Dave Dogface Brown – Brown's the name, Brown's the game, was his motto – glaring at the three of them.

He studied the girls for a moment, then motioned them inside. Putting his hand across Scruff Bag's chest, he added, 'Thanks for the business, Mick, see yer around,' and with that, shut the door in his face.

Fortunately for the girls and their long-lost virginity, Dave had just been chilling out to *White Rabbit* by the one and only JA, and was feeling cool. The only fly in the ointment to disturb his Karma was this incessant whirring sound. Was it the onset of tinnitus or was the stereo on the blink?

"aven't seen you girls on me patch before. Yer new?'

Linda and Clare looked at each other. Who said it was going to be easy?

'Yeah,' replied Linda, taking the initiative, 'we've moved down from Kings Cross, change of scene, change of air. More politicians and judges to swing a cat at, cruising around, so the filth are crawling all over the place, looking to make a name for themselves. I mean, respectable girls like us can hardly make a living no more. We don't need the hassle.'

Dogface chuckled. 'Don't blame yer.' He stretched back in his armchair. 'You'll get no 'assle in this part of town. The Plod are a dozy bunch of buggers, don't know their arses from their elbows, and the doziest bugger of them all is the station gaffer, 'ot 'ands Spinks they call 'im, too busy groping the new recruits to bother with the likes of me.'

Linda and Clare exchanged knowing glances. 'Yeah, we've heard he's a randy old git.'

So 'ow much yer want?'

'Two twenty bags and a ten bag for Mick.'

'Good old Mick, never knowingly paid for 'is fix in all the years I've known 'im. Let's see the colour of yer money, then.'

Linda extracted the marked bank notes, handed them over, and Dave left the room, returning a minute later with three wraps. 'Enjoy, girls, it's the best shit south of the river.'

'Thanks, Dave,' said Linda. She paused. 'Are you the main dealer in these parts?'

Dave's expression changed. "oo wants to know?' he asked. There was menace in his voice.

'It's just if we want another bag, do we come to you?' The girls were beginning to feel threatened, so they got up to leave.

'Speak to Mick, 'e knows the score. Now, on yer bikes, girls, I've got things to do.'

Linda and Clare didn't need a second invitation as they clattered back down the stairs and out into the street. It wasn't until they were well away that they stopped and hugged each other, both shaking uncontrollably.

Mick, standing in the shadows on the other side of the road, saw the girls hurrying past and was about to call out, but there was something about the way Biggles growled that made him stop. Linda and Clare were so excited about their first undercover assignment, they'd completely forgotten about Mick, and never gave him a second thought. They didn't see him following them back to the station, or watching them from the doorway as Linda punched in the security code to the inner door, on their way to report personally to Hot Hands.

Fortunately for the girls, Sergeant Major, vigilant as ever at the front counter, spotted Mick through the glass pane just as Mick moved out of sight. The phone rang.

'Sergeant,' it was Hot Hands. 'Bring in the video recorder and let's see what we've got.'

In his office, as Len entered with the recorder, Hot Hands was leaning forward, almost as excited as the girls as they recounted their exploits, but for different reasons. The low-cut blouses were bringing him out in a hot flush.

'If Dave's not the main dealer on the patch, then he's certainly one of them,' Linda was bubbling on, 'and now we know where he lives, we can go back any time.'

'That's right,' Clare nodded, not wishing to be left out.

The peep show as evidence against Dave was a disappointment. As ill luck would have it, Linda had her handbag pointing backwards, giving the viewer a close up of two of Clare's most prominent features. It was a video that Hot Hands would watch many times over in the privacy of his office – for training purposes only, of course. Clare, for the most part, filmed Linda's bottom, with only the occasional glimpses of Dave relaxing in his armchair.

The sound recording was no better, as little could be heard over the incessant whirring noise. Only snatched pieces of conversation could be heard, something about the filth looking to make a name for themselves, and politicians and judges on the prowl for a bit of totty.

Hot Hands was disappointed and made no bones about it. 'Incompetent, that's what it is. It's virtually unusable!' He glowered at Sergeant Major. 'I blame you for this, sergeant, they should have had a dummy run.' Len was unmoved. After all, he'd heard it all before. When things went right, Hot Hands took all the credit, but when they went wrong, it was everybody's fault except his.

Hot Hands leaned back and stared at the ceiling. 'Still, all is not lost. We've got the drugs, this Dave has got our marked notes, we know where he deals from, so all we need now is his supplier.'

'Sunning himself on the Costa del Sol, I shouldn't wonder,' said the sergeant. 'You'll not lay a finger on him.'

'Don't be so negative, sergeant. With the girls on the team, it's only a matter of time.' He beamed expansively as the girls nodded in agreement.

'Just as a matter of interest,' said Len Major, 'how did you girls find Dave so easily?'

'A stroke of luck, really,' replied Clare. 'We saw this bloke selling the *Big Issue*, and we took it from there.'

'What? Mick Rafferty? The druggie in Mare Street? With a dog called Biggles?'

'Yeah', replied Clare, 'how did you know?'

There was a deafening silence.

'What's the problem, sergeant?' asked Hot Hands.

'I saw Mick Rafferty in the doorway, not ten minutes ago. What was he doing there?'

Linda and Clare stared at each other. Then it dawned on them. 'Oh shit,' said Clare, 'we promised him a ten bag, but in all the excitement we forgot about him. He must've followed us back.'

The colour drained from Hot Hands' face. Suddenly he was on his feet, foaming at the mouth. 'You incompetent idiots, you've blown your cover! You want excitement?! I'll give you excitement! You'll be directing traffic for the rest of your miserable lives!'

'It's too late for recriminations, sir,' said Len, trying to salvage something from the wreckage. 'We need a squad round there now.'

'So what are you waiting for, sergeant? Let's go, go!'

With the girls showing them the way, and Spinks in the lead car spearheading the raid, they were outside Dave's flat in a matter of minutes. But Mick had already tipped him off, and as the boys in blue burst in, the flat was as clean as a whistle.

Hot Hands, having caught his breath after the exhausting climb, took immediate charge. 'Right, I want this flat searched from top to bottom, starting now, and as for you, sunshine, you're nicked.'

'Nicked? What for?' asked Dave in all innocence. 'And besides, where's yer warrant? I know me rights.'

'The only rights you need to know, sunshine, is that you're bang to rights. Now get him out of here!'

Hot Hands accompanied Dave back to the station, confident of a strong case, and he wanted to be in at the kill, to claim the credit and the headlines. 'Right, Sergeant, book him in, and I want a full strip search.'

Ten minutes later, one of the searching officers emerged from the cell with a brown lump in a tamper proof bag. Hot Hands was almost triumphant as he inspected the offending article from a safe distance.

'Where did you find this, constable?' he asked.

'In the suspect's back passage, sir.'

'And what, pray tell me, is it?' he asked Dave, now standing at the cell door in the regulation force issue paper suit.

Dave peered at the object. 'Looks like a turd to me.'

Len and the constable just managed to stifle a laugh, but Hot Hands was not amused.

'Wrapped in cling film? Don't play the joker with me, sunshine. I wasn't born yesterday.'

'That's not what I 'eard, Inspector,' replied Dave, enjoying the moment.

The search of the flat revealed nothing, and, worse still, no sign whatsoever of the marked bank notes. Unbeknown to Hot Hands and his team, Dave also rented the flat next door, where he kept the bulk of his stash, money and drugs paraphernalia. Mick was hauled in and given a verbal spanking, but he denied ever meeting the girls and was released without charge. As far as Hot Hands was concerned, it cut down on the paperwork and they had a strong enough case without him.

Which was where I came in.

AFTER MY REVIEW of the evidence, I turned to Dave's statement. 'As I understand it,' I said, tentatively, 'your defence to the charge of supplying is a simple denial, and the girls obtained their drugs from some other source to fit you up. Is that correct?'

Bootsy, temporarily forgetting which side he was on, glowered.

Dave nodded. 'You got it in one,' he said.

'You thought they were prostitutes.'

'Right on, man. That's what they told me, yeah. Any other time I'd'a' been 'appy to oblige, but I wasn't up for it, if yer know what I mean.'

So far, so predictable.

'But I don't quite understand your defence to the charge of possession,' I said. 'After all, the lump of cannabis resin was found secreted in your back passage.'

'Yeah, so they say,' replied Dave, 'I was gobsmacked when they found it.'

'And you thought it could have been a turd?' I continued, with a straight face.

'Yeah, got it in one.'

'Well,' I pressed on, 'it's been analysed, and it's a lump of cannabis resin.'

'Must've been a plant, that's what I think. There's no knowing what Plod will get up to.'

This was more than Bootsy could bear. 'There's only one turd here, matey, and it's you!'

Time to reassert myself before Bootsy went over the top.

'So how are you coping with prison?' I asked, trying to defuse an ugly situation.

'Not bad, thanks man, but the shit was awful when I first got remanded. As soon as I'd arranged me own supply, no problem, if yer know what I mean.'

Dave sniffed loudly and wiped his nose on the back of his hand. A pinch of brown before leaving that morning was working wonders, and he was cool, if yer know what I mean.

I decided not to press the matter, especially as Bootsy was making a careful note with 'malice aforethought.'

'Needless to say, anything discussed here in conference is subject to client confidentiality' – I looked pointedly at Bootsy – 'so you can speak freely. Just out of interest, didn't you suspect they might be police officers? Flat feet, 'ello, 'ello, 'ello and all that? Short of them taking out their pocket books and pencils and making notes as they went along, I would have thought it was pretty obvious.'

As far as Bootsy was concerned, this conference was going from bad to worse, and it showed. He was about to say something, but obviously thought better of it.

'Hey man, they were cool chicks,' Dave replied, 'and besides, I was stoned, know what I mean? A line of brown brings on a kaleidoscope of colours and inner peace.'

A rare treat, I thought, *for those privileged enough to witness it.*

Court Ten, on the fourth floor, was like second home to His Honour Bertrand Trubshawe, known affectionately as Bertie Trubsnore for his endearing habit of falling asleep when not actively involved in the proceedings. As he was seldom actively involved in the proceedings, he fell asleep a lot. In a strange sort of way, it seemed to help rather than hinder the trial process, and was to be commended to his more interventionist colleagues.

He was not exactly cast in the mould of the new breed of judges so favoured by the Lord Chancellor's Department, all work and no play and doing everything by numbers, but he didn't visit brothels, or download child pornography from the Internet, or have a mistress, or get falling-down drunk at judicial functions; in short he led a blameless life, so he was tolerated, even humoured. The bonus for the Lord Chancellor's Department was that his cases were hardly ever referred to the Court of Appeal, as a somnolent judge can't really cock it up.

My opponent was the Prosecutor in Residence, William 'Boyo' Williams from Lamb Buildings, a man with his roots firmly planted in the Welsh foothills. He did nothing but prosecute, Grade Three, and by dint of careful personnel management and regular visits with police officers and members of the CPS to the wine bar round the corner, he avoided the fate of other lesser mortals who came and went like the seasons. In his early fifties, with dark, wavy hair, bushy eyebrows and a very pink face, coloured over the years by too many large glasses of Sauvignon Blanc, he had a loud, mellifluous voice, as if about to burst into song at any moment, probably something about welcomes in valleys or green, green grass of wherever.

With the court assembled, I glanced over to Boyo. Sitting behind him was the prosecution team. Hot Hands was there, not as a witness but an interested spectator, along with the officer in the case, a DC Munro, and the CPS law clerk, ready to take notes, fill in forms and report back to the reviewing lawyer. All I had on offer was the truculent Bootsy Farmer, still smarting from the conference, and my determination to keep him firmly in check.

With the jury empanelled, Boyo opened the case for the prosecution. It was a fair summary, if a tad too long, and just as Trubsnore's head was beginning to droop, Linda was called to give evidence.

With Hot hands smiling encouragement, and Dave semi-supine in the dock and right out of it, Linda gave her evidence well enough, and then it was my turn to cross examine.

This was the signal for Trubsnore to push his notebook away and settle down for the first of his daily naps.

'You were dressed that night for what purpose?' I said.

'We were undercover.'

'Yes, I appreciate that, but how were you dressed?'

'In plain clothes.'

'A low-cut, revealing blouse, a mini skirt that would make a face flannel look like a horse blanket, fishnet stockings and platform shoes, is that right?'

Linda, paused, clearly embarrassed by the description. 'Something like that,' she replied.

'In short, you and your colleague were dressed like prostitutes, or "slappers" to use the common parlance. That's right, isn't it?'

Linda, was on the defensive. 'We were just playing a part.'

'And you were chosen for this undercover assignment, not for your experience but for your obvious female attractions?'

'In part, I suppose.'

'Which part do you suppose?'

Boyo rose to his feet. 'Really, your Honour, are these sexual innuendos appropriate?'

'Moving on,' I continued, ignoring Boyo, 'you told the defendant that you had come south of the river to escape the clutches of politicians and judges hassling you for sex in King's Cross?'

Trubsnore jerked himself into life. 'What's that you say? Judges hassling you for sex?'

'It was only an act, your Honour. We were playing a role.'

'I should hope so too,' Trubsnore was not amused. 'The very idea! Members of the jury, I direct you to disregard such a disgraceful suggestion! Proceed, Mr Potts.'

'Thank you, Your Honour. What brought you to the defendant's flat?'

'We were taken there by Mick Rafferty, a well-known local junkie,' replied Linda, regaining her confidence.

'You had never been to the flats before that night, had you?'

'That's right.'

'And you had never met the defendant before that night, had you?'

'No, we hadn't.'

So far, so good, I thought, but was I making any real progress? Time to find out.

'These flats are notorious in the area?'

'What do you mean?'

'Well, for a start, they're a regular stamping ground for prostitutes plying their trade, aren't they?'

'I wouldn't know,' replied Linda.

'Really? And yet you had been stationed barely half a mile away for the best part of two years?'

'Well, yes, but we weren't involved in prostitution.'

'I should hope not.' A few titters from the jury.

'That's not what I meant.'

'It comes down to this, doesn't it? You went to the flats dressed as prostitutes, you were invited into the defendant's flat dressed as prostitutes, and you actually told the defendant you were prostitutes from Kings Cross?'

'Yes, but I've already explained that.'

'And he asked how much did you want?'

'That's right.'

'For sex.'

'That's not true.'

'You said twenty pounds each for a quickie, he said it was too much and showed you to the door, that's right, isn't it?'

Trubsnore opened one eye. 'Twenty pounds for a quickie, Mr Potts? What does that mean?'

'Your Honour, it means sexual intercourse lasting less than five minutes.'

Trubsnore chuckled. 'Not much for your money, then? No wonder the defendant declined the offer.'

Boyo was up on his feet. 'Your Honour, the witness does not accept the suggestion that such an offer was made, so your Honour's speculation is irrelevant.'

'Kindly allow me to decide what is relevant or irrelevant, Mr Williams.' *One in the eye for Boyo*, I thought. 'Please continue Mr Potts, but I hope there's a point to all this, as the jury and I are in danger of losing the plot.'

'Of course, your Honour.' Turning back to Linda. 'I suggest you were there offering sex.'

'No, we were not. We were there to buy drugs. Sex didn't come into it. We handed over fifty pounds…'

Trubsnore was taking an unusually active part in the proceedings, even if he was on the wrong tack. 'So if twenty pounds buys you a "quickie", what does fifty pounds buy?'

Boyo thought about objecting, but changed his mind half way up.

'Can you help His Honour?' I asked mischievously.

'No, I can't,' she snapped back. 'You're deliberately trying to confuse me. The fifty pounds was for drugs, we handed over fifty pounds and the defendant gave us the drugs. How many more times do I have to say it?'

Trubsnore, still awake, rebuked Linda. 'Just answer counsel's questions, and leave the comments to me.'

'I'm sorry, Your Honour.'

'Very well. Continue Mr Potts, but let brevity be your watchword.'

'Thank you, Your Honour. You say the defendant sold you the drugs, but are there any fingerprints to support your allegation?'

'No.'

'His flat was searched from top to bottom. Was anything found?'

'No, but…'

'So these drugs could have come from anywhere?'

'Yes, but…'

'Other than your word for it, there is no independent evidence to connect these drugs with the defendant, isn't that right?'

'No, but…'

'Thank you, no further questions.'

Clare was next up to bat, sticking resolutely to the script, and then the searching officer was called to give evidence. Trubsnore had fallen back into a fitful doze, only to wake up as Boyo was waving the sealed tamper proof bag in front of the jury.

'What have you got there, Mr Williams?' he asked in a spirit of enquiry.

'A lump of cannabis resin, Your Honour.'

'Really? Pass it up.' Feigning a passing interest, Trubsnore removed it from the bag, inspected it carefully, smelled it, and then replaced it into the bag. 'And remind the jury where exactly was it found, Mr Williams?' he asked in all innocence.

Boyo paused. 'Does your Honour *really* want to know the answer to that question?'

Trubsnore paused, looked at the offending article, then back at Boyo, then, with an agility that belied his years, leapt up from the Bench and headed for the door.

'All rise,' intoned the usher at the judge's departing back.

Ten minutes later, and with the colour drained from his face, Trubsnore returned to court and the trial resumed.

DAVE DECLINED to give evidence, whether sitting or standing up, just as he'd declined to answer questions when arrested. It wasn't cool, and, besides, he'd rather yawn, and be withdrawn, and watch them gallop by.

My efforts to persuade the jury that Dave was not a drug dealer were undermined in large measure by the sight of my client, slumped in the dock, spaced out, eyes glazed, head snapped back and humming a selection from The Greatest Hits of Jefferson Airplane quietly to himself.

The jury were out for nearly three hours before returning verdicts of guilty by a majority of ten to two. Dave was sentenced to three years' imprisonment, and, having spent twelve months on remand, would be out in no time at all.

It was a victory of sorts for everyone. Mick was minding the store in Dave's absence, and business was brisk. Dave had extended his client list by several dozen amongst his newfound friends, and Mick was pushed to keep up with demand.

Hot Hands had his five minutes of glory on the steps of the court, and the girls got their promotion.

Bootsy greeted the verdict with smug satisfaction. He may be gamekeeper turned poacher, but his heart still belonged to the Met, and the best bunch of lads you'd never wish to meet. You crossed them at your peril. As for Smart Alec lawyers, they're all the same, all mouth and no trousers, and not worth spit! As Churchill once said, a policeman's lot is not an 'appy one, and he was right. Give credit where credit's due, that was his motto, and if you can't stand the heat, get out of the kitchen.

Within twenty minutes of sentence being passed, Boyo, in full song, was in the wine bar, clutching a bottle of Sauvignon Blanc and tomorrow's brief and making merry with the officers in the case and the law clerk from the CPS.

As I made my way back to Chambers, I reflected on my time at the Bar and what the future might hold for me.

As Dave Dogface Brown would put it, the answer, my friend, was blowin' in the wind. Problem was, he'd forgotten the question.

Chapter Eleven

LOVE IS IN THE AIR

IT WAS A MEMORABLE week in my life as the pace quickened. I had been instructed to represent an eighteen-year-old yob charged with mugging a group of schoolboys and relieving them of their pocket money and a BMX bike.

Without Bootsy's firm hand on the tiller, the youth had decided to chance his arm with the jury, but it was an uphill struggle. I was pushed to make a fist of it, especially as the school kids all knew the defendant from earlier encounters in the playground, and the BMX was found in his auntie's shed. But the best evidence came from a veritable vision of loveliness, Camilla Foster-Ward, who was on her way to a modelling assignment in her Audi TT and witnessed the whole incident. Unlike many who would simply drive on, she stopped to comfort the kids and left her name and address with Plod.

From the moment she swayed elegantly into court, the defendant's fate was sealed. Whatever else the jury were going to make of the school kids, they were totally captivated by the fragrant Camilla and every word she uttered. The defendant went crashing down in record time.

To refresh my spirits after such a depressing ordeal, I popped into a nearby wine bar. As luck would have it, I found Camilla inside, eating alone at a corner table. My heart skipped a beat and, taking a deep breath, I went over and introduced myself. She didn't seem hugely impressed, but nodded to the chair opposite and I sat down.

As the wine loosened my natural reserve, we chatted easily about this and that and, mercifully, very little about the case. I had attacked her evidence as nought but a tissue of lies – not quite so crudely, but that was the thrust of it – but she was a forgiving sort. In fact, she found the whole experience amusing and light relief from earning obscene amounts of money on the catwalk. I was smitten, not just by her natural beauty, but also by her confident and relaxed manner. Was it love at first sight? I thought so, but asking her out was a different matter entirely.

Camilla was way up there out of my league, but then, stranger things had happened, and I'd watched *Four Weddings and a Funeral* several times, where the fashion model in the big hat had fallen for Hugh Grant, albeit by a very circuitous route. And what did Hugh Grant have that I didn't?

I could see it all, the two of us snapped secretly by the paparazzi whilst cavorting on the beach in Barbados, or coming out of Stringfellows – or, better still, Annabel's.

As she got up to leave, it was now or never. Offering to pay for her meal was a big mistake, and she made that very clear. She was rich, independent and only willing to be indulged on her own terms. But my gesture obviously struck a chord, and my invitation to dinner was not dismissed totally out of hand.

'Look,' she said casually, 'I'm having a few friends round for supper tomorrow night. Why don't you come along. That's if you've got nothing better to do?'

I could hardly believe my ears. 'Thanks, that would be great.'

Camilla gave me her address. 'See you about nine,' and with that she was gone.

Fortunately for me, I was out of court the next day 'working on papers', as the clerks euphemistically referred to unemployment, and I was able to concentrate on the evening ahead.

A gesture of some sort was *de rigueur*.

Perhaps a bottle of Chateau Plonk, wine you never dreamt of drinking yourself but which was passed on round the drinks party circuit like an unexploded bomb until eventually, with the off-licences and pubs closed, some unlucky sod actually uncorked the noxious liquid and passed out from the fumes. A safer bet would be flowers and chocolates, not very imaginative, but less likely to cause offence. But a moment's reflection exposed the folly of that idea. You don't give chocolates to a model. What would Hugh Grant take – besides his enormous sex drive and smarmy ways? As I had neither, that was of no help at all.

Shortly after nine that evening, and clutching an expensive and elaborately-presented corsage, I rang the doorbell to a delightful mews house just off the Portobello Road where the supper party for a few friends was in full swing.

It was not what I'd expected at all. Some drop-dead gorgeous whom I had never seen before opened the door, and, leaving it open, swayed back inside without a word. I followed her into the living room, jam-packed with forty or fifty beautiful people straight from the pages of *OK!* and *Hello!* magazines, screaming at each other over the primordial beat of Ozzy Osbourne and Black Sabbath.

Glancing round the room, I spotted Camilla, draped across a sofa and being nuzzled by… Oh my God, it *couldn't* be! It *was*! Hugh Grant himself! His star was waxing mightily at that time, with another one of those rip-roaring Richard Curtis hits in the can – not the one with Julia Roberts, the one with Emma Thompson – and his foppish hair and self-deprecating smile were unmistakeable.

Camilla waved and beckoned me over. 'So glad you made it. You know Hugh, of course. Hugh, this is Toby, that absolute darling of a barrister I was telling you about. Very good, and very grand. Had me quivering like a jelly!'

'Now that, my darling,' purred Hugh, batting his eyelids, 'is something I wouldn't have missed for the world.' He gave us both his crinkly-eyed, million dollar smile. 'Good to meet you, Toby,' he lied, probably – though doubtless out of the most gentlemanly of motives. 'Now, Millie, I must love you and leave you. Got things to do. See you next time around.' And with a long, lingering, parting kiss, he sloped out.

With the departure of my main rival, I handed over the corsage. 'Oh Toby,' said Camilla, 'how absolutely divine! You shouldn't have. Now, there's lasagne and salad in the kitchen. Help yourself, and there's champers all over the place. Then I'll introduce you around.'

It was one of those parties where you roared at the person standing right in front of you, they roared back, and neither of you were any the wiser. Still, I went through the motions, and smiled and nodded a lot.

It was past two in the morning before the party began to disperse, I was exhausted, and decided it was time to go. But Camilla was having none of it. 'Don't be so wet, Toby. Stay the night.'

It was an invitation no red-blooded male could resist, but I did my best to appear as though this happened to me all the time. 'Are you sure?' I said. 'Won't that be a frightful inconvenience?'

Camilla smiled indulgently. 'Have another glass of champers, and I'll get rid of the stragglers.'

An hour later, Camilla led me upstairs to the master bedroom.

'I'm going to have a shower,' she said. 'There are condoms in the bedside drawer, all sizes and flavours, so help yourself. See you in five.' Her dress fell lightly from her exquisite shoulders and, as she was about to close the bathroom door, she turned and added, seductively, 'I prefer raspberry.'

This was not at all what I had expected. I wasn't a complete novice in these matters, and had had my fair share of flings at university. Well, two, actually, but I was a shy and sensitive boy, I got that from my mother, so it usually took me weeks, if not months, of courting, before the moment was right. And now, confronted with the most beautiful girl I'd ever met, would I be up to it?

I opened the drawer to find three packs of condoms, labelled small, medium, and large, all in assorted flavours. I found myself on the horns of a dilemma. Which size to choose? I couldn't help but notice the pack of large condoms nearly empty, speaking volumes for Camilla's previous conquests. The small pack was unopened, so if I took one, I'd be the laughing stock of Notting Hill and never live it down. Safer to choose the medium size, mercifully already opened, so long as it didn't cramp my style.

I had just slipped it on and was getting into bed when Camilla appeared, completely naked and ready for action.

I like to think I gave a good account of myself during two hours of active and unbridled passion, until finally, drained of all emotion, I fell into a deep and exhausted sleep.

I awoke to find Camilla putting the finishing touches to her makeup, ready for the day's shoot.

'Help yourself to toast and coffee,' she said, standing up and checking her dress for creases in the full-length mirror. 'If you're really hungry, there's cold lasagne and warm champers,' she giggled. 'Mrs Do-For-Me will be here at nine, so if you leave before she arrives, slam the door behind you, there's a darling.'

I propped myself up on one arm and gazed at her sleepily. 'What a wonderful party,' I smiled lovingly, 'and what a wonderful night.' I paused. 'So when do I see you again?'

Camilla smiled back, tossing her hair. 'Easy, big fella!' she replied. 'Let's not rush into anything we can't handle.'

'But I'm hopelessly in love with you,' I replied, surprising even myself, 'and I can't live without you.'

'And I love you too,' she replied, bending over the bed and kissing me lightly on the forehead to avoid smudging her lipstick. 'Now I must get going or I'll be late.'

'It's my birthday on Friday. I'm having a party, nothing as grand as yours, but it should be fun. Will you come?'

'Sure, it sounds great.'

I was excited. 'Gray's Inn, starting about seven thirty. Shall I pick you up?'

'No need, I'll find it, don't worry. Now I really must be going. See you on Friday.'

I had planned to celebrate my birthday in style. Several chums were to assemble in Gray's Inn Common Room to kick start the evening's activities, then on to Henekey's Wine Bar on High Holborn for champagne and oysters, and then, well-refreshed, to the Mille Pini Italian Restaurant just off Theobalds Road, where the basement had been reserved for food, wine and laddish behaviour.

I had bragged to my inner circle about Camilla, about how we were hopelessly in love and, as they would see for themselves, how she was the most beautiful girl in the world. I was greatly looking forward to showing her off, and watching their envious glances as we wined and dined and cavorted the night away. And then, to round off a memorable night, back to her place for another bout of passionate lovemaking. I'd even bought my own supply of condoms in Camilla's favourite flavours. I could hardly wait.

No sign of Camilla at Gray's Inn, but then, I reasoned, not easy to find, tucked away as it was behind a small arched entrance off High Holborn. Leaving a message with the barman in case she showed up late, my friends and I moved on to Henekeys, but still no show. Hoping against hope she would come breezing through the door at any moment, I considered the various options. Perhaps she'd been detained on a late shoot, yes, that was it, and as she didn't have my number, there was no way of letting me know. Never mind, perhaps she'll catch up with me at the Mille Pini. After all, the night was yet young, and she was very much a party animal.

The Mille Pini Restaurant, or Thousand Pines for the linguistically-challenged, may have called itself an Italian Restaurant, but there the similarity ended. The waiters were all Cockney to a man, but to maintain the Italian theme, had been rechristened, so Paul became Paulo, Fred Frederico, John José and so on, with Bill the owner, a lateral thinker, calling himself Manuel. They had also been schooled to speak Italian, which consisted of adding the letters 'a' or 'i' after almost every English word they uttered. So when taking the order, Paulo, or Frederico or José, whichever, would say: 'Wadda you wanna eata?' and wave their hands around. You could almost smell Naples.

The chef, Jock McTavish, was Scottish, with flaming red hair and a temper to match, who swore like a trooper and threw knives around, mostly in the direction of the long-suffering kitchen staff. But he made a Spaghetti alla Vongole to die for, his cannelloni was always fresh and, best of all, by London standards it was cheap and cheerful.

And so we dined, and drank, and sang badly, and danced the conga round the tables and into the small hours and, eventually, I fell into bed with only my unused condoms for company. Still, there'd be other times, I was sure of it.

I HAD PROMISED to spend what remained of the weekend with my parents, and, if all had gone to plan, to take Camilla with me. Next weekend, perhaps.

I arrived on the six o'clock train and decided to walk the mile to the house. It was a pleasant early summer evening, and I needed the exercise to loosen the hangover and expel the overpowering taste of garlic still clinging remorselessly to my breath.

After kisses and hugs, and the usual comments from my mother about how thin and tired I looked, I went upstairs to shower and dress for dinner. Smart casual was the order of the evening as I joined my father in the drawing room.

'So, my boy,' he said, with an indulgent smile. 'How's it going? Still glad you joined the Bar? I know a good solicitor, member of Rotary, who may have an opening if you want me to put in a good word.'

I returned the smile, remembering my father's dismissive description of barristers as pompous upper class idiots in fancy dress; nothing he'd seen or heard over the past two years had persuaded him to change his opinion.

'Thanks, Father,' I said. 'I'll bear it in mind, but for the time being I'm enjoying my work. Can't say I'm winning many cases, but it's only a matter of time.' Or so I hoped.

'Well,' replied my father, 'you can't make bricks without straw. If it's really what you want, then stick to it. Your mother and I are very proud of you, you know that.'

'I do, and thanks for everything.' I took a sip of champagne and glanced through to the dining room. 'I see the table's laid for six. Is that ominous?'

'Didn't your mother tell you? She's invited the Sandwells.'

'Oh no, don't tell me, Susie Sandwell on parade, yet again.'

My father smiled. 'You can't blame your mother for trying. She thinks it's time you met a nice girl and settled down. And besides, you have a lot in common.'

'Actually, I have a girlfriend,' I replied, my chest swelling. 'She's a top model, absolutely stunning, name's Camilla Foster-Ward, you may have heard of her?'

My father shook his head.

'I'd hoped to bring her down for the weekend, but she was unavoidably detained at the last minute. You know what life can be like for a top model, on call twenty-four hours a day. Still, you and mother will meet her soon enough.'

Just then the doorbell rang, and my mother hurried through from the kitchen to greet the Sandwells.

George Sandwell, now in his late fifties, was also in accountancy and a fellow Rotarian. The two families had known each other for as long as I could remember, and, like me, Susie was an only child. She was also the same age as I, so we'd spent many days together in our respective gardens, splashing happily in the paddling pool, running naked round the lawn, and, of course, our first kiss, aged four, had been lovingly captured on celluloid for posterity by my proud mother and now enjoyed pride of place in the family album.

As we grew up, I remembered Susie as a rather gawky teenager, not unattractive but not sufficiently stunning to arouse any serious interest when I was exploring my sexuality. No doubt she felt the same about me. We went away to different schools, and different universities, so we saw little of each other as we ploughed our respective furrows. Susie had spent the last year in Lesotho, comforting the less fortunate and rubbing shoulders with royalty, in the hard-partying but orphanage-building shape of Prince Harry, and had only just returned.

'Evening, George', said Sandwell, walking into the drawing room, 'are you well?'

'Yes, thanks, George,' replied my father. 'You?'

For years, when I was growing up, I had believed that all accountants were called George. It seemed to go with the territory.

Next came Mrs Sandwell, and, bringing up the rear, Susie, under the close supervision of my mother, clutching hold of her in the manner of a trainer leading his horse around the saddling enclosure. That was uncharitable, I had to admit, as Susie looked stunning. Not in Camilla's class – but then, who was? She was tall and slim, lightly-tanned from her time abroad, with shining light brown hair and hazel eyes. She had a beautiful smile, which lit up her whole face.

After the obligatory 'Mwah Mwah' all round, the champagne was poured, all the usual pleasantries exchanged and presents opened. Susie gave me an African wood carving of a warrior with a huge erection, which had the ladies blushing and the men folk roaring with laughter. It was a surprisingly enjoyable evening, helped enormously by Susie's charm and easy manner. She described her time in Lesotho, complete with appropriately discreet titbits about Prince Hal, and I was prevailed upon to recount some of my more interesting cases. That didn't take long.

'What I want to know, Toby,' said George Sandwell as the cheese board was passed around, 'is how you can defend all these ghastly criminals when you know they're guilty?'

'Not my decision, Mr Sandwell,' I replied, pompously. 'That's why we have trial by jury. They decide where the truth lies, and for the most part, it seems to work. The prosecution bring the case, they have to prove it beyond a reasonable doubt, and it's the defendant's right to be acquitted if there's a reasonable doubt. That's the system, warts and all.'

'I was called to jury service once,' Mrs Sandwell chimed in.

'And did you enjoy it?' I asked.

'Well, I got through two of Jilly Cooper's books, cover to cover, during my two weeks, and met some delightful people, but we did have one trial.'

'Oh yes? And what was that about?'

'It was a policeman charged with dangerous driving. We were told he was going ninety in a thirty mile an hour speed limit. Apparently all to do with familiarising himself with a new car.'

'And did you find him guilty?'

'Oh no, he was such a nice man, and you've got to support the police, haven't you? Besides, the black recording box, you know, the box that records the speed of the car, had mysteriously gone missing, and nobody could find it. All rather curious.'

'So you don't think the missing box had anything to do with police corruption?' I was wearing my defence counsel's wig.

Mrs Sandwell was horrified at the suggestion, and said so, but I was on a roll.

'And what would have happened if a pedestrian had stepped off the pavement just as the policeman was speeding by?'

My father had had enough. It was getting too confrontational. He shot me a glance. 'Well, I don't know anything about these legal niceties, but you've just told us the prosecution bring the case and must prove it. So if they couldn't prove what speed the police officer was going, he was entitled to be acquitted. Well done, Molly,' he beamed encouragingly at Mrs Sandwell. Before I could come back, he rose from his chair. 'Coffee in the drawing room.'

'What a good idea,' said my mother. 'Toby, will you look after Susie, and I know Molly will help me in the kitchen.'

I'd been a bore, and I knew it. It was one of Nick Ridley's golden rules; when you leave chambers, take off your wig and gown.

The mood lightened with the arrival of the coffee, and the two Georges helped themselves to large brandies. I chatted idly with Susie, but my thoughts were elsewhere. When would I see Camilla again? Should I wait for her to contact me? After all, she knew my name and could look me up in the Bar Directory. Or should I give it a couple of days and call round to her house, on the pretext I was passing and thought I'd just drop in?

When it was time for the Sandwells to leave, I exchanged the usual pleasantries with Susie, about how lovely it was to see her again, and how we must keep in touch, but they lacked sincerity and it showed.

I slept fitfully, awoke early, and decided on a brisk walk round the village. On the way back, I bought a selection of the Sunday papers, and planned a leisurely browse after breakfast. I was feeling better already.

The thunderbolt that hit me right between the eyes, and cut me to the quick, was to be found lurking in the Atticus column of *The Sunday Times*. I stared, seeing but not believing, at the photo of Camilla and Hugh Grant, emerging from Annabel's in the early hours of the morning. With trepidation I read the short report. The top model and Britain's favourite film star had spent an intimate evening at Annabel's, and were seen leaving at about the same time as I was flopping into bed with my unused condoms. I was devastated. I should've taken the last large condom when I had the chance, just to spite Super Stud.

It finally, and painfully, dawned on me. I was nothing more than a one night stand, and once I'd served my purpose, to be tossed aside like a used whatever!

My first reaction was one of blind anger. I wanted to go round to her house, bang on her door and give her a piece of my mind, the ungrateful girl! But then, when I'd calmed down, I analysed the situation. Camilla had made no promises, and, besides, could we ever be happy together? She led a fast-track life, modelling, and jumping into bed, and jetting here and there with the jet set, and the idea of settling down to domestic bliss and kids would be anathema to her. It would destroy her, and, anyway, she'd want to call the kids Apple, or Tiger Lily, or, worst of all, Hugh!

I'd get over it and move on with the rest of my life. No point dwelling on the past, count your blessings, as my mother was fond of saying. And so I did. I had a loving family, I was a member of the best set of chambers in the Temple, I smiled as I remembered Gazzard's comment, and I was beginning to make my mark, or so I hoped.

'Come on, Toby.' I hadn't seen my father come into the room. 'Time for a pint whilst your mother's cooking lunch. I always feel I'm under her feet if I don't go out.' He winked.

The pub was busy, as it always was before Sunday lunch, with husbands and fathers getting out from under feet. Whilst supping our first pints, my father nudged me and indicated a corner table. I looked over to see Susie, relaxed and laughing with a Hugh Grant look-alike and in animated conversation. God! The man was everywhere. Susie looked up, saw me and smiled.

'Go over and say hello,' said my father.

'But she's with someone.'

'I can see that, but it's rude to ignore her.'

At my father's insistence, I went over.

'I don't think you've met my cousin Rupert, have you?' Susie asked. 'He's down for the weekend.'

What a relief. Now why did I feel that?

'Good to meet you,' said Rupert, standing up. 'I promised to help Aunt Molly, so I'd better get going. See you later.'

I stood there for a moment, feeling awkward. 'Can I buy you a drink?'

I brought the drinks over and sat down. 'I wanted to apologise for my behaviour last night,' I began, 'and especially to your mother. I was being pompous and rude. I just got carried away.'

'That's alright, Toby. Mummy thought you were charming,' Susie put her hand on mine, 'and so did I.'

After lunch, and feeling more relaxed than I'd felt for a long time, I tossed *The Sunday Times* into the waste bin and looked over to my mother. 'Do you mind if I come down again next weekend?'

'Not at all, dear, it's always a pleasure to see you. Any special reason?'

'Er, I've invited Susie out for dinner next Saturday, and she's accepted.'

Chapter Twelve

QUEEN'S COUNSEL

AT TEN THIRTY-SIX on the night of November the fifth, or, as Berger would say, at twenty-two thirty-six hours, the sergeant on duty at Wood Green Police Station received a telephone call.

'I think I've killed my mother,' said the voice, before the line went dead.

The call was traced, police and ambulance dispatched, and, when they broke in, they found Andrew Stubbs sitting in a chair, staring vacantly at the badly-injured and motionless body of his mother, and nursing an empty, two-litre bottle of cider. The unfortunate woman was taken to hospital, where she never regained consciousness and died nine days later.

Andrew was charged with her murder and remanded in custody. After the usual preliminary hearings, trial was set at Wood Green Crown Court in front of the newly-appointed Mr Justice Greengross, better known as 'The Grocer', and as dry as a sea biscuit.

Life for me couldn't have been better. Camilla was but a distant memory, and romance with Susie was definitely blossoming. Her pace suited me, long walks in the woods holding hands, romantic dinners when finances allowed, a stolen kiss and a cuddle, whispering sweet nothings in her ear. It was all my dreams come true. I loved just holding her, never wanting to let go.

But let go I must, at least during the week, as there were battles to fight and dragons to slay. That Wednesday evening, just as I was preparing to leave chambers, Fred beckoned me into the clerks' room.

'Got an interesting case for you, Mr Potts,' he said, pointing to a large volume of papers in front of him. 'I'm returning your brief for tomorrow at Barnet Magistrates Court. One of the pupils can cover it for you. This is much more important, and, who knows, could do you the power of good. Murder,' – I felt weak at the knees – 'fixed for trial on Monday.'

My God, so little time, and was I ready for the ultimate challenge? I thought so, and with my incisive cross-examination and impassioned final speech to the jury, who could say otherwise?

'You're being led by Sir James Bingham of Queen's Counsel, no less.'

I felt a little disappointed at not taking centre stage, but then, even junior counsel have their part to play, and holding the hand of such an eminent silk would be a challenge in itself. A quiet word here, a suggestion there, earning the approbation of the great man, I could see it all, possibly even a mention in the press and media: 'Sir James Bingham QC, ably assisted by Mr Toby Potts, the rising star of the profession, secured a glorious acquittal in the teeth of the evidence'. That would do nicely.

'His junior had to drop out at the last minute,' Fred continued, bringing me back down to earth with a bump, 'so his bad luck is your good fortune. Consultation with leader has been booked for tomorrow at four thirty in his chambers.' And, with that, Paul handed over the papers.

I studied the four lever arch files. Forget about that drink at Henekeys, it was going to be a long night.

Sir James 'Jumbo' Bingham QC was a legend in the profession, and larger than life in every sense of the word. Six foot three in his red-stocking feet, and weighing in at twenty-four stones, he cast a giant shadow, and his courtroom triumphs were the talk of the profession. Now in his late sixties, but still a formidable adversary, he was generally regarded as one of the finest advocates in silk, but he had a fearsome temper and didn't suffer fools gladly.

Clutching my files, I was shown into the great man's room promptly at four thirty. Sir James peered at me over several double chins, and smiled. 'So you're Potts?' he said, nodding towards a chair. 'Sorry to have landed you with this brief so near to trial. Wretched juniors, don't know where their priorities lie, too busy making money!'

He paused, taking a long hard look at his new junior. 'So, are you up to speed, Potts? Got it boxed?'

'I think so, Sir James', I started tentatively. 'I've been through the papers twice.'

'Good, good,' he boomed, 'now let's see what we're up against. Our client Stubbs is a very troubled young man, and according to the reports from the trick cyclists who've prodded and poked him for the past six months, everybody has an opinion to offer whilst saying nothing relevant at all.'

He scrabbled amongst his papers and found what he was looking for. 'The list of possibilities is endless. His father died when he was twelve, his mother was over-protective, he was bullied at school, he was awkward with girls, he has low self-esteem and, hardly surprising, unemployable. A total recluse by all accounts.' Sir James read on. 'His only pleasures in life seem to be drinking White Lightning cider to excess, smoking the occasional joint and listening to Wagner. *Wagner!*' he snorted. 'Enough to depress anyone! Huge, leaden-breasted women with horns coming out of their ears staggering around the stage and belting out cacophonous arias and being chased by booming men with spears, and all the while competing for air space with the orchestra hell-bent on drowning them out! And to cap it all, the whole thing's sung in Kraut!'

He paused to regain his breath. 'I was taken to the Ring Cycle once, some years ago, by a failed politician.' Jumbo was in reflective mood. 'Damned if I can remember his name, but I made my excuses and managed to slip out before the half-time whistle. Worst night of my life!' He bellowed with laughter. Drying his eyes with an enormous spotted red handkerchief, he looked warily at me. 'You're not a buff, are you by any chance?'

'No, no Sir James, definitely not,' I replied.

'Good, good, wouldn't want to tread on junior toes so soon in our professional relationship. To my way of thinking, the only natural language of opera is Italian, don't you agree? The most tuneful language on earth, it's divine. No wonder Rome is the centre of the Christian universe. But I digress. Back to the plot.'

Sir James flicked through more papers. 'I've been to see the lad in Brixton Prison, totally pointless exercise. Since his arrest he hasn't uttered a single word, so no help there. Bit like that chap found wandering on a beach in Kent, you know the one, it was in all the papers, never spoke a word but played the piano like Rubenstein. Fortunately for those listening, he didn't include Wagner in his repertoire, thank the Lord!' Again the bellow of laughter and the spotted red handkerchief. 'But there the similarity ends. As far as I know, our punter doesn't play the piano, in fact, he doesn't do anything except stare at the wall, poor blighter.'

'So his defence is insanity?' I suggested, trying to be helpful and appear up to speed.

Not helpful at all, as Sir James made abundantly clear. His smile vanished in an instant. He had an idiot for a junior. 'Insanity? What on earth are you prattling on about? There's no such defence to a charge of murder, as you should know all too well. Didn't they teach you anything at Law School?'

He glowered at me and then composed himself. 'If, however, you mean diminished responsibility, and if you had bothered to read the reports from the trick cyclists, they are unable to form any opinion as to the defendant's mental state, and who can blame them? After all, how can you certify somebody as suffering from abnormality of the mind when he remains as silent as the grave? A virtue in some, which I suggest you follow.'

Oh dear, I thought, feeling thoroughly depressed and humiliated, *bang goes the mention in* The Times.

'You have much to do before Monday, so let me detain you no longer. Now, we shall meet, promptly at ten-thirty, when we can reappraise the situation and take it from there.'

'I'm sorry to interrupt, Sir James, but the trial is listed to start at ten-thirty.'

'The trial, Potts, will start when I am good and ready.' Sir James leaned back in his chair. 'For reasons that wholly escape me, the trial is listed at Wood Green Crown Court. Until I accepted instructions in this case, I have to confess I'd never heard of the place. Do you know it?'

'I've been there twice, Sir James, but not long enough to make a lasting impression.'

Jumbo's cold manner changed, and he chuckled. 'Bad as that, is it?'

I nodded.

'I blame this new Lord Chancellor… complete jackass, if you ask me. He wants to make us "user-friendly", all singing from the same song sheet. Can't be doing with the man! I was at the Bailey last week, and, do you know, I saw a notice on the board headed "Do you have a complaint about the judge?" My dear boy, I didn't know where to begin!'

Another bellow, and out came the red spotted handkerchief again. 'And the Bar Council is no better, bunch of chancers waiting to climb aboard the judicial bandwagon. He threw down his pen in disgust. 'Anyway, I'm too old a dog to teach new tricks. Now, to more important matters, what about the scoff?'

I smiled. 'I've never been there long enough to explore the culinary delights, Sir James, but I'm not hopeful.'

'Nonsense, Potts, you give up too easily. I am delegating to you the supremely important task of seeking out the best watering hole within hailing distance of this ghastly court. Do not fail me, on pain of death, or worse! And no foreign muck that looks like something you tread in during a country ramble. English, French at a pinch, or better still, *la Bella Italia*. You have your orders. Now off you go, and I'll see you on Monday.'

SADLY FOR ME, preparing for trial to meet Sir James' exacting demands meant spending my weekend in London and away from Susie. She was very understanding, of course, and thrilled at the news of the awesome responsibility falling on my slender shoulders. 'They must think you're very good, Toby,' she said on the phone that evening. 'How exciting!'

Needless to say, I had been somewhat economical when describing my role in the trial, but no need to bother Susie with trivial details. Fortunately for me, the law library at Gray's Inn was open over the weekend, so I plunged into *Black's Medical Dictionary* and made copious notes of all the medical terminology. Why couldn't doctors use plain English? It was just showing off to use all these Latin words and totally unnecessary, and besides, Latin was a dead language. *Quite witty*, I thought to myself, as I pored over the *post mortem*.

The prosecution pathologist was having a field day with the poor woman's fractured tibia, haematomas around the parietal region of the cranium, extensive comminuted fracturing over the body including the left ulna and right clavicle, and grazing over the left patella. He concluded that death occurred as a result of a subdural haematoma, which, according to Dr Black, was bleeding from the brain into the cavity of the skull, causing massive brain damage. The subdural haematoma was the result of blunt trauma, such as a blow or blows with a fist or a foot. The defence pathologist agreed.

Sir James was right, of course. In the face of the defendant's silence, the trick cyclists were unable to offer a positive opinion but could find nothing to suggest he was unfit to plead or stand his trial. So be it, let battle commence!

WOOD GREEN MIGHT have been a leafy suburb once upon a time, but was now conspicuous by the absence of any wood or any green. Rows upon rows of terraced houses, crowded together and fighting for space, were the hallmark of this unattractive part of north London, wedged between Muswell Hill and Tottenham. There was the now obligatory shopping arcade, and dozens of ethnic restaurants and fast food outlets from every corner of the globe.

I took the task set for me very seriously indeed, and was determined to impress Sir James with the results of my researches if nothing else. For the most part, the various authorities I'd consulted confirmed what I'd suspected all along, that Wood Green was a gastronomic desert. English food was confined to a handful of pubs dotted here and there, but I couldn't quite see Sir James leaning on the bar and munching his way through last week's shepherd's pie, or the *plat du jour* with chips. The French had absented themselves altogether, and who could blame them? But there was one possible nugget in the wash pan that might just fit the bill, an Italian restaurant named La Bella Notte. I arrived early, very early, to reconnoitre the terrain, and found it situated in a small precinct of shops, travel agents and building societies. It was closed, of course, at nine in the morning, but from the outside looked clean and respectable, with a varied menu boasting authentic Italian cuisine. To my great relief, it also met two essential requirements: it was open at lunchtime, and was within ten minutes walking distance from the court, taken at a leisurely pace.

Whilst waiting for Sir James to arrive, I discovered that prosecution counsel was Giles Warburton QC, a recently-appointed silk and still feeling his way. He was in his late forties, of average height and build – in fact the word 'average' had been invented to describe him – with fair hair swept aggressively back, and an aquiline nose with nostrils that flared when he was under pressure. As he was cutting his teeth on steady CPS fare, he took himself very seriously indeed, not a natural bedfellow for Sir James. By ten-fifteen Warburton, nostrils flared, was fussing around like the school prefect, clicking his teeth and clearly agitated.

'I really think this is most discourteous of your leader,' he kept saying, turning on me. 'There's so much to discuss before the trial, and Mr Justice Greengross will want to start promptly at ten-thirty.'

Warburton paced up and down the hallway with his junior, the infamous Paul Newman from the CPS who had decided to instruct himself. Not a good idea as it transpired. As the saying goes, the advocate who instructs himself has a fool for a client, but the CPS were slow learners. As the hour approached, Warburton and his junior were joined by his lordship's clerk and the court usher, and together the four of them paced up and down, glancing frantically at the main door.

At ten-thirty, as promised, Sir James arrived and made his way magisterially through the main door, accompanied by the senior partner of the defendant's solicitors. I rushed forward to greet him and carry his bags as Warburton and his posse closed in.

'Sir James,' Warburton smiled thinly, 'or may I call you Jumbo?'

'No, you most certainly may not!' replied the great man, 'and who the blazes are you?'

'I am Giles Warburton, QC' – he added the letters as though still getting used to the idea – 'and leading counsel for the Crown. I was hoping to discuss the shape of the trial with you before we begin.'

'As to the shape of the trial, as you rather quaintly put it, I suggest you call such evidence as you believe will prove the guilt of the defendant, and I shall rebut it. Isn't that the way it's usually done? Now, I shall robe. Then a cup of strong coffee whilst my junior goes to see the defendant in the cells. If he deigns to say anything, which I doubt, I shall be informed immediately.' That said, Sir James made his way to the third floor and the robing room, leaving the posse speechless.

The court usher was the first to break the silence. 'What shall we tell his lordship? He told me he wanted to start at ten-thirty sharp.'

My first encounter with the defendant was depressing in the extreme. Andrew Stubbs, a 26-year-old man, totally traumatised, with lifeless, sunken eyes set in a cadaverous white face, sat staring vacantly at the wall. His hands trembled visibly as I explained what was about to happen, and how he was represented by the best silk in the country, and if he had any questions now or at any time during the trial, he had only to ask. Nothing. As I got up to go, I touched Andrew's hand and smiled reassuringly. To my surprise, the hand stopped trembling for just a moment, there was a flicker of understanding in his eyes and the faintest trace of a smile, and then he was gone again.

The court assembled at five-past-eleven, and The Grocer was not best pleased. He almost sprinted into court, and began by addressing counsel in a high-pitched voice with a querulous and irritating edge to it. 'This trial was listed to begin promptly at ten-thirty, and it is now five minutes past eleven. Whatever the reason for the delay, I propose starting each morning from now on promptly at ten. Is that clear?'

Sir James eased himself to his feet. 'Your lordship displays a commendable devotion to duty and an example to us all. However,' he paused for dramatic effect, 'if your lordship is determined to sit each morning at ten, then you will do so without me.'

The Grocer's mouth snapped open as Sir James continued at his most urbane. 'That being so, I doubt if the Court of Appeal would look favourably on a conviction secured, in part, during my absence.'

The Grocer was about to say something, but Sir James cut him short. 'Unlike your lordship, who is accommodated in agreeable and, I hope, comfortable, lodgings nearby, we lesser mortals must rely on the vagaries of public transport. In addition, as head of chambers, I have many duties to perform, both before and after the court sitting, and these cannot be abandoned on a whim.'

I was loving every minute of it. The Grocer was not. 'So what do you propose, Sir James?' he asked, testily.

'My clerk informs me that the most convenient train with first class facilities leaves Kings Cross Station at five past nine, arriving at Wood Green at five minutes past ten. After a ten minute journey by car to court, I then need time to consult with my lay client, in the unlikely event that he should choose to speak to me, and with my learned junior. Let me assure your lordship that, with goodwill on all sides, the trial can resume each morning at ten-forty-five.'

The Grocer sat, grim-faced, knuckles white, absorbing the enormity of Sir James's statement and the man who'd just made it. 'Very well, Sir James, but I shall insist on no more than an hour for the short adjournment.'

That was worse than questioning Sir James's progeny, and you did so at your peril. 'No, my lord,' he replied, 'that will not be possible.' He smiled graciously. 'Whilst your lordship will avail yourself of the judicial dining room, we lesser mortals must find sustenance elsewhere. I am confident that if we rise promptly at one, we should be able to resume the afternoon sitting at two-thirty.'

The Grocer was onto a hiding to nothing, but still he blundered on. 'In that case, Sir James, I propose making up the time lost by sitting until four-thirty.'

'No, my lord, that will not be possible. With the good offices of my instructing solicitor, if we rise promptly at four, and no later,' he added with emphasis, 'then I should be able to catch the four-twenty train back to the Temple. I am obliged for your lordship's indulgence, and unless there are any other matters, I suggest we delay the trial no further and empanel the jury.'

Game, set and match! Sir James sat down, signalling the end of the discussion. It was pure theatre, and a real *tour de force*.

The Grocer, put firmly back in his box, chose discretion as the better part of valour, nodded towards the jury bailiff and the trial began.

Warburton opened the case for the prosecution in meticulous detail, no doubt wishing to impress those who sat behind him with his command of the case and all its complexities. It was boring but clinically efficient. Sir James occupied the time by doodling, whilst I took a careful note. With the court clock nudging twelve, and Warburton still in full flow, Sir James turned round to me. I leant forward, expecting some incisive comment about the law or the evidence. 'What about the scoff, Potts?' he asked, in a stage whisper. 'Have you got it sorted?'

All eyes in the jury box turned to Sir James as Warburton hesitated, stumbled and then waited, expecting an objection to something he'd said.

'I think I've found a reasonable Italian restaurant about ten minutes' walk away,' I whispered back.

'Good boy,' he beamed expansively. 'Have you booked a table?'

'Not yet, Sir James.'

'Then get to it.'

'What? Now?'

'Yes, now!'

Conscious that I was now the centre of attention, and avoiding his lordship's withering gaze, I rose, bowed, and sidled out of court.

Warburton, put out, turned to the Grocer for moral support. 'I pause, my lord, in case my learned friend wishes to raise an objection.'

'Do you, Sir James?' asked the Grocer in that high-pitched voice of his.

'No, thank you, my lord. Objections will almost certainly be taken when my learned friend calls his evidence, but as his opening speech is not evidence in the case, I see no point whatsoever. However,' he added ominously, 'the jury and I will remain vigilant.'

The moment the hands on the courtroom clock struck one, and with Warburton in mid-sentence, Sir James rose. 'Is this a convenient moment, my lord?'

The Grocer looked up. 'Very well, Sir James. We will resume at two-thirty.'

In no time at all, Sir James was ready for the off. 'Right, Potts, lead on!' he boomed, and striding out at a formidable pace, we reached La Bella Notte in six minutes flat. I had forewarned the restaurant of the impending arrival of the great man, and, as luck would have it, we had the place to ourselves.

Sir James entered with a mighty flourish. 'Buongiorno, Signore', he enthused, 'Lei è il padrone?'

The owner, Mario, was in awe of this great English baronet, an honour and a privilege, and after all, great men in Wood Green were as rare as hen's teeth.

'Si, sono io, milord. É un piacere accoglierla nel mio ristorante.'

'Piacere mio. Di dov'é Lei?'

'Di Verona, milord.'

'Ah, Verona, la città dei sogni con l'opera migliore di tutta Italia.'

'Lei é stato a Verona, milord?'

'Tante volte, ed ogni volta é sempre meglio.' Sir James embraced Mario in his massive arms. 'Adesso, padrone, parliamo di affari importanti. Vorremmo due bottiglie del suo Barolo ed un bell'antipasto. Poi vorrei dei cannelloni e dopo, una cotoletta alla milanese. Non abbiamo molto tempo, dunque, vorremmo mangiare alla svelta, grazie.'

'Subito, milord,' replied Mario, bowing low as we sat down.

The meal was superb, and the wine exquisite, although my appetite was no match for Sir James's.

'I wasn't sure if you wanted me to invite your solicitor, Sir James,' I said, in between mouthfuls of cannelloni, 'so I didn't. I hope I did the right thing.'

'Absolutely, my boy,' Sir James replied, refilling his glass. 'Henry Paige has been instructing me for the past thirty years, he's an excellent solicitor and a first rate colleague. But we have different roles to play, and we respect the professional boundaries during the trial. I've watched their erosion over the years, and today, I'm informed, it's not uncommon for barristers with indifferent practices to actually tout for business, taking solicitors out for lunch or dinner, inviting them to their homes, and, for all I know, letting them sleep with their "partners" – as they're now known in common parlance.'

He snorted in disgust. 'The Warbler's a case in point, and, even as I speak, is no doubt eating in the works canteen with that self-important twerp from the CPS. Might get him his next brief, but if he stops kissing arse that's the end of him. A dangerous and demeaning game. Sadly, there's too many mice chasing the same piece of cheese, too many who shouldn't be in the profession at all. Don't go down that road, my boy, that's my advice. If a solicitor won't brief you unless you fawn all over him, he's not worth the candle. Padrone,' he bellowed, pushing the empty plate away from him, 'il dulce per favore.'

AFTER *CAFÉ ESPRESSO DOPPIO* and a large *Vecchia Romagna*, it was time to return to the fray. True to his word, Sir James entered court at exactly two-thirty, and the trial resumed.

Warburton, or 'The Warbler' as Sir James had christened him, was ready to put the final touches to his speech. and was checking and cross-referencing his notes.

'Had a good lunch, old boy?' enquired Sir James, feeling in expansive mood.

'More of a working lunch, Sir James,' he replied. 'No time to leave court, so my junior and I ate in the Bar Mess'.

Sir James winked at me. I was already fighting to stay awake.

The Warbler concluded his opening speech and then called the evidence. The rest of the afternoon was taken up with the preliminaries, finding the body, the arrest of the defendant, lurid photographs and a plan of the room showing the exact position of the body when it was found. Sir James asked a few perfunctory questions, nothing incisive, simply showing the flag.

At five-minutes-to-four, Warburton rose to call his next witness.

'My lord,' Sir James rose slowly from his seat, 'this witness may take a little time, and, as we've made such splendid progress, may I suggest we adjourn until the morning? The jury have had enough for one day.'

Nice touch, I thought.

'Very well, Sir James.'

Tuesday was the day of medical evidence, starting with the psychiatrists. As there was broad agreement, only two of the four were called, both sporting bow ties and looking as mad as hatters. The defendant's mental state was dissected down to the last nodule, with lofty statements about dysfunctional atrophy and amnesiac-related memory loss associated with high anxiety paranoia. It was all complete gibberish to me, but they confirmed that the defendant was fit to plead and fit to stand trial. Sir James asked a few questions, just to get the sympathy vote, but no more. As far as the trick cyclists were concerned, not one suggested a disposal under the Mental Health Act in the event of a conviction.

Next came the medical evidence, starting with the paramedics who attended the scene. Sir James showed some interest in their findings and treatment, and in particular, their patient's comatose state. He highlighted this particular aspect of their evidence, I didn't know why, but assumed it must be important. The Warbler asked no questions in re-examination, so like me he hadn't seen its relevance.

Back to the ever-welcoming Mario and more excellent Italian scoff, and then more of the same in the afternoon. The Warbler called the doctors who treated Mrs Stubbs on arrival and who admitted her to the intensive care unit. As senior housemen newly-qualified, they trotted out all the Latin jargon, word perfect, which The Grocer, after searching inquiry, translated for the jury. This part of the evidence held no terrors for me, and I was itching to chime in and show off the fruits of my labours. They had also prepared diagrams, copies available for the jury, one between two, showing the extent and severity of the assault.

After the court adjourned for the day, and with Sir James departing for the station, I reviewed the evidence. Using the same forensic skills I thought Sir James would apply, I simply couldn't spot the defence. The prosecution could prove beyond a shadow of a doubt that Mrs Stubbs was seriously assaulted by the defendant and had died, nine days later, without regaining consciousness. Cause of death was a brain haemorrhage. The statements of all the medical witnesses, and there were many, indicated she had received constant and expert attention during those nine days, and that the damage inflicted by the defendant was simply irreversible. In the absence of a defence of insanity, and I wasn't going to revisit that particular low point, there was no defence to the charge of murder. But I couldn't believe Sir James was simply going through the motions. That would achieve nothing, and certainly wasn't in the defendant's interests. I was missing something... but what? Perhaps manslaughter? Time to go back to chambers and consider the possibility, just in case Sir James wanted my input.

THAT MOMENTOUS Wednesday began when Warburton called as his first witness the consultant in overall charge of the intensive care unit. His evidence confirmed the medical evidence already given and simply drew the strings together. He also confirmed the cause of death. Then Sir James got up to cross-examine.

'Mr Rowbotham,' he began, 'when the deceased was admitted to the intensive care unit, she was, and remained, deeply unconscious?'

'That's correct.'

'We can agree, can we not, that the other injuries to her body, about which we have already heard detailed evidence, were not life-threatening?'

'Correct.'

'So for the purposes of my cross-examination into the cause of death, we can concentrate on the head injuries?'

'I agree.'

'Very well.' He paused, looking down at his notes. 'Now your considerable experience will tell you that, in most cases, even after a severe beating, the patient normally regains consciousness within a relatively short period of time, possibly within ten to fifteen minutes of the assault. Do you agree?'

'In general terms, yes, but...'

'Good. So the fact that the deceased was deeply unconsciousness on admission suggests two things, does it not? Firstly, that she had sustained an injury to the brain, certainly a subdural haematoma, or, worse still, an extradural haematoma? And secondly, you would agree, these haematomas build up after a head injury of this sort over a period of hours, anywhere between two to three hours, sometimes much longer?'

'In broad terms, I would agree with your analysis, and that coincides with our clinical findings. Shortly after her admission, we conducted a brain scan and found a subdural haematoma.'

'Explain that for the benefit of the jury – and,' he added, with heavy irony, 'for his lordship.'

'Well, a subdural haematoma arises as a result of damage to the membrane between the brain and the skull, which manifests itself in bleeding. As the skull is fixed, and the brain is not, the bleeding as it accumulates presses down onto the brain, and in severe cases forces the brain down towards the base of the skull and the spine.'

'And without surgical intervention can prove fatal?'

'Yes, but as you know, there was surgical intervention within four hours of admission. We drilled into the skull and the accumulation of blood was evacuated, thereby relieving the pressure on the brain. This is standard procedure in these cases.'

'Excellent, Mr Rowbotham, I was not going to suggest otherwise.' Sir James smiled reassuringly. 'And, in the vast majority of such cases, with the pressure relieved and the bleeding stemmed, the patient will make a full, albeit slow, recovery, do you agree?'

'I agree.'

'And in the case of the deceased, following the operation, she remained critical but stable. So pausing there for a moment, there was every expectation that the operation had been a success?'

'Yes.'

'And yet, sadly, the deceased died nine days later as a result of the very same subdural haematoma we've been discussing?'

Rowbotham was on the defensive. 'If you're suggesting...'

'I'm not suggesting anything, Mr Rowbotham, I'm simply stating a fact and inviting you to accept it.'

The doctor paused, sensing a trap but not seeing it coming. 'Put like that,' he answered cautiously, 'I would have to agree.'

'Thank you. So what the jury need to do now, with your help of course, is to resolve the apparent contradiction between a successful operation to relieve and stabilise her condition, and the deceased's subsequent death from the self-same haematoma?'

'Well...' Rowbotham was now firmly on the back foot. 'There could be any number of explanations...'

'With respect, Mr Rowbotham, there could be only two reasonable explanations for death. Either the operation was not the success you claim it to be, or something happened during the deceased's time on the intensive care unit.'

Rowbotham's eyes narrowed as he envisaged a medical negligence action against his hospital, and all the adverse publicity. 'The deceased received the best possible medical attention, and I resent any implication to the contrary.'

Sir James was having none of it. 'I am not here to defend the good name of your hospital, Mr Rowbotham, but to get to the truth, so bear with me.' Back to his notes. 'After the operation, the deceased showed every sign of making a slow and steady recovery, that's right?'

'Yes.'

'So on the face of it, the operation was a success?'

'I have no doubt about that.'

'Excellent, so in your opinion, the jury can ignore inadequate or incompetent surgical intervention?'

'Absolutely.'

'Then let us turn to the second explanation for death. Something happened between operation and death.'

'Such as?'

Sir James held up three sets of papers. 'Usher, give these to the witness, and copies for his lordship and my learned friend for the Crown. Taking a moment to digest them, Mr Rowbotham,' he continued, 'kindly confirm they are the hospital records of the deceased.'

Rowbotham flicked through the pages. 'That would appear to be so.'

'Is that a yes?'

'Yes.'

'Good. Now for the benefit of the jury, each time an event occurs with a patient, indeed, each time the patient is visited, a note is made to this effect, is it not?'

'Correct.'

'So these notes provide a running narrative of the patient's stay?'

Rowbotham nodded in agreement.

'And they are hand-written by the nurse or doctor visiting the patient and at the time of the visit?'

Again, Rowbotham nodded.

'Some of these notes are difficult to decipher.' Sir James smiled at the jury. 'This is not unknown in the medical profession.' Rowbotham wore the pained expression of a man who'd heard that one many times before. 'But if I can draw your attention to twenty-three-twenty on day seven…' He paused. 'Do you have it?'

'Yes.'

'Can you read it out for us?'

Rowbotham peered at the entry. 'Patient on floor, returned to bed, still unconscious.'

I made a careful note. This was dynamite, although I wasn't sure why. Rowbotham looked visibly shaken.

'Have you seen that entry before?'

'I must confess I haven't, but then, I was never asked,' he added lamely.

'Never *asked?*' Sir James retorted, staring at The Warbler. 'The prosecution never once asked you to read these notes? Extraordinary!'

The Warbler rose. 'That was a comment, my lord,' he bleated.

'And a well-aimed one, Mr Warburton,' replied The Grocer.

Good for you, I thought, warming briefly to the man.

'So if you have never seen this entry before, can I assume that it was never brought to your attention at the time?'

'Well, yes, but…'

'Your hospital beds are two and a half feet from the ground, are they not?'

'I haven't the faintest idea.'

'We've had them measured, my lord,' Sir James glanced at the Bench, 'so perhaps you will take it from me?'

'If you say so.'

'And, furthermore, the floor in the intensive care unit is linoleum with a concrete base, do you agree?'

'So I believe.'

'So what we have here, I suggest, is a patient making a slow but steady recovery, who falls from the bed, bangs her head on the hard concrete floor, thus starting a fresh bleeding into the skull, which, if not spotted in time, could be fatal. That's right, isn't it?'

Rowbotham had the air of a defeated man. 'It's one possibility,' he replied, in almost a whisper.

'It's more than that.' Sir James was at his most scathing. 'It's a probability! Take your time, but you will see from the notes there was no further surgical intervention from the time of the operation shortly after the deceased's admission to her untimely death. And there wouldn't have been, as nobody had sought fit to bring this significant event to the attention of the doctors, correct?'

'No, but...'

'And looking at the notes after her fall from bed, her condition, from slow but steady recovery, worsens dramatically, and she died at three in the morning of the ninth day. Yes, thank you, Mr Rowbotham, no further questions.'

I wanted to leap to my feet and applaud my learned leader. It was a wonderful display of forensic cross-examination.

A cathedral silence fell over the court as Warburton got to his feet. 'I have no questions in re-examination,' he said. 'Does your lordship have any questions?'

'No, I do not. The witness may leave the court.' The Grocer turned to the jury. 'There are matters of law to discuss, members of the jury, so please leave, and I'll call you back when we are ready to continue.'

The Grocer was commendably brief and to the point. 'Unless you seek to persuade me to the contrary, Mr Warburton, I shall direct the jury to find the defendant not guilty of murder.'

The Warbler was not going to throw in the towel without a fight. 'I do indeed seek to persuade your lordship to the contrary,' he said. 'The hospital records are public documents, and examined by both parties, so the fall from bed takes nobody by surprise. There are two possibilities for the jury to consider, the first that the deceased died as a result of the injuries sustained by her at the hands and feet of the defendant, the other is *novus actus interveniens*. It is a matter for the jury.'

The Grocer, elevated to the High Court on the back of a thriving commercial law practice, had had enough of tibias, tabias and flatulas to last a lifetime, and the thought of grinding through that lot in his summing-up appalled him. Sir James had thrown him a lifeline, and he grabbed it. 'No, Mr Warburton, I am against you. It cannot be right to leave two equally consistent causes of death to the jury.' He turned to Jumbo. 'Sir James, can you resist a verdict of inflicting grievous bodily harm, contrary to section 20 of the Offences against the Person Act 1861?'

'No, my lord, I cannot. This is a tragic case where the defendant has lost the only person who ever really loved him, and made the more tragic by the regrettable and avoidable events in hospital.'

'Tragic, indeed. I shall be making a report for the consideration of the Director of Public Prosecutions, and no doubt there will be a full inquiry. Turning to the defendant, and given the fact that a conviction to section 20, at the very least, was inevitable, I have in mind a sentence of three years' imprisonment.'

The jury were called back into court and duly returned their verdicts as directed. Then, after the formalities, it was off to La Bella Notte.

'Potts,' Sir James roared across the robing room, 'now the trial's over, go and find Henry and invite him to join us.'

Just then, Warburton came in.

'We're off for a spot of scoff, dear boy... come along and drown your sorrows.'

Warburton's face lit up. 'That's very kind of you, Sir James, if you're sure it's not too much of an imposition?'

'Not at all, a pleasure.' Sir James hesitated. 'What about your junior, Mr Newboy?'

'He's gone back to the office to file a report.'

'Well, there's a blessed relief. Each one to his own.'

Mario excelled himself, and to my delight and surprise, Warburton turned out to be a very agreeable companion, particularly after the third bottle of Barolo. It was nearly four when we left to go our separate ways.

For me it was the experience of a lifetime. Sir James moved on to the next case, the next triumph, and Warburton, after a period out in the cold, also moved on. Newman reviewed himself favourably, of course, but determined never to sit behind counsel again. Next time he'd go it alone! Why buy a dog when you can bark yourself?

And, as for Andrew Stubbs, he remained as silent as the grave into which he consigned himself.

Three weeks after the trial, his lifeless body was found hanging from the bars of his prison cell.

Chapter Thirteen

BACK TO SCHOOL

WHEN THE BRIEF came my way to represent Joseph 'Call me Jack' Masters, I found myself on a steep upward learning curve, peering into the unknown world of comprehensive education. I had been one of the fortunate few to have been educated privately, and whilst Rougemont College was not exactly a major league player it provided me with the necessary tools and a kick start into the big, wide, world.

Jack Masters had always wanted to be a teacher, and not just because of his name. He'd had all the advantages of an affluent upbringing, a happy family life, a good private education, and then straight into a teacher training college. His parents had hoped for better, perhaps something in the City, but a child who actually knew what he wanted to do in life from an early age was a rare commodity, so they bit their tongues, put on a brave face, and smiled encouragingly. All this and more was contained in his lengthy proof of evidence, described by my solicitor as 'background information'.

Jack was also a man with a mission. His parents blamed their son's English teacher for all that nonsense, a remarkable man with an obvious gift for communication and a great motivator. He brought alive the classics, from Shakespeare through to the hugely boring James Joyce, and several stops in between. In their book, anybody who could bring alive the works of James Joyce deserved a medal.

Jack's parents boasted no particular literary pretensions. If they were to read at all, it was during their annual two-week pilgrimage to that delightful little village in Provence, populated by quaint little Froggies wearing striped jerseys and berets and reeking of garlic and body odour. Some grave and weighty tome such as Jilly Cooper was more their cup of tea, or even Jeffrey Archer. And besides, when at home, they watched *Newsnight* and *Panorama*, which were the same as heavy literature without the effort of turning the pages.

But Jack was cut from a different cloth altogether. His mission in life was to bring enlightenment where there was darkness and ignorance, so he eschewed the easy life of private education, with polite, well-mannered children calling him 'Sir', listening attentively in class, doing their homework on time, and moving effortlessly towards good grades in their exams, and opted instead for the state sector. To add spice to this otherwise unleavened fare, and a rod for his back, he applied for a teaching post at a bog-standard comprehensive school in Cowley, within striking distance of the dreaming spires of Oxford and the meadows of Christ Church College.

As far as his parents were concerned, it added insult to injury, but then, it wasn't their decision, so they went with the flow, hoped this would get it out of his system and that he'd go on later to find a decent job in the profession with real career prospects. After all, their son as an Oxford don would be something they could brag about at one of their endless dinner parties, a real feather in their social cap.

St. Jude's Comprehensive School had as part of its catchment area the less salubrious quarters of Cowley, and, in particular, the notorious Blackbird Leys estate. Quite what St Jude had done to suffer this second martyrdom, when he should be enjoying eternal redemption and a well-earned rest, was never fully explained by the local education authority, but then, such are the burdens of sainthood.

Vicky's mum Kylie was no different from scores of other young mums on the estate. Her dad had left home when she was a babe in arms, off to look for work, or so he said, and never returned. Kylie was only 16 when she gave birth, and a slap on the bottom from the midwife was just about the most affectionate gesture Vicky had experienced in her short and troubled life to date. The lucky father could have been any one of four during the weekend of conception, but no-one stepped forward to claim the prize, and besides, Kylie wasn't fussed. They were all complete deadbeats and only after one thing which, needless to say, they got in full measure.

But unprotected sex had its compensations. No sooner had Vicky been born than the caring agencies gathered in force. Housing benefit, income support, child allowance, and special needs payments ensured her financial security, and health visitors and the social services did the rest. It was an offer too good to pass up, and Kylie quickly added three more to her brood, until the caring agencies persuaded her to call it a day and shut up shop.

Vicky grew up in her mother's image, and by the time she enrolled at St Jude's, aged 12, she was already street-wise. At primary school, she'd excelled at the practical side of her education, like hurling abuse at the teachers, throwing her school dinner onto the floor in favour of a large bag of salt and vinegar chips, and chasing the other kids around the playground. Her vocabulary hardly advanced beyond the four letter word, so academic progress was slow.

By the time Vicky celebrated her 15th birthday, she'd reached the high water mark in her formal education. The three Rs were firmly on the back burner, where they were to remain, but if the sixty seven positions during the sexual act were ever to become part of the GCSE syllabus, she was predicted an A grade with distinction.

The Governors of St Jude's, in consultation with the Head Teacher, decided that mixed ability classes should be actively encouraged. After all, this was the very ethos of the comprehensive system, with the dullards benefiting from exposure to the more gifted pupils and being thus inspired to reach beyond their natural intellectual vacuity. Quite what the more gifted pupils were to derive from this social engineering was never satisfactorily explained.

And so it was that Vicky and some of her soul mates found themselves at the back of Jack's class, and, on any view, it was a bridge too far. Jack was in his second year at St Jude's, and, despite a first year marked more by failure than success, he was determined to persevere. After all, he kept telling himself, Rome wasn't built in a day. Getting his pupils to march out of step across desktops was the easy part, but getting them to think for themselves, or even think at all, was the real challenge, and there was still much work to be done.

The Head Teacher, eager to curry favour with the Governors and promote St Jude's as a progressive school without equal in the county, accepted Jack's suggestion that his class should study the works of Nietzsche as their specialist subject, with particular emphasis on the great man's philosophical need to understand the infinite chaos underlying primitive life if we are to understand the future of our evolution.

Not that the Head knew anything about him at all, he could barely spell the bloke's name. He'd heard of him, of course, just as he'd heard of Proust and all that humbug about rediscovering lost time. It was all foreign gibberish to him, and eminently forgettable, along with Goethe and Sartre and that lot, but it looked good on the *Curriculum Scholae*, so he gave Jack's idea his qualified blessing and turned to the main business of the day, trying to bring forth order out of the infinite chaos underlying primitive life and prevent Ms Baxter from being goosed, yet again, during playground duty. To his mind, these were self-inflicted wounds, as Ms Baxter's ample posterior was barely hidden beneath a skirt far too short for her age and build, but, in these politically-correct times, there was nothing he dare say without a sexual discrimination claim hitting the fan.

Jack's first two lessons were dominated by attempts, largely unsuccessful, to get the kids to spell Nietzsche's name correctly. Once inscribed in large capital letters on the blackboard, three of the class of forty-six got it right first time, with the others coming on side in dribs and drabs.

It was a mistake, as Jack had to admit in hindsight, to offer the phonetic spelling 'Neetsher' to help those at the back of the class, as once the seed was sown it was the devil's own job to uproot it. The great man's nickname 'Fritz' was easier to remember, as it coincided with the British stereotype of all things German, but Jack's attempts to move the class onto a higher intellectual plain met with deep-seated resistance and/or apathy. The first two weeks of study could best be summarised in one sentence: 'Fritz Neetsher woz a Krawt'. A poor return on Jack's investment.

It went from bad to worse, and, by the end of the third week, Jack could barely make himself heard above the general mayhem. Other teachers began to complain that the noise was disrupting their classes, which was nonsense, as they needed no help in that regard. But Jack was an easy target, as he tried to reason with the unreasonable, still clinging to the mistaken belief that his passion for literature and philosophy was infectious. It wasn't.

Vicky, who hadn't even mastered the spelling of Nietzsche in its phonetic form, was bored rigid, and her idle mind turned to more important matters, like boys, and sex, and chips, not necessarily in that order. She had her priorities in life, and Jack wasn't one of them.

That particular morning, Jack's class started where it had left off the day before, with a few bright sparks at the front showing interest, a grey area in the middle showing total indifference, and the two back rows showing the usual overt hostility, with Vicky, as ever, the ringleader. Finally, something snapped. Jack marched the length of the classroom, and placing his hand firmly behind Vicky's neck, propelled her out into the corridor before her feet could touch the ground. There was a stunned and sullen silence from the remaining forty-five pupils as he returned to the uneven struggle. For a few minutes, at least, he had earned the respect of the class, but it wasn't to last.

Vicky didn't turn up the next day, which was ominous, and Jack's reaction was one of apprehension mixed with relief. Still, he told his solicitor, he'd done nothing wrong, and following his firm handling, class discipline improved overnight. It was almost a pleasure to be teaching again, rather than wasting so much time on crowd control. It was like waking from a nightmare, but, unbeknown to Jack, his nightmare was just beginning.

At the end of the second day of her continuing absence, Jack was summoned to the Head Teacher's office.

'Bad news, I'm afraid,' said the Head. 'Vicky's made a complaint against you, and her mother has reported the matter to the police.'

'What!?' Jack couldn't believe his ears. 'I put her out of my class because she was disruptive, as always. I should have done it sooner. So what's the problem?'

'She's going to be formally interviewed tomorrow, but from what I gather, she claims you assaulted her when removing her from your class, and once out in the corridor, you indecently assaulted her by fondling her breast.'

Jack was horrified. 'I can't believe this is happening,' he said.

'I'm sorry, Jack, but you know the school rules. I have no choice but to suspend you with immediate effect until the matter is sorted out. Ms Baxter will cover for you in your absence, but I doubt if Neetsher will survive the ordeal. By all accounts, she knows less about him than Vicky, which isn't saying much. If only she'd wear more appropriate attire,' he mused, 'those short skirts and meaty thighs are most distracting.' He paused to mop his brow. 'Still, that's the least of my worries. If this drags on, I'll have to get in a supply teacher.'

His concern for Jack's welfare was gratifying.

Acting on Vicky's complaint, Jack was duly charged with common and indecent assault, and the case sent to Oxford Crown Court for trial by jury.

BASIL WHEATCROFT had been at the same Oxford College as Nick Ridley, my former pupil master, had qualified as a solicitor the year before Nick was called to the Bar, and they'd remained good friends ever since. When Jack turned to Basil for help, Nick was tied up in a long fraud trial, so the brief was returned to me. It was a high-risk strategy, given my inexperience in such a serious case, but Basil was persuaded.

I was understandably nervous as I arrived at court that Monday morning, with the Press buzzing around like flies. The trial was listed before the Recorder of Oxford, His Honour Judge Francis Coker QC, nicknamed 'Chuckles' because of his inability to laugh at anything, least of all at himself. Tall and distinguished, with silver hair framing a pink, fleshy countenance fixed into a permanent scowl, he was an interventionist by inclination, frequently interrupting counsel and witnesses alike to make telling points, usually in favour of the prosecution – all, of course, in the interests of justice and steering the jury in the right direction. He came from the old school which believed that the police didn't arrest and charge the innocent, and that if a defendant had the temerity to plead not guilty and waste his time and public money, then let him suffer the consequences. By all accounts, Jack and I were in for a rough ride.

The court convened promptly at ten-thirty. Chuckles sat down and glowered at me. 'So what's the defence, Mr Potts?' he snapped, knowing full well the answer.

'Does your Honour have a copy of the Defence Statement, where the defence is clearly set out?' I said.

'I never read the Defence Statement, Mr Potts, it's invariably humbug and a waste of my time.'

'In that case, the defendant admits using minimum but necessary force to remove the complainant from his class, as she was being disruptive, but totally denies indecently assaulting her.'

'So how does he account for the finger marks on the girl's left breast when she was examined by the police surgeon?'

'The defendant does not have to account for anything, your Honour.' A bold outburst, but I was not going to be browbeaten, and Jack needed all the support he could get. 'This and other issues will doubtless be fully explored in the course of the evidence.'

'Don't get clever with me, Mr Potts. It ill behoves you or your client.' Chuckles flicked through his papers. 'Has the defendant been advised of a reduction in sentence if he pleads guilty, and the real risk he runs of a substantial sentence of imprisonment if he is convicted by the jury?'

I was beginning to feel punch-drunk, and the trial hadn't even begun. 'He has, your Honour, and he's also been advised that as he hasn't committed the offence charged, he should plead not guilty, confident in the knowledge that he'll receive a fair trial in your Honour's court.'

There was a long pause, during which Chuckles gave me a very thoughtful stare. 'Very well, be it on his own head. Now, is the defendant on bail?'

'He is, your Honour, and I ask that bail continue until further order.'

'You may ask, Mr Potts, that is your prerogative. Whether I accede to your request is a different matter. These are serious allegations...'

'Not yet proved, your Honour.'

'Yes, yes, I know that'. Another long pause. 'What is known about the defendant? Do you have his antecedents?' I handed them up. 'A man of good character with no convictions recorded against him. Educated Highgate School London.' Chuckles looked up and studied the defendant intently. Very slowly, almost imperceptibly, his countenance softened. 'Is that Highgate Public School?' he asked.

'It is, your Honour,' I replied.

'I'm not addressing you, Mr Potts. Do sit down and stop interrupting.' I did as I was told. 'Highgate, eh?' Chuckles continued, reliving the happiest days of his life. 'We used to play you at soccer, Mr Masters.'

Jack was still in a state of shock, but quickly recovered his composure. 'Which school was that, your Honour?'

'Shrewsbury.'

'The Salopian fixture was the highlight of the soccer calendar, your Honour, and always keenly contested.'

Good man, I thought, *lay it on with a trowel, we need all the help we can get.*

'I can imagine. You played, no doubt?'

I offered up a silent prayer.

'I did indeed, your Honour. I had the distinction of captaining the school first eleven in my last year.'

Who said prayers are never answered?

'I trust we thrashed you,' said Chuckles with a gleam in his eye.

Another silent prayer.

'An honourable draw, your Honour, but a memorable match.'

Hallelujah! Praise the Lord!

In a ground-breaking moment of seismic proportions, Chuckles actually chuckled. 'I see you were teaching a course on Friedrich Nietzsche, Mr Masters. One of my favourite philosophers.' *This is getting better by the minute*, I thought. 'I particularly like his treatise in *Also Sprach Zarathustra*.'

'A seminal work, your Honour, but my favourite must be *Die Götzendämmerung*, a thought-provoking criticism of the Greek tradition's overemphasis on reason.'

'Thought-provoking indeed, and, in different circumstances, we could debate for hours. But, sadly, we must return to the business in hand.' Chuckles turned to address me. 'Of course Mr Masters may have unconditional bail, Mr Potts, and if at any time your client needs a break, he has only to ask. Now, if you're ready, I suggest we empanel the jury.'

The prosecution chose to call first the battle-weary Head Teacher to set the scene, after which, it was my turn to cross-examine.

'It's correct, is it not, that Vicky was a well-known troublemaker at school?'

'That's correct.'

'I have here the school incident book which you have produced to the court. Her name appears several times for disruptive behaviour.'

'Correct.'

'And reported not just by Mr Masters, but by almost every teacher who had the misfortune to come into contact with her.'

'That would appear to be so.'

'When you questioned the defendant about the incident which gives rise to the charge of common assault, he told you she was being disruptive, yet again.'

'Correct.'

'He also told you that when asked to stop talking, she told him, in her words, to "fuck off"?'

'That is what he told me, and I have no reason to disbelieve him.'

Good man, I thought. *Keep it coming.*

'She was asked to leave the class, and when she refused, Mr Masters used minimum and necessary force to remove her, do you agree?'

'Well... er... no.'

Chuckles was out of the traps like a greyhound. 'What do you mean, no?'

'Well, your Honour, the school rules are quite specific about physical contact between staff and pupils. There is to be no physical contact whatsoever. It's Department of Education policy, as set out in their policy document entitled 'Memorandum for Teachers – Forward Together', and provided free of charge to each new member of staff.

It is mandatory reading, needless to say. I have a copy with me if you're interested.' And with that, HT, as he was known to one and all, produced a 312-page manual from his battered briefcase, covering every aspect of school life – the how, when, where and what to do in any given situation.

'If Mr Masters is forbidden to touch the recalcitrant pupil, and she refuses to leave his class, what is he supposed to do?' Chuckles glowered at the unfortunate HT.

'The rules are quite specific. He is to bring the class to an end and refer the matter to me. By the authority vested in me and the Governors by the local education authority, and acting on behalf of the Department of Education, I shall then decide the appropriate response.'

'Which is what?' snapped Chuckles, irritably.

'Well, your Honour, there are a number of responses, starting at page 243, paragraph 7.'

Chuckles opened the manual. 'Have you received a copy of this document, Mr Potts?' he asked.

'I have, your Honour.'

'Looking at page 244, paragraph 2, it deals with physical contact between staff and pupils in the playground. Is that the section to which you wish to draw my attention?'

'Well, actually no, but it deals comprehensively with all aspects of physical contact between teachers and pupils. If I can refer you back…'

'Before you do so, this section clearly states that if a pupil falls over and injures herself, the teacher on duty must not touch the pupil, but must summon the designated first-aider – whatever that might mean.'

'Every school has a designated first-aider, your Honour, trained in first aid,' HT added, helpfully.

'But what happens if the pupil has cut herself on broken glass and has severed an artery, and what if the designated first-aider is taking the day off, suffering no doubt from post-traumatic stress disorder?' said Chuckles. 'A common complaint, no doubt, at your school,' he added waspishly. 'Is the pupil left to bleed to death?'

'There is no broken glass in my school playground, I can assure you of that!'

Chuckles was having none of it. 'We are losing the plot, whatever the state of your playground. Mr Masters is accused of assaulting this pupil. You're telling this jury that if a teacher gives the recalcitrant and abusive pupil a well-deserved clip around the ear, he'll be suspended and finish up in a court of law?! How can you possibly defend such an asinine policy?'

'I don't devise the policy, your Honour,' replied HT lamely, 'I simply implement it.'

'That doesn't wash with me. Mr Potts, you have a submission, no doubt?'

I didn't. 'Your Honour, I…?'

'You do indeed, and quite right, too. Members of the jury, there is simply no case to answer on the count of common assault, and I direct you to find the defendant not guilty. It simply beggars belief, does it not?'

In fact, it didn't, as most of the jury had kids at St Jude's, and if any teacher gave their kid a good clip round the ear, there'd be hell to pay. Discipline and GBH were the sole preserve of Mum and Dad, no matter what some toffee-nosed judge had to say on the matter. Still, it was his court, and who were they to argue? The not guilty verdict was duly entered.

'Now let us proceed to the *gravamen* of this case, namely the indecent assault.'

AS A CHILD witness – and Vicky qualified as a child, just – she had been video-interviewed in a purpose-built suite. The police interviewer, accompanied by the resident social worker, struggled to retain her interest, as he gently teased out the complaint that gave rise to the charge of indecent assault. As the groping of the left breast, according to Vicky, had happened when she and Jack were alone in the corridor, it was her word against Jack's.

Once her pre-recorded evidence-in-chief had been played to the jury, I began my cross-examination via a video link. Vicky sat slumped down in a ghastly, magenta-coloured sofa, surrounded by cuddly toys, empty crisp packets, Coca Cola bottles, and damp nappies, looking for all the world as if she were in the back row of Jack's class, bored and resentful. It was not a pretty sight – though I felt it would be helpful to the defence.

I started softly. As Nick was fond of saying, keep the witness on side for as long as possible before putting the boot in.

'Now, Vicky,' I began, smiling into the camera link in my most engaging manner, 'why did you wait two days before telling your Mum what you say Mr Masters had done to you?'

'Cos I woz embarrassed.'

'But from what I've been told, you're not a girl who's easily embarrassed about these sort of things, are you?' There was a resentful silence. 'Are you?'

'Wadda yer mean?'

'Well, you told the police Jack squeezed your left breast after he put you out of his class on the Monday morning. You didn't come into school the next day, Tuesday, and you told your Mum on the Tuesday evening, that's right, isn't it?'

'So wot?'

'Young lady,' Chuckles interrupted. 'Counsel has to ask these questions, and we'd get on much faster if you simply answered them, do you understand?' Another resentful silence. 'Try again, Mr Potts.'

'So what did you do on the Monday after school?'

'Same as always.'

'Which was what?'

'"ad me tea, then went down the Community Centre.'

'And what did you do down the Community Centre?'

'Same as always.'

Chuckles was getting fidgety. 'The question is simple enough, young lady,' he snapped. 'What did you do on the Monday evening?'

'I've already told yer,' she snapped back. A wellspring of sympathy for Jack was beginning to wash over Chuckles as he pictured the Herculean task of trying to communicate with the odious girl on even the most basic level. He was about to wade in again, when Vicky let out a long, bored, sigh. 'We listened to music and 'ung around.' At last, ignition, and lift off.

'And who do you hang around with?' I asked.

'Me friends, 'oo do yer think?'

'Girls and boys?'

'Yeah.'

'And are you popular with the boys?'

'None of yer bizness.'

'Yes, it is, so answer the question.' I was surprised by my own firmness, but it seemed to work.

'Yeah.'

'Yeah what? Are you popular with the boys?'

'Yeah.'

'And do you have a boyfriend?'

'I've got loads,' she shot back. Wrong answer. Suddenly her defences were down.

'Do you have a special boyfriend?'

'Yeah.' Her eyes lit up. 'Darren.' Lucky Darren.

'And do you have a kiss and a cuddle with Darren round the back of the Centre?'

'Yeah, sometimes.' Now she was on her guard, the defences back up again.

'And did you let Darren give you a kiss and a cuddle that Monday night?'

'Can't remember.'

'Yes you can, Vicky. And did you let Darren fondle your breasts?'

'No I didn't.' The reply was too quick.

I felt I had done enough. I'd sown the seeds of doubt, time to call it a day. 'No further questions, your Honour.'

Chuckles was impressed, and it showed.

The next witness was Dr Priscilla Goodbody, the police surgeon who'd examined Vicky and found the incriminating finger marks around her left breast. She was clinically efficient, and her findings were potentially damning.

I started tentatively. 'Vicky is a well-developed young lady for her age, is she not?'

'I don't know what you mean,' she replied, unhelpfully. She knew exactly what I meant, but the extra income she earned as a police surgeon was not to be lightly thrown away by agreeing with defence counsel.

'It's a simple enough question, doctor,' interrupted Chuckles, acidly. 'The jury and I have spent the best part of an hour watching a video-taped recording of a very well-developed 15-year-old girl, so what do you mean when you say "I don't know what you mean"?'

Goodbody was taken aback. She wasn't used to being handled quite so roughly, but the judge was the judge, so better dance to his tune. 'Yes, your Honour.'

'Yes what?'

'Yes, Vicky is a very well-developed girl for her age.'

'And may I add, a very well-developed girl for any age, is she not?'

Goodbody paused. This was not how it should be going. 'Yes, your Honour, you could say that.'

Chuckles was on a roll. 'When Vicky presented herself for examination, did you ask if she was sexually active?'

'Not specifically, but I got that impression from her language and demeanour.'

'I'm sorry, Mr Potts, I interrupted your cross-examination. Please continue.'

'Thank you, your Honour.' Time to climb on board the bandwagon. 'From your examination, and I am referring to your clinical notes...'

'Clinical notes?' Chuckles interrupted yet again. 'What clinical notes?'

'The doctor's clinical notes disclosed to the defence as part of the unused material, your Honour,' I replied.

I had learned much from Sir James in the trial of Stubbs, among them where medical issues are raised, always study the clinical notes.

'If they are part of the unused material, Mr Potts,' Chuckles retorted, 'then I do not have them, as well you should know.'

'I apologise, your Honour. Perhaps my learned friend for the prosecution could oblige.'

A set was duly passed up.

Chuckles flicked through them. 'It all looks complete gibberish to me. Anyway, what did you want to ask the doctor?'

'Doctor, I am looking at page three of your notes, where you refer to a small livid mark around Vicky's left nipple, and faint marks on her right breast, and yet there is no mention of these in your witness statement. Why not?'

Goodbody felt trapped, which she was. 'I... I... I was asked to examine Vicky to see if there was any medical evidence to support her complaint against the defendant that he had fondled her left breast. There was, and I wrote my statement accordingly.'

'But, doctor,' back came Chuckles, at full gallop, 'if Mr Potts, learned counsel for the defence, had not bothered to decipher your clinical notes, and had relied solely on your witness statement, he could have been seriously misled?'

'I wouldn't put it like that.'

'Wouldn't you indeed!' Chuckles pushed back from the Bench and glowered at Goodbody.

'Your findings, I suggest,' I continued, 'are more consistent with the groping of both breasts and a possible love bite around the left nipple, would you not agree?'

'Possibly.'

'Possibly? At least I hope you'll agree that the livid mark around the left nipple and the faint finger marks on the right breast were not caused by the defendant?'

'I agree Vicky made no such complaint against the defendant,' she replied lamely.

We were on the home straight now, and things panned out in our favour from there on.

After the verdict, which the jury took less than half an hour to return, Jack was gracious enough to thank me for all I'd done.

HT came over to offer his congratulations. 'I never doubted you for a moment, Jack,' he burbled, sounding less than convincing. 'You've earned a well-deserved rest, so take time off, and we'll see you back after half term.'

'I'm sorry, HT,' said Jack, coolly. 'But I don't think Nietzsche and I are ready for St Jude's. No offence, but you'll get my letter of resignation in the post tomorrow morning.'

'I can understand how you're feeling,' HT replied, 'but at least sleep on it. Act in haste, Jack, and repent at leisure. I wonder who said that?' he mused. 'It wasn't Neetsher, was it?'

Jack got a job teaching English at Highgate, with polite, well-mannered children calling him 'Sir', listening attentively in class, doing their homework on time and moving effortlessly towards good grades in their exams. Every October, Chuckles appeared on the touchline for the Salopian soccer fixture, where he and Jack enjoyed many a happy hour discussing Nietzsche, morality, ethics, and the rich vein of German literature. Chuckles may have been a ghost from the past, but a very welcome one for all that.

As for me, there was so much to learn, and so little time. Now who said that?

Chapter Fourteen

GOING FOR GOAL

I AM NOT a soccer fan. Soccer was not on the sports curriculum at Rougemont College, as the Headmaster and Governors considered it too rough, and more a game for hooligans. But I had to learn the noble art of the national game, and learn it fast, if I were to do justice to 'Nutter' Nugent, the star of Alchester Town Football Club.

According to my instructions, it all started with the draw for the FA Cup, one of the premier tournaments of the football calendar, and involving the great, the good, and the downright awful of the English and Welsh clubs. Minnows and sharks together, all names went into the hat for a chance of Cup glory, and a memorable win against all the odds.

The eagerly-awaited draw for the third round – the point at which the top teams enter the competition – was made by Sir Malcolm Sweet, the Chairman of the FA, and known to one and all as Sweet FA. It was the match of the century, between Alchester Town FC and the all-conquering, all-mighty Manchester United. It was the stuff of dreams, and almost too good to be true.

Alchester Town had been languishing at the foot of the third division for as long as anybody could remember, and on any view, they were a naff team. The first XI – they fielded a full-strength outfit when Nobby Fowler could be bothered to turn up – was a team of honest journeymen more interested in the day job than international fame and stardom. It was a chance for a bit of exercise on a Saturday afternoon, a hot bath, and a few bevvies at the Three Horseshoes before trudging home to 'er indoors and the screaming kids.

Then along came Jarvinder Patel, the Midas of Alchester. He took over the corner shop, which, like the team, was dead on its feet, and transformed it overnight. Somewhat predictably, he called it Xanadu. He sold everything from newspapers to magazines of dubious provenance for which top shelves were invented, sweets, alcopops, fruit and veg, soft and hard drinks and greetings cards with smutty messages. He knew what the English liked, and if you can't beat them, join them, was his mantra. Not sure who said that first.

Next came the takeaway curry shop, which, according to some locals, was the best thing you could do with the stuff, but, again, it flourished and profits soared. Finally, there was the cash-and-carry outlet, selling to local tradesmen at heavily-discounted prices and open all hours. Everything he touched turned to gold... except for Alchester Town FC.

It was Fred Basset, the outgoing chairman, who had persuaded Jarvinder to pick up the torch and run with it. After twenty years of keeping the flickering flame alight, Fred had had enough and was ready to move on to a comfortable and well-earned retirement.

To Jarvinder, Fred was the key to the door. He was a past president of the Rotary Club, a past captain of Alcester Golf Club, and a past mayor. If it was there, Fred had been past it. Jarvinder's money and brand new Mercedes didn't, of themselves, bring him the social status he craved in his adopted town, so he jumped at the chance of taking over the football club. Not that he knew anything about football, but it was a showcase where he could expose himself to the townsfolk, so to speak. In return for Fred's controlling shares and the promise of a substantial injection of cash, Jarvinder secured pole position in the directors' box, a dubious honour, where he could all but freeze to death every other weekend and try to look interested.

The local press made it headline news, which was good for business, with lots of photos of the 'new saviour' of the club, standing in the water-logged centre circle, holding a ball and surrounded by most of the team. Nobby Fowler, as usual, had forgotten to turn up.

Alchester Town's stadium was built, or more precisely, put up, in 1912, in the days when every town had to have its own club. Few improvements had been made over the decades, but at least Fred Basset had done his bit. A new team kit, new goalposts, and upholstered, water-resistant seats for the directors. Nobody could accuse Fred of being tight with his money.

Jarvinder, however, was more ambitious, reasoning that if the team did well, it was good for business. In his first two years at the helm, the club shop was given a facelift, and new ablutions, affectionately christened the 'Jarvinderloos'.

As in the way of these things, the team was known as the Gollies, but nobody knew why. One seasoned wag suggested it was a reference to those rare occasions when the team scored a goal: 'Golly, they've scored a goal,' but that was generally discounted. If their nickname had anything to do with their goal scoring prowess, it was reasoned, they'd be known as the 'Blooming Adas!'

Jarvinder did what he could, and even named a curry 'The Golly Good Curry', special offer, Saturdays only – but, like the team, it was hardly a runaway success. His suggestion that it be served to the lads as a half-time snack was firmly vetoed. Whilst it might have kept the opposition at arm's length, the sight of eleven players running around aimlessly, and not necessarily in the right direction, was unlikely to improve performance.

In spite of his best efforts, the team remained firmly rooted in the bottom half of the division, lurching from one crisis to another, and the average weekly attendance was disappointing. Something had to be done, so Jarvinder summoned Dapper Dave Johnson, the team coach, to a meeting.

Dapper Dave, so called because of his penchant for wearing cheap gold jewellery, sharp suits, a permatan from the bottle, and chomping on gut-wrenching cigars, was in the twilight of his career, but he was all the club could afford, so he was tolerated more than loved by the board and fans alike.

'What we need, Guv,' said Dapper Dave, 'is a new striker of proven quality to bang the ball into the back of the net, not just twice a season, but week after week.'

'Looking at the results, what we are wanting is somebody to stop the ball going into the back of *our* net, not just twice a season, but week after week,' responded Jarvinder, who had done his homework.

'True enough, Guv,' said the manager, 'but success breeds success. The lads need to know that if they boot the ball up field, there'll be somebody to take it on, know what I mean?'

'So what are you suggesting?'

Dave was excited. 'I've heard on the grapevine that Nutter Nugent may be available. He's a household name.'

'Not in my household,' replied Jarvinder, distinctly unimpressed.

Bloody foreigner, thought Dave, but he pressed on. 'Nutter's got the pedigree, he used to play in the second division for Notts County, he was their top scorer for three years running, and he's now being offered on a free transfer, so no money up front, that's the good news.'

'And what's the bad news?'

'Well, we'll have to help him relocate and pay his wages.'

Jarvinder heard alarm bells ringing. 'How much?'

'He wants a thousand a week.' The thud was Jarvinder's jaw hitting the desk. 'But I reckon we can get him for seven-fifty,' said Dave, hastily. 'After all, if you pay peanuts, you get monkeys, and we've got enough of them already to open our own menagerie. He's not exactly inundated with offers' – Jarvinder was doing mental arithmetic as Dave continued – 'so we could offer him a twelve month rolling contract, and I reckon it could make all the difference.'

Jarvinder was in reflective mood, not saying yes, and not saying no. It could be a real coup for the club and, more to the point, his popularity in the community would soar, but this was not a decision to be taken lightly.

'And what's more, Guv, with a player like Nutter, we'd double gate receipts overnight.'

That was music to Jarvinder's ears, and the clincher. 'Alright,' he replied, 'I am leaving you to make contact, but not a penny more than seven-fifty a week, and I hope he is worth it. By the way,' he added, 'why is this gentleman calling himself Nutter?'

'Well, it's a measure of his standing in the sport,' Dave lied, 'he does things with his head other players only dream about.'

At least that part was true. Nutter Nugent was infamous for launching himself headlong at the opposition with a ferocity second to none, and if the ball happened to get in the way, it was a bonus.

NUTTER'S ARRIVAL was certainly the publicity coup Jarvinder had hoped for, plenty of photo opportunities, and a small but welcome run on 'Nutter' replica shirts. Even better news on the pitch, as Nutter crashed in the goals, whilst crashing into the goalie, the goalposts, the back netting, and anything else that stood in his way. For those of a delicate disposition, it was a sickening sight, but sales of the Golly Good Curry rocketed. After all, if you could stomach a Golly Good Curry, you could stomach Nutter's antics. Results improved, and for the first time in living memory, Alchester Town climbed into the top half of the division. And even Dapper Dave got it right, as gate receipts doubled. At last Alchester had a team worth shouting about.

Alchester had progressed steadily through the first two rounds of the Cup. Their first scalp was lowly Bathpool Rovers, seen off comprehensively at home after their goalkeeper was carried off unconscious in the third minute following a goalmouth incident involving Nutter. The linesman thought about flagging for a foul, but, when he saw Nutter advancing towards him, thought better of it, and his flag stayed down. The away team surrounded and jostled the referee, screaming for justice, but as he was adjusting his bootlaces at the time, he saw nothing amiss. Bathpool didn't boast a reserve goalie, so the team physiotherapist was dragooned into action, against his better judgment, and after that it was like shooting fish in a barrel. Five-nil.

Next came Coleswell Wanderers, away, a needle match if ever there was. Nil-all until the last five minutes, when Nutter launched himself at their centre-half like an Exocet missile. Fortunately he saw Nutter coming, and took life-saving evasive action. Nobby Fowler, who'd turned up for such an important fixture, had just punted the ball hopefully into the centre as Nutter was in full flight. More by luck than good judgment, his left ankle made contact with the ball, which fizzed into the back of the net, closely followed by Nutter. It was a moment to savour.

So much for the minnows, now for the big boys! And so to the dream tie, and at home to boot. Jarvinder, embracing the football ethic, was over the moon, as was the whole town. Excitement reached fever pitch as the great day loomed. Volunteers with garden forks were conscripted into improving the drainage, but with only limited success. The directors' box was given a fresh lick of paint, supplied at special discount rates by Jarvinder's cash-and-carry, and new seat covers were installed. The thought of sitting next to Sir Bobby Charlton was almost too good to believe, and Jarvinder was determined to make the most of it. Copious quantities of Golly Good Curry were laid on for the half-time bash, together with a full-bodied Rioja for the menfolk and a cheeky little Chardonnay for the ladies, again supplied at special discount rates by Xanadu. And, as if that were not enough, Sky Sports and BBC Television were to film the match, Sky broadcasting it live, and the BBC showing highlights at three the following morning.

The great day dawned, and the ground was packed to overflowing. Sadly for Jarvinder, Sir Bobby failed to show, so he found himself wedged between two complete nonentities, not in his game plan at all. A sizeable contingent of Man U supporters helped to swell the numbers, and they were carefully cordoned off in their own enclosure like a contagious disease. Man U had elected to field their reserve team, collectively worth in excess of £10 million, but there was a sense of disappointment in the home crowd, who had paid to see the real stars. Still, their team was captained by Scholesy, with Giggsy, Smithy and Butty on the bench. Hang on a minute, hadn't Butty been transferred? Must be a lookalike.

Finally, after what seemed like an eternity, the whistle blew, and they were underway. The Gollies, having won the toss, elected to kick off. Dapper Dave's tactics, explained in words of one syllable, were crude but effective. Don't let them settle on the ball, keep harrying them, run them off their stride. For once in their lives, the team responded, and, for a while, the tactics worked. Man U's reserves, used to playing quality football, with skilful one-twos, close control and intricate step-overs, found themselves flattened, with or without the ball, as the Galloping Gollies clattered into them. It was like lambs to the slaughter, and, by the tenth minute, the pea in the referee's whistle was burning red hot. And then it came.

Twelve minutes precisely, and the stuff of legends. A clearance down field from Man U's goalkeeper fell into the centre circle, where it stopped dead in the mud. Nobby pounced on it like a dog on a rat, and without a moment's hesitation, punted it back up field. He was good at that – it was his party piece. Nutter set off like a steam train, taking no prisoners on the way, and as he thundered into the penalty area, the ball hit him on the back of the head and looped majestically over the advancing goalie and into the net.

The crowd erupted. Nutter set off on his victory lap, pursued by the rest of the team, and slithered ten yards into the corner post, which snapped like a rotten twig. The Man U supporters were stunned into silence, but, as Dapper Dave was fond of saying, football's a game of two halves.

And so it proved to be, with Man U scoring four goals in the second half as the Gollies began to tire. Nutter's frustration turned ugly. There was an off-the-ball incident where a Man U player received an elbow in the face, fracturing his nose, and all hell broke loose. This time there was no reprieve, and Nutter got the red card. Red was also the colour of the mist before his eyes as he sloped off to an early bath, but not before gobbing at the linesman.

The FA took disciplinary proceedings, and banned Nutter for three matches. But there was worse to come. Having viewed the tape of the incident, the Crown Prosecution Service initiated a criminal investigation, and Nutter was charged with assault occasioning actual bodily harm, and common assault on the linesman. At a preliminary hearing, Nutter pleaded not guilty to both charges, and elected trial by jury at Croydon Crown Court.

Finding myself 'unexpectedly' available for the trial, I was briefed to represent him.

CROYDON CROWN COURT, another purpose built *Palais de Justice*, is about as attractive as Croydon itself, i.e. not very. It is a dormitory town, full of banks, building societies, egg box hotels, and multinational conglomerates, attracted by the lower ground rents and overheads, but within easy striking distance of the City. As far as I could see, it had absolutely nothing to commend it. It was totally anonymous, the sort of place you drive through, without stopping, to get somewhere else, and to add insult to injury, not even a football team worth spit.

Nutter's defence to the charges was blunt and to the point, rather like his football. The elbow in the face was accidental. He was back-peddling, anticipating another Nobby belter up field, when he stumbled into the Man U player, lost his balance and put his elbow out to steady himself. It happens all the time, mate, know what I mean?

As for gobbing at the linesman, every player gobs, on average once a minute, it goes with the territory. In fact, there was a television programme not so long ago called *Gob of the Month*, featuring the various techniques employed by players as they gobbed their way through ninety minutes, ranging from the short, staccato gob, through the one-nostril snot expectoration, to the full-blown, back-of-the-throat, roll-it-round-the tongue traditional gob, and several other permutations in between. Nutter went for distance, which was why his gob hit the linesman square amidships from a dozen paces. It wasn't Nutter's fault the daft bugger got in the way.

The trial was to be presided over by Mr Recorder Sheldon, a local man with his own chambers in Croydon. He'd levelled out early in his career, and, with a combination of age and mediocrity now rooting him firmly in the third division, he was ideally suited to the task at hand. By reputation, he was fair, if somewhat pedestrian in his approach, a bit like Nobby Fowler. The prosecutor, Harold Trumper, came from the same chambers, so was part of the home team.

Trumper met me in the robing room. 'What we need here,' he said, 'is a jury well-versed in the niceties of the game, I'm sure you agree. With your client's defence of accident, they'll need to decide if the elbow in the face was part and parcel of the run of the game, or a deliberate and malicious act.'

'I agree wholeheartedly,' I replied. 'No point having twelve housewives who go shopping as soon as football comes on the television. A joint approach to the judge, perhaps?'

'Leave it to me,' said Trumper confidently, 'Sheldon will do as he's told.'

'And does he follow the game?'

'Oh yes, been a Southampton supporter all his life, poor chap. No wonder he's old before his time.'

With Sheldon's agreement, the jury panel was duly vetted, in spite of some mutterings of discontent from the ladies. Not one of those selected declared support for either team. Most had never even heard of the Gollies, which was hardly surprising, but all followed the game to a greater or lesser extent.

After his opening speech, Trumper addressed the judge. 'Your Honour, it is my intention to show the televised match to the jury in its entirety.'

'Really, Mr Trumper? Is that necessary? After all, the jury are only being asked to decide what happened during two isolated incidents.'

'Yes and no, your Honour. That is correct regarding the allegation of ABH. However, regarding the allegation of common assault, Mr Nutter claims that when he expectorated at the linesman, it was one of many during the match...'

'Just pause there, Mr Trumper, whilst Mr Potts takes further instructions.'

I was beckoned over to the dock by an agitated Nutter. 'What's all this expecting stuff he's on about? It's a stitch up if you ask me. I want a retrial.'

'Calm down, Mr Nugent, it's just a pompous word for spitting. Leave it to me.' I turned back to the judge. 'The defendant is confused by my learned friend's use of the word "expectorated", your Honour.'

'I agree with him, Mr Potts. Mr Trumper, this is the third division, not the High Court. Let's keep it simple.'

'As your Honour pleases. It is the Crown's case that the offending evacuation of spittle' – not much better, if you asked me – 'was deliberately aimed at the linesman who had flagged for the foul and, in the eyes of the defendant, was directly responsible for his dismissal. By comparing that evacuation with others during the match, the jury can make up their own minds.'

'Very well. Members of the jury, you have heard what is proposed. I shall therefore adjourn until 2.15 this afternoon, when we shall all watch the match here in court.'

At 2.15 precisely, the jury filed back into court. I wondered if I should insist on the commentary being turned off in case it influenced the jury, but as the commentator hailed from the dark side of the Gorbals and was totally incomprehensible, the risk was minimal. I also noticed that, to a man, they were all carrying bags with them from the local Spar store. As soon as the lights went down, there was an audible rustling, and the distinct sound of cans of lager and packets of crisps being opened. As they settled down to enjoy the match, the smell of salt and vinegar was almost overpowering.

It is strange but true that, with the obvious exceptions of Old Trafford in Manchester and the entire Far East, Manchester United Football Club is disliked with an abiding passion. It may have something to do with the fact that they are the biggest, and sometimes the best, club in the world, conquering all before them. So it was clear, from the opening minutes, where the jury's sympathies lay. It was not just the Englishman's love of the underdog, it was their dislike of mighty Man U.

When the goal arrived, with several replays, that had the entire jury and Nutter on their feet, whooping with delight, and it was all Nutter could do not to embark on a victory lap around the court. Sheldon thought about trying to restore some order in the court, but thought better of it. He didn't want cans of lager being lobbed at him from the direction of the jury box. The match continued, and as Scholesy did one of his trademark double-footed tackles, there was a roar of outrage from the jury, and a chant of 'Off! Off! Off!'

There was an audible groan when the first of Man U's goals went in, and a plaintive shout of 'Offside ref!' from the back row. Then came the elbow incident. It looked pretty deliberate to me. Nutter was backing into the Man U player, as he claimed, but the ball was nowhere to be seen. Out went the elbow, down went the player like a pole-axed heifer, clutching his face and streaming blood. It was not a pretty sight. The jury fell silent, absorbing the enormity of the assault and Nutter's flying elbow.

Finally, the gobbing incident. As lawyers are fond of saying, the defendant was in evidential difficulties. Instead of making his way to the tunnel and the Jarvinderloos, Nutter seemed to walk deliberately towards the linesman before 'evacuating his spittle' at him. I was not hopeful.

I called Nutter to give evidence, and he was true to form, taking the jury through the match, using the highlights and replay buttons to make his point. Some of the fouls were pretty horrendous. In the early part of the match, before the Gollies tired, the Man U players were going down like nine pins.

Then came the foul that led to the charge of ABH.

'Right, your Honour and members of the jury,' he continued, clearly excited, 'I've got Ramondo, their left-back, crowding me, and I'm backing into 'im, to give meself room to break, know what I mean? A player of my experience needs to be ready for anything. And as I'm backing into 'im, 'e's pushing into me, and I lose me balance. Now, what would you do?' he said. 'Do you mind if I demonstrate, your Honour?'

'If you think it will help, by all means do so,' replied Sheldon, ever anxious to please the crowd.

Nutter stepped out of the witness box and beckoned the usher. ''ere, mate, come and stand behind me.' The usher reluctantly complied. 'Now, you start pushing into me, know what I mean, and I'm backing into you, see? Then I'm about to wheel away, right, you're right up close, I lose me balance, out comes me elbow, and pow!'

Fortunately for Nutter, the usher declined to press charges for a chipped tooth and a badly-swollen cheek, which, in the circumstances, was very decent of him.

The jury were out for over two hours before acquitting Nutter of ABH, reasoning, as they must have done, that if you play for Man U, you deserve everything you get, and more. But they convicted him of common assault. After all, the linesman was only doing his job.

Sheldon fined Nutter a week's wages, and another week's wages in compensation. I was bemused, but Nutter was well pleased with the result. A definite score draw, with the moral advantage to the home team.

I declined his offer of a celebratory night out with the lads at the Three Horseshoes – despite the fact that they had booked strippers – and our paths never crossed again. But I kept a casual eye on those scores written in very small type, and positioned deep inside the sports pages of the nationals, and was pleased, in a proprietorial sort of way, to see that he continued to bang the ball into the backs of nets up and down the lower divisions with varying parts of his anatomy for some time afterwards.

Nutter lasted another two seasons with the Gollies before hanging up his boots. He bought a small pub, where the picture of his victory lap was prominently displayed, and, at the drop of a beer mat, he'd regale his long-suffering customers with a blow-by-blow account of his finest hour and twenty minutes.

I was quietly pleased with my own part in the whole affair, coming as it had at the end of a very busy period for me. My career was definitely on an upward trajectory.

Chapter Fifteen

TIME OUT

SINCE BEING TAKEN on as a tenant at Brick Court, I'd worked non-stop. I wasn't complaining, at least there was work to be had, but with my nose buried in *Archbold* and the daily cut-and-thrust of the courtroom drama, I'd neglected the lighter side of life. Time to smell the roses and feel the grass beneath my feet. It was also time to play Bar politics. I was constantly reminded that it was as much who you know as what you know, and being seen in the right places was essential to sharpen my professional profile.

Gray's Inn was a good starting point. Each year, in July, the Inn hosted a Reception, followed by a Ball, and by all accounts, the latter, at least, was spectacular. It boasted an ox roast, a live band of which only the likes of John Peel had ever heard, a disco, and fireworks for the grand finale.

The Reception, in contrast, was a turgid affair, but the setting was quintessentially English. The green sward of The Walks stretched right up to Theobalds Road, and was planted with enormous lime and plane trees, together with an ancient catalpa which, according to legend, was either planted, or sat on, or played under, by the equally legendary Sir Francis Bacon, the darling of 16th century philosophy and the favourite of King James the First. He was also a formidable advocate and latterly Lord Chancellor, who dabbled in the natural sciences and Aristotelian polemics, and for which he was generally rubbished. Proof, if proof were needed, that you should stick to what you do best, but at least he died in his own bed. Those who, from time to time, visited the catalpa, walked around it in a reverential hush, like some holy shrine. They'd heard of him, of course, but they weren't quite sure why. Americans from Baconsville, Nantucket, were regular pilgrims to the site.

After touching base with the Under-Treasurer's office, and upon payment of the princely sum of £25, I eventually received my embossed invitation to the Master Treasurer's Reception, and immediately set about my plan of action. There was no published guest list, and worse still, no lapel badges, in the best traditions of the American convention circuit, so I would have to feel my way.

My plan of action was simple. I had two hours to put myself about, to get noticed and known by the great and the good whilst avoiding the boring old farts. The third hour was the social graveyard, as those still there would be far too inebriated to remember the time of day, or Bacon and his poxy tree, let alone my name or anything else about me.

The problem about distinguishing between the great and the good and the boring old farts was they all looked the same. How was I to tell the difference between the Lord Chief Justice and some old buffer from the Outer Hebrides? It was a nightmare scenario.

I arrived twenty minutes after kick-off to make the maximum impact on arrival. Unfortunately, all the other guests must have had the same idea, as I joined the long queue snaking through the enormous wrought-iron gates and up to the reception line. I spotted none of my contemporaries, and must have been the youngest there by at least forty years. No matter, at least I would have the field to myself, to exploit and explore at my leisure.

From my place in the queue, it was also a good vantage point to sort the wheat from the chaff. The reception welcoming party consisted of the Master Treasurer, Lord Justice Maurice Oldland, the Presiding Judge of the Admiralty Division, and his fragrant wife Madge, looking for all the world like a younger version of Barbara Cartland.

To my untutored mind, the Admiralty Division was all about slapping speeding tickets on ocean-going tankers, with the occasional high seas collision to leaven the bread, lots of oil sludging on to pristine white sandy shores, and flapping cormorants being hosed down by local worthies from the RSPB. All very commendable, but not exactly my idea of a good day out.

The outgoing and incoming Master Treasurers were also there to greet the guests, and bringing up the rear was Rear-Admiral

'Salty' Matravers, retired seadog and now the Under-Treasurer. From seadoggy to dogsbody, all in one effortless stride. As I watched, those who were passed along the reception line like hot potatoes with barely a nod of recognition could be firmly placed in the boring old farts category. Those who lingered, and who were treated to a few words and a welcoming smile, were prime targets for my plan of action. I tried to memorise as many faces as I could before I, too, was passed down the line in record time and out the other side.

Armed with a lukewarm glass of South African Chardonnay and a *bonne bouche* of some description, I set off in search of my first target. As luck would have it, a distinguished-looking man, dressed in pinstripe trousers and a lightweight summer jacket, had just detached himself from a group of acquaintances and was making his way to the marquee for a refill. Time to pounce.

'Good afternoon, sir,' I said, respectfully. 'May I introduce myself?'

'Good Lord, boy, whatever for?' he replied, without breaking his stride.

Pompous jackass, I thought, as I stared at his retreating back. Undaunted, I pressed on, and spotted a splendid old buffer sporting a Panama hat, sitting alone in the shade. Perhaps it was Lord Denning, the retired Master of the Rolls. One way to find out.

'Good afternoon, sir. May I introduce myself?'

'No need, my boy,' replied the splendid old buffer, peering at me from beneath the brim of his hat, 'I know you well. Now don't tell me, let me guess,' he continued, looking me up and down, 'it's Paul Featherstone. Haven't seen you in a while. What are you up to?'

'Well, actually, sir, it's Toby Potts.'

'Can't say I know the chap,' replied the splendid old buffer, looking around him in confusion. 'Which one is he? Still, there are so many coming to the Bar these days, it's difficult to keep track of them all.' *Why bother*, I thought, but how to slip away graciously? Too late. 'Sit down, Paul, and tell me all the latest gossip.'

'I'm in Gazzard's chambers, sir, and greatly enjoying it.'

'Ah yes, Gazzard,' he mused, 'Palmer and Camley Borough Council. You know it, of course?'

'Indeed I do, a landmark case in public negligence…'

'Yes, yes, as Gazzard was fond of reminding us at every opportunity.' He paused. 'Is the old fool still alive?'

'Still alive, and still head of chambers,' I replied.

'Can't think why on either score. Should have punted off years ago. Peaked after the Palmer case, don't you know. Couldn't abide the chap at any price. Waiter!' he bellowed at the Master Treasurer, 'another bottle of that revolting Chardonnay, chop, chop. You'll join me of course?' he added, smiling indulgently.

This was the encounter from hell, and not in my plan of action at all. 'That's very kind of you.' What else could I say?

'Those were the days. Gazzard took over his father's set, and I opted for service overseas. You know, of course, I was Chief Magistrate of the Solomon Islands for twenty glorious years.' His eyes misted over. 'Service over and beyond the call of duty, but somebody had to do it. Did I tell you, Paul, when I arrived, a bevy of bare-breasted maidens, every one a virgin, or so they claimed, swam out to meet me and carry me aloft on a bed of palm tree matting.' He was off, and there was no stopping him. 'Damned decent of them. The whole island turned out to greet me. The King was particularly solicitous, and offered me three of his wives. Such a generous man.'

'And did you accept?'

'That, Paul, is between me and my Maker,' and he chuckled. 'We had the death penalty in those days, and public flogging, so the responsibility was considerable.'

I was horrified. 'You didn't condemn anybody to death, did you, sir?'

'Heavens, no,' he laughed, 'they were such a gentle people. Generally speaking, it was unpaid work for the community, that sort of thing. If you stole from your neighbour, you had to work for him until you'd paid off the debt. It was all very civilised.'

'And what about Old Blighty?' I asked. 'Didn't you miss it?'

'Good Lord, no. Would you?' He had a point.

Just then there was a stir in the Walks and a frisson of excitement ran through the assembled guests. The Master Treasurer, on his way over with another bottle of wine, stopped in mid-stride.

'Go and grab that bottle from the idiot waiter, there's a good chap, Paul. Looks like he's distracted. So difficult to get good staff these days.'

I got up, relieved the Master Treasurer of the wine, and returned. I half-thought of making a run for it, but that would be rude, and besides, the splendid old buffer was far more interesting than listening to the usual shop talk. As I poured another glass for each of us, I spotted two familiar figures out of the corner of my eye, and my heart skipped a beat. Up the Walks strode Jumbo Bingham and Archie Scott-Malden, larger than life in every sense of the word. Judging from the Master Treasurer's reaction, it was as if royalty had arrived. The other guests were spellbound.

'Mo!' bellowed Jumbo. 'Hope we're not too late.'

'Not at all, Jumbo, a delight to see you both. How are you, Archie?'

'Passably well, thanks, Mo. Picked a good day for it,' he continued, looking up at the cloudless sky, 'but then, God always smiles on the Admiralty Division.'

'So they say, Archie, but I couldn't possibly comment. Now, a glass of wine,' and he beckoned over a waiter.

Jumbo inspected the contents as if he were being offered a poisoned chalice. 'You're not seriously expecting us to drink this, are you, Mo?' He took his arm conspiratorially. 'What's the point of being Master Treasurer if you can't enjoy the perks from time to time? Now,' he continued, lowering his voice, 'I happen to know you have a particularly fine '71 Veugeot laid down in the cellars waiting for a moment such as this. Six bottles should suffice. And we need some crusty French bread and a slab of mature cheddar, and thee and Madge beside us. What more fitting way to end the term, don't you agree, Archie?'

'I agree,' laughed Archie, 'and have nothing further to add.'

'Good man, Archie, and breaking the habit of a lifetime. Now go to it, Mo, and with any luck, by the time the wine has caught its breath, all these ghastly people you've invited will have drifted off.'

'Please, Jumbo,' Mo whispered, 'keep your voice down, or you'll get me sacked.'

Jumbo bellowed with laughter, and with the Head Butler duly dispatched on his errand, Mo began to lead them to his table.

'If it's alright with you, Mo,' said Jumbo, taking his arm, 'I'm not in the mood to socialise. Besides, your guests look a very dreary lot. Archie and I need gaiety and laughter to do justice to your magnificent wine.'

'Give me ten minutes and I'll join you.'

Jumbo looked around and spotted me. 'Aha, I see a young friend of mine. Come on, Archie,' and to my trepidation, they bore down on me, with the remaining guests open-mouthed in astonishment.

'Archie, this is Toby Potts, a splendid lad and my saviour in Wood Green. By the way, I received a delightful letter from Mario after the trial, accompanied by a very drinkable bottle of wine, very thoughtful of the chap.'

'Hello, Toby,' said Archie, 'do you mind if we join you?'

'A great honour, but this isn't my table. This kind gentleman invited me to join him.'

'This kind gentleman, as you delicately put it, is Mungo Fitzgerald, the toast of the Pacific.'

Mungo rose slowly from his chair and lifted his hat in salutation. 'Jumbo, dear boy, and Archie, what a pleasure. Now, if you will excuse me, the heat and this atrocious wine have had a debilitating effect upon my *sang froid*, so I shall leave you in the company of my charming friend Paul Featherstone. Until the next time.'

'Dear old fellow,' said Jumbo, as Mungo tottered off, 'and the last of a dying breed. Mark you, they say that about me,' and he roared with laughter. 'Now, to the business in hand, where's that wine?'

As if on cue, the Head Butler approached, bearing the fruits of his search, and carrying the bottles of vintage Clos de Veugeot with much the same care as Mungo had been carried ashore by that bevy of bare-breasted maidens, and closely followed by the crusty bread and cheese. Mo, not wishing to miss out on a drop of this liquid nectar, quickly made his excuses and joined them, with Madge in tow.

'Come on, Madge, plant those firm, tight, buttocks on this old man's lap,' boomed Jumbo.

'I shall do no such thing, Jumbo,' she replied, colouring visibly.

'That's not what you used to say when we were students together,' he quipped.

'That was light years ago,' she smiled, 'and a lot of water has gone under the bridge since then, so behave yourself.'

'I have my orders,' he laughed, 'so I shall do my best. Now, Toby, do the honours, there's a good chap. Mo, have you met?' and he waved his hand in my direction.

'Only briefly. A pleasure, young man.' The Master Treasurer extended his hand as I rose from my seat.

I was in the presence of greatness, and totally overwhelmed.

'It's been a great privilege meeting you again, Sir James,' I said, not wishing to intrude, 'but I think I should be going.'

'Nonsense, dear boy. Yours is the spirit of perpetual youth and the future of this God-benighted profession. Without you, we are nothing, so stay, and let us old fogies enjoy a few moments in your company. You shall be our Peter Pan, our Dorian Gray.'

And so the wine flowed, the most exquisite I had ever tasted. Far from the dry old stick I had imaged, Sir Maurice was the soul of wit, giving as good as he got from Jumbo, and loving every minute. Sir James had that rare gift, an infectious sense of humour and a love of life, which in combination was irresistible.

As the third bottle was poured, Sir Harry Hogswell loomed out of the gathering gloom. 'Just popped over to thank you, Master, for such an enjoyable day.' He eyed the bottle of Veugeot enviously.

'Ah,' boomed Sir James, 'Mr Justice Hogswell, as I live and breathe. Still putting the world to rights, I hope?'

'One does what one can, Sir James,' he replied tartly.

'With your lordship on the Bench, there is no safer pair of hands.' He grinned mischievously. 'Let me introduce you to my friend Toby Potts, that is, unless you've met already?'

I stood up, and immediately recognised the pompous jackass who'd cut me dead. It was a moment to savour.

'No, I don't think we've met, unless we spoke earlier,' I said, my eyes holding Sir Harry's for just long enough. 'A great pleasure, my lord.'

'Please, Toby,' he replied, obviously embarrassed, 'no formalities here. After all, we're all equal on these occasions.'

'Exactly the expression I was clumsily groping for.' Jumbo was unstoppable. Hogswell turned on his heel and marched off. 'There goes Mr Justice Hogswill, a man who was never born, but simply dug up at the age of 55, a fully-formed high court judge. I could never abide the man! Now, dear hearts,' Jumbo was back to his most expansive, 'a toast, to good friends, good wine, the exuberance of youth, and the loveliest woman I never made mine.' There was a glint in his eye as he gazed affectionately at Madge. 'Still, my sweetheart, if you had to settle for second best, you couldn't have chosen a finer man than Mo.' Mo laughed. 'To the victor, the spoils! To Mo and Madge!'

THE GRAY'S INN BALL the following night was bound to be an anti-climax, but with Susie at my side it was to be a memorable weekend, and one I would never forget.

We met at the Savoy, where Susie's father had booked a room for her. The thought of his beautiful daughter spending the night in some impoverished barrister's grotty little flat off the Earls Court Road was more than he could bear. The fact that his beautiful daughter had spent the best part of a year sleeping under the stars in Lesotho simply didn't enter into his calculations.

Susie looked stunning, and I was not the only one to think so, judging from all the envious glances I received throughout the night. We formed a table of eight, gorged ourselves on ox roast and salad, and danced the night away. John Peel's rock band was nothing if not loud, and it gave me the chance to show off my 'solid gone' act as we gyrated round the floor. After a good workout, we made our way back to the marquee, where the lights were now dimmed as the DJ played a succession of slow, romantic, numbers. I was lost in a world of my own, holding Susie tight, just happy to have her and to hold her.

Back at our table, chatting easily about nothing in particular, we were interrupted by the arrival of the Head Butler.

'With the compliments of the Master Treasurer,' he announced gravely, placing an ice-cold bottle of champagne in front of us. Reverentially, he opened the bottle, poured two glasses, bowed gravely, and withdrew.

I was astonished and delighted, and looking round the marquee, spotted the Master Treasurer in the corner. I made my way over. 'It's exceedingly generous of you, Master. Will you and Lady Oldland care to join us?'

'A kind thought, Toby,' he smiled, 'but the night belongs to the young, and besides,' he added, looking at his watch, 'it's past our bedtime.'

'It may be past your bedtime,' Madge retorted, 'but Toby is about to ask me to dance, and I suggest you do the same with his absolutely divine girlfriend.'

Mo needed no second invitation, and after two numbers, we exchanged partners and danced, cheek to cheek, until the lights went up. After the fireworks, the four of us finished the champagne, and then it was time to go. Madge had taken Susie by the arm and was chatting to her as if they'd been friends for life. Mo and I followed a few paces behind.

Mo smiled, and turned to me. 'Madge and I have had a gloriously happy life together, but there are times, when she's with Jumbo, she wonders what might have been. They were very much in love in those early days, but, for one reason or another, it never happened, and I think they both regret it more than they can say. So if you'll take the advice of an older but well-meaning man, don't make the same mistake, my boy. Susie's adorable. If you love her, as you obviously do, don't let her get away.'

Back at the Savoy, I gave Susie a long, lingering, kiss. 'It's been a wonderful evening, and I don't want it to end, but I suppose I should be getting back home.'

'Toby, you're very sweet, but if you think I'm going to sleep alone in an enormous double bed in the best hotel in town, then think again.'

After a late breakfast and more champagne, I put my arms around Susie and gazed adoringly into her eyes. 'I can't think of one reason why you would want to... I mean, I'm an impoverished barrister and likely to remain one... so I can't promise you much... in fact...'

Susie put her finger to my lips. 'Yes, Toby darling, the answer is yes.'

Chapter Sixteen

THE WEASEL

IT WAS THE ambition of all aspiring barristers to cultivate a stable of solicitors to call their own, who would love, honour and cherish them till death, or retirement, did them part, and I was no exception.

It all went back to the days of the blessed St Thomas à Becket, before his untimely martyrdom at the hands of King Henry and his merry men. There's nothing quite like a gory slaying in the House of God to move you rapidly up the beatification ladder, and St Thomas was no exception. But before his elevation to heavenly grace, he was the king's favourite, and as such, enjoyed rapid promotion of a more temporal kind. After a few non-descript jobs to whet the appetite, he was appointed Lord Chancellor. Not that he knew anything about the law, a precedent set for generations to come, and it wasn't until the 19th century that judges were expected to be learned in the law and not simply make it up as they went along.

But his heart was in the right place, and, feeling the urge, as is the way of saints, to do something for the Great Unwashed, Thomas started his own court, which he named the Court of Chancery. It was an overnight success, and everybody with a gripe, real or imagined, trundled off to the Court to argue the toss and await the Lord Chancellor's judgment. The Court became a victim of its own success, with litigants jostling and pushing and shouting the odds. It was a complete shambles, so Thomas was forced to introduce a few simple rules to restore some semblance of order. To keep the disgruntled litigants out of his face, with abusive shouts of 'Do you want some!?' and 'What's your fucking problem!?' hurled at him from close proximity, he erected a stout wooden barrier, or bar, between himself and the rabble. Those with an eye on the main chance and who claimed a familiarity with the law offered their services as advocates and pleaders, for a modest fee, of course. When called upon by the Lord Chancellor to address him, they had to do so at the Bar.

It soon became bruited abroad that the chances of successful litigation were greatly enhanced by employing this new breed of barristers, as they had the ear of the Court and were reasonably literate, an irresistible combination. But as the litigants far outnumbered barristers, and as barristers could only plead one case at a time, it was the devil's own job to get the right man at the right price, and successful barristers found themselves very much in demand. How times have changed.

Something had to give, and it did. Enterprising touts began offering their services, introducing the favoured few to the barrister of their choice in return for a slice of the action. It was a cosy arrangement that suited both parties, and these touts became known as solicitors.

I could boast only one solicitor who favoured me above all others, but I had to start somewhere.

Derek Finnan was a sole practitioner, operating out of his own kitchen in Camberwell Green, and relying on day-to-day support from the likes of Bootsy Farmer. To help him on the paperwork, he engaged the services of Jane Hodges, known affectionately as Topsy. She was celebrated by one and all for her purposeful and business-like manner and her magnificent hairdos, a triumph of lacquer over gravity.

My professional relationship with Del began when I was instructed to represent a wide boy clocked at over 120mph on the M1 motorway in his Porsche.

Appearing at St Alban's Magistrates Court, I put in a compelling plea in mitigation, lots of guff about the breadwinner with a young family, needs the car to sell insurance to the world and his dog, will lose his home and his job if he can't drive. To my amazement, it worked, the wide boy kept his licence and paid my fee of £50, there and then, in cash from the back pocket. Within the hour, the grateful client phoned Del to sing my praises, and from that moment on the dye was cast.

As the clerks were fond of saying, if you provide a service, sooner or later, a plum will fall into your lap. Put another way, better to be working on dross than sitting in chambers chewing the fat. No doubt about it, the clerks had a way with words.

Del didn't like clients who wanted to plead not guilty. It was time-consuming, with forms to be filled out, statements to be taken and some sort of defence to be cobbled together on the kitchen table. A plea of guilty was far neater, almost clinical in its simplicity, go to court, take your medicine and move on. Del was in it for the quantity, not quality. If it couldn't be turned round and the taxed bill submitted to the Legal Services Commission in seven days flat, Del didn't want to know. That is, until Danny 'The Enforcer' Bloom came into his life.

Although I didn't know it at the time, Danny was about to provide me with that long-awaited plum. Problem was, by the time it fell into my lap, it was putrid and rotten to the core.

DANNY WAS THE product of his time. Born and raised in Camberwell, with little or no formal education, he couldn't see the point, all that crap about Neetsher, and the bloke didn't even speak English, and who was he to tell the likes of Danny about the infinite chaos underlying primitive life? Danny knew all about primitive life. After all, he lived in Camberwell.

After leaving school with no qualifications, Danny joined the Green Youth Club and excelled at boxing. He wasn't big, but he was very stocky, all muscle from the tips of his toes to the space between his ears. He even thought at one stage of turning professional, until he met The Weasel.

The Weasel was a small time hoodlum and infamous on the Green. Protection, prostitution, gambling and drugs were controlled with ruthless efficiency from his club, fetchingly named the Copa Cabana. The Weasel was a fan of Barry Manilow, and what was good enough for Barry was good enough for him, know what I mean?

He modelled himself on Al Pacino in *The Godfather*, even down to the brilliantine hair, the loud, pinstripe suits, and the two-tone shoes. The videos had pride of place in his penthouse suite above the Weasel and Trouserleg Public House, one of his many haunts. It was also the origin of his nickname, but those who used it in his presence did so at their peril. 'Boss' was a safer bet, or better still, Don Cornyony, although that could have been a misspelling. Nobody saw fit to ask.

The Weasel was always on the lookout for enforcers, and Danny fitted the bill. He was duly summoned into the presence and made an offer he couldn't refuse. On the downside, it was unsocial hours, no sickness benefits and the pension plan was dead in the water, like those who crossed his path. But the money was good, all cash-in-hand with no deductions, two free drinks a night with nosh at the Copa Cabana, selected dishes only, and the occasional torrid tumble with a girl of The Weasel's choice, at special knock-up rates.

To oil the wheels, The Weasel also had a handful of bent coppers on the payroll, and, in return for party favours, he was left very much to his own devices.

Then, one day, somebody stood up to be counted.

Yu Flung Dung, which meant something else in Cantonese, ran a dry cleaning business just off the Walworth Road, on the edge of The Weasel's patch. For the first two years he'd been willing to pay a modest sum to keep the peace, but when the rate doubled overnight Mr Dung drew a line in the sand and refused to pay. Billy 'Fingers' Malloy, one of The Weasel's collectors, got two fingers back when he called, and a good spanking into the bargain.

Time for The Enforcer.

Danny and three mates, all chiselled from the same block of granite, paid Mr Dung a visit, put him in hospital and firebombed his premises. No half-measures when The Enforcer came to call.

As luck would have it, a new superintendent had been appointed to the Green barely six weeks earlier, and he had The Weasel firmly in his sights. He'd obviously been speaking to Hot Hands Spinks, just down the road in Hackney, and was damned if he was going to let Hot Hands steal all the headlines. Besides which, the thought of

Hot Hands getting promoted over his head was more than a body could bear. Time to clean up the cesspool, and grab a share of the limelight.

Mr Dung knew The Weasel and his gang well. Most of them brought in their sharp suits to be dry cleaned, six for the price of five, and The Weasel's Fedora hat was a regular visitor.

Mr Dung, a brave if foolhardy man, was willing to give evidence, so, in a blaze of publicity, The Weasel, The Enforcer and his three mates were all arrested. As Del was duty solicitor that day, he represented the footsoldiers and sat in on the interviews with the police, where they all went 'no comment'. The Weasel had his own brief, 'up west', who danced to his tune, know what I mean?

I was instructed to make a bail application on behalf of Danny. The others had been scattered round the manor to other lucky solicitors, as Del couldn't cope with more than one client at a time. The crush round the kitchen table would have been unbearable, not to mention the run on the coffee and the chocolate digestive biscuits.

The application was an unmitigated disaster, and refused in short order. The CPS had thrown the book at Danny, conspiracy to commit GBH with intent, GBH with intent, blackmail, intimidation, threats to kill, and arson. Still, Danny could draw comfort from the fact he was not alone, as the remaining foot soldiers were similarly charged, and even The Weasel was in the frame, but not for long.

The Weasel's brief from 'up west' had instructed the oleaginous Noël Cantwell, he of Snaresbrook fame, to represent him at the preliminary hearing. With no evidence that Danny and his mates were acting on his orders, and the only evidence connecting The Weasel with Mr Dung's business being a Fedora, the occasional sharp suit, and several pairs of over-starched boxer shorts, the CPS were onto a hiding to nothing, and, gritting their teeth, withdrew all charges.

That left the foot soldiers, and a round kitchen table conference was called by The Weasel to review progress and determine the way forward. After all, languishing in prison as they were, the boys needed to know their defence, and, once decided, to begin singing from the same song sheet.

Del's kitchen was situated in a small terrace off Bethwin Road, and a stone's throw from the Green. Outside No. 27 was a small brass plate announcing 'Derek Finnan – Solicitor' and a phone number.

I arrived promptly at 2pm and was met at the door by Del.

'So good of you to come to my humble abode, Tobes,' he enthused, leading the way into the kitchen. Del motioned me to a chair and sat down opposite, looking agitated. 'I hope you don't mind, but The Weasel has invited himself to sit in on our little discussion. As you know, Danny and the boys work for him, and he wants to see them right. You've read the committal bundle, no doubt?'

'Yes, but I'm missing Danny's proof of evidence. I don't know how to advise him, or how to prepare the case properly, until I know that.'

'You've wisdom beyond your years, Tobes, but all in good time. That's where The Weasel can help, put flesh on the bones so to speak. Oh, and before he arrives, a word to the wise, don't call him Weasel. Best stick to the formalities. He likes to be called Don Cornyony.'

'You must be joking,' I laughed.

'With The Weasel, you don't joke unless he jokes first.' Del was deadly serious. 'It's not easy for either of us, Tobes, I know that, but this is my living, and The Weasel's a part of it.'

Just then, the doorbell rang, and Del jumped up like a startled rabbit. 'That'll be The Weasel now, so better leave the talking to me,' he said, and with that he hurried out.

I could hear Del greeting The Weasel effusively, and a few snatched words of conversation.

'He's young, but bright, and a fast learner...'

'So long as he learns to jump through me 'oops, Del, that's all that matters. Danny's one of my best boys, and 'e deserves the best.'

'And he'll get the best, you've my word on it.'

'You givin' that girl of yours a portion, Del?' he asked, as Topsy walked past the open door and out of sight.

'No way, Don, why do you ask?'

'She wants to let 'er 'air down a bit, that might do the trick.'

Del laughed nervously. 'Now what about Spud? He can wait in the front room if you like, there might be some boxing on Sky Sports.'

Spud, one of a rapidly dwindling band of faithful retainers, was so-called because of his uncanny resemblance to a large potato.

'Nar, Spud can stay outside and swat any tosspot warden what tries to slap a ticket on the motor.'

The kitchen door opened and in walked The Weasel. It was like something from a time warp. In his late forties, he was short and wiry, with jet-black, brilliantined hair and a thin, cruel face. He was wearing Aviator sunglasses, which he removed slowly and put into the top pocket of his sharp, pinstriped suit jacket. Across his scrawny shoulders was draped a yellow cashmere coat, which Del offered to hang up.

'Yeh, but be careful. That cost more than you make in a month.'

Again, Del's nervous laugh. 'Let me introduce you to Danny's counsel, Toby Potts. Toby, this is Mr Don Cornyony.'

I extended my hand, which The Weasel ignored. He turned to Del. 'You were right, Del, 'e's young alright, but does 'e know 'is arse from 'is elbow?' It was as though I wasn't there.

'Sit down, Don,' said Del, fussing around him like a mother hen. 'How about a coffee?'

'I'd rather 'ave a vodka on the rocks.'

'Sorry, Don, fresh out, but I can get Topsy to run down the off-licence if you want.'

'Nar, next time perhaps. Right, let's get down to business,' he continued, fixing me with his beady eyes. 'So, what's the score, sunshine?'

'Toby's read all the papers, Don, and is well up to speed…'

'Shut it, Del!' snapped The Weasel, 'I want to 'ear it from the boy.'

I smiled through gritted teeth. I'd taken an instant dislike to The Weasel, and it could only get worse. But one look at Del's pleading expression persuaded me to tread lightly. 'Well,' I began cautiously, 'if Mr Dung gives evidence and comes up to proof…'

'Wadya mean, sunshine, come up to proof?'

'It's an expression we use,' I said pompously, 'meaning if he says in court what he says in his witness statement…'

''e's got all the lingo, Del, I'll give 'im that. Yeah, go on.'

'Then Danny is almost certain to be convicted, and the same goes for the others.'

There was a long silence, with The Weasel deep in thought. 'So,' he said finally, 'the cheeky little Chink is an important witness?'

'Crucial.'

Another long silence. 'So what if we whack 'im? Are the boys home and dry?'

I was horrified. 'You can't be serious, Mr Cornyony!'

'Calm down, sunshine,' The Weasel replied, but there was a cold edge to his voice. 'Just testing the water.'

I felt I was in the conference from Hell, and was getting badly out of my depth. I didn't like The Weasel dictating the terms, but I had no choice. I was treading a fine line between humouring Del and keeping The Weasel off my back. Best to press on.

'I haven't viewed it yet, but there's CCTV footage, or so I'm told, showing Danny and the boys arriving at Mr Dung's premises shortly before the incident.'

'No there ain't,' The Weasel interrupted.

'Well, according to the witness statements and the list of exhibits, there is.'

'Take my word for it, sunshine, there *ain't*.' The Weasel's expression spoke volumes. 'So, what's the bottom line?'

Again, that uneasy feeling, as I continued. 'Well, I can't rule out a cut-throat defence.'

'I like the sound of that. Meaning?'

'How sure are you that all four will stick together? After all, they have different solicitors and different counsel, and if one or other decides to do a deal to save his own neck and blame the others, or, worse still, give evidence for the prosecution, it's a whole new ball game. It could put you in the frame.' Time to stir the pot.

'That won't 'appen,' replied The Weasel.

'Why not?' I asked naïvely.

'Cos it's more than their lives are worth.'

There was a long pause.

'Alright then,' I said, breaking the silence. 'Danny has two choices. He pleads guilty to something acceptable to the prosecution and gets credit for an early plea of guilty, or he takes his chances with Mr Dung.'

'And if he goes down?'

'He's looking at double figures.'

Another long pause. 'Right then, so what's Danny's defence?'

'I don't understand.' Things were turning nasty again.

'It's a simple question, and Del tells me you're a fast learner, so let me spell it out to you in words of one syllable.' The Weasel's favourite form of communication. 'If the Chink comes up to proof, as you call it, 'ow does Danny talk 'is way out of it, or, more to the point, 'ow do you talk Danny out of it? After all, you're 'is brief, and you're there for the money, that's right, ain't it?'

'Somewhat crudely put, Mr Cornyony. However, if I were Danny, I'd have two choices. Either I wasn't there, so Mr Dung is mistaken, or I was there with three other thugs, and in the course of assaulting Mr Dung so severely I put him in hospital for four weeks and emerged without a scratch on me, I was acting in lawful self-defence. Now, Mr Cornyony, you're an intelligent man, which defence would you choose?'

The Weasel didn't like multiple-choice questions, he usually got them wrong. He liked things in black and white. He was watching a travel programme on television the other day, and to win an all-expenses paid holiday he had to answer a simple question: 'In which Italian city is the leaning Tower of Pisa? Is it: (a) Rome? (b) Venice? (c) Pisa, or (d) Naples?' Alright, so how was he to know it wasn't a trick question? And besides, Naples is full of towers, some straight, some leaning.

Del, sensing The Weasel's unease, and knowing him a whole lot better, rode to the rescue. 'Well, it's obvious, Tobes, Danny goes for mistaken identity, isn't that right, Don?'

'Yeah, Del, stands to reason,' The Weasel replied, nodding vigorously in agreement, 'and without the CCTV' – why was he so sure, I wondered – 'it's the Chink's word against ours, and we outnumber 'im four to one.'

'Probably not your best point, Mr Cornyony, but no matter.' I had had enough, and wanted to end the conference on a high note. 'Of course, all this is hypothetical, and until Del and I go and see Danny in Brixton, we don't know what his defence will be.'

'Yes, we do,' replied The Weasel, and on that, he was as firm as the Rock of Gibraltar. 'Right, Del, my time's valuable and I've got calls to make.' He turned to me. 'Don't screw it up, sunshine,' he added ominously, 'I've got a lot riding on this result, and I don't like disappointments.'

After The Weasel had gone, Del flopped back into his chair and mopped his brow. 'I need a drink,' he said, and, pouring himself a large scotch, pushed the bottle towards me. 'I wouldn't want to go through that again.' He paused, and looked intently at me. 'Question is, Tobes, are we up for it?'

'Whatever else, Del, I'm keeping a packed suitcase under the bed, ready for a quick getaway,' and we both laughed nervously.

Del looked reflectively into the bottom of his glass, and then looked up. 'Yeah, I know what you mean, but don't worry. If it goes pear-shaped, I'm coming with you.'

I DIDN'T SEE The Weasel again until the day of the trial. In my case, absence did not make the heart grow fonder.

Surprise, surprise. When Del and I went to visit Danny on remand, his instructions were clear. He wasn't there, it's a case of mistaken identity, and he was gutted – *gutted*, I tell you! – to find himself in the frame. And surprise, surprise, the other three were saying exactly the same thing.

The trial was listed before His Honour Judge Hew Goldsmith at Inner London Crown Court, south of the river on the Borough Road. The court had absolutely nothing to commend it, dumped as it was in the back of beyond, and not a decent hostelry for miles around. However, for me at least, it had two redeeming features. It was close to the Temple, and it made a welcome change from Snaresbrook.

According to robing room gossip, Goldsmith was very popular with the Bar. Polite, unfailingly courteous, patient beyond measure, and above all, fair.

The three other defendants were separately represented by Cantwell and two others from his set, known to one and all as the Twilight Chambers. As Danny was last on the indictment, this meant I could feed off my more experienced colleagues and, all being well, simply adopt their cross examination. Easier said than done. Cantwell, as befitting his self-important status, was first in the batting order, and had the lion's share. Still, knowing Cantwell as I did, I was sure he felt equal to the task.

With the jury empanelled, the case for the prosecution was opened by Brendan O'Hara, the darling of the CPS with his beguiling Irish lilt and making his mark. If he succeeded, this would mean an unremitting diet of prosecution work, a fate worse than death in my book. All those reviews by the likes of Paul Newman, and 'Advocate Evaluation' forms by the score, but then, as Churchill once quipped, shit happens, and somebody has to clean it up. Or was that Bootsy in one of his more florid moments? And did it matter?

And then, the moment we had all been waiting for, as Mr Dung was called to the witness box. You could cut the atmosphere with a knife, something The Weasel was working on.

Mr Dung was a small, dapper man, in his late fifties. He walked across court with a pronounced limp, but had otherwise fully recovered from his injuries. The usher thrust the Bible into his hand and instructed him to read the words from the card.

Mr Dung, slowly and deliberately, took out his reading spectacles, and then looked up. 'I no believe in God,' he announced. 'I believe in Buddha.'

Goldsmith, smiling indulgently, looked over to Brendan. 'Do we have an oath in Buddha, Mr O'Hara?' he asked.

'I'm afraid not, your Honour.'

'Such a pity the witness wasn't asked in advance to state his religious beliefs, but no matter.' He turned back to Mr Dung. 'I apologise for the discourtesy, but I wonder if you would be willing to affirm, Mr Dung?'

'What you mean?' The affirmation card was thrust into his hand.

'Take your time, Mr Dung, and kindly read the words on the card.'

Dung took the card and peered long and hard at it. 'I do solemnly, sincerely, and truly affirm that the evidence I give shall be the truth.' He looked up and beamed. 'OK, Joe?'

'Well,' observed the judge, blinking slightly, 'there we are. At least we've made a start. Pray begin, Mr O'Hara, unless there are any objections.'

'Thank you, your Honour.' Turning to the witness, he asked, 'Is your full name Yu Flung Dung?'

Cantwell oozed to his feet. 'Your Honour, my learned friend begins his examination-in-chief with a leading question.'

'He does indeed, Mr Cantwell, but, if I may venture an opinion, a relatively uncontentious one. However,' he continued, before Cantwell could reply, 'you and I will remain vigilant to ensure the rules of evidence are strictly applied. Pray continue, Mr O'Hara.'

'Thank you, your Honour. Mr Dung, before your premises were destroyed by fire…'

Cantwell oozed to his feet again, but Goldsmith was equal to the task. 'I feel, Mr O'Hara, you had better proceed on the assumption that everything is in issue, that way we'll get on faster. Let me see if I can help. Mr Dung, what do you do for a living?'

'Raundly,' replied Mr Dung, helpfully.

'Is that laundry?'

'That's what I say, raundly.'

'Well, there you have it, Mr O'Hara, Mr Dung does raundly for a living.'

'I am obliged, your Honour. And what do you do now for a living?'

'Nothing.'

Progress at last.

'Why not?'

'Business burn down.'

Almost too good to be true.

'Tell the jury about that, will you?'

'Tell the jury what? And who is jury?'

'They are the twelve ladies and gentlemen over there who are to decide the case against these four accused.' O'Hara waved in their general direction, as Yu Flung Dung bowed deeply. Some of the jurors nodded deeply in return.

Cantwell oozed to his feet.

'Yes, yes, Mr Cantwell,' Goldsmith's patience was being tested, and as yet, no runs on the board. 'Enough of the guided tour, Mr O'Hara, shall we move on to the *gravamen* of the case?'

'Of course, your Honour,' O'Hara replied. 'Can you tell the jury how your business burned down?'

'No.'

'No? Why not?'

'I in hospital at time.'

'And why were you in hospital?'

'That right.'

'What's right?'

'What you say.'

'But I haven't said anything.'

'OK, Joe,' and Mr Dung beamed expansively.

Throwing caution to the wind, O'Hara plunged in. 'Were you getting treatment for your injuries?'

Cantwell was up like a jackrabbit, and even I spotted that one.

'Your Honour, I am concerned at the attempts by my learned friend to assist the witness as he gives his evidence. Whilst they are laudable and well-motivated, it may be that some of the answers are being inadvertently misrepresented, thus denying my client a fair trial.'

'Quite so, Mr Cantwell. Mr O'Hara,' Goldsmith turned to O'Hara, 'I imply no criticism of Mr Dung, but the defence may well have a point, and I am anxious above all else to ensure a fair trial. In the circumstances, therefore, I am going to adjourn until tomorrow morning. Will you please arrange for an interpreter?' The judge turned to Mr Dung, and speaking slowly and loudly, said, 'We're having a little difficulty understanding you, Mr Dung, and as your evidence is very important, it is vital we understand everything you say.'

Mr Dung was not amused. 'My English velly good,' he retorted.

'Then the fault is entirely ours. May I enquire, do you prefer Cantonese or Mandarin?'

'Cantonese', he snapped, 'Mandarin silly ranguage.'

Promptly at 10.30 the next morning, and with Mr Dung and the interpreter side by side in the witness box, the trial resumed.

'You were telling the jury you were in hospital, getting treatment for your injuries. Can you tell us why you were in hospital?'

'I assorted.'

'No, no, Mr Dung,' said Goldsmith, 'please wait for the interpreter, and he will give your answer.'

There followed a few minutes of animated conversation in Cantonese, or so it was assumed. Finally, the interpreter turned to the judge. 'The witness says he assrorted, your Honour.'

'That's what I said, assrorted,' echoed Mr Dung, triumphantly.

Goldsmith raised his eyes to the heavens. 'Yes, yes, Mr Dung, but to be clear, are you saying *you* were assaulted, or conversely, did you assault somebody *else*?'

Further animated conversation. 'Witness say *he* was assrorted.'

'And who assaulted you, Mr Dung?' O'Hara pressed his advantage. There was an audible hush in the court.

'Those men there,' he replied, pointing to the four defendants in the dock.

This time, even I joined the mass uprising.

'Yes, yes, gentlemen,' Goldsmith's Job-like patience was being pushed to the limit. 'I am aware of the rule against dock identification, and I shall direct the jury to disregard the witness's last answer.' He turned to the jury. 'Members of the jury, we have strict rules of evidence, and one of them forbids a dock identification. It is nobody's fault, but the identity of those responsible for assrorting, I mean assaulting, Mr Dung, must be proved by admissible evidence and by no other means. I hope that is clear. Mr O'Hara?'

'Can you describe the men who assaulted you?'

'No need, they sitting over there.'

This was going from bad to worse, and Goldsmith's patience was reaching breaking point. 'Please just answer the question, Mr Dung.'

'I have…'

'And please wait for the interpreter.'

'Ok, but I no need interpreter.'

'Let me be the judge of that, Mr Dung.'

'Ok, Joe, you judge.'

'Thank you,' Goldsmith sighed. 'Now let's begin by describing the colour of their skin, and please don't say, no need, they sitting over there, otherwise I shall have to stop the trial. Alright?'

The interpreter jabbered away. 'The witness say, OK, Joe, you judge.'

'Good, now what's the answer to my question?'

More jabbering. 'The witness ask, what question?'

'Can he describe the colour of their skin?' Goldsmith snapped.

More jabbering. 'The witness say yes.'

'So what was the colour of their skin?' Goldsmith repeated through clenched teeth.

'White,' replied Mr Dung.

'Please wait for the question to be interpreted, Mr Dung!' The veins on Goldsmith's forehead were beginning to stand out.

'I no need, my English velly good.'

The judge's pencil snapped in his hand as they jabbered away. 'The witness says, no need, his English velly good.'

Goldsmith took a deep breath, counted to ten, composed himself, and then turned to O'Hara. 'I'm sorry, Mr O'Hara, I interrupted you. Pray continue.'

'Thank you, my lord. So how many of the men who assaulted you were white?'

This time, Mr Dung waited for the interpreter. 'All four.'

'Excellent.'

'That's a comment, your Honour,' interrupted Cantwell.

'You have been warned, Mr O'Hara,' replied the judge wearily.

'And what else can you tell us about the four white men?'

More jabbering. 'The witness says, all white men look same to Chinese,' said the interpreter. 'But,' he added, 'witness say, look at men in dock, the four men who assrorted him their spitting image, if not men in dock, then their twin brothers, right down to silly striped suits.'

'And how many times had you seen these men before the night you were assaulted?' O'Hara hurried on before the inevitable objections.

'Many times,' replied the interpreter, after a quick conference. 'The witness say men bring in silly striped suits once a month, regular as clockwork, six for price of five, special offer.'

Goldsmith was curious. 'You say six, Mr Dung? To whom did the other suits belong?'

'Witness say, Fingers Malloy and The Weasel.'

'The Weasel?'

'The witness say, boss of gang, sitting in public gallery,' and Mr Dung pointed him out. This was The Weasel's worst nightmare, public exposure in a court of law, as he rose and left with as much dignity as he could muster, all eyes following his bright yellow cashmere coat slung casually across his scrawny shoulders.

Cheeky little Chink, he should have whacked him months ago when he had the chance.

O'Hara felt he was on a roll at last. 'And can you tell the jury why the four white men, who looked the spitting image of the four defendants, right down to their silly striped suits, assaulted you?' He was suddenly enjoying every moment at the sight of clear blue water. Cantwell squirmed, but there was nothing he could do.

Mr Dung waited for the interpreter. 'The witness say protection, my lord.'

'Protection from what, Mr Dung?'

'The witness say,' the interpreter continued, 'if no pay protection money, they burn down shop.'

'And did you pay protection money, Mr Dung?'

'No.'

Game, set and match. 'No further questions.'

'Before you sit down, Mr O'Hara,' said the judge, 'Mr Dung has referred to the men who attacked him wearing silly striped suits. Do you have any evidence to support him?'

'I do, your Honour. Following the assault on Mr Dung, all six, who included Mr Malloy and the man known as The Weasel, were arrested, and six striped suits were seized. I have them in court.'

'Pass them up.'

After a lot of pulling and tearing at the tamper proof bags, the suits were revealed in all their glory, and duly passed on to Mr Dung, who immediately identified them from his own dry cleaning marks inside.

They were passed back to the judge, who held one aloft. 'Very striking, Mr O'Hara. I wonder if they glow in the dark?'

Cantwell rose to his feet. 'That is a comment, your Honour, and wholly inappropriate.'

Goldsmith had had enough of Cantwell and his oily ways. 'It is indeed a comment, Mr Cantwell, and as I am the judge I shall feel free to comment as I see fit. I shall be directing the jury in due course that they are free to accept or reject my comments, as they are the judges of the facts. Now, unless you have any further submissions,' he turned to the usher, 'pass the suits to the jury for their closer inspection.'

That done, Goldsmith turned back to O'Hara. 'What other evidence do you call?'

Brendan stood up. 'There was to be CCTV footage of the defendants, or their twin brothers, entering Mr Dung's laundry at the time of the assault, your Honour, but when the master tape was removed from the police property store for copying, it had been taped over. I am still waiting for an explanation. Needless to say, there will have to be a full investigation.'

Better ask The Weasel, I muttered.

'Very well. Is that your case?'

'It is, my lord.'

Cantwell and his cronies did their best to shake Mr Dung's evidence in cross examination, all smoke and mirrors, but he was having none of it. When it came to my turn, there was nothing left to say, as I flapped around like a wet hen in a thunderstorm. I was going nowhere fast, and I was simply prolonging the moment of truth.

The jury were itching to convict, and they did so in record time. My prediction was right on both counts, as I reminded myself of the advice given to The Weasel round Del's kitchen table. If Mr Dung came up to proof, they'd all be convicted, and they'd get double figures. He did, and they did, twelve years each.

Cantwell oozed back to Twilight Chambers, muttering darkly about the Court of Appeal, but it was an empty gesture.

With his foot soldiers out of the way, The Weasel's empire crumbled. Three detective constables resigned, and their resignations were accepted with immediate effect. Mr Dung became a hero on the Green. His Raundly was rebuilt, and business was better than ever.

Danny Bloom, taking advantage of his enforced leisure time, retrained as a plumber. After all, he was good with his hands, and according to word on the street, a good plumber could earn more than a criminal barrister. What's more, it was daylight robbery *and* legit. What more could he want?

Six months later, The Weasel was found dead in an alley behind the Copa Cabana, knifed through the heart following a turf war with local drug dealers. With no enforcer to protect him, he was easy meat. By a strange twist of fate, Mr Dung bought the club and turned it into the finest Chinese restaurant south of the river.

As for me, I went back to the day job to await the next plum to fall into my lap. Del and I remained good friends and colleagues, with a steady flow of work. Topsy let her hair down, became pregnant, and joined Del's practice as his sleeping partner. An irresistible combination.

Chapter Seventeen

THE GALLOPING GOURMET

IT WAS ONE of those days when Gazzard, the Head of Chambers, chose to put in an appearance, and such days were not entirely popular with chambers. For a start, he occupied the only parking space, much coveted by the senior members; he also occupied the best room, used to impress privately paying clients in conference, and, as a man with nothing else to do, he sat at his desk with the door open and collared anybody and everybody who happened to cross his line of sight to chat away endlessly about this and that, either of which led, inevitably and inexorably, to Palmer v. Camley Borough Council.

On this particular day, it was my turn, as I tried to sneak past on my way to lunch.

'Come in, dear boy,' Gazzard beckoned. 'Are you a chambers solicitor?'

'Er, no, I'm a tenant,' I replied.

'Are you indeed? And in whose chambers?'

'Yours, Gazzard. You were kind enough to take me on.'

'Was I indeed? So you'll be…?'

'Potts, Toby Potts.'

'Can't say I remember the name.' Gazzard was really losing it, I thought. 'So how are you enjoying life as a tenant? Keeping busy?'

'Fairly busy, thank you, highs and lows, but mustn't complain.'

'Nobody complains in my chambers, boy! The best set in the Temple! If you can't make it here, then you shouldn't be in the profession.'

'Quite so.'

Gazzard studied me with suspicion. 'So, what did you want to talk to me about?'

This was going nowhere. 'Well, actually, I was on my way out to lunch.'

'Lunch? Can't be doing with it! Besides, rich food gives me dyspepsia. There's too much self-indulgence in these chambers, with long lunches and wine. I won't be having it, do you hear?' He glared at me.

'Well, as they say, Gazzard, good food is like music to the soul.'

'Poppycock!' he snapped, as he leaned down and retrieved a tin from under his chair. 'A heavy lunch with wine dulls the senses, and, in this profession, and particularly as a tenant in my chambers, there's no room for dull senses.'

'A sobering thought indeed, Gazzard,' I replied mischievously, 'but, according to Henry Fielding, "it is widely conceived that too much wine will dull a man's senses, and that is indeed true, in a dull man".'

Gazzard didn't appreciate the humour or the wit of this upstart youth, or Henry whatsisname, and he allowed it to show. 'A word of advice, young man,' he said, gravely, 'you'll get nowhere espousing such flippancies. I didn't get where I am today by worshipping at the shrine of Bacchus. Be in no doubt, you must remain active and alert throughout the day, as I was when I appeared in the House of Lords in the case of Palmer v Camley Borough Council. You know it, of course?'

'I do indeed, and the leading case on public negligence.'

'Quite so.' Gazzard looked pleased with my response as he wandered down memory lane. 'For as long as I can remember, I've got by with a cheese and onion sandwich and a piece of fruitcake. My wife Mildred makes them for me, don't you know?' *Lucky Mildred*, I thought, *but at least it gets him out of the house and from under her feet.* 'I used to have an apple, but the teeth can't cope any more, keep coming out with every bite,' he chuckled. 'Here, boy,' he said, pushing the tin towards me. 'Help yourself – but not the fruitcake.'

For the next ten minutes, we sat together, munching Mildred's sandwiches, and saying nothing. Meanwhile, in another part of town, food of a different variety was being contemplated, under the close supervision of Jock McTavish.

JOCK, HE OF MILLI Pini fame, had decided that his future lay elsewhere, so he'd been saving his pennies in pursuit of his dream, to open his own restaurant and join the big hitters in the culinary world. Once established, that same world would be his oyster, or lobster, or whatever, with the rich and the famous beating a path to his door, and bookings being taken two years in advance. Then the TV series, which he had thought of calling *Jock's Spot*, but, on mature reflection, that sounded too much like an athletic support, so he'd come back to that one. With the series a runaway success, the companion cookbook would follow, brim-full of delicious recipes lovingly photographed in colour by Patrick Lichfield if he was still with us, someone else if he wasn't, together with a cover photograph of Jock himself, displaying a few tufts of electric red chest hair over his apron, to give the recipes that 'Man Appeal'. He could see it all, and it was only a matter of time.

As luck would have it, The Greasy Spoon was up for sale, and affordable. Just off the Portobello Road in Notting Hill, it was an ideal location, and with a complete hose-down and some remodelling it could be up and running in no time. Contracts were exchanged, and Jock and his nervous 'small business' bank manager set about the transformation. What he needed was a theme, perhaps with a Scottish flavour, which was more than you could say for the food, but the bank manager quickly vetoed that idea. Being a Sassenach who'd never ventured north of the border, Scottish food was all about glutinous bowls of porridge oats, haggis, and Arbroath Smokies, and great slabs of venison and mounds of neaps and suet, which might be alright for those hairy Scots in skirts with nae knickers, but not for the rich and famous, so keep it simple, and keep it international. The bank manager gave way on tartan-covered chairs, but that was as far as he was willing to go, and Scottish piped pipe music was definitely taboo.

The choice of name became a nightmare, as various permutations were tried and rejected. Le Gavroche; good name, but the Roux brothers might have something to say on the matter. Jock on the Square; same problem with Gary Rhodes, and besides, there wasn't a square for miles around, so confusing for the punters. Brazz; 'fraid not, some bloke in green wellie country down Somerset way had got his handle on that. Brown's; which the bank manager Mr Brown particularly liked, had been taken. The eponymous Jock's; too Scottish, and anyway, they'd been through that before. Smith's; wasn't there some lass who cooked a bit and owned a football team, possibly the Gollies? They were getting nowhere fast.

How about The Aurora, suggested Mr Brown, who'd just watched a television programme all about the spectacular light sensation seen in both hemispheres at night, and, as he explained, Jock's restaurant would be a culinary night-time sensation, or so he hoped. Jock was sceptical, as he didn't know his aurora from his borealis, but Mr Brown was enthusiastic, and he who pays the piper calls the tune, although Mr Brown remained adamant, no piped music.

The Aurora opened its doors to a blaze of publicity. Acting on Mr Brown's advice, the opening night was to be a celebrity affair, with specially-invited guests and a handful of food critics to write pages of wonderful reviews and fill the tables for months to come. A publicity agent was engaged to ring round the usual celebrities, those who wouldn't turn down the chance of free scoff and their photos in the tabloids.

The celebs weren't exactly 'A' list, in fact Jock didn't recognise any of them. A few television presenters, a chat show host or two, and that twerp from the National Lottery. There were also some freeloading politicians, either yesterday's men on the way down, or tomorrow's men on the way up, or so they hoped, with dolly birds in tow and definitely not their wives. Mr Brown occupied a corner table, where he spent the night picking nervously at his food and drinking mineral water, all the while number-crunching into his personal organiser.

Of greater interest to Jock were the food critics, two of whom put in an appearance. There was Michael Windbag, more a self-professed gourmet, who insisted on having his photo taken with Jock and his staff, Windbag to the fore. Jock could handle him, give him double portions of everything and keep the wine flowing, and Windbag would come up trumps. The chances of him remembering what he'd eaten the next morning were remote in the extreme.

The critic Jock and his fellow chefs feared the most was BB Fish, presumably a *nom de plume*, otherwise a very silly name, who wrote a syndicated column for most of the Sunday broadsheets. The tabloids were for intellectual pigmies. It was common knowledge that Fish could make or break a restaurant, such was the power of his pen. Jock half hoped he wouldn't turn up, but he did, accompanied by a very attractive girl he called The Blonde. Fair enough, as that was obviously her colour for the night, and certainly better than calling her The Weasel. His table had been carefully selected, not too bright to draw attention to himself, and not too dark to avoid the originally presented dishes as they exploded in a symphony of mouth-watering harmony. He looked tired, almost liverish, perhaps The Blonde may have had something to do with that. Windbag hooted at him from across the room, BB Fish studiously ignored him.

With the benefit of hindsight, it would have been better if BB had come once the teething troubles had been ironed out, but too late for regrets. The Head Waiter, Gaston from Belgium, was good, but the others were on a sharp upward learning curve.

Gaston's English was not conversationally fluent, and when taking the order he kept referring to The Blonde as The Blob, which BB Fish found singularly unamusing. Not an auspicious start.

Still, Jock rated the evening a success, with his guests singing his praises and making the usual complimentary noises as they stumbled out into the cold night air. He stood at the door, beaming effusively and thanking them for eating and drinking him out of house and home. Windbag, the last to leave, approached him for the traditional photo call, and Jock looked round for BB Fish and The Blonde to join them for a real moment to savour, but to his horror, they were nowhere to be seen. Damn! They'd left early, and nobody had bothered to tell him.

The following Sunday, Jock bought all the broadsheets and, pouring himself a strong black coffee, sat down to know his fate. It was not good, but worse still, it was not fair. They say that one man's meat is another man's poison, but this was no consolation. BB Fish's remarks about the service were not too wide of the mark, but his niggling complaints about Jock's food were nothing short of outrageous, with gratuitous comments like 'stodgy', 'insipid' and 'uninspiring' peppering his column. Worse still, he claimed a stomach upset the next morning from the medley of seafood on cracked ice, briefly earning him the soubriquet of The Galloping Gourmet. Not all the comments were negative, and he was nothing short of effusive about Jock's fruits of the forest Pavlova drizzled with a raspberry coulis and a splash of Grand Marnier, but, overall, it was damning with faint praise.

It was not all doom and gloom, as Windbag gave him a good write up, and the photo call was welcome publicity, but the epicureans would go with BB Fish. Jock had half a mind to phone and give him a piece of his mind, but he didn't have his number, and, anyway, it would do more harm than good.

As Jock sat fulminating, the phone rang. It was the publicity agent. 'Thought you might like to know,' he said, 'I've had great feedback on your big night. I rang round the celebs we invited, and to a man and woman, very positive and very upbeat. Looks like you've got a winner.'

'Then you haven't read BB Fish's column about me in the Sunday broadsheets?'

'Er… yes, but it's not the end of the world, Jock, and Windbag had some nice things to say about you, so cheer up. After all, hardly anybody reads these critical broadsides, and fewer still take them seriously, and it'll soon be forgotten. If you want my opinion, the likes of BB Fish would find something negative to say about the Garden of Eden, it goes with the territory.'

He was half right, as bookings remained strong, but with no sign of the TV series on the horizon BB's column continued to rankle with Jock. He was like a dog with a bone, lightly seasoned with garlic, no doubt, and cooked slowly in a casserole. The bone, that is.

Mr Brown, ever the efficient 'small business' bank manager, had kept all the bills and costed them down to the last penny. The total outlay for Jock's big night was just in excess of £7,000. Let's hope it was worth it.

SIX WEEKS LATER, Jock was taking the night off, and had accepted an invitation to join his friend and fellow chef Alphonse for dinner at Chez Alphonse, a fashionable bistro in unfashionable Battersea. Like Nico before him, Alphonse was trying to civilise the natives and was failing miserably, but his bistro attracted the 'A' list in their droves, and he was minting it.

As luck would have it, for me at least, Del and Topsy were also dining there that night, celebrating Crispin's first birthday. Del was like a fine wine, he didn't travel well, so Battersea was as far as he was prepared to go for overpriced nosh. Good God! Del kept saying, have you seen these prices, and even the house wine was off the Richter Scale. Topsy told him to belt up, called him a tight-fisted bastard, and proceeded to order the most expensive dishes on the menu. To rub salt into the wound, she also ordered a bottle of '82 Puligny-Montrachet, because she liked the name, modestly priced at £130. After all, it wasn't every day Crispin celebrated his first birthday. If egg and chips and a pint of bitter had been on the menu, Del would have gone for it. Such a Philistine!

Jock and Alphonse were enjoying the warm foie gras with crispy bacon in a rich, wine sauce, with a very drinkable bottle of St Emilion, cheeky yet delicate, with just a hint of fresh gooseberries, when Alphonse looked up and nodded across the room. 'I see a friend of yours is dining with us tonight.'

Jock turned round to see his Nemesis, seated with the same attractive girl, this time calling her The Redhead, and just about to order. It was a red rag to a bull, as Jock got up.

'Leave it, Jock, he's not worth it, my friend.'

'Don't worry, Alphonse, I'll just go over and introduce myself,' he lied, and with that, he marched over and stood, arms folded, smouldering with pent-up anger, just waiting for the fuse to be lit.

'As I live and breathe,' he snarled, 'the great food critic himself, the high-and-mighty BB Fish, or is it Haddock?!'

BB Fish looked up, taken by surprise. 'Have we met?'

'Have we met?! Oh, yes, my friend, we have! I'm Jock McTavish, the owner of The Aurora, and you wrote a column about my restaurant a few weeks ago. Remember?'

'Actually, no, but so what?'

The other diners were beginning to feel uncomfortable as the temperature began to rise.

'So what?! You called my food stodgy, insipid and uninspiring, that's what!'

'Then it must have been.' Wrong answer.

'I'll show you stodgy, you big prick!' and with that, Jock grabbed a roll and stuffed it into BB's face. The Redhead screamed hysterically and fell backwards off her chair. BB, who used to be a prop forward for London Irish before he took to food, leapt to his feet and aimed a hard punch at Jock, catching him right between the eyes. But Jock was made of sterner stuff, as he came back, crashing over the table, fur and feathers and skin and hair flying in every direction. The diners ran for cover as Alphonse, shouting Gallic obscenities, and his waiters, tried to prise them apart. Eventually they were bundled outside, the police were called, and Jock was charged with assault with a bread roll, freshly baked that morning as Alphonse was keen to point out, using locally-sourced ingredients, and affray.

Jock's fortunes were at an all-time low. He was just beginning to break even after the £7,000 opening night, but his antics in Chez Alphonse cost him dear. With the damage caused during the affray, and refunds to the terrified diners, he was faced with another unwelcome bill, this time in the region of £3,000. At least Del was well pleased, as there was no charge for the meal or the bottle of Puligny-Montrachet.

Del also banked with Mr Brown, and used his 'small business' expertise from time to time, so he wasn't surprised when asked to represent Jock, best rates for miles around. Sadly, Del couldn't oblige, as he might be called as a witness, but recommended a colleague, who in turn, and at Del's insistence, briefed me, young and inexperienced, but best rates for miles around.

Jock didn't have much of a defence, in fact, he didn't have any defence at all, and the damage to his reputation was already there to be seen, or read, on the inside pages of the tabloids. Headlines such as 'Jock's away' and 'Fishy business at the Bistro' had done the rounds.

I met Jock in conference at my chambers, and it was not a happy encounter. I explained, as diplomatically as I could, that stuffing a bread roll, even a freshly-baked one, in BB Fish's face, was unlawful, whereas BB's response in hitting Jock was lawful self-defence. The affray, by using unlawful violence and putting the diners in fear of their personal safety, was also made out, and there was no choice but to plead guilty and throw himself on the mercy of the court. It was a case of confess and avoid, an expression I'd read somewhere in *Archbold*, it sounded rather grand and gave me the air of a man with wisdom beyond my years.

As for Jock, he wanted to put the whole sorry mess behind him as quickly as possible, and pick up the pieces of his ruined life, or what was left of it.

'You know what rankles most of all,' he sighed, 'is this bastard Fish claiming in his column I gave him food poisoning from my seafood platter.'

'Yes, I read that. He got the trots, and called himself the Galloping Gourmet. Not helpful. So what about it?'

'Well, my bank manager retained all the bills from the opening night, for tax purposes he said, and I've got BB Fish's bill here.' He pushed it across for my inspection. Thanks to Mr Brown and his meticulous accounting, starter, main course, the Pavlova, coffee, wine and the ubiquitous mineral water were all itemised.

'He didn't have the seafood!' I exclaimed. 'He had the wild duck terrine with a cherry confit!' Looking at the bill carefully, in case I'd missed something, I looked up at Jock. 'I can see why you were so angry. And that's why you confronted him?'

There was a long pause. 'Er... actually, no, I hadn't seen the bill until the other day.'

'Oh dear.' That was the confess part, so where was the avoidance?

'But it's still fucking slanderous!' Jock's notorious short temper was beginning to surface. He'd make a terrible witness. 'He shouldn't be allowed to get away with it!' he ranted, slamming his fist on the desk.

After mature reflection, as we say in the profession, I proposed a possible way forward. 'From what I've heard, BB Fish is a fair man' – Jock snorted in derision – 'so I have a suggestion.'

'Alright, but it better be good.'

'His column is intended to be controversial, I have his last six here, and that's why he's paid a king's ransom,' I added enviously, 'but I doubt if he's deliberately malicious.'

'Don't you believe it! He's a...'

'Hold on a moment, Mr McTavish. At least he should be given the chance to put the record straight, and, who knows, he may wish to reconsider his position. After all, a conviction for assault and affray, in a restaurant, could cause all sorts of problems with your licence, to say the least, as well as the damage to the future success of your business.'

'You're right there, laddie. So what do you suggest?'

'I'd like to contact BB Fish, through our solicitor, of course, and see if we can reason with him. I suggest, initially, you keep well away. We certainly don't want another incident, and you have a notoriously short temper.'

'What me!' he exploded, 'I'm a fucking pussycat, laddie!'

I looked hard at Jock, and then we both started laughing.

'OK, do what you think best,' and with that, Jock stood up, gave me a bone-crunching handshake, and made to leave.

'Just one final question, Mr McTavish, and it's not intended to be impertinent.'

'Aye?'

'How good a chef are you?'

For a moment, Jock bristled, but it was a fleeting moment. 'The best, laddie. Does that answer your question?'

A WEEK LATER, my solicitor and I duly presented ourselves at the offices of *The Sunday Times* and were shown into an enormous conference room, where BB Fish was waiting to meet us, together with a representative of the Crown Prosecution Service. Probably the ubiquitous Paul Newman, pen poised and ready to complete his 'conference evaluation' form, in triplicate. BB was not as I had imagined, tall, broad shouldered, with a rugged, rather knocked-about face and an easy smile.

After the introductions, I came straight to the point, and produced the offending bill.

BB was mortified, and checked his diary for the day in question. He was aghast. 'You're quite right.' He paused, studying the diary intently. 'How could I have made such a mistake?'

Newman shifted nervously in his seat. This wasn't how it was supposed to go.

'I have it,' he continued, 'lunch at Longmeads, a rather pretentious place just behind the Ritz, you may know it?' he looked up.

Don't be so ridiculous, I muttered, *on my income?!*

'Yes, I see it now. I had the seafood platter at Longmeads, absolutely ghastly, so bad in fact, I decided not to review it. No wonder poor Jock McTavish was so angry.' My solicitor and I exchanged knowing glances. 'I've done him a great injustice.'

Newman shifted even more nervously in his seat. This wasn't even confess and avoid, and to make matters worse, it was in front of Jock's barrister and solicitor.

It was damage-limitation time. 'I wonder if I might make a suggestion?' I began tentatively.

'Which is?'

'You, Mr Fish…'

'Please call me Harry. BB Fish is my *nom de plume*. Silly really, but I'm stuck with it,' and he laughed.

'Thank you,' I smiled. 'Now what Mr McTavish deserves is to put the record straight, so I suggest as follows. He tells me he's the best, so let him prove it, to you of all people. I read your column regularly,' I lied, but time for some ego massaging, 'and I know you're a hard-hitting man but also a fair man. Let him cook you the meal of your choice, and then write it up in your column, no punches pulled, no favours asked, just fair.' BB nodded. So far, so good, now for the hard part. 'I also ask you in your column to set the record straight about the seafood, and,' I gulped, 'to drop the charges against him.'

Harry looked intently at me, then laughed out loud. 'You're a hard man, Mr Potts, but you're on!'

'Just a minute,' said Newman nervously, 'shouldn't we discuss it first?'

'Nothing to discuss. It's a brilliant idea, so long as we both understand, no punches pulled, if you'll forgive the expression, and no favours asked. And of course, you'll be there as well to see fair play.'

I laughed. 'Not on my income, and besides, I'm saving my pennies to get married.'

'Then you and your fiancée will come as the paper's guests, I insist on it. It's the least I can do, and we need some female company to lighten the mood. It promises to be a memorable evening.'

And so it was. Jock was as good as his word, he was the best. The finest food, the finest wines, Jock on his best behaviour, and Susie captivating one and all. It was the mother of all meals, and to cap it all, BB had arranged for a photographer to capture it all for posterity.

The following Sunday, and with trembling hands, Jock read BB's column. He couldn't have written it better himself, and on the back page of the main section, a photograph of BB and Jock, shaking hands and smiling broadly.

True to his word, BB withdrew his complaint, and Newman, with his star witness jumping ship, dropped all charges, and Jock's reputation was restored. With BB's column up in lights of Aurora proportions, bookings were being taken two years in advance, and a television series in the pipeline.

A few months later, a package arrived for me in Chambers. It was a case of Veuve Clicquot champagne and a book of Jock's favourite recipes, lovingly photographed in glorious colour by Patrick Lichfield, if he was still with us, or someone else if he wasn't, with Jock beaming out from the front cover.

Inside, Jock had scribbled: 'To Toby Potts, my very good and learned friend. Nothing stodgy, insipid or uninspiring about you, laddie! Five stars in anybody's book, and mine in particular. Every future success, you deserve it!'

Chapter Eighteen

AHOY THERE ME HEARTIES

AUGUST WAS A QUIET time for the profession. The High Court had closed for the summer, with only a Vacation Judge holding the fort for emergency applications, and a skeleton staff drifting around aimlessly and wishing they were somewhere else.

The Crown Courts ticked over, but as most of the villains were on holiday in Spain it was plain fare, with applications, mentions, and the occasional review hearing under drug treatment and testing orders. This involved former drug addicts, high on life or whatever, turning up with their urine test certificates and either being congratulated for keeping to the straight and narrow, or reprimanded for returning to their nasty habits. I did a couple, but I was there for window dressing, as the probation service made all the running. The excitement was almost too much to bear, and I was back in Chambers by midday, hoping the next day would bring riches beyond measure.

I enjoyed, or rather endured, long lunches in Gray's Inn Hall with chums who'd also succumbed to the siren call of their senior clerks, and then it was back to Chambers to reread those two briefs adjourned from yesteryear and never destined to see the light of day. I browsed through the occasional dusty law book, chosen at random, or the latest supplement of *Archbold*, brim full of new Acts of Parliament and helpful comments from the editor, but it was hard work, and my heart wasn't in it.

This was my first summer as a full tenant, and unlike my senior colleagues washing around Tuscany, braying a few words of pidgin Italian, pestering the natives and drinking overpriced espressos in Sienna town square, I had elected to remain at the masthead, a steady hand on the tiller, and wait for all those returns to come flooding in, or so the clerks reasoned, in that rather skewed way of theirs. The sort of returns being returned to me were the sort of returns I'd like to return to somebody else, but I persevered.

'Take my advice, Mr Potts,' said Fred, 'with the competition out the way, there'll be rich pickings to be had, and by the time term starts again you'll have stolen a march on them.'

He couldn't have been more wrong, but I wasn't about to tell him that. You argue with the senior clerk at your peril. Fred, needless to say, spent the whole month of August in his villa just north of Benidorm, which left Mike, the first junior clerk, and Paul, the monosyllabic grunter, in charge of the shop.

By the end of the second week, and the diary for the third looking as blank as the expression on Paul's face, time to make a stand.

'I'm thinking of taking next week off, Mike,' I ventured tentatively, 'with not much going on, I thought I'd spend a few days in Cornwall.'

Mike drew in his breath sharply. 'You're the governor, Mr Potts,' he lied, 'and you're at liberty to take as much time off as you wish. But,' he warned, 'you can bet your bottom dollar something juicy will come in for trial Monday, and you'll be kicking yourself for months to come.'

'Something juicy, you say? Such as what?'

'Too early to say, Mr Potts,' Mike replied, in a matter of fact sort of way, 'if I had a crystal ball, I wouldn't be doing this job now, would I?'

'Can't argue with that, Mike, and neither would I. OK, then,' I said, with as much spine as a jellyfish, 'let's see how next week pans out.'

On Friday evening, the phone on my desk rang. It was Mike. 'Got two cases for you on Monday, Mr Potts,' and, for no obvious reason, he sounded well-pleased with himself. 'Breach of probation, Snaresbrook, first on at ten, then not before two, Croydon, committal for sentence, prosecution. That's a hundred-and-thirty-five quid for a day's work. Not bad if you can get it. I told you it'd be worth your while staying on.'

I didn't know what to say, so I didn't, but by Tuesday I really had had enough.

'If you can spare me for the rest of the week, Mike, I'm going to spend a few days with my fiancée in Cornwall. I've been neglecting her, and we've got a wedding to plan, so I'll phone in on Friday, if that's alright?'

Mike was not amused. 'Paul, fetch the diary.' Paul brought over a large book and set it down in front of him. 'Right,' he continued with thinly-disguised contempt, 'Mr Potts of Counsel, Wednesday AWAY,' he wrote in large capital letters, 'Thursday AWAY, Friday AWAY.' He looked up and smiled, or what passed as a smile. 'Have a good time, of course this means I'll have to return your work at very short notice, but I'll do my best. After all, that's what clerks are for.'

I felt like that bloke with the four feathers, but I wasn't going to be bullied, well, not all the time.

Happily, Susie was up for it. 'I know a divine little hotel in St Mawes, called the Rising Sun,' she said excitedly. 'Mummy and Daddy used to stay there years ago. They may have a room, so leave it to me, and see you later.'

'WE'RE IN LUCK,' Susie told me delightedly when she picked me up from the station. 'Apparently the best room in the hotel was booked for the week by some hugely important barrister who stays there regularly when he's in court at Truro. His trial had to be adjourned, as the defendant was on holiday in Spain, so the room is ours. It's going to be such fun!'

We set off the next morning after an early breakfast. 'I reckon we should be in St Mawes by mid-afternoon, then a Cornish cream tea and a stroll through the village. What could be better?'

It turned out that several million other motorists had decided to take a short break in Cornwall at the same time, so the journey was long and tortuous, and we eventually pulled into the Rising Sun car park just before seven. After a shower, though, our spirits soon revived, and we went down for a stroll along the seafront before dinner.

St. Mawes was enchanting. It was a delightful fishing village where nobody fished any more, and was now a tourist resort, boasting the mightily expensive Tresanton Hotel on the road up to the castle, and a few more modestly priced hotels down on the front. Feeling in holiday mood, I took Susie into the Tresanton for a drink, and, when I got the bill, rather wished I hadn't.

As we strolled back to our hotel, I noticed a large, 60ft ketch, named *La Estella*, a little distance from the shore, just outside the harbour wall, and listing badly. It was very much the talk of the bar as we sat down to peruse the menus. Four men, obviously out-of-towners, were huddled together in one corner, talking in whispers over pints of some Cornish brew. All the locals had an opinion to offer – rather like barristers, only better-informed – but from what we could glean, the ketch was loaded down to the gunwales and had run aground on a sandbank.

'It'll be ten in the morning, earliest, afore the tide's 'igh enough to free 'er, I reckon,' ventured one ancient mariner.

'You be right, Bill,' added another. Barnacle Bill be right most of the time when it come to boats. The others nodded knowingly.

'It's all so wonderfully quaint, darling,' Susie whispered, squeezing my hand.

Bloody Townies, muttered the locals.

We went into dinner, to be met by La Patronne of the hotel, Annie Short. She was cook *par excellence*, bottle washer, car park attendant, front of house and, judging from her paintings on the walls, an accomplished artist. Shades of The Aurora, but without the histrionics. Susie let slip that I was a barrister. Mrs Short pricked up her ears. 'So you'll know Mr Harvey-Jones, a very eminent barrister who stays here all the time? So charming, and so witty, our favourite guest, and a very generous tipper.'

'Er, no,' I replied, 'I don't practise in this area, I'm afraid. I'm from London,' I added, rather grandly.

'Yes,' said Mrs Short, loftily. 'We have heard of it. Now, if you'll follow me, I'll show you to your table.'

In spite of the initial *froideur*, the meal was excellent. The waitress, a rather gawky girl plucked at random from the local stock, was very pleasant and attentive, and, by the time pudding was served, Mrs Short was doing her rounds.

'An excellent meal, Mrs Short,' I said, anxious to make amends, 'absolutely delicious.'

Mrs Short was not the sort of woman you addressed in the vernacular unless specifically invited to do so.

'I'm so glad you enjoyed it. Now, coffee and brandy in the lounge? Mr Harvey-Jones always has coffee, a large *espresso*, brandy and his favourite Havana cigar in the lounge, and he always brings his own supply of Bendicks chocolate mints. I don't suppose he'll mind me offering you one.'

'That's very kind of you, Mrs Short,' said Susie, ever the diplomat, 'such a treat.'

This Harvey-Jones chap, I thought, sounded like a complete pain in the arse, but when in Rome and all that. Just to be awkward, I helped myself to two mints, under the watchful and disapproving eye of Mrs Short and the gawky waitress. As we were leaving, Mrs Short, as ever in close attendance, mentioned breakfast.

'Mr Harvey-Jones takes his breakfast promptly at eight, full English with fried bread, to give himself plenty of time to get to court. Shall I expect you at the same time?'

'Oh, no thank you,' replied Susie, smiling, 'we're on holiday.'

'Are you indeed?' she said, somewhat sniffily, as if eminent and hugely-important barristers never took a holiday. 'Mr Harvey-Jones is such a workaholic, but, then, he is exceptional. We finish serving breakfast promptly at nine-thirty.'

'If she mentions Harvey-Jones once more, I'm going to throttle her,' I muttered on the way out.

There wasn't much to do in St Mawes of a night. We had the choice of returning to the bar to listen to tales of derring-do on the high seas from Barnacle Bill and his motley crew, or joining the queue at the Fish and Chip Bar opposite the hotel. The Ship and Castle Hotel round the corner was running Bingo, but last 'eyes down' was at nine. It was the sort of hotel where all the inmates were in bed by nine-thirty, doors locked promptly at ten, and no room service. There was nothing for it but to retire to bed and make passionate love to Susie, my preferred option, as it had been since the moment we arrived.

I sat bolt upright. It was either a cat being neutered, or an infant child in the next room screaming for its early morning feed. I glanced at the bedside clock. Four thirty. Another screech. I put my head out of the window, and staring at me on the ledge, barely three feet away, was a seagull the size of a London bus, eyeing me malevolently. I tried to shoo it away. The gull stared back, with one of those 'Bloody Townie' looks, gave another ear piercing screech, and lifted off, defying all the natural laws of gravity, winging slowly out to sea.

That bird should not be flying, I thought, watching its progress, it was positively dangerous for its health. But there was progress of another sort that caught my eye. Down below, and pulling gently away from the quayside, were three of the men I'd seen in the bar the night before, rowing a small dinghy out towards *La Estella*, which was still listing, and still stuck on the sandbank.

WE CAME DOWN for breakfast at nine-fifteen, well within Mrs Short's deadline, and ordered the full English with fried bread. That went down well with all three of us. The morning was fine, warm and sunny, so we took our coffee onto the terrace and drank in the invigorating sea air. Just as we were contemplating a walk up to the castle, giving the Tresanton a wide berth, the harbourside erupted into a picture of frenzied activity.

First on the scene was a Customs launch, rounding the head and making straight for *La Estella*, which was beginning to right itself but was still stuck on the sandbank. Then three police cars, blue lights flashing and sirens blaring, and containing probably the entire Cornish Constabulary, shot past us and slammed to a halt at the end of the quay. All eyes now turned to *La Estella*, where, after much heaving and ho-ing, the three men were taken from the boat and into the waiting arms of the Constabulary. It was all tremendously exciting.

Over the next four hours, a total of eight tons of cannabis resin, all neatly baled and stamped 'Produce of Morocco – Enjoy', and with a street value of sixteen million pounds, was unloaded from La Estella.

In the bar that night, the hubbub of excitement reached fever pitch. One of the Customs officers who'd raided the boat was a local, Ronnie Dorkins by name, so he was holding forth in a most knowledgeable way, to the rapt attention of the assembled multitude. 'Afore they set sail from Morocco,' he was saying, 'we 'ad a tip off they'd be putting into Plymouth for victuals and refuelling, and then on to Tilbury, where the drugs were to be unloaded. As 'apchance would 'ave it, there was a freak storm in the Bay of Biscay, and La Estella 'ad to make for the nearest port. That's why she ended up 'ere in St Mawes.'

'Stands to reason,' growled Barnacle Bill, and the others growled in unison.

'But I'm 'ere to tell you,' Ronnie dropped his voice in conspiratorial fashion as the assembled multitude leaned forward, 'the CIS...'

''oo be the CIS, Ronnie?' asked Bill.

'They be the Criminal Investigation Service, Bill, very 'ush, 'ush,' and he tapped the side of his nose, 'you never see 'em, you never know they're there till they pounce, you know what I'm saying 'ere? They're like James Bond, licence to kill.'

'Ooh, arr,' muttered the assembled multitude.

'They're masters of disguise, blendin' in. They 'ave eyes *everywhere*. For all we know, they could be sitting in 'ere, even as I speak.'

All eyes turned to me, seated with Susie at a corner table by the door, and the assembled multitude shifted uneasily.

'So the CIS 'ave been tracking the boat from the moment she left Morocco.' Ronnie downed his pint of bitter and looked expectantly at the barman. 'And them what masterminded the venture are being watched, even as I speak. They call 'em barons, you know what I'm saying 'ere?'

'Ooh, arr,' muttered the assembled multitude.

'So what'll 'appen now, Ronnie?' asked Bill, 'and what about the crew?'

'Can't say for sure yet, but the crew to a man are denying all knowledge of the drugs, claim they must've been loaded on board overnight when they was all fast asleep. I say, pull the other one, that's what I says.'

'Don't be too 'asty', counselled Bill, playing the devil's advocate, 'me and the lads saw the four of 'em, sitting over there, larger than life, without a care in the world. They'll get some expensive barrister to defend 'em, I shouldn't doubt.'

'Four, you say, Bill? But there were only three on board when we arrived. Sounds like one's got away.'

Once again, all eyes turned to me, 'e being a stranger in these parts.

Ronnie downed the rest of his pint in one. 'You and the lads could be witnesses, Bill,' he replied, 'might even be on telly.'

'Ooh, arr,' chorused the assembly.

'Now, I must be going,' he said, giving me one last look. 'There's work to be done,' and with that, he hurried out.

For the remainder of our stay, we were treated with exceptional deference and free drinks in the bar, lots of forelock tugging from the locals as they moved quickly to one side.

Opinion was divided. There were mutterings from some about 007 and Miss Moneypenny, and my licence to kill, although I didn't look like no natural-born killer. One even claimed to have seen a suspicious bulge inside my jacket, where my Walther PK handgun was kept. Others reckoned that if I wasn't 007, maybe I was the fourth man, brazening it out and reporting back to the barons. It was the most exciting thing that ever happened in St Mawes since the great storm of '63.

Come Friday evening, I phoned Chambers.

'Sorry, Mr Potts,' said Mike, without a hint of sincerity, 'but you're out of court on Monday. It's very quiet at the moment.'

'Ooh, arr,' I muttered, feeling duly chastened.

After breakfast on Sunday morning, it was time to head for home. As a memento of our stay, I bought one of Mrs Short's paintings as a present for Susie. Mrs Short was delighted. Apparently, in all the years Harvey-Jones had been staying, he'd never once expressed an interest in her paintings. Too busy expressing an interest in himself, no doubt. One up to me.

'All being well, we should be home by tea time,' I said. Wrong again, and it was just before ten when we finally arrived back.

The following Wednesday, as I walked into Chambers after an exciting afternoon at Bromley Magistrates Court, Mike looked up.

'There's a message for you, Mr Potts. Somebody called Mr Tomkins phoned, said it was urgent, wouldn't say what it was about, but asked you to ring back as soon as you came in.' He paused. 'Nothing for me to worry about, I hope?' he asked, his curiosity getting the better of him, 'you've paid your annual subscription to the Bar Council, haven't you?'

'Oh, yes, Mike, a long time ago.' The name Tomkins meant nothing. 'Perhaps it's a solicitor wanting to instruct me in a murder most foul, you never know.'

Mike was unimpressed. 'Quite so, Mr Potts, you never know,' and he returned to his work.

'Mr Tomkins? Toby Potts.'

'Thank you for returning my call, Mr Potts,' replied the disembodied voice on the other end of the phone, 'I work for the CIS' – my throat went dry – 'and we're investigating the seizure of a large quantity of cannabis resin in St Mawes last week.' There was a pause. 'We understand you were staying at the Rising Sun for a few days when the seizure was made, so if you could spare me the time to come in and make a statement, I'd be greatly obliged.'

Another pause.

'Yes, of course,' I croaked.

'Thank you. Shall we say six o'clock tomorrow evening? I wouldn't want to interfere with your busy practice. You know where we are, just the other side of Westminster Bridge from the Houses of Parliament. Come to reception and ask for me by name. And, by the way,' he added, 'congratulations on a good result at Bromley.' And with that, the line went dead.

I began to perspire, for no reason at all. The building referred to by Tomkins was the Headquarters of MI5. Everybody knew it, or they certainly did after the outgoing Director-General, or M, as she was known, broke cover and lined her pockets with a turgid book about it. And how did Tomkins know about Bromley, where I'd saved the defendant from a richly-deserved spell in detention for breaching an Anti-Social Behaviour Order? Were they following me, and if so, why?

I'd done nothing wrong, I kept telling myself, and had nothing to hide, and all that nonsense about a licence to kill was just nonsense – wasn't it? Perhaps the CIS had been tipped off about me being a natural-born killer. Worse still, what if they thought I was somehow involved, perhaps one of the barons Ronnie was talking about, down there to oversee the operation? Should I have a solicitor present, just in case? Should I speak to Gazzard? Probably not, as Gazzard would ask me to resign from Chambers on the spot. Nick Ridley was my obvious choice, but, like all senior members of Chambers, he was on holiday abroad and somewhere far out of mobile range. And what about Susie? Would she ever speak to me again? More to the point, would she come and visit me in Belmarsh prison, reserved for Category 'A' prisoners and those deemed a threat to national security?

I spent a restless night, tossing and turning, as I considered my options and my future. I hadn't the courage to phone Susie, at least not until my meeting with Tomkins, when things would become clearer. The poor girl, as I pictured the ordeal ahead. It was Senator McCarthy and the fifties all over again.

'Is your fiancé, or has your fiancé ever been, a member of the Communist Party?'

I'd just returned from a committal for sentence at Southwark Crown Court, a bundle of nerves, when the phone rang. It was Del.

'Tobes', he said excitedly. 'I've got some good news. There was a drugs bust down in Cornwall last week.' I froze to the spot, my worst nightmare coming back to haunt me. 'The bust of the century, it was. Over eight tons of cannabis resin recovered from a boat marooned in some poxy little harbour, I forget the name…'

'St. Mawes,' I added, helpfully. 'With a street value of sixteen million pounds.'

'Yeah, that's the one, so you read about it?'

'I didn't have to, Del, I was there.'

'Lord love us, Tobes, whatever for?'

'It was quite by chance, but that's another story. The CIS want to interview me about it this evening.'

There was a long pause. 'Is there something you're not telling me, Tobes? You're not involved, are you, or perhaps you'd rather not say.'

'Of course I'm not, Del. You sound like a solicitor.'

'It has been known. So what's the score?' I explained my predicament. 'Then you'll have to cancel your appointment, and now!'

'Why?'

'Cos I've been retained by the London end of the conspiracy, and I'm instructing you, that's why.'

It took a moment to sink in. 'My saviour, my knight in shining armour, Del, you're the best!' Now Tomkins could go whistle. 'Tell me more.'

'Well, as you may know, the drugs were due for Tilbury when they were intercepted in Cornwall. Customs and the CIS had arrest warrants for two men here in London who they say were the brains behind the importation, and we're representing one of them.'

'That's brilliant, Del.' I was very excited for a number of reasons. 'So who's representing the other?'

'Nobody at the moment. They'd had the house under observation for days, but when they went in Mr Big was nowhere to be found, vanished into the night. Probably in Spain by now, sunning himself on the Costalot.'

'So what's our man's role in all this, where does he fit in?'

'They're saying he's the banker, sorted out the purchase of the drugs and the boat and arranged all the finances. I'm glad he's not my banker, strikes me as a complete dipstick, but you know what they say, still waters run deep and all that.'

'What's his name?'

'Terry Knowles.'

'And what's his defence?'

'"*I Knowles nothing about it*",' and Del laughed. 'Anyway, brief on its way for a preliminary hearing at Camberwell Green Magistrates

Court next Tuesday, so see you then, and ring Tomkins now before you forget.'

Not something I was likely to forget.

Mr Tomkins was not amused. 'You are, of course, a barrister, albeit according to my records, young and inexperienced, so far be it for me to offer you legal advice, but have you considered your position? After all, you are very close to this case, perhaps closer than you imagine.'

Again the dry throat. Why did I feel so guilty when talking to this man?

'Thank you for your concern, Mr Tomkins,' I said, trying to sound calm and in control, 'and, needless to say, if at any time I feel professionally embarrassed, then of course I shall withdraw At the moment, I don't see a problem. After all, I was there quite by chance, and simply witnessed the arrest of the crew.'

'Yes, I was meaning to ask you about that.' There was an ominous pause. 'Had you ever visited St Mawes before?'

'Well no, it was a spur of the moment thing...'

'Quite so.' Again the ominous pause. 'According to my information, you were booked to work all last week, but then suddenly decided to take a few days off, on the spur of the moment as you put it, and just happened to be in St Mawes when the crew of *La Estella* and their cargo of drugs put into port.'

'They deny all knowledge, I suppose you know that?' As soon as I'd said it, I wished I hadn't.

There was another long pause. 'Yes, I do,' replied Tomkins. 'The question is, though, Mr Potts, how do *you* know? That information is not yet a matter of public record.'

This was going from bad to worse, time to shut up and bale out. 'I'm sorry I can't help you, Mr Tomkins, but in the circumstances I can't discuss the matter further. I'm sure you understand. Now I've detained you long enough. Goodbye,' and I put down the phone.

I was perspiring heavily and feeling sick. I'd done nothing wrong, so why was I shaking like a leaf? I was being treated like a criminal, or certainly a suspect. I immediately phoned Susie and told her the whole story.

'They might contact you for a statement,' I said, 'so I thought I'd warn you.'

'It's too awful for words, darling, no wonder you're upset. They think you're a drugs baron, how ridiculous!' She paused. 'You're not, are you?' she asked, giggling.

'Very funny, Susie, but we must be careful what we say to each other. Our phones might be tapped.'

'Now you're just being melodramatic, Toby, and, anyway, it's against the law.'

'And so is importing eight tons of cannabis resin, but it happens.' I took a deep breath. 'I'm just asking you to be careful, that's all.'

'Of course I will, darling, now will I see you at the weekend?'

'Unless I've been arrested and held *incommunicado*, in which case, bring a fruit cake with a file inside,' and we both laughed nervously.

To my great relief, Mr Tomkins and his conspiracy theories were never heard of again, but for a while, I kept looking over my shoulder:

> *Still as they run they look behind,*
> *They hear a voice in every wind,*
> *And snatch a fearful dread.*

It was as if they had never been, but there was a respectful gait to Mike's tread that I had never seen before, and all the more welcome for that. 007 was alive and well and swaggering around the Middle Temple.

Eventually, with Del surprisingly proactive and me following in his wake, the dipstick cut a deal with the prosecution. Knowles, who'd been laundering drugs money through offshore accounts for years, agreed to plead guilty to the single charge of being concerned in the importation of the cannabis resin in return for a half-hearted promise to give evidence for the Crown if Mr Big were ever arrested. As that was remote in the extreme, it was a calculated risk and an offer too good to refuse. He got a remarkably light sentence, and was well pleased.

Aided and abetted by their barrister, too clever by half in my opinion, the crew abandoned the defence that some unknown party had loaded eight tons of cannabis resin onto their boat without their knowledge whilst they were having supper and a well-earned kip at the Rising Sun, and instead put forward the defence of necessity.

They claimed the drugs were destined for a country beyond the jurisdiction, and they were forced by the storm to seek shelter in St Mawes to avoid death or serious injury. Whilst superficially attractive, their defence was immediately holed below the Plimsoll line when the prosecution recharged them all with trafficking on the high seas, under some obscure International Co-operation Act I had never heard of, but then, as it was none of my business, it didn't matter. Just as well, really. To put it bluntly, they were dead in the water, so to speak, and had no option but to plead guilty.

As for Mr Big, he remained as elusive as ever, just like the Scarlet Pimpernel and that bloke in *The French Connection*.

Now who said crime doesn't pay?

Chapter Nineteen

THE PORN KING

I WAS IN GOOD SPIRITS. After the long summer vacation, the courts were busy again and work was picking up. Susie and I had decided on a Spring wedding, and a date had been set. This was the signal for both sets of parents to rush around like wet hens in a thunderstorm and in a heightened state of panic. After all, there were only eight months until the big day and so much to be done. It was also an excellent opportunity to touch base with long-forgotten relatives, dead or alive.

Fortunately for me, I had other more pressing matters to attend to, like earning a living and keeping my intended in the manner to which she was accustomed. On that front, the work was getting better, with more solicitors briefing me, and some even sending me work in my own name. My overdraft remained perilously close to the maximum agreed, with no sign of a significant move in the right direction, so it was very much 'hand-to-mouth', but I was not alone.

Fred had returned from Benidorm, looking like an overcooked lobster, and with the reins of power firmly back in his grasp, Mike returned to what he did best, a hive of activity and little to show for it. Paul was Paul, as predictable as summer rain, grunting away and waiting interminably for a shot at the big time.

In that regard, he and I were kindred spirits.

Peter Rolls, of Rolls Royce & Co, Solicitors to the Gentry, and anybody else with cash up front, had briefed chambers over the years with a variety of work, some civil, some matrimonial, and occasionally, very occasionally, crime. Peter didn't want his firm associated with the riff raff, and the criminal elements were usually moved on as quickly as possible, for an introduction fee of course, to the likes of Del and that lot. After all, Peter hadn't spent his early years in practice, searching the length and breadth of the land for a partner with the name Royce, for no good reason. Rolls Royce by name, and Rolls Royce by reputation, that was his motto, and although Gerald Royce lacked Peter's dynamism and his great vision, he was competent enough without being spectacular. He left that to Peter.

Their offices were just north of Cambridge Circus in Charing Cross Road, a stone's throw away from Shaftesbury Avenue and luvvieland. They picked up some contract work when the luvvies fell out of luv and started bickering, as well as the occasional breach of copyright, and personal injury, when one of the luvvies fell down an open trap door. That would have been right up Gazzard's street, were he still practising. The firm also specialised in wills, Gerald Royce's department, advising luvvies who wanted to give their wealth, or lack of it, to some obscure dogs' home or retired donkeys' sanctuary. It was all too, *too* divine, my dear.

Larry King provided entertainment of another sort, far removed from the smell of the greasepaint and the roar of the crowd, in his outlet in Meard Street in the heart of Soho. Larry catered for the dirty raincoat variety of life, something for every taste and prurient pleasure in his video shop, fetchingly named King's Video Shop. A lot of thought went into choosing that name.

When Larry wandered in off the street one afternoon, Peter Rolls' first reaction was to show him the door. But Larry was a cash buyer, bundles of it in his hot, sweaty fist, so, against his better judgment, Peter took him on.

When Peter contacted Chambers, it was Mike who recommended me, perhaps still wary of my 007 label and my close encounter with the CIS, and besides, with Rolls Royce & Co not wishing to be publicly associated with crime, and definitely not this sort of crime, Peter wanted to keep it low profile.

Poor me, forever destined to be low profile.

The brief was duly delivered to chambers, and it made for interesting reading. Larry's shop had been raided by the boys from the Obscene Publications Unit at Scotland Yard, following an anonymous tip off from a killjoy calling himself 'Deep Throat'. Quite what he was doing in Larry's shop in the first place was never explained, perhaps the video jammed just as it was reaching its climax, and the anonymous punter had been denied a refund. Larry had four invariable rules. No kids, no animals, no cheques, and no refunds, a simple and effective business policy, with no exceptions.

During the raid, over three hundred videos and DVDs had been seized, and Larry was arrested and charged with publishing obscene articles for gain. The prosecution had chosen five videos as a representative sample, ranging in their titles from *Babes in the Wood*, *What the Butler Sore*, and *Nymphs and Shepherds Come Again and Again*, through to *Life on the Ocean Rave with Captain Horny Blow Job* and *Erection Night Special*, presented by David Dimple Bottom.

Larry King's video shop had everything the lusting heart desired, and more. On public display in the main shop were magazines of every size and description, in full colour and leaving nothing to the imagination. After a period of idle browsing, the favoured few, about two thousand at the last count, were admitted to the inner sanctum, the Holy Grail, where, for a modest subscription, explicit videos were available, for purchase or hire, to suit every perversion. Viewing booths were set aside for previews, maximum two minutes, with a maximum of five videos per session, after which, the selections were made and carried from the shop in a plain, brown paper bag. It was all very discreet.

Peter Rolls arrived early for the conference, and without Larry, who was left to make his own way to Chambers. Peter may be willing to represent him, but he was certainly not going to be seen with him.

Rolls looked like a cross between John Gielgud and Noël Coward, a felt trilby hat with an enormous brim, a startling lemon yellow suit with pink shirt and matching socks, suede shoes, and a silk scarf knotted lightly around his neck, fluttering provocatively in the breeze as he walked, and every movement accompanied by extravagant theatrical gestures.

He sat down and immediately engaged me with a troubled expression.

'Now, Mr Potts,' he began, 'I've brought the offending articles with me for your perusal,' and, dipping into his briefcase, he removed the five videos with all the care of a surgeon removing a malignant and highly contagious growth. 'You'll need to view them in due course, you poor lamb,' he continued.

'I suppose you've watched them already, Mr Rolls?' I asked.

'Absolutely not, young man! What do you take me for?!'

A competent solicitor preparing his client's defence might be a good starting point, I thought, but I wasn't about to make an issue of it.

'I mean, it's all too, too, distressing. I wonder if I've done the right thing, after all, this is not the sort of work Rolls Royce cares to be associated with,' and he threw back his head in disgust.

'I'm sure Mr King is in excellent hands, Mr Rolls,' I replied, anxious to ingratiate myself.

'I have no doubt of that. We are not called Rolls Royce for nothing, you know.'

'Absolutely.'

'Now, I have here a transcript of each video, lovingly prepared by the prosecution,' he continued, dipping back into the briefcase and removing a large bundle of papers. 'I have skim-read some of them, and I have to warn you, Mr Potts, they are filthy, yes, there's no shying away from the word, filthy!' he added for emphasis, and back went the head again. 'Absolutely disgusting!'

'Well,' I said, trying to put a positive gloss on the matter before Larry King's arrival, 'I suppose beauty is in the eye of the beholder, and each man to his own.'

'Very droll, I'm sure, but I beg to differ...'

Just as Rolls was about to launch into a diatribe on the concept of absolute morality, Paul knocked and entered.

'Mr King has arrived', he grunted, 'shall I show him in?'

I looked enquiringly at Rolls. 'Shall we get under way, Mr Rolls?'

'I suppose so,' he sniffed, 'the sooner we start, the sooner we can get this whole unfortunate business behind us.' Not quite how I would have put it.

Larry King was a showman of sorts, but not in Peter's class. A short, fat man, almost round, with thinning hair combed across his head to hide his balding pate and meeting in a small widow's peak somewhere off-centre, he sported a loud, multi-coloured waistcoat with gold buttons, and his remarkably small feet were encased in black, patent leather shoes, with gold buckles. A jovial man with a moist handshake, he acknowledged Rolls with a wink and sat down.

'This is Mr Potts, Larry, your barrister,' said Rolls, making the introductions.

'A pleasure, squire'. Larry paused. 'You're very young, are you sure you're up for it?' Again, not quite how I would have put it.

'I haven't had any complaints so far,' I lied, 'but if, after the conference, you have any doubts about my ability to represent you, please say so.'

'I will, squire, I will. After all, Pete,' he turned to Rolls, 'this is my livelihood we're talking about here.'

Peter Rolls winced. To address him by his Christian name was a privilege for the favoured few, but to address him as 'Pete' was unforgivable. What an absolutely ghastly little man.

'I fully understand, Mr King,' I said. Hardly a vote of confidence, so it was time to impress with my grasp of the law. 'Now,' I continued, 'turning to the allegations, you're charged with offences under the Obscene Publications Act…'

'I know that.'

'Yes, of course.' This was not going well, time to assert myself. 'But I need to know you understand all the relevant implications, so if you'll bear with me?'

'Fair enough, you're the boss.' That's better.

'Now the prosecution have to prove that you had these videos to sell or rent for gain.' I looked up. 'I don't suppose they'll have any difficulty there. And, secondly, they have to prove that the videos tend to deprave or corrupt persons who watch them. Presumably, you say they don't?'

'I haven't a clue, squire,' replied Larry, somewhat disarmingly. 'You don't think I watch this crap, do you? I mean, it's complete garbage, but I provide a sort of social service, for all the inadequates out there, and what they do in the privacy of their own attic is up to them. I should add,' and he did, 'that I have a lot of self-satisfied customers.'

'With the obvious exception of one,' I quipped, 'otherwise known as 'Deep Throat'.'

'Yeah, slimy bastard, spoiling everybody's fun. If I get my hands on him…'

'Now,' I hurried on, 'I think we might watch excerpts from the videos, to get a flavour of what we're up against, if you catch my drift.' Larry didn't, but no matter. 'According to the transcripts, each video runs for approximately sixty minutes, so if we were to watch them all from beginning to end, it might be emotionally draining for all of us.'

'Amen to that,' said Rolls, already feeling faint.

'Fair enough, squire, you're the boss.'

WORD THAT THE videos were to be played spread like wildfire to the clerks' room, and I lost count of the number of cups of tea and plates full of digestive biscuits brought into the conference room over the next hour, service over and above the call of duty.

We started with *Babes in the Wood*, which, according to the transcript, was a tale of four lesbians and a dildo romping in the wood. There was very little plot, in fact, there was no plot at all. As soon as the girls reached the woodland glade, they got their kit off in record time, and set about enjoying each other's company. The dildo was passed around like a joint of cannabis, and much fun, accompanied by moaning and groaning and lots of passionate embraces, was had by all.

I was no prude, but the sheer size of them all simply beggared belief.

'Do you think it's trick photography?' I asked, in between mouthfuls of tea and digestives.

Peter Rolls spent most of the time, feigning utter disgust, throwing his head back theatrically, whilst keeping his eye on the action. Such a dutiful solicitor.

Captain Horny Blow Job was one more for the boys, with Seaman Stains and Roger the Cabin Boy performing unnatural acts to the accompaniment of jolly nautical ditties. But the *piéce de resistance* was undoubtedly *Erection Night Special*. This explored the very limits of human proclivity and beyond. My eyes began to water, Peter Rolls was uncharacteristically silent, and even Larry let out a low whistle, as yet another tray of refreshments came winging, unannounced and unrequested, into the room.

'Well,' I said, as the curtain came down and the lights went up, 'that's the knob, I mean the nub, of it, Mr King.' I paused. 'I don't think we can go with the statutory defence, so we'll have to go with deprave and corrupt. We say they don't, the prosecution say they do, and it's for the jury to decide.'

'Yeah.' Larry was deep in thought, or so it appeared. 'So what's this statutory defence?' he asked at last.

'As I say, I think it's a non-starter, unless we've missed something in all the excitement, but,' and I opened *Archbold* at the relevant section and began to read, 'if we can show that the videos are for the public good on the ground that they are in the interests of drama, opera, ballet or any other art, or of literature or learning, the person publishing the articles for gain, that being your good self, shall not be convicted.'

'So why not?' Larry was excited. 'I mean, there's drama aplenty, will he stick it to her or won't he? And in *Babes in the Wood*, the girls are up on their toes from time to time, great little movers, if you want my opinion.' I didn't. 'Then you've got opera, well, in *Life on the Ocean Rave*, there's singing of sorts, all those sea shanties, as they shag to the sound of music, and as for *Erection Night Special*, that's got to be educational. Am I right, Pete, or am I right?'

Pete was having a fit of the vapours, and well out of it, as he dabbed his forehead with an enormous silk handkerchief.

'It's an interesting argument, Mr King,' I said, not wishing to crush him. 'Let me think about it, and I suggest we discuss it again nearer the time.'

THE TRIAL WAS listed at Middlesex Crown Court, and presided over by His Honour George 'The Glums' Clutterbuck, so named because of his perpetual morose mood and gloomy expression. The prosecutor, Bernie Bernstein, was home-grown, a CPS lawyer, self-selected on the basis that not even he could cock it up. All he had to do was press the start button on the video recorder, sit back and enjoy himself, then stand up and tell the jury that the videos were filthy, disgusting, tending to deprave and corrupt, and sit back down again. Not even he could get that wrong, and besides, he'd written it down, word for word, and rehearsed it several times in front of the bathroom mirror.

Peter Rolls, determined to distance himself from the whole sordid mess, had instructed an agent who, in turn, had delegated Bootsy Farmer to come and sit behind me. It was just like old times, which I had tried to forget.

No question of copping a plea on this one, Bootsy was well up for it, and raring to go.

With Larry firmly planted in the dock, The Glums addressed counsel's bench, where, to my surprise, Bernie had taken up residence. Shouldn't he be sitting one row behind, reserved for solicitors and other lesser mortals? The cheek of the man.

'Gentlemen,' he droned, 'I propose asking the jury panel if they feel able to discharge their duty, especially the ladies, in this distasteful matter. I had a similar case recently where three lady members of the jury asked to stand down halfway through the first video, for obvious reasons. These cases can be very distressing, the more so for those of a delicate disposition.'

Enquiries were made, and eventually eight robust blokes and four women, game for anything, were selected. The videos were played, with appropriate breaks in between for all parties to compose themselves. Then it was my turn to open the defence.

'I am going to ask your Honour to take a view,' I began pompously.

'I thought that's what I'd been doing for the past five hours, Mr Potts.' He was not intending to be funny.

'I'm sorry, your Honour, that's not what I meant. I invite your Honour to turn to Chapter thirty one, paragraph sixty three, in the current edition of *Archbold*.' I waited whilst The Glums found the page. 'I submit that these videos, taken as a whole, are not such as to tend to deprave and corrupt persons who see them.'

'But isn't that a matter for the jury?'

'I submit that your Honour is a person…'

'That is not an assumption you should make lightly, Mr Potts.'That, too, was not intended to be funny. 'I take the view that the persons referred to in the section are represented by the twelve members of the jury, and it is for them to decide. Now if we were discussing a film like *Polyanna*,' his all-time favourite, and he always cried at the end, 'then your submission would have obvious merit, but that is not the case here. Let's hear what Mr Bernstein has to say.'

Bernie got to his feet, a mounting sense of panic seizing him. This wasn't in the script, so he hadn't rehearsed it. 'Er… Um… Er, your Honour…'

'Yes, thank you, Mr Bernstein. I am afraid I am against you, Mr Potts. Now shall we get on?'

I was down, but not out. 'Before we do so, your Honour, may I enquire if you propose leaving the statutory defence to the jury, in any event?'

The Glums was taken aback. 'How so, Mr Potts?'

'Well,' I continued, doing my best to humour Larry, 'the *Babes in the Wood* had a certain balletic quality, I'm sure you agree…'

'What?! Are you referring to the four maidens prancing around in the buff and waving a long, cylindrical, rubber object about the place?'

'That was obviously a stage prop, your Honour, to enhance the action…'

'It certainly did that, Mr Potts, but what do you say about *Life on the Ocean Rave*? Where is the defence there?'

'Opera, your Honour,' I replied, keeping a straight face, 'and I refer to the excellent and melodic singing in a nautical vein running like a golden thread throughout the video.'

'As far as I could make out, Mr Potts, the excellent and melodic singing in a nautical vein, as you describe it, began with the lyrics:

'T'was on the good ship Venus,
By George, you should have seen us,
The figurehead was a whore in bed,
And the mast a rampant penis.'

I said nothing.

'Any further submissions, Mr Potts?'

'Finally, your Honour, *Erection Night Special*, I suggest, has a strong, educational quality to it.'

'It was certainly an eye-opener, Mr Potts, but its educational merits are highly dubious. However, in fairness to the defendant, I shall direct the jury on the statutory defence, and leave it to them to decide.'

The jury were out for most of the next day, and at three o'clock, sent a note to the judge.

The Glums read it out: 'We are hopelessly divided eight to four, and no chance of reaching a verdict. Can we go home?'

He addressed counsel's bench. 'I have no option but to discharge the jury from returning a verdict. Mr Bernstein, I take the view there is no point having a retrial. It's a waste of public time and money. Whilst the videos are undeniably explicit, I've seen much worse in my time.' He coughed, and added, 'In my professional capacity, of course,' almost too quickly. 'I doubt if any jury, properly directed, would consider them tending to deprave and corrupt. Mr King, stand up. I am entering verdicts of not guilty on each charge, and you are free to go. The five videos and the remainder seized by the police will be returned to you. Good Day.'

'I'm well pleased with the result, Squire,' said Larry outside court, pumping my hand warmly. 'Now, to show my appreciation' – for a moment, I was half hoping for a wodge of sweaty money, to help with the wedding and all that – 'I'm going to give you the five videos as a present. Watch them at your leisure, and think of me affectionately.'

I was underwhelmed, and speechless, and thinking of Larry affectionately was the last thing on my mind. Once he had waddled off, Bootsy, ever attentive, volunteered to take charge of the offending articles, and was last seen hurrying home.

Larry's business went on as usual, and to his delight, eight new members signed up in very short order.

They looked vaguely familiar, but where had he seen them before…?

Chapter Twenty

JINGLE BELLS

IT WAS THAT time of the year again, and how quickly it comes round. In fact, said my mother, who had a knack of stating the obvious, it seems to come round earlier and earlier each year, and this year in particular, with the wedding plans still in their infancy, it was most inconvenient.

It was early November, and the stores were already decked out in tinsel, with fairy lights, greeting cards, artificial trees, and presents to suit all the family, with nothing to pay for six months. It was Christmas, or so screamed Noddy Whatsisname from that pop group back in the seventies, with the nation's yuletide favourite belting out from every retail outlet in the country. Another year of the great British public gearing themselves up, once more, to the dubious delights of over-indulgence in the name of our Saviour Jesus Christ. Who?

My in-tray was not exactly groaning with work, and little on the horizon to meet the extra expenses of the festive season.

It was a hard and unrewarding slog, as I travelled the length and breadth of the metropolis in search of an honest crust. Relaxing weekends were spent with Susie and keeping out of the way of the parents as much as possible.

Just as I was resigning myself to ending the term with a whimper, the case of George Albert Spencer unexpectedly landed on my desk. It was a moment of great excitement, not least because the brief was addressed to me in my own name, with no also-rans to muddy the waters.

My instructing solicitor was Duncan Campbell, another one-man band, who'd been in court at Middlesex during my submissions on the artistic merits of Larry's videos, and was singularly impressed with my forensic skills, for all the wrong reasons. Whatever else, he'd liked my style and delivery, the name stuck, and the rest, as they say, is history.

George Albert Spencer's whole life revolved around Christmas. In short, it was his reason for living. During eight memorable weeks of the year, George was Santa Claus personified, as he took on the look and persona of the ubiquitous fictional – I assume there are no children reading this (Ho! Ho!) – character. The remaining forty-four weeks were simply a precursor to the big event, a time to put his house in order, to get the elves motivated, the workshops in the North Pole igloo-shape and ready to roll, and Donner and Blitzen and Rudolf and the other reindeer fed and watered and ready for a hard day's night.

During those forty-four weeks, he jealously guarded his weight to just the right Ho! Ho! Ho! proportions, his Santa suit was kept in mothballs and a protective covering, lovingly taken out each week to be brushed and aired, and his beard kept long and bushy and white and as clean as possible under sometimes difficult circumstances. Bread and soup, kindly supplied by the Salvation Army, were his particular bugbears in that department.

But these were no more than distractions, which he tolerated with good humour until, on the twenty-third of October each year, he reported for duty at Hardy's department store on Regent Street, ready to bounce children of all ages on his knee, under the watchful eye of Santa's beefy helper, otherwise known as Mel from security. For eight weeks, he wove his magic for the endless queues of snotty kids who pulled his beard, poked his stomach, made indelicate remarks about his breath and the all-pervading smell of mothballs, and asked for ludicrously expensive presents such as PlayStations, DVD players, computers and season tickets to watch Chelsea beat all-comers. George went Ho! Ho! Ho! at each and every request, and promised to do his best if they'd been good children. That was the ultimate cop-out, and, by the time the little darlings had torn open their presents on Christmas morning with a discernible sense of grievance, Santa was safely back in the North Pole enjoying a well-earned rest.

It was a cold, wet, November night, and a few minutes to ten. Sam Wellard was about to close his corner shop, when in walked Santa Claus. Without hesitating, he walked straight up to Sam behind the counter, and pointing to a large protuberance bulging inside his trouser pocket, growled, 'This isn't a joke, I've got a gun, so empty the till, now!'

Sam was having none of it. He'd spent the whole of the day working his butt off, and he wasn't about to hand over the fruits of his labours to some beery Bozo from Neverland, or anywhere else. Reaching under the counter, he produced a baseball bat, special offer £9.99, and swung it, catching Santa a glancing blow on the forearm. This was not in the script, so Santa, taking fright, scampered off empty-handed, down the street and around the corner. Sam immediately called the police and set off in pursuit.

As luck would have it, there was a patrol car in the immediate vicinity, and Santa was soon spotted nearby, running at a lively pace for such a big man. One of the officers gave chase, felled Santa with a rugby tackle, and arrested him. Sam arrived a minute or so later, and immediately identified George Albert Spencer as the man who'd tried to rob him. After caution, Santa replied, 'Ho! Ho! Ho!'

When interviewed by DC 'Five' Watts, so-called because he was incredibly dim, George denied any involvement, claiming it was a case of mistaken identity, and, besides, he was the real Santa, and Santa didn't behave like a common criminal. To prove his point, George offered to bounce DC Watts on his knee, an offer the constable declined. As far as Watts was concerned, Santa was a sandwich short of a picnic.

'So you're saying you're the *real* Santa Claus?' asked the sceptical detective.

'I most certainly am,' replied George.

'That's a lie. Everybody knows it's Richard Attenborough, and he lives on 34ᵗʰ Street in New York,' said DC Watts. Besides being incredibly dim, he was also an impressionable lad.

'An impostor,' trumpeted George, 'and a charlatan!'

'Alright then, if you're the real Santa, ask me what I want for Christmas, and, if I get it, I'll personally apologise.'

'Ok, so what do you want for Christmas?'

'Something about five foot four,' said the policeman. 'Big up front, playful and easy over will do nicely.'

'That's disgusting!' retorted George.

'If you think that's disgusting, mate, just wait till I unwrap her,' replied Watts, leering.

'And are you going to be a good boy?' asked Santa.

'Course not, that'd spoil the fun.'

George was charged with attempted robbery and remanded in custody, to await his trial at the Old Bailey.

Duncan Campbell and I went to see George in conference, and, in spite of his predicament, he was in remarkably good spirits. We found a man in his middle fifties and surprisingly cultivated for somebody in his straightened circumstances.

'So, Mr Potts,' said George after the introductions, 'you are to defend me. You look very young, if I may say so.'

'It has been said before, Mr Spencer,' I replied, wearily, 'but Alexander the Great conquered most of Asia Minor before his eighteenth birthday, so youth is not necessarily an obstacle to success.'

'Well said, Mr Potts,' George laughed heartily. 'I feel we shall get on splendidly.'

'Thank you for the vote of confidence, which I hope isn't misplaced. Needless to say,' I continued, 'the circumstantial evidence is quite strong, so I cannot guarantee an acquittal. Let's consider the case against you together.' I flicked through my notes. 'You were arrested, only minutes after the attempted robbery, running away from the shop…'

'Pause there, Mr Potts,' George interrupted, 'I was not running away from the shop, rather I was running towards a Number Nine bus, which was about to pull away from the bus stop. That would have taken me to the Salvation Army Hostel in Bermondsey where I was staying at the time. Such kind people,' he added reflectively.

'Not exactly five star de luxe,' quipped Campbell, smirking.

'May I remind you, Mr Campbell,' George chided, 'that Jesus Christ was born in a stable.'

Campbell, duly chastened, shut up.

I continued with my review of the evidence. 'Next we have the large salami found in your trouser pocket when you were arrested, which the police say was an imitation firearm.'

'Quite so, Mr Potts, and positively ridiculous. I had bought it that very night, to leaven the bread when I returned to the Hostel and the banquet awaiting me.'

'And finally, a mark on your right forearm, which the police say was caused by a blow from the baseball bat.'

'I was rugby-tackled to the ground, Mr Potts. That was not my only injury, you know.'

I didn't, and made a note to examine the doctor's attendance record relating to the period George spent in police custody.

'That's very helpful, Mr Spencer,' I said, 'and Mr Campbell and I will follow up the matters you've raised. Now, looking ahead, I doubt very much if your trial will be listed before the New Year. There's a considerable backlog of cases at the Bailey waiting to be tried, and we must take our turn.'

'Fear not, Mr Potts,' George replied, 'I am confident I shall be tried before Christmas, and in your young but capable hands I shall be acquitted. After all, I am innocent. Thereafter, I have pressing business to attend to, with not a moment to lose.'

'Barking mad, if you ask me,' muttered Campbell on the way out.

'Possibly,' I replied, 'but they said that about Jesus Christ when he claimed to be the Son of God, and who are we, mere mortals, to unfold the mysteries of the Almighty?' There was no answer to that.

To my amazement, Spencer's trial, as he had foretold, was listed at short notice in the last week of sitting before the Christmas recess. A window of opportunity had appeared following the collapse of a terrorist trial, when one of the defendants had slipped through the net, travelled unchallenged on false documents through Dover and Calais, and was last seen heading for ports of call east of Suez. It was late on Friday evening when Mike informed me of the Monday listing, guaranteeing a stomach-churning weekend as I went over the case line by line, rehearsing each and every point, covering every angle.

MONDAY MORNING dawned grey and bleak, the pavements washed with rain, and a cold, biting wind, as I walked the short distance from Chambers to the Bailey. As I robed, I espied a familiar face, grinning inanely at me across the room.

'Hello, Tony,' whined Ronald Berger, my former pupil master. 'What brings you here?'

'It's Toby actually, Ronald,' I replied, giving him a wintry smile, 'and I'm here to represent George Spencer.'

'Are you, by Jove? Then we have the pleasure of doing business together, as I prosecute. It's going to be interesting, to see if the pupil can teach his master a few tricks.'

'Quite so, and I shall listen in awe as you open the case and call your evidence, whilst the jury and I will remain ever vigilant.'

Berger smiled. 'Well put,' he said, before adding, flippantly, 'I can see I'm in for a rough ride. We're before Mr Justice Boniface, you probably don't know him,' he continued, trying to pull rank, 'but I know him well of old. Off the Bench we're good friends, but on the Bench he shows no favouritism, and rightly so. Firm but fair, they say, so don't let him intimidate you. You'll need to be at your sharpest if you're to get anywhere with him. Open and shut case, but you don't need me to tell you that.'

'Ah, yes, "Sourpuss",' I replied. 'My first case with you in pupillage, when you prosecuted Sir Adrian Browne. I remember it as if it were yesterday.'

Berger's inane grin vanished in a trice. 'See you in court,' he whined, before trotting off. First blood to me, and a moment to savour.

It was all frighteningly *déja vu*, Berger locking antlers with Sourpuss all over again, and me thrown in at the deep end. It was as if everything I'd done before had been a rehearsal for this defining moment in my career. Suddenly I felt desperately inadequate for the task that lay ahead. Steadying myself, I determined to see it through.

Promptly at ten-thirty, Court One assembled, as Boniface sloped into court and slumped down in the judicial throne, glaring at one and all, and decidedly irritated at the thought of trying an attempted robbery with a salami. This was not why High Court Judges were appointed, and the blithering idiot responsible should be strung up. Did he have the power to so order, he wondered, or had the law changed? Parliament in its wisdom set too heady a pace for the Honourable Mr Justice Boniface. Just when he'd mastered some new piece of legislation, along came another to trouble him and interfere with a good round of golf.

The court clerk addressed the defendant. 'Are you George Albert Spencer?'

The defendant rose. 'I prefer to be known as Santa Claus, as that is my real name,' replied Santa.

'Your preferences are of no interest to this court,' snapped Sourpuss, setting the mood nicely, 'so unless and until the contrary is proved, you shall be known as George Albert Spencer, and,' he added menacingly, 'if you know what's good for you, I advise you to proceed on that basis. Do I make myself clear?'

'Crystal clear, my lord,' Santa smiled back soothingly. *For the love of God, George*, I muttered to myself, *don't offer to bounce him on your knee, and don't ask him what he wants for Christmas.*

'Mr Potts.' I shot to my feet. 'Are you satisfied that the defendant is fit to plead and stand trial?'

'Absolutely, my lord.'

'Then let him be arraigned.'

George duly pleaded not guilty, and sat back down.

'Now,' continued Sourpuss, in much the same vein, 'who prosecutes?'

Berger rose to his feet, grinning inanely. 'I do, my lord.'

'Mr... er... McDonald.' Sourpuss, somehow failing to recognise his good friend. 'Are you ready to proceed?'

'Berger, my lord,' bleated Berger.

'Moderate your language, Mr McDonald,' said Sourpuss, goggling, 'or I shall hold you in contempt! Remember you're in a court of law, and what's more, *my* court of law!'

'No, no,' Berger added, hastily. 'Your lordship misunderstands me. My name is Berger, Ronald Berger, and I prosecute.'

'Then why does it plainly say "McDonald" here on the slip of paper handed to me by the usher? It reads Mr R McDonald for the prosecution, and Mr T Potts for the defence.' Sourpuss allowed himself a little chuckle – a rare beast not often spotted in the wild. 'I suspect you've been the butt of a few jokes about that over the years, Mr Potts,' he chortled.

'I think I can explain the misunderstanding, my lord,' whined Berger. 'The usher, surprisingly, did not immediately recognise me, despite the fact that I am routinely instructed for the prosecution at this court.' Berger here allowed his chest to swell with his own sense of self-importance. 'So when he asked my name, I told him it was Berger, as in McDonald's. They are a fast food outlet,' he added helpfully.

'I'm aware of that, Mr Burger. After all, I do have grandchildren.'

This statement was greeted with an audible gasp of disbelief.

Sourpuss scribbled heavily on the slip. 'I am now writing B..U..R..G..E..R.' Ham was about to say something, but thought better of it. 'In future, it would help all of us if you provided your correct details.' He turned to the long-suffering usher. 'Empanel the jury, we've wasted enough time as it is.'

I couldn't help myself as I stifled a smirk at Berger's expense. Ham noticed, and was not amused.

The jury panel filed into court and sat at the back, waiting to be called.

The court clerk rose. 'Let the defendant be upstanding.' George duly obliged. 'Prisoner at the Bar, the names I am about to call are the names of the jury who will try you. If you object to them, or any one of them, you should make your objection known before they come to the Book to be sworn, and your objection shall be heard.' The clerk then turned to the jury panel. 'Members of the Jury in waiting, answer to your name as it is called, and take your seat in the jury box as directed by the usher.'

Damn! I kicked myself. I'd forgotten to tell Santa about his right of challenge. I rose swiftly from my seat, bowed to Sourpuss, and made my way hurriedly to the back of the court and the dock.

Sourpuss, predictably, was not amused. 'What on earth are you doing, Mr Potts? Leaving us already?'

'I'm sorry, my lord, but I omitted to advise the defendant on his right of challenge.'

'Really, this is intolerable. Do get on, and let's have no further interruptions.'

Now it was Berger's turn to smirk at *my* discomfort.

Santa leant over the medieval spiked surround of the dock as Toby approached. 'Calm down, Mr Potts,' he said soothingly, 'his bark is worse than his bite. Underneath the gruff exterior lies a heart of gold.'

'I wish I could agree, Mr Spencer, but in any event this isn't the time for pleasantries. Now, if you want to challenge any juror who is called to try you, for whatever reason, let me know before he takes the oath. Is that clear?'

'Absolutely,' replied Santa.

I made my way back to Counsel's bench, bowed and sat down as the court clerk rose and called out the names of twelve jurors. They were a mixed bunch. From their appearance and demeanour, four were clearly from Middle England, and pillars of their community. They would lean towards the prosecution.

The next four looked as if they'd wandered in from the day job, greasing nipples and clogging up the M4 with forty-four ton juggernauts, honest horny-handed sons of toil, wishing they were somewhere else, and likely to go with the defence.

Finally, four floating voters – an open-toed libero-pinko with a pony tail and a corduroy jacket, an earth mother with a dress made from recycled waste, a young and attractive polytechnic student with an earnest expression and spectacles with varifocal lenses, and a transvestite who could swing either way. He, or she, sporting a two-day stubble, looked particularly fetching in a two-piece outfit with matching handbag and accessories.

It was my task, on instructions, to challenge three of the jurors. Had they ever visited Hardy's department store during the Christmas season, and, if so, had they ever bounced on Santa's knee? Santa thought they looked familiar. Each challenge was met with a flat denial. Santa may be able to swing the lead in Neverland, but not at the Old Bailey.

Once empanelled, the jury settled down to listen to Berger's opening.

'Mem'jury', he began, as if addressing the wife of some Middle Eastern potentate, 'I appear on behalf of the prosecution, and my learned friend Mr T. Potts appears for the defence.' The penny having finally dropped, Berger thought he'd break the habit of a life time and try to be witty. Wrong move.

'I'll do the funnies in my court, thank you, Mr Berger,' said Sourpuss, singularly unamused. 'Now do get on.'

Berger, duly chastened, did as he was told, and whined on about the strength of the case against the accused, adding, as an aside, that the prosecution must prove the case, but in all the circumstances, it was a mere formality. He then called his first witness.

SAM WELLARD took the oath, and promptly sat down. As somebody who spent the whole of his working life on his feet, it was a welcome relief. But Sourpuss was not in the business of bringing relief to those who came before him, and he scowled down.

'Do you suffer from an infirmity, Mr... er... Wellard?' he asked testily. Sam, not immediately conversant with the word, stared back, grinning foolishly. 'You're sitting down, Mr Wellard, so I ask again, do you have an infirmity?'

Time for Berger to intervene. 'It's usual for witnesses to give their evidence standing up, Mr Wellard,' he whined, 'so his lordship is wondering why you're sitting down?'

'Well,' said Sam, not one to mince his words, 'there's a chair right be'ind me, plain for all to see, mate, so if you don't want me to sit down, what's it doing 'ere?'

The judge looked harder still. 'Why are you calling Mr Berger "mate", Mr Wellard? Do you know him?'

Sam peered long and hard at Berger, obviously thinking this had something to do with the evidence he was about to give, perhaps a sort of courtroom identification, so he took his time, much to Sourpuss's irritation.

'Well, Mr Wellard, do you know Mr Berger, or not?'

'Face looks familiar, mate, but the man I remember was taller...'

'This is intolerable! I am certainly not your mate, and never likely to be. You will address me as "my lord" or "your lordship", and when answering questions from Mr Berger, best say nothing at all. Now let's get on.'

'Are you Samuel Frederick Wellard?' Berger began, uncontroversially. Silence. The clock ticked onwards. Berger stared at Wellard, who stared back. Eventually, Berger gave in. 'Please answer the question.'

'I'm sorry, mate,' replied Sam, 'but my lordship 'ere told me not to say nothing to you.'

Sourpuss threw down his pen. 'That's not what I meant at all. Are you deliberately trying to obfuscate the issue, Mr Wellard?'

Sam couldn't remember the last time he tried to obfuscate anything, and was beginning to feel hard done by. Here he was, a public-minded citizen, doing his bit for law and order, and all he was getting was verbal flak from some overdressed old codger wearing a ridiculous, ill-fitting toupee who couldn't even speak the Queen's English, what with infirmity this and obfucking that, and the like. He had half a mind to jack it in and go back to the shop for some peace and quiet. And besides, he'd left his missus in charge, wrestling with the complexities of the new electronic till he'd installed for the Christmas rush, and who was going to cook his dinner?

Sourpuss determined to move things forward, decided on a different tack. 'Let me see if I can help, Mr Wellard,' he said through gritted teeth, 'I hope we can all agree your name is Samuel Frederick Wellard?'

'Yeah, my lordship.'

'Good,' progress at last, 'and you are here to tell us that on the thirteenth of November last, a man dressed as Santa Claus tried to rob your shop, that's right, isn't it?'

'Yeah, my lordship, got it in one.'

Alarmed at the way things were going, I felt I should say something, so taking my courage in both hands, rose from my seat. 'My lord, I am somewhat concerned that your lordship is leading the witness.'

'Somebody has to lead the witness, Mr Potts, otherwise we shall be here until next Christmas. Correct me if I am wrong,' he continued icily, 'but the defence here is one of mistaken identity?'

'That is correct, my lord…'

'Good, then resume your seat, and let's have no further unnecessary interruptions. Now, Mr Wellard, in your own time and words, tell the jury what happened.'

At last, English that Sam could understand, and he was off like a long dog. With any luck, he'd be back at the shop by twelve. A vain hope, as it transpired.

'Not so fast, Mr Wellard,' snapped Sourpuss, 'I have to take a careful note of what you're saying.'

Sam, aware the proceedings were being tape-recorded, was about to say something, but thought better of it, as he waited for the judge to catch up. At a snail's pace, Sourpuss, and Berger, when he could get a word in edgeways, took Sam through the events of that night. Then it came to the concealed weapon.

'I'm going to show you an exhibit, Mr Wellard…'

I was up on my feet in a flash. 'I object, my lord. That would be leading the witness.'

Sourpuss agreed. 'You must first lay the ground, Mr Berger, as well you should know.'

Berger grinned inanely. 'Can you describe the protuberance in the man's pocket?'

'Prer what?' asked Sam.

Sourpuss took over. 'You saw something sticking out from inside his pocket. Can you describe it?'

'Oh, right, I follow. There was something sticking out from inside his pocket. He said it was a gun.'

'And what was it?' asked Berger.

'How do I know? He never took it out. It could've been a gun, or his finger, or Santa's big dick for all I know.'

'Or a salami!' trumpeted Berger.

I was back on my feet.

'Point taken, Mr Potts,' said Sourpuss, glaring at Berger. 'Mr Berger, that is a wholly improper suggestion, and assuming it is your intention to invite the witness to compare a salami with Santa's big dick, I shall direct the jury to disregard it.'

After a few more questions, it was my turn to cross-examine.

'Mr Wellard,' I began soothingly, 'you run a busy corner shop selling a variety of goods, assisted only by your wife, is that correct?'

Before Sam could reply, Sourpuss intervened. 'Really, Mr Potts, you must adopt the basic principles of cross-examination in my court. Assuming of course, that you are familiar with them,' he added acidly. 'You have just put three questions to the witness. Which one do you wish him to answer first?'

Oh dear, I thought, *public humiliation, and so soon*. 'I'm sorry, my lord.' I turned to Sam. 'You run a corner shop, is that correct?'

'Yeah, mate.' Sourpuss glared, and was about to say something.

'My lord,' I said, quickly. 'I have no objection to Mr Wellard calling me "mate", if that puts him at his ease. After all, it can be quite an ordeal giving evidence in your lordship's court.'

'Yeah, too right, mate,' agreed Sam, 'good on yer.'

It turned out to be an inspired move, as I now had Sam on my side – and, hopefully, Sourpuss back in his box.

'And at this time of year, when the attempted robbery took place, the shop was busy?'

'Too right. Rushed off me feet.'

So far, so good. 'And when the attempted robbery took place, it was at the end of a tiring day?'

'Yeah, I was absolutely knackered!'

'And when this man came in, dressed as Santa Claus, he came straight up to the till?'

'Yeah.'

'And before you could draw breath, he was demanding money from you?'

'Yeah, that's right.'

'And almost immediately, you grabbed a baseball bat and swung it at him?'

'Yeah.'

'And then he ran off?'

'Yeah.'

'So you had the man in your sights for no more than a few seconds?'

Sam's eyes narrowed. He may be a fool, but he wasn't a complete fool, and he could see what was coming. 'Long enough to recognise him if I saw him again, mate.'

Damn, I thought, *wrong answer*, but I shouldn't expect everything to go my way. Time to try a different approach.

'As a rough estimate, how many men dressed as Santa Claus were operating in your area that night?'

'Can't say for sure, a dozen or more, maybe, but I know most of them by sight. They're always hanging around, day and night, and,' he added gratuitously, 'the robber wasn't one of them.'

'So you'd never seen the robber before, is that what you're saying?'

Sam realised, too late, that he'd walked into that one, but had to agree.

'And the complete stranger who attempted to rob you was dressed in a traditional Santa outfit?'

'Yeah, but…'

'So the only part of his face you could see were his eyes?'

'Yeah, and they were evil, know what I mean? I'm not likely to forget them in a hurry.'

'Can you remember anything else about the man?'

'Yeah, his breath smelled of alcohol. He looked drunk to me.'

'Finally, Mr Wellard, were you ever asked to see if you could pick out the man on an identification parade?'

'No need to, mate, the police nicked him within minutes. They asked me if that was the man, and I identified him there and then.'

'So you did, Mr Wellard, but you identified the wrong man.'

'No I didn't, mate, as God is my witness.'

'Are you suggesting, Mr Potts,' Sourpuss interposed, 'there should have been a formal identification parade, with ten or more Santas lined up, all dressed identically?'

'I am, my lord. Where identity is in issue, it is the defendant's right.'

'That's a bit far-fetched, isn't it, if they all look the same?'

'With respect, my lord, no. All high court judges dress identically, but they don't all look the same.'

That remark could have gone either way, as Sourpuss glared at me. Then he smiled. 'Point taken, Mr Potts,' and nodded encouragingly. 'Do you have any further questions of the witness?'

'No thank you, my lord.'

After lunch, Berger called the doctor to give evidence about the mark on the defendant's forearm. In his opinion, it was consistent with a glancing blow from a blunt weapon such as a baseball bat.

'And equally consistent with the sort of injury sustained from a heavy fall onto a hard surface,' I suggested.

'I wouldn't say "equally consistent", but I certainly couldn't rule it out.'

Fair enough.

'And when you examined the defendant, you found other marks and abrasions consistent with a fall onto the ground.'

'That is correct, but the mark on the forearm stood out '

'Pause there,' said Sourpuss, making a careful note.

Finally, DC Five Watts was called to deal with the interview. His Christmas wish list had been edited out to avoid unnecessary embarrassment, otherwise the interview was uncontroversial.

At last, and to Berger's evident satisfaction, the salami was produced and became Exhibit One.

I was about to rise, but Berger waved me back down. 'One final question, Officer. When the Defendant was brought into the interview room, did you notice anything about his breath?'

'Yes, his breath smelled of alcohol.'

Damn and blast. I'd read through the custody record, but hadn't noticed the entry. A stupid and careless mistake, and potentially fatal. Best to leave it alone for now.

'No further questions.' Berger was well pleased with himself, as Sourpuss made another careful note.

'Just two questions,' I said, rising to my feet. 'Can you confirm that the defendant is a man of good character, with no criminal convictions recorded against him?'

'I can,' replied Watts, grudgingly.

'And can you confirm that, close to where the defendant was arrested, there is a bus stop with services to Bermondsey?'

'There's certainly a bus stop. I can't say if they go to Bermondsey.'

'Thank you, no further questions.'

'Very well,' said Sourpuss. 'Members of the jury, we will now adjourn until ten-thirty tomorrow.' And so saying, he rose and swept majestically from the court.

A visit to George in the cells was called for, as I had to deal with the alcohol evidence.

'I'm sorry I didn't bring it to your attention,' said George, 'although I assumed you knew. It was a cold night, and I had a nip of brandy before I set off home. As there is a strict alcohol ban at the hostel, I keep a small flask hidden away in Santa's grotto. It's not something I'm proud of, you understand,' he added. 'Santa is supposed to set an example to all the little children.'

'Yes, of course, I understand,' I replied, 'but we can't ignore it. The judge has made a careful note, and on the face of it, it's strong evidence for the prosecution.'

'Then of course I shall deal with it if you so advise. Such sadness, Santa with feet of clay.'

'I don't suppose the jury will hold it against you,' I added. 'After all, even Santa has to keep warm on a cold night.'

George smiled encouragingly, and we said our farewells. 'Till tomorrow then.'

BACK IN CHAMBERS, I reviewed my notes, and went through the evidence again, just in case I'd missed something else. As for tomorrow, I'd call the defendant, of course, and hoped George would keep it simple.

I also had witnesses up my sleeve – a doctor to say that the mark on George's forearm was consistent with a heavy fall against the kerb, and a ranking member of London Transport to deal with the Number Nine bus. Finally, the Adjutant-General of the Salvation Army Hostel in Bermondsey, to speak of George's gentle character and mild manner. That should be enough, God-willing, but nothing was certain in trial by jury.

And what of the jury, and what were they making of the case? I had kept half an eye on them during the day, and, following Nick Ridley's advice, had tried to identify the foreman, the man or woman to whom I should pitch my closing submissions. The four from Middle England were giving nothing away, and nobody had broken ranks. They smiled appropriately, nodded together, and made the occasional note as they exchanged glances. Of the others, I noticed the polytechnic student making copious notes yet keeping her own counsel. At first blush, a rank outsider, but coming up fast on the rail. One to watch, and not just because she had a pretty face.

I arrived early at court. Fortunately, Berger was nowhere to be seen, probably down in the CPS office receiving last minute instructions and a copy of his Advocate's Evaluation form.

It was now ten, Campbell had arrived, and together we went down to see George and give him his little pep talk. It was what Nick called the 'Punter Patrol', keeping the lay client happy and informed. George was up for it, and surprisingly calm.

Sourpuss had two applications, listed at the last minute, so instead of starting promptly at ten-thirty, we were kept waiting until nearly eleven, which did nothing for my nerves. Berger kept his distance, whining away to the CPS representative and Five Watts, glancing occasionally in my direction, and grinning inanely.

At last, the usher called us into court, and the trial resumed.

'May it please your lordship,' I began, opening the batting for the defence, 'I shall now call the defendant to give evidence.'

By my reckoning at least, George performed well. He stuck to the script, answered my questions, even about the nip of brandy, and gave a very good account of himself. He came over as the innocent victim of mistaken identification, and a decent, caring man. The jury seemed impressed, and even Sourpuss managed to control himself for the best part of an hour. I sat down, exhausted. Then it was Berger's turn.

'So as I understand your evidence,' he began querulously, 'you're the real Santa Claus, and the real Santa Claus doesn't go around robbing corner shops. Have I got it right?'

'Your perspicacity is a marvel to behold, Mr Berger,' replied George without a hint of sarcasm.

'Never mind the clever talk, what proof do you have?'

'Let me ask you a question, Mr Berger. Christians and Jews alike believe in Almighty God, and after a blameless life, they will go to Heaven, correct?' Berger stood in a sullen silence. 'Now, I ask you, have you ever seen God? Have you ever seen Heaven? Do you know where it is? Do you believe in celestial bodies with wings?'

'What has this got to do with anything?' snapped Berger, losing patience and the argument.

'So why not a real Santa Claus, who lives in the North Pole, and who delivers presents to good children with the help of flying reindeer? Just because you never see them, doesn't mean they don't exist. Was it not our Saviour who said to Doubting Thomas, because thou hast seen me, thou hast believed: blessed are they that have not seen, and yet have believed?'

'Fascinating though this ecumenical discussion may be,' interrupted Sourpuss, 'I wonder where this is getting us, Mr Berger, and does it really matter? The jury will have to decide whether the defendant attempted to rob Samuel Wellard of a sum of money, regardless of his beliefs or otherwise. Isn't that right?'

Berger was like a dog with a bone. 'The defendant claims to be the real Santa Claus, my lord, and therefore not capable of a criminal act. I'm suggesting he's not what he claims to be.'

'Quite so, I follow that, but your line of questioning is only relevant if you've inviting the jury to accept that there is a real Santa Claus, and the defendant is an impostor. Is that what you're suggesting?'

'Absolutely not, my lord. Santa Claus is a figment of the imagination, nothing more.'

There was an audible gasp from the jury, as Berger set about shattering all their illusions. This was not playing well.

'So I come back to my question, Mr Berger,' persisted Sourpuss. 'If, according to you, there is no Santa, real or imagined, does it matter what the defendant believes?'

'Very well, my lord.' Ham turned back to George. 'Let me ask you about the attempted robbery. The man was dressed as Santa Claus, and so were you, correct?'

'Correct.'

'Still dressed as Santa Claus, you were arrested close to the scene, correct?'

'So it would appear.'

'You had a salami in your pocket, which you used as an imitation firearm.'

'If you'll forgive the pun, Mr Berger, that's a load of baloney.'

The pun went right over Berger's head, a case of one flew over the cuckoo's nest, as he whined on. 'And minutes later, Mr Wellard identified you as the robber.'

'He did indeed, but the jury know that already.'

'And he identified you as the robber because you were the robber.'

'Wrong, and a clear case of mistaken identification.'

'He was right, wasn't he?'

'No, he wasn't.'

'Yes he was, so why not admit it?'

'You and I both know he was wrong, Mr Berger, so why should I admit to something I haven't done, just to please you?'

Berger sat down, looking decidedly miffed. I glanced over at the jury. On balance, I felt George had done well, but only time would tell.

The defence doctor and the ranking member of London Transport did their bit. Berger went through the motions, but there was little he could say.

The Adjutant-General ended on a high note, describing George in fulsome terms, a generous and noble man, and an example to one and all. Berger trotted out the 'real Santa' bit again, but the A–G was having none of it. Putting Berger firmly in his place, he quoted from the Book of Psalms: 'eyes have they, and see not, they have ears, and hear not'. In that respect, Berger had the hide of a rhinoceros and roughly half the intelligence.

After lunch, Berger made his closing address, heavily laced with 'mem jury' this and 'mem jury' that, and then sat down.

Now it was my turn to dazzle, cajole, charm, and persuade. Many a case was won or lost on final speeches, and I was determined to make this a memorable one for all the right reasons.

I'd learned a number of basic principles listening to others more experienced. Never be flippant, as the jury, for the most part, took their public duty very seriously, so opening my speech by telling the one about the judge and the usher was doomed to failure. Never be boring, as it insults the jury's intelligence and risks losing their sympathy and goodwill. Always engage eye-to-eye contact, and make each and every juror feel important. Never read from a prepared text, as the jury expect counsel to have all the facts at his fingertips. And, most important of all, never go on too long. Make the speech brief, to the point, leave them wanting more, and leave them with something ringing in their ears.

Making sure the jury were settled down and attentive before rising to my feet, I began with a review of the evidence, bringing the judge into the frame as much as possible. I reminded them of the obvious dangers of mistaken identification, and the failure of the police to conduct a parade. I praised Sam Wellard, as he'd gone down well with the jury in his down-to-earth, no-nonsense approach. But I reminded them that an honest and convincing witness can nonetheless be a mistaken one, and that his lordship would be giving them a careful direction.

'Finally, Ladies and Gentlemen,' I concluded, 'you have heard much during the trial about the defendant's beliefs, and a lively discussion initiated by my learned friend Mr Berger, for reasons best known to himself.' Nice little dig, without being disrespectful. A number of the jury nodded in agreement. 'Perhaps, in the context of this trial, it doesn't really matter, but there must be millions of children, of all ages, who, even as I speak, would be mortified to learn of Mr Berger's dismissive attitude.'

More nodding, as Berger looked down at his papers.

'As some of you will know, the Royal Mail handles over eight million letters every year addressed to Santa Claus, and it is a hard-nosed and insensitive man who lightly dismisses Santa as a figment of the imagination. Of course, I adopt his lordship's remark, and it would be foolhardy of me not to do so' – a few sympathetic smiles – 'that we are here to decide if the defendant attempted to rob Mr Wellard's corner shop, and not to decide if there really is a Santa Claus, and if this defendant really is Santa Claus.'

I paused for effect.

'But in one respect I beg to differ with his lordship, and for this reason. You have heard much about the defendant, especially from the Adjutant-General of the Salvation Army, one of the finest charities in the country.' Nice touch – everybody loves the Sally Army at Christmas. 'You have heard that, for eight weeks of the year, the defendant is Santa Claus personified. He bounces children on his knee, listens patiently to their hopes and fears whilst they pull his beard and poke his stomach and make outrageous demands of him. You have heard that after a long day at Hardy's department store, he makes his way home, or what he calls home, and, after expenses, donates his entire salary to the Hostel.' Another pause and a sip of water. 'So if the prosecution be right, this good, virtuous and noble man, in a moment of total madness, abandons all the principles he holds so dear, and for what? A wodge of sweaty money!'

Nearly there. 'If there is a real Santa Claus, holding dear all that *we* hold dear, and bringing happiness and laughter into our lives, then he is here with us today, sitting in the dock. Thank you for the care and attention you have brought to this case, and I invite you to find him not guilty as charged.'

I sat down, exhausted, but hoping I'd done enough.

'Thank you, Mr Potts,' said Sourpuss. 'Members of the jury, the hour is upon us, and I will not tax your patience any longer. I shall sum up tomorrow morning at ten thirty.'

'Court rise,' intoned the usher. Tomorrow would be another day.

SOURPUSS SUMMED up fairly, directing the jury on the law and making the obvious points for the prosecution and defence. True to form, he warned them of the dangers of mistaken identification in difficult circumstances, late at night, with only a fleeting glimpse of the robber. It was, he observed, and I had to agree, a classic case for a jury to decide. It was eleven thirty-three by the court clock when the jury retired to consider their verdict.

Now came the worst part, the interminable waiting, endless cups of coffee, pacing up and down outside court, wondering what the jury were discussing, how long would they be out, the dry throat, the clammy hands, and the churning in the stomach.

Campbell and I went down to the cells to see George, who was the calmest of us all.

'Whatever the verdict, Mr Potts,' he said softly, 'I couldn't have asked for a better advocate, and I am most grateful to you, and Mr Campbell, for all you've done.'

'You're very kind, Mr Spencer,' I replied. 'But whilst there's life, there's hope.'

'Spoken like a real Santa Claus,' he beamed back.

I smiled in return. 'Now,' I said, 'I gather from the prison staff that your good friend the Adjutant-General has come to visit you, so we'll leave now, and see you back in court.'

It was just after one when the tannoy crackled into life.

'No verdict will be taken in the case of Spencer until two-fifteen.'

Chance for a breath of fresh air as Campbell and I repaired to the Cock and Bull Tavern on Ludgate Hill for a pie and a pint. I prodded listlessly at my *plat du jour* and stuck to mineral water. I needed a clear head, whatever the outcome, but not so Campbell, who set about demolishing an enormous Guinness steak and kidney pudding, with chips, and a pint of the landlord's Old Peculier. How could he eat at a time like this, I wondered, but I kept my thoughts to myself. After all, Campbell may have earmarked me for his next big case, so best to keep in favour and smile ingratiatingly. Fortunately, with Campbell's mouth full most of the time, intelligent conversation was at a premium, and I preferred it that way.

We got back to court at ten-past-two, and I hurried to Court One for an update. I found the usher deep in the sports section of his favourite tabloid.

'Any news?' I asked, trying to stay calm.

'As quiet as the grave, Mr Potts,' he replied, sucking his teeth, 'I'll tannoy you when you're needed.'

My first instinct was to retire to the Bar Mess, slump into a chair and be alone with my thoughts, but that might appear rude, so I joined Campbell in the public canteen, bought us both a stewed coffee, and for the next hour, listened without hearing, to Campbell's life story.

It was catatonically boring, and, to make matters worse, the pie was beginning to repeat on him. On he droned, in between thinly-disguised burps, about the wife and kids, and life in the fast lane with his new Vauxhall Cavalier, which, on a long run, topped thirty miles to the gallon. If it hadn't been for the incessant churning in my stomach, I would've dozed off well before the tannoy called us back to court. It was twenty-past three.

As I walked into court, barely able to control my emotions, I spoke to the usher. 'Verdict?'

'I 'aven't a clue, guv,' he replied unhelpfully, 'I simply do what I'm told.' A rare breed indeed.

The jury filed back into court. I studied their faces for any indication, but there was none.

'All rise,' intoned the ever-obedient usher, as Sourpuss entered, a tad flushed around the gills after an expansive lunch chased down with two or three glasses of medicinal port.

The court clerk rose and addressed him. 'My lord, the jury have been deliberating for three hours and fifty-seven minutes.'

Sourpuss nodded, feigning interest. 'Let the defendant be upstanding.' Then, turning to the jury, he continued, 'Will the foreman please stand.' It was one of the honest, horny-handed sons of toil who rose, not my first, second or third choice, but no matter. What counted was the verdict, not who delivered it.

'Mr Foreman, please confine yourself to answering my next question either yes or no. Have the jury reached a verdict on which you are all agreed?'

'Yus.' My heart started pounding. 'Well,' he added, clearly overwhelmed by the ordeal, 'eleven of us are all agreed, and one disagrees.'

The eleven all glared at the transvestite, sitting prominently in the front row, resolute of countenance and clutching his or her handbag for moral support.

'Pause there if you will, Mr Foreman,' snapped Sourpuss, shaking himself out of his post-prandial torpor.

He was obviously dealing with the biggest idiot on the planet, so, speaking slowly and deliberately, he continued as though addressing a five-year-old at the back of the class.

'I must assume from what you say that you are *not* all agreed. That being so, the law now permits me to accept a verdict on which at least ten of you are agreed. Is that clear, or do you wish me to repeat it?' There was an irritable note to his voice, as he smiled through gritted teeth.

After a moment's reflection, enlightenment broke across the foreman's countenance like a shaft of sunlight behind a bank of dark clouds. 'No thank you, my lord,' he replied, confidently, 'so can we now return our verdict?'

'No, you cannot!' Sourpuss's patience was being sorely taxed. 'You must retire again and see if you can reach a unanimous verdict – that is,' he added with emphasis, 'a verdict on which all twelve of you are agreed. If that is not possible, then I can accept a verdict on which at least ten of you are agreed. Do I make myself clear? You can't sit in court and jabber away like a cartload of monkeys, you need to reach your verdict in the privacy of your retiring room.'

The foreman reflected on the enormity of this statement, and was far from convinced. 'As I see it, and from what your lordship is saying,' he blundered on, at his peril, 'you want us to retire, then come back into court and return a verdict what eleven of us already agree, when we could do that now, so I don't see the point.'

'Yeah,' muttered somebody from the back row, keen to get back to the day job.

There were rumblings of discontent at the palace gates. Time to placate the mob with a few well-chosen words. Sourpuss rose to the occasion, or so he hoped.

'Members of the jury,' he was at his most urbane, 'the law is the law, however ridiculous it may seem to you, so you must retire, as directed, and when you have reached a verdict, let me know.'

The jury retired, somewhat truculently, as directed, and before I had the chance to draw breath and calm my nerves, there was a loud knock. Reprising their role of a few minutes earlier, the jury filed back, and the court reconvened.

The clerk went into his routine again. 'Members of the jury, have you reached a verdict on which at least ten of you are agreed?'

'Yus', replied the foreman, 'but you know that already. We reached our verdict three hours ago.'

'On the charge of attempted robbery, do you find the defendant guilty or not guilty?'

'Not guilty, my lord. In our opinion, Santa is as innocent as the driven snow, and all eleven of us 'ave written letters to 'im, 'oping it's not too late, if you'll forgive the inconvenience,' he added, turning to George and smiling.

'The sooner I leave, Mr Foreman, the sooner I can attend to your each and every wish,' replied Santa. 'After all, there are only five days left before Christmas.'

Sourpuss interrupted this mutual admiration society. 'Mr Spencer,' he looked over to the dock, 'It gives me great pleasure to inform you that you are free to go. I shall rise.'

Just before he left court, the Honourable Mr Justice Boniface handed an envelope to the usher, and nodded in the direction of the dock. 'From the grandchildren,' he whispered. I was just able to make out the writing: 'To Santa'.

As soon as Sourpuss had left, the court erupted, with the jury to a man applauding wildly and crowding round the dock, such was their delight. Even Berger managed a wintry smile, although no visit from Santa for him. The only thing missing was Tiny Tim bleating, 'God bless us all, every one'.

For me, it was a moment to treasure, as George approached and gave me a big, warm, hug. Not a dry eye in court, and then it was time to go.

'My dear Mr Potts,' said George, 'I must now take my leave, as there is work to be done. I would like to promise you something special for Christmas, but you have gifts beyond measure that even Santa cannot match. You have the love of a good woman' – curious, I thought, I'd never mentioned Susie – 'and a warm and loving family. But above all, you also have the gifts of compassion, of caring for your fellow human beings, and real humanity. And fortunately for me,' he added with a chuckle, 'you also have the gift of the gab.' Shaking me firmly by the hand, he continued, 'Lay to rest the demons of your self doubts, as many great triumphs lie ahead of you, and, without you, justice and the search for truth will be the poorer for it. So fight on, we need you, we all need you.'

A few well-chosen words for Campbell, and then George took his leave.

Christmas Day dawned wet and windy, one of those days when the clouds scudded across the sky, threatening rain, as I awoke and made my way downstairs. It was a tradition in the Potts household to hang stockings above the fireplace, together with a mince pie and brandy for Santa, and a carrot for Rudolf. I had hung up my stocking for as long as I could remember, marvelling at the goodies

Santa had purchased for me at Marks and Spencer and other high street chain stores, the pack of three linen handkerchiefs, the socks, sweets, puzzles, games, fruit and nuts, all were part of the magic.

On this particular Christmas Day, I emptied the goodies from my stocking onto the carpet whilst my father poured Bucks Fizz, thrilling over the pack of three linen handkerchiefs, and as my mother was fond of saying, you can never have too many handkerchiefs. Then socks, sweets, and one of those puzzles where you move the pieces around to form a picture. Right at the bottom, and almost overlooked, was a small glass globe containing Santa on his sleigh, loaded with toys for all good children, and being pulled by Donner and Blitzen, and Dancer and Prancer, Comet and the one whose name nobody could remember, and Rudolf. When shaken, it snowed.

'How very thoughtful of you, mother,' I said.

'How strange,' she replied, taking it in her hand. 'I wonder where that came from?'

That evening, the two families assembled for Christmas dinner. Susie was looking radiant, all were perfectly relaxed in each other's company, although much of the conversation was dominated by the forthcoming wedding and the heightened state of panic as each day succeeded the next. Susie and I took it all in our stride, simply happy to be together. The turkey was brought in with great ceremony, the lights dimmed and the candles lit, I said grace, in Latin of course, and the feast began.

We all heard it. It was after pudding, as we were settling back, congratulating the ladies on the magnificent dinner, and ready for family charades. It was a quiet, yet incessant, tapping on the dining room window.

'I wonder what that could be?' asked Molly Sandwell.

'Probably the copper beech,' replied my mother, 'I've asked you more than once, George, to cut back the branches.'

'You have indeed, my dear,' replied my father, 'but as the copper beech is a good twenty feet from the house, I think it unlikely in the extreme. Perhaps learned counsel could take a view?' he added, nodding towards me.

I got up and peered behind the curtains, just as the full moon appeared through a bank of clouds, and for a moment, I could have sworn I saw a familiar figure at the bottom of the drive, smiling and waving and calling out 'Ho! Ho! Ho!'

It can't be, I thought to myself, *it must be a figment of my imagination.*

'Anything out there, Toby?' asked my father.

'Not that I could see. It must be the wind,' and so saying, I raised my glass in a silent toast to Santa Claus.

I would never forget George Albert Spencer. Whatever life might throw at me, whatever the future might hold, for three days I strode a small corner on the stage of life, and strode it like a Colossus.

THE END

Or is it?
As Bootsy Farmer might well say, quoting Churchill:

> This is not the end,
> It is not even the beginning of the end,
> But it is, perhaps, the end of the beginning.